Three Dog Night

THE DOGMOTHERS - BOOK TWO

roxanne st. claire

Three Dog Night
THE DOGMOTHERS BOOK TWO

Copyright © 2019 South Street Publishing

ISBN Print: 978-1-7339121-5-0
ISBN Ebook: 978-1-7339121-4-3

COVER ART: Keri Knutson (designer)
and Dawn C. Whitty (photographer)
INTERIOR FORMATTING: Author EMS

Critical Reviews of Roxanne St. Claire Novels

"Non-stop action, sweet and sexy romance, lively characters, and a celebration of family and forgiveness."
— *Publishers Weekly*

"Plenty of heat, humor, and heart!"
— *USA Today* (Happy Ever After blog)

"Beautifully written, deeply emotional, often humorous, and always heartwarming!"
— *The Romance Dish*

"Roxanne St. Claire is the kind of author that will leave you breathless with tears, laughter, and longing as she brings two people together, whether it is their first true love or a second love to last for all time."
— *Romance Witch Reviews*

"Roxanne St. Claire writes an utterly swoon-worthy romance with a tender, sentimental HEA worth every emotional struggle her readers will endure. Grab your tissues and get ready for some ugly crying. These books rip my heart apart and then piece it back together with the hope, joy and indomitable loving force that is the Kilcannon clan."
— *Harlequin Junkies*

"As always, Ms. St. Claire's writing is perfection…I am unable to put the book down until that final pawprint the end. Oh the feels!"
— *Between My BookEndz*

Before
The Dogmothers...
there was

The Dogmothers Series

Hot Under the Collar (Book 1)

Three Dog Night (Book 2)

Dachshund Through the Snow (Book 3)

And many more to come!

For a complete guide to all of the characters in both The Dogfather and Dogmothers series, see the back of this book. Or visit www.roxannestclaire.com for a printable reference, book lists, buy links, and reading order of all my books. Be sure to sign up for my newsletter on my website to find out when the next book is released! And join the private Dogfather Facebook group for inside info on all the books and characters, sneak peeks, and a place to share the love of tails and tales!

www.facebook.com/groups/roxannestclairereaders/

Chapter One

Alex Santorini leaned back on the lace-draped folding chair, scanned the terrace crowded with friends and family, and let his gaze move over the vineyards bathed in sunset yellows. He ignored the lively debate going on next to him, as two of his siblings and a few of their new "step" cousins argued the benefits of whiskey over ouzo. He preferred wine, like the glass of Pinot Noir in front of him.

Taking a sip, he savored the notes of oak, blueberry, cinnamon, and that hint of pepper. It was good. Not perfect, but then, what was? It paired well with the braised lamb, which, in his professional chef's opinion, needed more rosemary and less garlic, but the meal was more than serviceable.

His mother clearly hadn't needed Alex's skills in planning or executing the food and drink for her wedding. She had brought him in on an early planning meeting here at the winery, but a cocky-as-hell banquet chef had taken over the menu discussion. Alex had spent his time quietly admiring Overlook Glen Vineyards. Well, actually, it was the owner of this tiny but elegant winery whom he admired that day…and on any other occasion when he'd met Grace Donovan.

Tall, cool, with wheat-toned blond hair and eyes that reminded him of the blue-green waters of the Caribbean Sea, the woman had attracted and intrigued him from the moment they'd met.

He shifted in his chair, watching a group of friends chatting with the bride and groom, regaling the new Mrs. Kilcannon with a story that made her belly-laugh. He couldn't help smiling because nearly a hundred people—many of whom were branches of the same family tree—had gathered at this spectacular venue in the Blue Ridge Mountains to witness the vows and celebrate the union of Katie Santorini and Daniel Kilcannon.

Both his mother and her brand-new husband had lost the great loves of their lives, and neither had expected this second round of romance to bloom as they entered their sixties. Alex couldn't be happier for Mom, or the man who'd proven himself worthy of such a great lady.

But Alex's gaze didn't stay on the newlyweds for long, because the taste of the wine in his mouth spurred him to look for the woman who made it.

He'd gotten no more than glimpses of Grace since they'd arrived for the late afternoon wedding and reception, catching a flash of a sleek blond ponytail or a peek at long legs in a tight skirt when she glided past him in spiky heels. He'd brushed by her once and was rewarded with a quick, distracted smile that barely reached turquoise eyes and a whiff of something that smelled like a flower garden in summer.

He'd cracked a joke in passing, too, and then commented on the tablescapes that managed to capture the russets and golds of a North Carolina October, but his humor and compliments fell flat with her.

Which only made him want her more.

The toasts were made, dinner was served, and dancing had already started. It was the perfect time to...try again. All he needed was a good excuse to talk to her.

Sipping the wine, he let it linger on his tongue, this time picking up something different. Something... musty. Again, not a taste the average Joe would ever notice, but Alex wasn't average, and if there was one thing he could do, it was taste.

Maybe that's what he could talk to Grace about.

"'Scuze me," he murmured to his brother John, who just held up his hand and stayed deep in conversation with their sister, Cassie, and her fiancé, Braden Mahoney, who happened to be the groom's nephew.

Oh yeah. One too many Kilcannons, Mahoneys, and Santorinis at this table. He needed someone else completely. He needed Grace Donovan.

His siblings barely noticed that he grabbed the wine bottle from the table and headed across the fieldstone terrace. He hadn't gotten far when he passed two little old ladies rocking with laughter.

"You two look like you're having fun." He grinned at Yiayia, who, despite the Greek title, looked much less like a "grandma" than the woman next to her. Gramma Finnie, on the other hand, was the quintessential aging Irish lass, with white hair, bifocals, and a shot of Jameson's in her knotted old fist.

She raised that glass to him. "'Tis a happy day, lad."

"It sure is," he agreed, pausing to talk to the two women who'd become fast—if utterly unlikely—friends who were always up to some sort of trouble.

From the gleam in the gaze Yiayia pinned on him, tonight was no different.

"Where's Yianni?" his grandmother asked, using John's Greek name and looking past him.

"We're identical twins, Yiayia, not Siamese. I left him behind." He winked at her. "In more ways than one."

She tsked and shook her head, leaning closer to Gramma Finnie. "That's my Alexander. It's always a competition with his brother, that one."

He shrugged, not bothering to disagree. Although they worked side by side running three locations of his family's successful Greek restaurants, Alex and John still enjoyed a brotherly and mostly friendly lifestyle of one-upsmanship. Alex hated to admit it, but with John's genius IQ and easygoing personality, his older twin—by four minutes—had him beat at most things. Alex came in second everywhere but in the kitchen. And with women. Alex won in the woman department every time.

"Did you need John for something?" he asked.

Yiayia lifted a carefully drawn brow and shared a look with the other woman. "I wanted him to know that pretty Grace Donovan just headed back there." She pointed toward the back of the winery building where a stone archway led to the banquet kitchens.

"She did?" He filed that knowledge and mentally thanked his grandmother. "Why would John need to know that?"

"Just…"

"'Tis nothin', lad," Gramma Finnie said quickly, shooting a meaningful glance at her partner in crime.

But Alex knew exactly what that meaning was. Ever since their "success" with Cassie and Braden, these two fancied themselves Greek and Irish yentas, and the focus of their matchmaking efforts seemed to be the many grandchildren they had between them now that Yiayia's daughter-in-law had married Gramma Finnie's son.

But…wait. John and Grace? Oh, *hell* no. "Grace is back there, you said?" He was already moving in the direction of the kitchen.

"Quick." Yiayia flicked her fingers. "Tell your brother. It's his chance with the pretty vintner."

It's my *chance with her.* "Sure. I'll get right on that." He held up the bottle as a farewell and hustled straight toward the kitchen entrance, where a server came rushing out with a tray.

"Can I help you?" the young man asked, glancing at the bottle. "You need another at your table?"

"I need to talk to Ms. Donovan. About the wine."

"Oh, okay." He glanced over his shoulder, behind a wall that blocked Alex's view into the hallway. "This man has…his wine."

"I have this under control." Grace's calm, steady voice was at odds with the click of her stiletto heels on flagstone on the other side of that wall, matching the surprisingly strong beat of Alex's heart.

The server hustled away, and Alex used the final few seconds to brace himself for the impact of the woman, which was like a nine on the Richter scale, followed by a tsunami.

She came around the corner and stopped dead in her tracks at the sight of him.

"Oh, it's...you." Her eyes widened almost imperceptibly, while the slightest rush of blood deepened her creamy complexion.

Okay, then. Same scale, same tsunami. Good to know.

"Is anything the matter, Mr. Santorini?" she asked, instantly regaining any composure that might have slipped.

Not a damn thing was the matter. Not with her, anyway. He resisted the urge to let his gaze coast over her narrow but decidedly feminine frame, trying instead to think of a good reason for why he'd come marching back here with the wine. Maybe a chance to get her to show him the wine cellars?

"This wine won't work," he said.

"The Pinot Noir 1410?" She sounded stunned.

"Is that what you call this?"

She lifted one brow, sucking in a breath so her cheekbones were more prominent and glossy pink lips pursed in a little O, as if she were about to kiss... something. "It's from barrel number 1410, so yes, that's what we call it."

"You couldn't think of a more creative name?"

Her expression melted to something a little more like amusement. "So it's the name on the label that's bothering you, or what's inside? Because I'm confident the Pinot Noir is perfect for this meal."

"It's a little...lifeless."

She inched back. "That wine was made using the latest viticulture and oenology, measured with sulfur dioxide and genetically modified grapes."

"Sounds like a science experiment. I was hoping you could show me something else in your cellars." Too obvious? He tempered the invitation with a sly smile. "Maybe you have something with a, I don't know, cork?"

She sighed as if she'd heard it all before. "Actually, a screw-top doesn't make a wine less desirable. It's a proven scientific fact."

"Proven by who? The box-wine makers?"

She didn't laugh. "By the people who understand that corks allow molecules of air to oxidize the tannins. I'd cork a more complex wine, but not this one."

"Well, I'd *like* something more complex. Preferably a Shiraz for this course, but we could settle for a Merlot. I'm happy to look with you."

"*Settle*?" She searched his face for a moment, then took the wine bottle, their fingers brushing with a sweet electric shock. "I can assure you there's nothing wrong with this wine, Mr. Santorini. Maybe..." She glanced up, holding his gaze with a dare in her eyes. "There's something wrong with your mouth."

He almost smiled. "Are you serious? I'm a chef."

"Ah, just what I need tonight. Another temperamental chef."

"Got problems in the kitchen, boss?"

She blew out a breath. "My chef is...feeling the stress of the event."

Her chef was a pain in the butt, based on Alex's one and only encounter with the guy.

"Every time I go at it with him, I kind of want to..." She lifted the bottle over his head with a teasing glimmer in her eye. "Give him the first pour."

The way she said it, the way she looked right into his eyes, was like she'd just turned up the heat to an eleven. "You wouldn't dare."

He sensed the bottle tipping over his head. "It would give me so…much…*pleasure*."

Pleasure. Oh, he could give her that. Heat pooled low in his gut at the loaded word.

Without even realizing it, they'd inched close enough that he could smell jasmine in her hair and count the individual eyelashes that fanned almost to her brows. He couldn't look away.

"But I can only have one unhappy chef at a time," she whispered with a sigh of surrender, lowering the bottle. "I have a Shiraz."

Alex stood still, his whole body humming as they locked gazes. After a moment, he rubbed a knuckle under his lower lip where his beard itched. "I'd like a…taste."

"I'll arrange for the server to replace your wine." Shuttering her eyes closed, she stepped away, then headed back down the stone corridor, her heels clicking, her hair swaying, his whole body fighting the desire to follow.

He turned, though, loosening the tuxedo jacket, which suddenly felt too tight and too hot, frustrated at the strikeout.

"Every time," he muttered. "Every damn time."

As he headed back to the airy, open terrace, the sound of giddy laughter pulled his attention to the table where Gramma Finnie and Yiayia were clinking crystal like the Irish and Greek representatives from the UN had just signed a new trade agreement.

"What's all this about?" he asked as he passed

behind his grandmother, placing a hand on her shoulder.

Yiayia looked up at him with a spark in her dark eyes. "We were just toasting…" She gave a questioning look to Gramma Finnie, who nodded as if giving permission. "Frenemies."

"What the hell is that?"

"Pru says it means enemies who become friends," Yiayia said, referring Gramma Finnie's teenaged granddaughter who spent a lot of time with these octogenarians. "And then they become…" She waggled her eyebrows, cracking him up.

"We couldna' help overhearin' bits of your conversation, lad." Gramma Finnie tapped her ear under fine, white hair. "Mightn't have picked up every word with the music and talkin', but we got the gist of it."

"Which would be?"

"We told you she belongs with Yianni," Yiayia said.

He snorted. "So he can wave a spreadsheet at her? When I could cover her in kourabiedes?"

The older woman laughed. "You do make a mean cookie, grandson."

"But so much animosity there." Gramma Finnie pointed to where the conversation had taken place. "We simply couldn't tell if you two want to beat each other or—"

"Eat each other," Yiayia finished.

He threw his head back with a hearty laugh. "Well, as soon as I figure it out, I'll tell you." He leaned over and planted a kiss on Yiayia's head. "I don't know who or what turned you from a nasty old battle-ax to one of my favorite people, but thank them for me."

9

Yiayia looked up, all humor gone from her eyes. "I do. Every day."

He blew them a kiss and went back to his table, scanning the dance floor for any sign of Grace. None yet, but Alex loved a challenge, and he wasn't about to give up on this one.

Chapter Two

For the remainder of the evening, during all the dancing—especially when the Greek side of the wedding party took over the floor—and throughout the bride and groom's exit and the crew's quiet but efficient cleanup of the farm tables dotting the terrace, Grace carefully avoided Alex Santorini. She had enough problems tonight and didn't need a second battle with that man and his...his...

Intensity.

Yes, he had mesmerizing brown eyes that looked right through to her soul. And impressively broad shoulders that most women would love to cling to. And, of course, half his chiseled face was covered with that rough, sexy beard that only drew every eye to the soft, full lips it surrounded.

But none of those handsome attributes had an effect on Grace Donovan. It was something much more raw and terrifying that kept Grace at a distance. Maybe it was his easy humor or that bubbling passion for life that sparked in his eyes. Maybe it was how *not casual* his casual touch was, or the way he drew her closer so she could hear every nuance of his deep voice.

Maybe it was just that it had been eons since Grace had been with a man. And she'd sure never been with one who somehow made her think he could take off her clothes *and* take down her walls.

Walls and clothes would stay in place, thank you very much. All that chemistry was just nature's way of reminding her that she was thirty-two and had better start procreating, stat.

Well, nature could suck it. And so could Alex Santorini. She had a winery to run and the biggest opportunity of her professional career right around the corner.

So, she'd best go talk to her high-maintenance chef to remind him that they had a very important meeting on Tuesday, which might mean he'd have to work Monday to prepare, like it or not. Knowing Desmond Landsdown? Probably not.

But this wasn't any meeting. It was *the* meeting. The advance team for the event that would change the trajectory of this little winery and seal her success. Desmond damn well better give up his day off to prepare, because without him, she'd never make the short list for Scooter and Blue's wedding.

She still couldn't believe Overlook Glen had even made the long list for first review. But apparently, Blue, a capricious and unpredictable celebrity if there ever was one, wanted something small, understated, personal, and far enough off the beaten path that the paparazzi couldn't stalk the nuptials. Overlook Glen hit every one of those requirements.

But Desmond was nowhere to be found in the empty, but sparkling clean, kitchen.

"Desmond?" she called, opening the door to dry

storage, hoping to find him in that pantry. No luck. She tried the walk-in cooler, which was freezing and empty. Then the laundry, which was humming with linens being washed and dried, but no chef in sight.

Finally, she opened the back door and prayed he was chilling outside.

But it was quiet back here, the only sound the ambient noise of the last of the wedding-goers, the die-hards laughing and talking and refusing to leave even though the music had stopped and the bar had closed.

Desmond must have gone home, Grace decided. Fortunately, his home was a small cottage on the edge of the vineyard, just a few minutes' walk away. Grace was wearing the wrong shoes for a stroll down a stony path, but she didn't want to go all the way back up to her third-floor apartment in the winery house to get flats. And she didn't want to wait until tomorrow to make sure every perceived slight that had been inflicted on Desmond tonight was smoothed over and forgiven.

Yep, she often had to suck up to the moody chef, apologize for seventeen different people who pissed him off, promise to never again buy second-rate fontina, and stroke his massive ego. And still he threatened to walk at least once a month and twice during every wedding.

She wouldn't have minded, especially now that the season was just about over and most of the remaining events were smaller and held indoors. She could use freelance chefs for those. But she needed Desmond to win *the big one*, since he was far more talented than anyone she could hire locally.

She stumbled on a rock, but caught herself just as she came to the split in the path at the perimeter of the vineyard. The steps up to the terrace were about twenty feet in the other direction, close enough for her to still hear that last group of guests, but she headed the opposite way, toward the cook's cottage.

She breathed a sigh of relief when she saw a light in the window, hoping Desmond was having a late-night scotch and soda to calm down after a huge few days of banquet cooking.

"Des?" She knocked on the door, taken aback when it opened immediately.

The middle-aged man stood like he was about to step out and leave...with a suitcase in one hand. Oh *no*.

"Will you be back by Tuesday?" she asked, unable to hide a little note of fear and desperation.

"No. I won't ever be back."

"Desmond Landsdown." She put her hands over her mouth. "You *can't*."

"I can and I will. I'm meant for bigger and better things than North Carolina hick weddings with braised beef, and holy hell, were they dancing like Zorba the Greek out there? I thought the Hokey Pokey was bad."

Disappointment strangled her. "They're Greek."

"And the jig?"

"Also Irish." Did she really have to defend this big, loving, nice family who'd paid a lot of money for the pleasure of dancing however the hell they wanted? "Desmond, please. I know the sous chef I brought in didn't julienne the carrots to your liking and that those two new servers were a little pushy, but—"

He held up a hand. "It's just not enough for me. And you're not enough for me."

She felt her jaw slip open. "Excuse me?"

"You're so...crispy."

She was *crispy*? She just stared at him.

"Like bacon. Without the fat, of course."

"I'm...bacon?" She looked at the hand not holding a suitcase, half expecting an empty scotch glass. "What are you talking about?"

"I need to bond with my work family. It's one thing not to bond with minimum-wage servers, but tonight I realized that I just can't work for you, Grace."

She felt her back stiffen and bristle. "I thought we were..." Okay, not *friends*. "Doing fine."

"You are all wrapped up in your science and logic," he said. "Do you realize you refer to the seasoning with salt as an *enzymatic reaction*?"

"Well, it is, technically."

He shook his head vehemently. "I just can't connect with you. Hasn't anyone ever told you that?"

Hasn't anyone ever not *told you that?* would have been a better question. An age-old pain wrapped around her chest, squeezing so tight she could hardly breathe. "I do my best," she said on a rough whisper.

He just stared at her, his expression clear: Her best was not good enough.

She was going to have to pull out the big guns if she had a snowball's chance of keeping him on for another week. She took a deep inhale, lifted her chin, and looked him in the eyes.

"I was raised by foster families, Desmond. And never adopted. So, I admit that has made me...well,

I'm guarded. And, of course, I hold a degree in oenology, which is a science, and I tend to think scientifically, which might explain the enzymatic reaction. But I run a business, and you have a job here. How much do we need to have in common?"

He managed a shrug. "I want more from my life than a small-time mountain winery that makes its money on local weddings. I left a note inside where you can send my final paycheck."

"Desmond! You know what's happening this week. There's nothing small-time about Scooter Hawkings and Blue. Your name will be in *People* magazine. This will change everything for us. Blue is a household name."

"Blue? Pffft. A gimmicky *one* name. And her cotton candy music makes my teeth itch."

"Well, millions of people love her songs, and another bunch of millions love Scooter Hawkings."

He curled a lip. "Rednecks who drive pickups with gun racks and drink Jim Beam."

She closed her eyes, digging for composure in the face of his callous, bigoted generalizations. "This wedding is within our reach, Desmond. Nothing like it has ever happened here, and if we don't get selected as the venue, nothing like it ever will. I need you at that meeting on Tuesday."

"It's not just the meeting. You'll need me for the dry run, whenever they schedule it. And then for the actual wedding next year, with no date set yet. I literally will die if I can't get to a real metropolis by then."

"Just stay for the meeting, please." She sounded desperate. Well, she *was* desperate.

He shook his head and stepped all the way out of the cottage. "Not happening, Grace. I've got an interview at the Ritz-Carlton in Miami on Monday. I'm driving down there tonight."

He brushed by her and took a few steps, then turned back to her. She braced for one last chastisement, one more reminder that she was…crispy. Less than worthy of anyone's loyalty or love.

She swallowed, knowing that no matter what he said, it would be some version of the same thing she'd heard her entire childhood.

We've loved having you, Grace, but the system says it's best for you to move to another family now.

"You should know I've been feeding a pack of dogs."

She blinked at him. "Excuse me?"

"They started coming around here, and I…" He shrugged. "Anyway, if you see them, they're not mine, but they'll need food."

"Who do they belong to?"

"Beats me. They just showed up. Someone must have dumped them."

She closed her eyes. She sure knew what that felt like. "Okay. I'll keep an eye out for them."

He lifted a hand. "Sorry to leave you in the lurch, Grace. But it's better for both of us."

Wasn't it always?

She stood there and watched him walk up the hill toward the winery, tamping down an old sensation of…loss. There was no other word for it.

"Except this is business," she muttered to herself. "And most of the time, Desmond was a grade A douche, so it's not a loss at all."

Clinging to that thought, she headed back, following the path as best she could in the dark. But just as she reached the turn toward the back kitchen entrance, her high heel slipped on a stone, and she slipped, falling to her knees and landing hard on her palms.

"Damn it!" She bit back a small cry, hating that tears of frustration sprang to her eyes like she was a toddler who'd face-planted. Gritting her teeth, she pushed up and checked her knees and hands, which were bruised but not bleeding.

She could make it up the steps and across the terrace, the very shortest and safest way home. Except she still heard the strains of laughter and conversation of the last of her guests who were just unwilling for a perfect night to end.

But her imperfect night had to end, and soon.

She'd wait them out. They had to leave any minute, so she limped to the bottom step and dropped down with a heavy, noisy sigh just as a hoot of laughter rose from the group.

"Shane! How can you say that?" The man's voice echoed from the terrace. "Dad made us clean the storage barn and the kennels for a month just because you thought it would be hilarious to take some chick muddin' at midnight."

"You did?" a woman asked, not sounding too surprised.

"Of course he did, because that's how he got laid."

"Still works," the woman replied, cracking everyone up.

"Only if someone will take the baby for us."

"I got you covered, bro."

There was more laughter and some conversation she couldn't pick up, but she prayed this family's reminiscing and teasing would come to a blessed end. Closing her eyes, she pulled her bruised knees up to her chest and wrapped her arms around her legs, curling into the stone stairs, listening to the sounds of a family. A close, loving, large family with so many memories.

The lump in her throat was unwelcome, but no surprise. What would that have been like? To share a history with siblings like...

More tears threatened. Siblings like Bitsy and Jack.

"Is it that bad that you have to hide?"

She pushed her legs down and squinted into the moonlight, right into the face she'd been avoiding all night.

"Oh, hi. No, it's...not...bad." God, no. Nothing about Alex Santorini was bad. Especially since he'd lost the tux jacket and tie, and his shirt was open at the collar. "I just didn't want to interrupt the flow of their conversation."

"I think the only thing that flowed was the wine, which is why you've got campers on table six." He put one foot on the stair where she sat and leaned close enough for her to smell spice and the vineyard air on him. "I can get rid of them for you. Want me to?"

She almost said yes, looking into his impossibly dark eyes. She'd almost say yes to anything this man offered. "That's all right," she said, then she frowned and looked around. "What are you doing down here?"

"I'm the DD for this crew." He pointed up to the terrace and then sat onto the stair next to her. "They had one last bottle left, and I decided to take a walk through the vineyards while they finished. Is that okay? Against house rules?"

"No, it's fine."

"And you? Do you frequently lurk at the bottom of the stairs during events?"

"I had to talk to my chef." She pointed in the direction of the cottage. "He lives..." *Lived.* "Right there."

He angled his head, a question in his eyes. "Ah, yes. The thorn-in-your-rose-garden chef."

"Not a thorn anymore," she said dryly. "He's on his way to Florida for an interview at the Ritz-Carlton."

"No loss," he said, far too cavalier to understand just how much of a loss it was. "I thought that guy had ACS when I met him."

"ACS?"

"Asshole Chef Syndrome. Sadly, it's all too common in the business."

"He had a bad case." She dropped her head back with a grunt, thinking of nothing but that meeting on Tuesday. "Any idea how I can find a replacement *without* ACS really fast?"

"Full time? For this gig?" He squinted up toward the winery. "Shouldn't be too hard. There are chef job boards. Want me to email you some links?"

He did cook in a Greek deli, so maybe he knew someone qualified. "Yes, that'd be great. Just send it to the winery website. There's an email contact."

He leaned a little closer, just enough for their thighs to brush and send heat curling through her. "Or I could give it to you in person. Over dinner. That I made."

She didn't answer right away, mostly because the

thrill that traveled through her was a little irresistible, and she wanted to hold on to it before common sense wiped it away. "Thank you, but I don't think so."

He studied her for a long moment. "Got a great reason? Like another guy, or you hate beards, or you're still pissed about me sending back the wine? Because that was just a really lame excuse to try and get your attention."

Her eyes flickered in surprise. "It was?"

"I'm slick like that."

"You wanted to hit on me by insulting my wine?"

He shrugged. "I crashed and burned on all the standard attempts at humor and flirting. But dis the wine? Whoa, the woman notices you."

Another zing shot through her at the thought of him seeking her out or feeling the same attraction she did. "I noticed you the first time you walked into this winery, for a fundraising event with dogs." She couldn't help smiling. "There were oodles of cute dogs and hot firemen, but I noticed you."

"Then what's stopping you from saying yes to dinner?"

She was way too tired to lie. "You scare the hell out of me, Alex Santorini."

He drew back, obviously surprised by the answer, but then he broke into a wide smile. "Really? Okay. I like that."

"You like scaring me?"

"It's better than you not knowing I'm alive," he admitted. "What scares you?"

"Your...passion. I prefer to avoid it."

"Why? Passion is good. It's creative fuel. It's sexual fire. It's—"

She put a hand on his arm to stop him. "Passion is the opposite of science and logic, which I use as my guideposts to life."

"Your...guideposts. Not sure I ever thought about those. Might not even have them."

"You probably don't." She searched his face, taking in the angles of his cheeks, the near blackness of his eyes, her heart slamming her ribs now, while everything much lower sort of melted.

"And you have guideposts aplenty, I bet." He inched closer, forcing her gaze to drop to his mouth. "You know what I do to guideposts?"

"Mow them down?" she guessed.

"With passion." He leaned a little closer, and she didn't move away. Because all it would take was one more inch. One more second out here. One more—

"Alexander the Great!" A woman's voice cut through the tension stretched between them. "Where is our safe ride home?"

They both stayed completely frozen for a moment, then he slowly drew back. "I'm being paged."

And she was being saved from a big, big mistake. "Then you better go, Alexander the Great."

He grinned. "We're not done yet, Gracie."

The nickname cut right through her, forcing her to stand. "Yes, we are." She smoothed her skirt, ignoring her stinging palms. Sometimes, it hurt to build brick walls, but she knew when and how to do it.

"I'll call you?" he suggested as he stood, too, making her look up at him.

"Just send that email. That'll be good enough."

"Good enough is never good enough."

"In this case, it'll have to be."

He put a finger under her chin and lifted her face toward him. "Want my secret recipe for a good life?"

"Now that, maybe I could use." Tonight, anyway, when life felt anything but good.

"A little less logic and a lot more…passion."

She just stared at him, a little lost in those deep, dark eyes. "I'll…think about it." And she would. All night and tomorrow, she imagined.

He tapped her chin and turned around, taking the steps two at a time. "All right, you drunkards. Let's call it a night."

"To Waterford we go!" someone yelled.

"Let's go muddin'!"

"Are you out of your mind, Shane? Did you forget you have a nine-week-old baby at home?"

"Yeah, on second thought, count me out. How about you, Aidan?"

"I'm in. Who's gonna stop us? Gramma?"

"If I know Finola Kilcannon, she's firing up the four-wheeler right now."

The howls of laughter disappeared along with their footsteps, but Grace stood there for a few minutes, listening to the echo of a family and a feeling she'd never had, longing for it as much as she longed for that kiss.

Chapter Three

"I think Bitter Bark is letting us slide this morning." Cassie propped her elbows on the stainless-steel pass-through in the kitchen of Santorini's, looking at Alex. "Thank God we're slow, since I'm hung the hell over right now."

His younger sister's usual bright eyes did look understandably tired after last night's festivities. "How's Braden?" he asked as he slid a tiropita on the plate and considered some way to make the flaky egg-and-cheese pastry a little more gourmet and a little less Greek deli.

"All warm and cuddly in bed, waiting for me to come back to him."

"Ew." He made a face.

"What? We're engaged!" She fluttered the sparkling diamond on her left hand. "So can I leave early since I don't really work here anymore but I knew you were short-staffed?"

"Yes, you can go early, Cass." John walked in from the back office, adjusting his black-rimmed glasses as he peeked into the dining room. "There are exactly two tables alive out there."

Alex shot a look at his brother, a mirror image of himself right down to the close-cropped beards they grew to honor their father, the perennially bearded Nico Santorini, when he'd passed away.

"You think we should close early?" Alex asked, optimistic that he had a better way to spend his Sunday. Surely the Bitter Bark customers would understand. The entire town held Daniel Kilcannon and his whole family, which now included the Santorinis, on a pedestal so high a man could break his neck looking up at it.

"I have a walk-through with the new floor manager in Chestnut Creek," John said, referring to the original Santorini's Deli. "So I'm out of here in a few." Just then, the bell rang with the arrival of customers, making Cassie grunt with frustration.

"You're out," she said to John. "But the day laborers who dragged their booze-soaked butts in here out of love and pity have to stay."

"Just get the new arrivals served," John said. "Then we'll put up the closed sign."

"Hallelujah," Cassie sang as she walked out. "I'm going home to get lai—"

"Cassie." The double-older brother warning shot came out in perfect unison.

"Lazy," she finished on a laugh. "I'm going home to get *laz*y."

Alex was still smiling as she headed into the dining room, because he loved when his sister came in to help them out. It was rare these days, since her event-planning business was growing, but he always welcomed her spunky, sassy self in this kitchen.

It made him feel less...stuck. But, oh, he was.

Stuck at Santorini's Deli like the falafel burger he'd just tossed on the flat-top grill.

"You okay?" John asked, making Alex remember that even the slightest sigh would be picked up by twin radar. And the one he'd just let out wasn't slight, but then, Alex never did anything half-assed, even brood.

"I thought I'd work on some recipes this afternoon when we close," Alex said, flipping the chickpea and breadcrumb pattie he'd recently added to the brunch menu. "I bought all the ingredients at the farmer's market the other day."

"Yeah, I saw the Paris ham and Gruyère in the walk-in fridge. I knew that wasn't for our menu."

Because the biggest change on their menu since their grandfather opened the first Santorini's in 1953 was transforming a fried falafel ball into a veggie burger. "No menu changes" was one of the few demands their father had made from his deathbed.

"I just wanted to practice so I don't lose some croquette-making skills," Alex said. "I'd bring some to the Kilcannon Sunday dinner, but I take it there isn't one today."

"Cassie just told me the Kilcannon-Mahoney family texts were flying with a discussion of an impromptu gathering this afternoon for some Bloody Marys even though the big wedding was yesterday."

Alex choked a laugh. "Damn, those Irish give the Greeks a run for their money in the drinking department. You'd think they'd spend the day recovering."

"But we hold our whiskey so well, lad."

They both turned at the familiar brogue, spotting tiny Gramma Finnie on the other side of the pass-through and Yiayia only a few steps behind. Gramma clutched a squirmy brown dachshund he knew well, and even though he couldn't see the floor from his vantage point, he had no doubt Pyggie, their other doxie, was on a leash next to his own grandmother.

They were all frequent customers and never came without the dogs. Though they usually didn't bring them into the kitchen.

"Spanakopita coming right up," Alex said, knowing Gramma's order. "And, Yiayia? Can I interest you in a falafel burger?"

She made her best face of disapproval, but it just wasn't as effective since she'd discovered Botox. "A falafel burger? Alex, your father would be turning in his—"

Next to her, Gramma Finnie placed a subtle but firm hand on Yiayia's arm. "Agnes," she whispered. "Kindness, remember?"

"A falafel burger sounds…delicious." Yiayia's stiff shoulders softened, along with her tone. "But we're not here for food, I'm afraid. We need help."

His grandmother handed the leash to Gramma Finnie, who hung back while Yiayia rounded the pass to come back to the cooking area. Her husband had started the first Santorini's Deli back when it was *just* a deli, so her arrival in his personal space wasn't unexpected, but the desperate look on her face was.

"What's wrong?" he asked, aware that John and Cassie had moved in closer to listen.

"I've lost everything."

"What?" All three of her grandchildren asked the question at the same time.

In the doorway between the kitchen and dining room, Gramma Finnie sighed. "I fear that's a wee bit dramatic, Agnes," she said. "You've lost yer bag and the few dollars that were in it. Hardly everything."

Yiayia flashed a look to her friend. "I had photographs in there. And forty-dollar lipstick." She tried to frown. "I'm upset about it."

She didn't look too upset, but...Botox.

"Where did you leave it?" Cassie asked.

"The last time I remember, I put it under our table at the wedding. I don't know how I walked off without it, but I must have."

"Did you call the winery?" Alex asked. "I'll be happy to do that for you."

Gramma Finnie nodded. "Aye, we called. No one answered. 'Tis too far for me to drive."

Alex didn't argue with that. Finnie's driving skills—or lack thereof—were the stuff of Kilcannon family folklore that even the Santorinis had heard by now. "But I can," he said, his fingers already on the apron tie.

Grace Donovan, here I—

"John can," Yiayia said, narrowing her eyes.

"I have a meeting in the opposite direction," John said. "Anyway, you can drive that Buick boat out there, Yiayia."

Yiayia shook her head. "The mountain roads are too dangerous for me," she said.

"I was lost in the snow and nearly died out there last Christmas," Gramma Finnie added.

"Dangerous?" Cassie asked. "It's October. There hasn't even been a frost yet."

"I'll go." Alex flicked at his apron tie.

"No, no, no, Alexander." Yiayia's voice rose to that note it always reached when she wasn't getting her way. She pivoted to John. "You must go, Yianni."

"Alex just said he'd do it," John said, heading back to the office, ignoring the order.

"Let me get those dogs out of the kitchen." Cassie skirted around the pass to relieve Gramma Finnie of the leashes. "And y'all can fight it out. I'm not going, that's for sure, so I'd take Alex's offer."

"Alex has to cook!" Yiayia called after her.

"Not to mention..." Alex put a hand on Yiayia's shoulder. "I'm *not* the one you're trying to set up with Grace Donovan."

His grandmother's eyes flashed, and Finnie snorted a soft laugh.

When Yiayia opened her mouth to argue, Alex put his hand over her lips, careful not to touch her sticky lipstick. "You're wasting your time on John." He leaned down and whispered in her ear, "Grace Donovan already likes me."

Yiayia raised a carefully drawn brow. "Do you know how many times she made a beeline to avoid you last night? Finnie and I lost count."

"Proving she likes me."

"Oh, for crying out loud, Finnie, help me out here."

Gramma Finnie came closer, barely having to bend to see between the warmer and pass counter. "We've given it a great deal of thought and decided John's the one for her."

"She's not your type," Yiayia insisted.

"And we talked to her," Gramma added. "She's into science and stuff. He likes numbers and spreadsheets."

An age-old competitive streak shot up and down his spine. "You don't even want to give me a shot?"

Yiayia closed her eyes. "The Dogmothers can't fail, Alexander."

"The what?" He almost choked on a laugh. "You're serious?"

"As a heart attack," Yiayia said. "Which I almost had a few months ago, but because we had so carefully arranged for Braden and Cassie to fall in love, I was saved. Do you remember that?"

He studied her for a long moment, digging into his memory bank for all the ways he'd learned to handle his Yiayia when he was little. She'd been much nastier then, and more manipulative.

But he always knew how to get around her...then and now. The only thing that drove her more than the need to get her own way was the need for Santorini's Deli to run exactly as she said it should.

"You want to know what I remember?" he asked as he slid off the apron. "That you run a grill that makes mine look like a kindergartner was in charge."

Slowly, her gaze shifted to the cooktop. "Well, I surely wouldn't inflict that...*thing* on a customer."

"The falafel burger? It's a new menu item."

"You know how your father and grandfather felt about those."

"You're welcome to take over for a bit, while I run out to Overlook Glen Vineyards." He tipped his head. "To retrieve your handbag." *If it was even there.* "So, help us out, Yiayia?"

He pressed the apron into her hand, getting that look he knew so well, the one that said she knew she'd been outsmarted.

He smiled. "And you know how your son and husband felt about having a Santorini in the kitchen."

"'With a Santorini at the grill, there's always money in the till,'" she quoted, defeat in every word as she turned to Finnie with a plea in her eyes.

But the little Irish grandmother just clasped her hands on the top button of her baby-blue cardigan. "I think we should trust the lad on this one. You know, the Irish say, 'Love isn't logical.'"

He leaned in closer and gave Yiayia a kiss on the forehead, then frowned at her. "John? Are you kidding me?"

She glared at him. "A falafel burger? Are *you* kidding *me*? I think I just heard your grandfather cry from his cloud in heaven."

He was still laughing when he jumped into his Jeep Cherokee and headed back to Overlook Glen for round two. Or three. Whatever. He'd win the last one, and that was all that mattered.

Chapter Four

G race took her coffee to the terrace, still wearing her sleep pants and a T-shirt, safe in the knowledge that no one would see her this morning since Desmond had left for good. Her staff was all part-time, brought in for events as needed, and the harvest workers had long gone, though a couple of her best men had agreed to come and help with the press later this week now that fermentation was nearly complete.

So, she had the most important meeting in the brief history of her winery and her very first press without a vintner both in the same week. And she was alone. *What a surprise.*

Walking across the patio, she pushed a few chairs under the tables as she passed, pausing to pick up a stray flower that had fallen during last night's festivities. The cleaning crew would come tomorrow and make sure the place looked amazing for the big meeting, which she'd have to somehow manage without any assistance.

She could do it. That was how Grace Donovan had rolled her entire life. Well, most of it. The years she remembered clearly, anyway.

Grace's memory of life before she was a foster child was foggy and thin. Except for…Bitsy and Jack.

She shook her head, wanting the names and mental image to disappear. She didn't want to think about siblings she didn't know and might have invented. Didn't want to think about who she was before she was no one's child. How could she when the world she lived in now was so very beautiful?

Taking the steps down toward the vineyard, she paused to inhale the crisp autumn air and drink in the jaw-dropping view. She'd owned Overlook Glen Vineyards for just over three years, but she never took this vista for granted. Especially in October, when the blue foothills were tipped in every shade of gold and red from the peaks of the mountains on the horizon down to the valley below.

Her thirty acres were almost all stripped of their grapes now, but still boasted rows of green vines. In addition to the huge terrace where outdoor events were held, the property included the three-story, four-thousand-square-foot building that housed a massive kitchen, two offices, and a mini ballroom for indoor events on the first floor and her apartment on the third. The second floor had three more bedrooms and one bathroom, all empty now. But once she had money—next year, if she landed that wedding—she planned to add two more bathrooms and turn those into "bed-and-breakfast" suites for guests.

To this day, she couldn't believe her good fortune when the winery real estate agent had called with a secret "pocket listing" of a very small North Carolina vineyard that hadn't even hit the market yet.

The moment Grace laid eyes on the rolling hills of

neat grapevines and the gray stone walls and mullioned windows of the winery house, her reaction to Overlook Glen had been nothing short of visceral. Everything about the house, the wine-press building, the cottage, and, especially, the wine cellars had smacked her with a feeling she'd never known before.

Home.

And that wasn't a word she'd used often or casually, if at all. The buildings, land, view, and even the smell of the place tugged at her heart. Tears had sprung to her eyes the first time she'd entered the cold wine cellar corridor and touched the oak barrels. She'd inhaled familiar scents and felt the hard slate under her feet and cool air on her arms. *Home.*

She'd searched for almost a year, after getting her oenology degree, for a small, affordable family-run winery to purchase, with most of her effort focused on Upstate New York and Virginia. But when she saw Overlook Glen, there was no doubt this slightly run-down and shockingly well-priced property on a ridge over a verdant green valley was the one she wanted.

With the money Grace had saved on the bargain-sale price, she'd been able to make some basic repairs and renovations, update the kitchen, and invest in what she needed to launch a profitable event facility. In addition, she'd purchased newer winemaking equipment and had started bottling her own wine two years ago. For those harvests, she'd brought in a vintner, but this year—this *week*—she'd be calling the shots herself when they bottled the press that had been fermenting for a few weeks.

With another deep inhale, she navigated her way down to the tractor path that ran the perimeter of the vineyards, finding her way to the cottage much easier in the daylight than last night. Her knees were still scraped, but the only thing that really hurt was the knowledge that Desmond had left.

Maybe he'd changed his mind. Maybe he got a few miles away, realized he was being a prima donna and world-class jerk for leaving her high and dry, and came back.

But when she leaned over to peek in the tiny window, she knew that had not happened. The front room was dark and deserted.

Deciding to grab the note he said he left, she twisted the knob and opened the squeaky door. Or...was that the door? She frowned at the sound, which she heard again and realized wasn't the door. A soft mew or a...bark?

What had Desmond said about a pack of dogs? She froze in the doorway, looking around, half expecting wild wolves to jump out at her. For a moment, it was silent, then she heard that cry again, so soft it was nearly inaudible.

Didn't he say they were outside? Abandoned? Not his?

"Hello?"

She stepped into the tiny living area, peering into the adjacent kitchen separated by a small counter with two barstools, the only actual place to eat in the little house.

"Anyone home?"

She took a few more tentative steps, peering into the kitchen to see the back door was wide open. Oh great, Desmond. Anything could be in here, hiding around a corner.

Holding her breath, she kept walking, bracing for an animal to lunge at her, tentatively rounding the kitchen bar, waiting for a...

A single bark startled her, making her jump back just as a patter of footsteps tapped behind her in the hall. Spinning around, she fisted her hands and braced herself, then all her breath came out in a whoosh as her gaze dropped to the ground and landed on the tiniest ball of brown fur, with a wagging tail, giant eyes, and a pink tongue hanging out.

"Oh, you're just a puppy!" Instantly, she dropped to her knees, holding back so as not to scare him. "Hello there, little guy."

He barked again, a weak effort at best. Then he ran past her, circled around her once, and launched into the lid of a cardboard box a few feet away, landing on a purple checked blanket. That woolen cloth moved and fluttered as two more little furry puppies popped up, one white with a lighter brown head and a white circle on top, one all tan with a white snout. All three stared at her like she was their personal savior.

Grace leaned over to get a better look, but the white guy climbed out and scurried away, running through the kitchen, sliding on the linoleum, disappearing down the hall, and just as suddenly, he— she?—came back, reaching a dead stop in front of the box. Then the pup shot a playful look at Grace, dropped onto her back, and rolled over in a mewing, wagging, happy trance.

Laughing, Grace plopped to the floor by the box, enchanted. "A pack of dogs?" she asked incredulously. "Desmond called you three stuffed animals a *pack of dogs*?"

Dark Brown barked again, and the other one, the very color of peanut butter and fluff, tried and failed to follow her sibling out of the box, scratching at the blanket, but unable to get a hold.

"You need help, honey?" Grace reached for her, wrapping her hands around the warm, tiny belly. "What are you even eating?" Not much, by the feel of her ribs. "Did Desmond feed you?"

As she crooned and held the puppy closer, Brownie climbed out and made his way to her lap, nestling between her legs, while the third puppy kept darting around like a lunatic.

"How could he not tell me about you guys sooner?" She shook her head as she cuddled the peanut buttery one into her neck, getting bathed by a little tongue that was no doubt hungry for more than kisses. "And where is your mama?"

Dark brown guy looked up with a question in his eyes, as if he could say, *I wish I knew.*

Suddenly, the wild one slowed down, squatted low, and—

"Oh God, now we're peeing in the kitchen."

"We are?"

She nearly jumped out of her skin at the sound of a man's voice.

Desmond? Still holding the puppy, she tried to stand up just as Alex Santorini walked in, and suddenly her legs felt too weak to work.

"Because I have a hard and fast no-peeing-in-the-kitchen rule," he said, unfazed by the furry chaos.

She couldn't help laughing at that, maybe because a completely unexpected joy bubbled up in her at the sight of him. Or maybe it was the puppies. No, it was him.

"I found puppies."

"I see that." He started to crouch down as the puppy on her lap tried to scramble out. "Hang on," he said, grabbing a roll of paper towels on the counter and dabbing the yellow puddle. "Whose are they?" he asked as he tossed the paper towel in a trash bin and headed to the sink, with the brown dog right on his heels.

"Desmond, my former chef—"

He whipped around as he flipped the faucet handle. "He left puppies? What the hell?"

"No, he made a point of telling me they weren't his. He didn't say they lived here, just that he'd been feeding them." She stroked the bony body that still clung to her for dear life. "But they're so skinny."

He shook his hands dry and bent over to scoop up the dog at his feet, then folded right on the floor next to her, moving with remarkable grace and that effortlessness that he seemed to have about everything. Conversation, flirting, almost kissing. Alex made it all look so easy.

"C'mere, little one." He reached for Crazypants, but she scooted away, barking, wagging a tail, and then batting at Alex's hand with a paw.

"She, or he, is pretty playful," Grace told him.

"And what about this guy?" He stroked the one on his lap. "Baker's chocolate for days."

She laughed again, nuzzling the lover in her arms. "This one looks like peanut butter to me."

He watched the way the puppy bathed her chin and neck with licks. "Looks like he thinks you *taste* like peanut butter." There was something in his voice that sent a now familiar wisp of heat through her.

"What are you doing here?" she asked, realizing only now that she probably should have wondered that sooner. "How did you even find me down here?"

"I came around the back when no one answered the door. My grandmother left her bag at the wedding." He lifted the dog so they were face-to-face. "Did you eat her forty-dollar lipstick, little fellow?"

As cute as Alex was, Grace frowned at this news. "No one on the staff found a bag last night."

He sent her a sly look she didn't quite understand. "Shocking."

"No, it is. If no one reported it, then someone took it." She shifted the dog from one arm to the other. "I'll look in lost and found."

He waited a beat, then asked, "So, what are you going to do with these furballs?"

"I have no idea." She closed her eyes and pressed Peanut Butter to her nose for an inhale of puppy. "With the week I have ahead of me, I can't take care of them, that's for sure."

"Maybe they belong to a neighbor."

"Maybe, but none are close, and these dogs seem really young. Too young to be on their own."

"Well, they have each other."

She closed her eyes again, fighting an unexpected well of emotion. "Yeah, I guess."

"What kind of week do you have coming up? Another wedding?"

Blowing out a breath, she lowered the puppy onto her lap just as the crazy one came over, climbed onto her legs, and dropped her chin on Grace's thigh with a sigh that sounded like she'd waited her whole life for that spot.

Smiling, Grace petted the tiny head not much bigger than a golf ball. "I'm trying to land another wedding. A big one. But..." On a sigh, she looked at him, momentarily lost at how intensely he looked into her eyes. Like he was listening with his whole being and invested in every word. Did he have any idea how sexy that was?

"But...?" he urged.

"It's Scooter Hawkings and Blue. You know who they are?"

"Singers? Celebrities? Are they getting married?"

She chuckled. "Are you living on this planet?"

"In a Greek restaurant kitchen with no celebrity-gossip rags. They're getting married *here*?"

"You don't have to sound so stunned. This is a beautiful venue."

"I'm not and it is," he assured her. "It's just that...wow. I would imagine that is a big deal."

"It would be, if I get the business."

"So they're coming here this week?"

"Their advance people are, on Tuesday," she explained. "They're considering several wineries in western North Carolina for their wedding this spring because Blue was born out here." She closed her eyes. "And I have to bottle our harvest this week." She grunted. "Worst-possible timing. I might have to back out of the event."

"Are you out of your mind? That's got to be a game changer for you. Big names like that? Why would you back out?"

"I don't have a chef."

He inched back, dropping his chin to give her a *get real* look.

40

"What? I told you mine quit last...oh." She finally caught his drift. "No, I couldn't—"

"Of course you could. You need me here Tuesday for a meeting? Done. I'd love to cook for an event like that."

She searched his face, considering the offer. Considering how to tell him that, sorry, the guy who runs the Greek restaurant in town is not going to have the chops for a wedding of this caliber. "I don't know..."

"Oh, that's right. You're scared of me." He laughed softly. "I won't insult the wine. Or try to kiss you. Or...whatever you don't want me to do."

She couldn't even begin to imagine all the things she didn't want him to do, a few of which she'd already imagined while she was trying to fall asleep last night. But first things first, and she didn't want him to cook Greek deli food for an event that would attract major media attention.

"That's sweet of you, Alex, but—"

"Sweet schmeet. I want the job. It's kind of a chef's dream. I could—" Before he finished the thought, the puppy on her lap jumped up, leaped from her to him, and tried to crawl up his shirt, making him laugh. "You like that idea, kiddo?"

Well, Grace didn't like it. And now she had to politely talk him out of it.

"I better go look for your grandmother's bag," she said. "And feed these guys."

"You can't just give them regular food."

"You want to cook for them, too?"

He smiled. "I'd love to, but I might kill them."

Yikes. He really wasn't a good chef. "Oh, then..."

"Puppies need a special diet," he said. "I don't know what it is, and we don't even know how old these guys are. But we need to take them to Waterford Farm, because they'll know exactly what to do with them."

"Oh, that's right. Your mom's new husband owns a canine facility. I was there once to have some papers signed for their wedding."

"And I'm there often enough to know that puppies need special housing, because Molly, the vet, is always freaked about some kind of virus they can get. And they do need a specific diet if their mother's not around. And once they're healthy and old enough, Garrett Kilcannon can get them adopted to perfect homes."

"Home." The word came out before Grace took her next breath, getting a quizzical look from him.

"God knows what they've been through, Alex," she said. "When they last saw their mother or..." She didn't have to rationalize it. "I won't separate them."

"Okay, that's your call. But the first thing we should do is get them to a vet for some quality care. Right away. Now, actually. I'll take them if you want."

Her heart folded at the unexpected offer. Especially since she was sitting here wondering how to tell him his cooking skills wouldn't be good enough to fill in for her missing chef.

"We can take them there together," she said. "They'll be challenging for one person. But I'm not leaving them to get...separated. Siblings shouldn't be separated," she added, feeling the need to defend her position. "I would think as a twin you'd really get that."

"I was fine being away from John at a certain age," he said with a laugh. "They can stay together until they're older or you find their mother, but getting them placed in two or, more likely, three loving homes will be a breeze for the Kilcannons. It's what they do."

She stood after laying the warm puppy back on the purple blanket. "Okay," she agreed, not willing to argue the point now. "I'll get dressed and look for your grandmother's bag. Can you stay here with them? I won't be long."

"Sure."

As she walked a few steps, the weight of what she had to say pressed on her, along with the need to get it said and done. He *wasn't* the chef for this wedding. "Alex?"

"Yeah?"

"I think…"

His brows lifted expectantly.

"I think that you…"

It was going to hurt him, she sensed. And he'd done nothing to deserve that except run a Greek deli.

"Waiting," he teased.

"I think that you're really nice."

He lifted the dog he held to his lips. "Hear that, Choco? She likes me. You're a great wingman, little guy."

All she could do was smile. After all, he wasn't wrong. She did like him. That didn't mean she'd date him, kiss him, or let him cook for a major event. But, damn it, she did like him after all.

Chapter Five

The unvarnished truth was Grace Donovan didn't *want* Alex to cook for that wedding. That was almost as infuriating as the fact that she'd turned down a date with him. No, it was worse.

"What the hell?" he whispered to the puppies as he found bowls in the cabinets and made sure they all drank some water. Then he secured the little house and took them outside one at a time for business, still stewing.

She was practically crying for a chef, but the one in front of her wasn't up to par? Was she really that scared of him?

"Am I scary?" he asked the chocolate dog who peed in the grass for a good thirty seconds, then sniffed it for ten more before heading back into the house.

Nah, it couldn't be that she was scared of him. It had to be something else.

"Help me out, doggo?" he said as he carried the smallest and lightest of the three to a fresh spot of grass. The puppy responded with big eyes and a snuggle against Alex's ankle and an irresistible plea to be picked up. "Needy one, aren't you?"

She licked his face and stuck her little snout in his neck as if that was her way of proving him right.

Finally, he managed to get them all back in their carton lid, pressed into the purple folds of their blanket, and carried them back up to the terrace. Since Grace wasn't down yet, he set the box on one of the tables and texted Molly Kilcannon, his brand-new stepsister and one of the best vets in the county, to make sure she'd be at Waterford later. They exchanged a few texts, and he sent a picture of the pups, but in ten minutes they were all frantic to get free and run around.

One did, and he snagged it, and another tried, managing to get onto the table just as Grace came through the double doors that led to the terrace from the three-story house.

"I knew this was a two-man job," she joked, jogging closer to give him a hand.

She wore jeans and a teal sweater that matched the gaze she locked on him. With her long hair pulled up into a ponytail and almost no makeup except for some clear gloss on her lips, she looked fresh and beautiful.

"I could handle them," he said. "With leashes. Maybe a crate. And—yikes." The wild one escaped again. "Maybe some doggie Valium for the maniac."

She laughed. "I don't have any of those things, but I'll give you a bottle of wine for your help. Oh, I'm very sorry to say I scoured the lost and found and the whole terrace, reception area, and backrooms and didn't find a handbag. Is your grandmother positive she left it here?"

"I'll take it up with her, but, you, little devil…" He snagged the wayward puppy. "You are a wily one, little girl."

"You sure she's a girl?"

"I'm sure she's wired for sound." He held the puppy to his face and let her lick his cheek while her legs paddled the air and her white tail knocked back and forth. "Settle down, missy. Or mister. Molly will know what you are, other than *cray*."

Grace laughed. "You're definitely earning that wine," she said.

"Don't want wine," he said, lowering the dog to look Grace in the eye. "I want to cook for that wedding."

She paled a little. "That's…nice of you to offer. I'm really looking for a very specific kind of chef."

"A good one."

"Of course, but even more important, someone who can be at Overlook Glen full time. You never know what they'll need or when they'll need it. I'm looking to hire someone who'll be an integral part of my team, not a freelancer."

"By Tuesday."

She sighed. "I'll wing it Tuesday. It's better than bringing in someone who'll disappear before the next meeting."

"You're making a mistake," he said as he gathered up the box lid of puppies. "Because not only would you have the right chef, you'd have fun."

"Fun," she whispered the word.

"Buckle up, buttercup," he teased, bumping her with the box that was full of fun. "Could be a wild ride with these three."

He let the topic drop as they loaded the puppies into his Cherokee and headed to Waterford Farm. And it wasn't a wild ride, because the car lulled all three of their furry passengers to sleep, with one of them snoring so loud, Alex and Grace kept cracking up.

But he couldn't let the opportunity pass without a fight.

"So tell me about the event," he said after they'd been driving for a while. "The one you don't want my help with."

"Alex."

"It's okay. I can brainstorm with you, right? Give you some ideas for your big meeting on Tuesday?"

She shifted in her seat and gave a smile. "Of course. And that meeting is really just a chance for the advance team to walk the property, look at photos from other weddings, and talk preliminaries."

"But you'll give them food and wine?"

"I wasn't planning to," she said. "And the wine is definitely stressing me out."

"How so?"

"They want a custom wine," she told him. "Something just for the event that would be served and sent home with all the guests. They're wine people, and she's from North Carolina, so she wants to shine a light on the great wineries in our state."

He took the Bitter Bark exit and threw a glance at her, unable to hide his reaction. "Holy crap, what an opportunity."

Her return look was not as excited. "You see it as that. To me, it's a daunting challenge."

"Love me one of those."

She laughed softly. "Yeah, I bet you do. But this event…"

"But what? This shindig is what you do, right? It's like someone coming to me to make a signature dish.

What could be more exhilarating?"

"I've never made wine without a vintner," she admitted. "This is my first harvest on my own. We press later this week."

"Seriously?" He shot her a look of disbelief. "Man, you are under the gun this week." And still she didn't want his help.

"I was thinking that if I made the cut after the first meeting, I'd offer up the Pinot. The one you called lifeless."

"I told you, it was a ploy to get your attention."

"It might be a little lifeless," she said.

"It wasn't awful wine," he said quickly. "Just not perfect."

She huffed out a sigh in response.

"Why don't you use something else you have? What about the wine you're about to press?"

"It won't be ready to drink for eighteen months."

He frowned, thinking about that. "Look, I only know a little about making wine, but if you're pressing this week, doesn't that mean you'll have new wine? First press?"

She shook her head in immediate rejection of that idea. "No. Overlook Glen wines are aged."

"Pinot doesn't need to age."

She gave him a look that said exactly what she thought of that statement. "And skip the malolactic fermentation?"

He laughed softly. "Not sure what that is."

"It turns tart malic acid into a smoother lactic acid."

"So *that's* how you make that dreamy 1410," he teased.

"Shut up." She tapped his arm, but smiled. "And I would give it a better name. Like...Blue Hawk? You know, a mix of Scooter Hawkings and Blue?"

"Exactly what your competitors will do."

Dropping her head back, she laughed. "Shoot down every idea, why don't you?"

"Just trying to help. *If you'd let me.*"

"I told you, I'm cautious. And the commitment is more than you could make with your job. And I..."

"Am scared of me," he finished. "That's what you said last night."

"When you asked me on a date."

He reached over and put a hand over hers. "You're scared of me in your kitchen, too."

She looked him right in the eye. "Yes, I am," she said softly. "You are very...intense, Alex. A man of emotions and passion and deep, deep...feelings."

"Thank you." He squeezed his fingers a little. "I take all of that as a real compliment."

She sighed. "It's not...good for me to be around people like that."

He lifted his hand, waiting for the rest. There had to be an explanation. "Why not?" he asked when none came.

"Long story."

"I have time."

She shook her head. "I had a weird childhood," she said. "That's the short version."

"I want the long version."

She turned and looked into the back seat at the sleeping puppies. "They'll need names," she said.

"Crazy Ass, Chocolate, and Needy Nellie."

"No." She pointed at the box. "The brown one is

Jack. The wild one is Bitsy. And the one who needs the most love is…Gertie."

"What if you have their genders wrong?"

"Then we'll change the names to match what they are."

"You're the boss." He glanced in the rearview just as he pulled up to the wide, white gates with the WF logo on them. "Welcome to Waterford Farm, Jack and Bitsy and Gertie. They say it's a hundred acres of happy."

This time, she reached for him, closing her narrow fingers over his forearm. "Promise me one thing, Alex?"

"Anything."

"Don't let them get separated. Those three, Bitsy and Jack and Gertie? They have to stay together. Promise?"

"One condition."

She blew out a breath. "I told you, I can't—"

"You'll tell me the long version of your childhood story."

She just stared at him, then glanced into the back seat. "I kind of just did."

"What?" Now he was completely confused.

"Okay, I promise. I'll tell you someday."

"Someday soon."

She didn't answer, which he took as a yes.

As they drove in, Alex gave her a quick rundown on who might be at the house—but it couldn't be too quick once he reached the fifth or sixth or tenth name that ended in Kilcannon or Mahoney.

"How do you keep them all straight?" she asked on a laugh.

"John used to say we need a spreadsheet. Cousins left and right, couple of babies fired out in the space of a year, including two just two months ago. Now my sister is engaged to one of the firefighter brothers." He shook his head. "Sunday dinners are insane."

"I can't imagine." And that was the absolute truth. Nothing in Grace's life would have given her the ability to know what that kind of family felt like.

She shifted, turning to look around, getting a glimpse of a stately yellow farmhouse perched on a rise overlooking foothills with a totally different view than she had at the winery, but as beautiful as anything an artist ever painted on canvas.

The house itself, with three chimneys, dark green shutters, and a wraparound porch, looked like it belonged on the cover of *Southern Living*.

"I've only been here once," she told him. "Your mother gave me a quick tour, but I have a feeling I only saw a sliver of the pie."

"The property's amazing, but the facility? It's really one of the most impressive canine rescue and training sites on the whole East Coast. They train dogs and people who want to be dog trainers, have kennels that house dozens of dogs, a grooming studio, a full veterinary hospital, and a dorm for students who stay for weeks of specialized programs, some just to become dog trainers, some in law enforcement. There's a couple dozen dogs here on any given day." He gestured toward the three puppies crashed on their ugly blanket, made beautiful by their furry little bodies. "These guys'll fit right in."

"So you come here every Sunday?" she asked, still a little enchanted by the idea. "Everyone in the family does?"

"Usually. We close Santorini's early after Sunday brunch. After my mom started seeing Daniel, John and Cassie and I would come out once in a while, then more frequently, and now? It's just…" He shrugged. "Family, you know?"

She didn't answer because, no, she didn't know. Instead, she let her gaze drift from the house to a massive enclosed dog pen surrounded by clapboard outbuildings.

"Yep. There's a gathering." Alex tapped on the brakes as they reached a wide circular drive, which was peppered with a variety of trucks, cars, and one bright yellow Jeep Wrangler that had seen better days. "Liam, Garrett, Josh, and Darcy. Oh, that's Aidan's truck. I hope he and Beck brought pizzas from Slice of Heaven, because I usually bring the food." He squinted at the vehicles. "And there's Declan and Connor. Hell, more than half the family's here, and I know Cassie and Braden are on the way. Grandmothers can't be far behind."

"A full house," Gracie murmured on a sigh.

"Is that a problem?" There was far more surprise than challenge in his question, and it made her realize he'd never understand why the answer was *yes*.

"I'm kind of an introvert," she said with a self-deprecating laugh. It was only partially true, but telling him, *Big families put me into a tailspin*, would just be…*weird*.

He reached across the console to pat her arm. "Just stay with me every minute. I'm pretty much the polar opposite of introverted."

His fingers were warm and strong, and she couldn't resist putting her hand over his again for the sheer pleasure of more skin-on-skin contact.

"Thanks for your help with my abandoned-puppy problem," she said.

"Don't thank me." He jutted his chin over her shoulder toward the house. "Thank the puppy cavalry. Looks like Molly shared the news."

She turned to see at least eight adults, a teenager, one toddler, and three dogs heading down the drive to the car, led by an effervescent blonde she remembered as Daniel Kilcannon's youngest daughter, Darcy.

Oh boy. Grace closed her eyes for a moment, swallowed hard, and swore she would not let envy eat her alive. What would it be like to be surrounded by a virtual army of family? Nothing could ever hurt you, no one could leave, and the security would be... breathtaking.

Alex climbed out and gave a wave as he opened the door to the back seat. "I went looking for Yiayia's purse and found—"

"Puppies!" The squeal came from the beautiful dark-haired teenage girl named Prudence, the oldest of Daniel Kilcannon's grandchildren, who'd been quite the planning expert at several of the wedding meetings.

She tore ahead of the group, followed by a little boy who broke from his mother's grip and ran with Pru, a gorgeous German shepherd keeping pace.

"I want to hold one!" the little boy cried out. "I want to hold them all!"

As Alex carefully pulled out the carton of puppies and Grace got out of the passenger side, the lot of them descended like a human avalanche, laughing, joking, greeting, and cooing over the pups.

"Whoa, whoa, careful everyone," Alex said on a laugh, easing the box protectively against his chest, then lowering it to the ground. "These guys are young. And they're feisty. And—"

"So stinking cute!" Pru dropped to her knees, reaching her hand to the boy. "C'mere, Christian. These are just like baby Annabelle and my little brother, Danny." Grace could hear the pride in the girl's voice as she guided her little cousin's hand. "You know you have to be very careful with babies."

Behind them, tall, dark Liam, the oldest of the Kilcannons, dipped closer to give the toddler he held in his arms a closer look. "Look at the puppers, Fee," he whispered, making her squeal with delight.

"These are Labs," one of the Kilcannon brothers announced. That must be Shane, since the woman next to him wore a pink baby wrap, with a little bald head peeking out of the fabric. That would be the nine-week-old who kept him from going muddin' at midnight.

"And maybe some shepherd," Liam added.

"What they are is gorgeous." Another brother came closer, this one wearing a beat-up old hat.

Despite the crush of interest, not one person, not even the little boy who looked to be about seven, reached in to touch the puppies. It was clear this whole clan loved and respected dogs.

"My mom'll be right out." Pru looked up at Grace. "As a vet, she should be the first to handle and examine them. They can't be on the grass because of diseases, at least until they're completely cleared by a vet."

Alex and Grace shared a look.

"We might have broken that rule," Alex admitted.

"I found them in my cook's cottage," she explained. "And he's gone, so we don't have any idea who they belong to, or what they've been through."

"Someone just left them?" Christian asked, voicing with childish dismay what all of their faces said.

Liam leaned over, clinging to the armful of pink confection he held, putting one hand on the little boy's shoulder. "Son, this is why I tell you dogs beat people every time."

"What are their names?" Christian asked, shifting from knee to knee, obviously itching to pick up a puppy.

Alex, down on one knee next to the box, pointed to the almost-all-brown one. "If we have the genders right, this is Jack. And this..." He drew a little circle over the brown and white head. "This is Bitsy. And this little girl is Gertie, the sweetest of all."

As the chorus of greetings rose up, Grace reached for his shoulder, pressing a hand of gratitude on that strong muscle. He looked up, smiling.

"Did I get them right?"

"Perfect," she said, feeling her heart swelling over the fact that he cared so much about the names she'd given them, without even knowing why.

Just then, a woman walked over from the house, mahogany curls bouncing with each step, a broad-shouldered man next to her who looked no less masculine despite the tiny baby in his tattooed arms. This was Molly the vet, Grace recalled from an earlier introduction, and her husband, Trace, who trained therapy dogs.

"All right, let me at them." Molly worked her way through her siblings, cousins, in-laws, and daughter to get to the box, her pretty face brightening at the sight of the dogs. "Look at what we have here."

Molly didn't dive in and touch them, either, Grace noticed. But she fell right to her bottom and eased the box very close. Awake now, all three puppies started squirming and threatening to jump, but the lovely vet seemed to have a magical, calming presence, and her soft whispers settled them down.

"Pru, Christian, we need some crates to get them to the vet office. There are clean ones with fresh blankets in the back storage area. Oh, and pull a bag of puppy chow, please."

Without being told twice, the kids took off.

"I really did bring them to the right place," Grace mused, getting smiles from the group around her.

"And we'll get them adopted." The man in the hat stepped forward, taking it off so Grace could see that his dark good looks were as arresting as his brothers'. "I'm Garrett," he reminded her. "And when word goes out in my rescue network that we have these three, we'll have good homes as soon as Molly clears them for adoption."

Grace looked up at him, defiance lifting her chin. "They have to stay together."

His eyes widened a bit. "That could be a challenge."

"It's not negotiable," Alex said simply. "They've been through too much to be separated."

His statement seemed to be enough to end the subject and shift the attention back to the puppies, chattering about their breeds and health and personalities.

But Grace didn't hear much of it. Instead, she gave into a wave of gratitude toward Alex for his support on the subject. Affection had never been her strong suit, but Alex sure made her want to change that.

So she just inched her shoulder a tiny bit into his and smiled.

What Alex didn't know was that minuscule gesture was the equivalent to a full-on, openmouthed, kiss on the lips. Which suddenly felt…possible.

The fact was with this man, and this family, anything seemed possible.

Chapter Six

Molly would let only one of them in the exam room at a time, so Alex let Grace do the honors, and she seemed grateful. Ever since he'd come to her defense about separating the puppies, he'd felt a thaw from her in the form of more frequent smiles and a light in her eyes.

Warmed by that and assured that she'd be fine in the vet office alone, he headed to the house, hoping to get some time with his older brother, Nick, who hadn't been in the greeting committee, but had been staying at Waterford for the wedding festivities. Nick had flown in from Africa, where he worked as part of Doctors Without Borders. Their youngest sibling, Theo, had stayed here, too, but had had to report back to his Navy duty early that morning, so he'd taken a red-eye after the wedding.

Of course, Alex had talked to Nick a few times this week, but there was always a crowd. Even if that group was only his siblings, Mom, and Daniel, there'd been no real one-on-one time with his oldest brother. And, to be honest, Alex sensed there was still a slight discomfort where Nick, Mom, and Daniel Kilcannon were concerned.

Not long after his mother and Daniel started seeing each other, both families had been rocked by the news that Nico Matteo Santorini *Junior*, also known as Nick, was not the son of Nico Matteo Santorini *Senior*. Nick was, in fact, Daniel Kilcannon's offspring, conceived when Mom and the young vet student dated briefly in college, before she dropped out to go home and marry Dad.

The worst of the shock waves had passed in the ensuing months, and if anything, the three families were tighter than ever. Daniel, of course, had embraced the idea of another son. But Nick had struggled, no matter how much he'd tried to hide it. And Alex wanted to talk to him and see how he was doing, how things were going in Africa, and why he rarely mentioned the woman he'd told them months ago he loved.

As he approached the wraparound porch, the door opened, and Declan, the oldest of the three Mahoney men, who'd all followed in their father's footsteps to become firefighters, stepped out and greeted Alex.

"Have you seen my brother?" Alex asked after they had a quick hello.

"I think he just took Goldie out back for a walk," he said. "Poor thing's a wreck when your mother and Daniel aren't around."

"I'll find him. Thanks." As Alex started toward the door to cut through the house, Declan put a hand on his arm and shot a thumb outside. "Go this way, or you'll get dragged into a Mario Kart competition."

He smiled and nodded his appreciation for the tip,

hustling around the house, right past a snoring Rusty, Daniel's longtime Irish setter companion.

Alex spotted his brother's tall, lanky form and the dog about a hundred yards away on a path that led to the woods. "Hey, Nick," he called. "Want company?"

His brother turned and broke into an easy smile, the powerful genes of Daniel Kilcannon so obvious now. For Nick's entire life, they all—including his parents—had had no idea Nico Santorini wasn't his biological father. If not for Cassie's Christmas present of one of those online DNA tests for all the Santorinis to take, they might never have known.

But they knew now, and Alex wondered, not for the first time, how this life-changing news had altered his steady, stable doctor brother. *Half* brother, to be technically accurate. And definitely one of the greatest big brothers to ever live.

"I heard you came bearing puppies," Nick said as Alex approached, offering up an easy, brotherly hug. "A little like bringing sand to the beach, don't you think?"

Alex chuckled. "Where would you take three furbabies found abandoned in a winery cottage?"

Nick's dark brows lifted. "Sounds like you had an interesting morning."

"Extremely," he agreed. "You?"

He just shrugged, letting Goldie bring him to a stop so she could sniff and pee.

"I haven't had a chance to really talk to you," Alex said. "I miss you, bro."

Nick smiled and gave Alex's back a pat. "I miss you, too."

"Yeah, it's been a long rotation. You thinking about

coming back soon?" When Nick didn't answer, Alex narrowed his eyes. "Don't want to leave her, do you?"

Nick huffed out a soft breath. "Lucienne has no interest in living in the States," he said simply, referring to the French anesthesiologist he'd met about six months ago in the mobile medical unit where he worked in the Central African Republic. "I couldn't even persuade her to come to this wedding, and it wasn't for lack of trying or time off. She had the time, but no interest."

Nick made no effort to hide the disappointment in his voice.

"Shame," Alex said. "Last time you came home, it sounded like the relationship was serious. What changed?"

Nick shot him a look.

"The news about Dad? And Daniel?" Alex guessed. Why should that change anything? When Nick remained silent, Alex fell into step with an equally long stride and tried to think of how to get his brother to open up. "Africa has gotta be a tough place to carry on a normal relationship," he finally said.

"Oh, CAR is not normal," Nick said on a dry laugh. "Which is what Luci loves about it. About…us." He looked out toward the horizon, his jaw locked, his eyes tapered to slits, his thoughts about seven thousand miles away. "She lives for anything…unorthodox. Nothing normal for my Luci. The less like a traditional relationship, the better."

Alex threw him a look. "I imagine that's exciting."

Nick looked skyward. "It was, for a few months. Then it got exasperating. The idea of a ring, wedding, vows, and a marriage contract makes her hair curl."

Ring? Vows? *Marriage contract?* Alex almost choked. "Oh, sorry. I thought I was talking to Nick Santorini, bachelor to his last breath, saving the world one disadvantaged patient at a time."

Nick let out a sigh. "Those two things are not mutually exclusive, but hey. Things have changed, and not just because I had another birthday last week that put me so deep into the forties, it's a little scary."

"Forty-three. Not scary. So this is about Daniel Kilcannon?"

Nick kicked a stone on the path with his work boot. "Yep."

"How so?"

"I'm not the man I thought I was for forty-two years, Alex. And I often wake up and feel like I've lost Dad twice."

"Man, that sucks." It was bad enough to remember the night they gathered around that bed and said goodbye to the greatest Greek who ever lived. Feeling that loss all over again must have kicked poor Nick in the nuts. "But how did it change your relationship with Luci?"

"Well, it's kind of hard to admit, understand, or explain, but since you asked, I'll tell you." Nick slowed his step and turned to look Alex in the eyes. "For some reason that I cannot possibly explain, finding out Daniel Kilcannon, not Nico Santorini, is my father has made me want to have children."

Alex choked softly. "Whoa. Wasn't expecting that."

"Neither was I," Nick said on a laugh. "I was happily planning to go childless my entire life. But then I found out that my DNA is...half Irish. Half complete stranger. Half not what I thought. And all that has made me want to do is be sure I stamp that sucker on another human and make sure that this single, thin limb of the family tree gets to continue. Think I'm crazy?"

A little. "I think you've changed," Alex said honestly. "And I'm sure you've given a lot of thought to what a responsibility a kid would be and how tough it would be in your current lifestyle."

"How could I not? Luci reminds me every time I say a word about it. Fact is, mention kids and she practically laces up her running shoes and heads for the door. She does *not* want children, ever. Which was why we were a great match until…" He shrugged, then turned to Alex. "If I leave the program and come back to the States and return to private practice, I'll lose her. If I don't, I'll never have kids."

"And there's no compromise?" Alex asked.

"Not her favorite word," he admitted.

They turned and headed back to the house, the sounds of dogs barking and laughter rolling over the hill toward them.

"Have you talked to Daniel about this?" Alex asked.

"No. Haven't told anyone. Wouldn't have told you, but I just spent an hour trying to get through to the mobile unit in CAR, only to find out Luci's not on duty and no one knows where the hell she is." Low-level fury darkened his voice, and Alex understood Nick's need to unload. "It's not a safe country, and she loves nothing more than to…go off and explore. Like it's freaking London or something."

"She's smart, and I'm sure she's safe," Alex said. "But maybe you should get Daniel's opinion."

"Because he's my father?" There was just enough resentment in his tone for Alex to know he hadn't yet embraced this new normal.

"Because he's a smart guy. He gives great advice and really seems to understand this whole..." He made a sweeping gesture to include everything, from the raucous group on the back porch to the dogs in the pens outside. "Family thing."

"Well, no, he's kind of busy this week." His gaze shifted to the right, past Alex. "Is that your puppy girl?"

He turned and caught sight of Grace crossing the wide lawn from the vet's office, talking to Yiayia and Gramma Finnie.

"She's not a girl," he corrected. "She is one very... enigmatic woman."

"Enigmatic?" Nick gave him a playful jab. "Run, don't walk, little brother. The last thing you need is a woman you don't quite understand."

"Good to know, Nick."

Nick put a hand on Alex's shoulder and nodded his goodbye, taking off toward the house. That left Alex to decide whether he should follow him, or go snag Grace before the "Dogmothers" persuaded her to marry John.

It was a no-brainer, but as he walked toward Grace and the two old ladies, he had to wonder just what had the three of them so deep in conversation.

Grace remembered the lost purse the minute she saw the older Greek woman coming toward her.

"Oh, Mrs. Santorini." Grace held out her hand in apology. "I couldn't find your handbag anywhere. I'm so sorry."

"We heard you found puppies, though."

She smiled, amused and a little amazed at the way news traveled in this family. "Three of them." She gestured toward the vet office she'd left a few minutes ago, before the kids, Prudence and Christian, had taken her on a tour of the kennels. "Molly's running some more tests, so I wanted to find Alex."

Gramma Finnie's white brows lifted. "Alex? Why do you need him?"

A question she'd asked herself for that whole kennel tour. "Oh, well, we took a guess on genders, and it turns out we were right."

Yiayia inched back. "*We?* You're a *we* now?"

Grace felt the heat rise to her cheeks and cursed her fair-skinned tendency to blush. "He showed up right after I found the puppies, so…" She shook her head. "Anyway, about your purse. I feel awful, but I promise I'll contact every server who worked last night, and Overlook Glen will—"

"Tell her, Agnes." Gramma Finnie nudged her friend with an elbow.

The other woman shuttered her eyes closed on a sigh. "You didn't find my handbag because I didn't lose it," she said. "It must have been all that delicious wine you served."

"And the Jameson's," Gramma chimed in.

"And the dancing. When I do the sirtaki, I lose my mind." Yiayia gave a quick laugh. "So it turns out I hung the bag on the back of my bedroom door when I got home and never looked there. It was my mistake."

"Oh, well, I'm so relieved." Grace put a hand over her chest, smiling. "I thought someone might have taken it."

"The only thing taken is my pride," Yiayia said. "And to think Alex had to drive all the way out there."

"But I'm glad he did. I'm not sure I could have gotten those puppies here by myself."

"John wanted to come." Yiayia reached out and put a hand on Grace's arm. "He really did. But he had a meeting."

"That's all right, I—"

"But he's inside now, lass." The little grandma flanked Grace's other side. "So you can talk to him right this minute."

"Okay." She drew the word out, trying to let them down easy. "But I really should find Alex and..."

"Oh, Alex." Yiayia flicked her hand like Alex was a bothersome gnat. "You know, John can take you home when you leave. No reason for Alex to make that drive twice in one day."

"It's not that far, but..." Grace looked from one to the other. "If it's a problem for Alex, then..."

"Oh, he'll want to go cook," Yiayia said. "He was planning to do that all afternoon anyway. Trying out those crazy recipes he learned in France. Did you know my Yianni has a master's degree in...something very difficult? I can't remember what. He's very intelligent. And handsome."

Wait. Did she just say... "Alex trained in France?"

"Oh, he just disappeared for years over there," Yiayia said. "He finally came home when his father got ill."

"He studied cooking in France?" Why wouldn't he mention that?

"Which is why he's always trying to fancy up the Santorini's menu," Yiayia said. "And hang those awards, not that something called *Les Lebey de la gastronomie* would impress our customers. They want spanakopita!"

"He won a *Les Lebey* award?" Which was, if memory served her, the equivalent of an Oscar in French cuisine. "That's amazing."

"It is," Gramma Finnie agreed. "But John is the logical one. No passionate outbursts for the lad, just a cool, steady, quiet way about him."

"That's...nice." And if Grace were looking for a husband, like she was beginning to suspect these little old ladies seemed to think, those would be terrific attributes. But she was looking for a chef. A *Les Lebey* award?

"Oh, here's Alex now," Gramma Finnie said.

Yiayia tugged on Grace's arm. "Let's go in the house, dear."

Just as he approached, with a gleam of humor in his eyes, Molly stepped out of the vet's office and called for Grace.

"I have some test results," she said, coming closer with a clipboard at her chest. "Would you like to come and talk about them?"

She glanced at Alex, who was instantly at her side. "I'll go with you."

Out of the corner of her eye, she caught Gramma and Yiayia exchanging a most unhappy look. Alex must have caught it, too, because as the two women retreated, Alex whispered, "What was that all about?"

"It was about John."

He rolled his eyes. "They're nothing if not relentless."

"You won a *Les Lebey* award?"

He slowed his step. "The student's version of it, yes. Yiayia told you that?"

"It slipped out in the John sales pitch."

That made him laugh. "Does it change anything?"

"It might," she admitted. "Let's go find out about the puppies. Good news, though, we had the genders right."

He stayed next to her after Molly ushered them into a small waiting area lit softly to highlight the dog pictures on the wall—photos of all the Irish setters in the family, Pru had informed her earlier.

Across from them, Molly spread some papers on the coffee table. "Preliminary test results are a bit of a mixed bag," she said. "But the good news is they are relatively healthy, and any problems are treatable with medication, love, food, and time. Jack—the brown one?"

Grace nodded, so happy that the little leader of their pack could be named Jack.

"Jack has a low-grade fever, and that's most concerning to me. Were there signs of vomit or nausea?"

Grace shook her head. "I didn't see any, but I don't know how long they were in the house or…wherever they've been."

"What could cause a fever?" Alex asked.

"Parvo, which can be dangerous and would make him super contagious. The other two don't show symptoms, but I want to watch them. So they need to be in separate kennels until the blood tests come back tomorrow."

"How about the others?" Grace asked, surprised at how tight her chest was, considering she'd known these puppies for less than two hours.

These abandoned *puppies.*

"Bitsy? The kind of frantic one?" Molly asked.

Alex and Grace shared a look and a laugh. "Yep," Grace confirmed. "That's...Bitsy." Even saying the name gave her a little thrill.

"She's got a cough, and again, that could be a cold, or a sign of distemper, which we can't vaccinate against yet. I can treat the symptoms with meds, and we'll get a test back tomorrow as well. The good news is the quiet tan one—Gertie, right?"

Gertie. The first name that had come to mind, as she couldn't exactly call the puppy *Grace.*

"She checks out perfectly, though I'd want to keep her under observation in case she picked up parvo from her brother. But I can vaccinate them all for that sometime this week, based on my age estimate."

"How old are they?" Alex asked.

"At most, six weeks. More like five." She blew out a breath and tapped her notes. "They're at a very delicate stage. Just about ready for early separation from their mother, but not completely. The first four weeks are so critical for learning social skills—with dogs and humans—from the mother. If they've been separated from her too early, they risk health issues their whole lives, including susceptibility to disease. If we could do anything for these little guys, it would be to reunite them with their mother. The sooner, the better."

Grace's heart hitched. "We have no idea where their mother might be."

"My brother Garrett might be able to help," Molly said. "He has a lost-dog network that's second to none. He'll get on social media, and the word will spread all over this side of the state. If someone lost the puppies, it's not out of the realm of possible that they could show up to claim them."

"Who loses puppies?" Grace asked.

Molly angled her head, her thick curls falling, a sad look in her eyes. "It's rare, but it does happen. As a brand-new mother myself, I sure hope the puppies were accidentally separated from their mother and not just *left* at your property. Dumping a dog is as bad as dumping a child, in my opinion."

Grace closed her eyes, almost ashamed at how the puppies' plight hit home with her. It was silly, nothing she would ever admit, but now that they were named and lost and...

"What should we do, Molly?" Alex asked, putting his hand over Grace's as if he could sense the turmoil inside her.

"Leave them here for a few days at least," Molly said. "We'll take great care of them. And we'll get Garrett moving on social media. We've had situations where a kid was in charge and the puppies got out, so a family could be searching for them. They're not purebred, so I don't think these come from a breeder, but I will say they're solid, healthy dogs likely from strong parents. Puppies born to strays are often weaklings, and these aren't. I actually think they've been protecting each other, instinctively keeping each other alive. So let Garrett post pictures, descriptions, an address of where they were found, if you're okay with that."

"Of course," Grace said.

Molly gathered her papers, a slight frown on her face. "Are you planning to keep them or let us find them homes?"

"I don't know, but I do want them to stay together. Always."

Molly's gaze flickered with the same surprise she saw in Garrett's eyes when Grace made that announcement. "Have you ever owned a dog?" she asked.

Three, over the course of her unorthodox childhood. And one by one, she'd had to say goodbye to the dogs and the families they belonged to.

It's best this way... It's how the system works... It's for your own good.

"No dog of my own, no."

"Because three's a commitment," Molly warned with a soft laugh. "And these three, if they are a shepherd-Lab mix like it appears, could get sizable when full grown. If you want one, that's doable, but—"

"They need to stay together." There was no debating that now that they had these names and had been taken from their mother. "But can we discuss who owns them later?"

"Of course!" Molly reached across the table and took her hand. "I didn't mean to overwhelm you. Plus, you and Alex have done exactly the right thing with these puppies, and they'll all survive and thrive because you acted so swiftly and compassionately."

Grace managed a smile, aware that Alex had put his hand on her back and added some pressure.

"I know they're in good hands," Grace said, pushing up.

"Want to say goodbye to them?" Molly asked, gesturing her toward a door that led to the exam rooms.

"Of course we do," Alex said, guiding her with that comforting hand.

The puppies were in a room in the back, at eye level in separate crates against the wall. When Alex and Grace walked in, Jack barked, Bitsy started jumping, and Gertie just looked up and made that mewing sound.

"Hey, you guys." Grace went straight to Gertie's pen, closing her fingers around the wire mesh. "You okay, little one?"

She got the most pathetic look in response.

At Jack's crate, Alex stuck his nose right in front of the puppy's. "You're in charge, big boy. Make sure your sisters are happy."

Grace felt her chest crack a little.

They both stepped sideways and stood side by side in front of the last puppy, Bitsy.

"What kind of a name is Bitsy, anyway?" Alex asked, wiggling his finger in the crate so the puppy could nip at it. "Sounds like a spider."

How could she ever tell him that she didn't have any proof, but believed in her heart she had a little sister she'd called Bitsy? She couldn't. He'd think she was as crazy as anyone else she'd ever told. "It's her name," she said defiantly. "Itsy Bitsy." Just like the sister she might have imagined.

The puppy fell on her back, rolled twice, then jumped up and panted in Alex's face.

"Crazy Daisy would be better," he joked.

"I like Bitsy."

"Okay, then." He smashed his face against the crate, and Bitsy licked his nose. "You chill out, Bitsy. And take care of that cough."

Grace took a step back, regarding him with no small amount of wonder.

"What?" he asked, sensing her gaze on him. "I like them, too, you know."

"I know." She slipped her hand into his, a move that was both utterly out of character for her and so right. "Now, will you tell me a little bit about this French training you've had?"

"With pleasure. Can we go back to the winery now?"

"Sure. Are you in a hurry?"

"Just keeping you away from John." He winked at her. "Let's go, Gracie."

She should have nipped the name in the bud, told him right then and there that it brought back murky memories that confused and confounded her. She also should have let go of his hand and kept her distance and stopped flirting with him. She should have stopped letting him soften her heart and touch her soul and make her want to kiss him.

But she just smiled, gave his fingers a squeeze, and let him lead the way.

Chapter Seven

Based on her questions, Alex realized that Grace had seriously underestimated his culinary skills. Although he answered everything, he downplayed his work, always a firm believer in "show, don't tell" when it came to cooking. She hadn't yet offered him the assignment he wanted so much, but she would. She *had* to once she tasted his food.

Back at Overlook Glen, he allowed her to give a quick tour of the large house that was at the center of the winery, even though he really only wanted to see the kitchen. But he walked through the first-floor wing that consisted of a tasting bar and a function space for parties of twenty or so, a conference room, and a small office crowded with antique furniture but offering a spectacular vineyard view.

On the other side of the two-story reception hall and curved stone stairs, Grace led him down a hallway, then slowed her step as they reached the double doors of the banquet kitchen.

"Warning," she said, pushing them open. "It's cavernous."

"Cavernous?" Alex came to a dead stop in the

doorway, blinking at the fading afternoon light that poured through mullioned windows that filled one wall.

"I know, it's huge," Grace said.

His head swiveled from side to side as he took in the stainless steel, the equipment, the storage, the *space*. "Cavernous?" he repeated, a little speechless at it all. "Try…glorious. Extraordinary. Incredible, and holy shit, is that an eight-burner Viking stove *and* a Blodgett bakery deck oven?"

"You sound like little Christian when he saw the puppies."

"Of course I do, because, oh man, the pastries I could make." He took a few more steps, stretching his hands out to get it *all*.

"You think you could cook in here?"

"Cook?" He snorted a laugh. "I could do more than cook in here. I could make art in here. I could perform in here. I could…" He placed both hands on the massive prep counter, the size and scope of which he hadn't touched since he'd left France. "I could change lives with the food I make in this kitchen."

She laughed, her eyes light and bright as she watched him walk around. "Change lives? That's pretty extreme."

"So's my food. Especially if I have free rein in this piece of heaven that I've been dreaming of for years."

"I hate to admit it, but if we don't have an event, all this equipment isn't getting used. I have an apartment on the third floor with a small efficiency kitchen that meets my needs."

He moved slowly toward the Viking, glancing up to inspect an industrial-size hood that could suck the smoke out of a burning building.

"I had to replace the appliances when I first bought the winery," she told him. "I knew I wasn't going to make a profit on wine for a few years, but there isn't anything quite like this around Bitter Bark, Chestnut Creek, and Holly Hills. I got such an incredible deal on the purchase that I could afford to sink some cash into this kitchen, and then I renovated the reception hall and terrace for parties and weddings."

"Money well spent," he whispered as he pulled the oven door down and peered inside and pictured dough rising to near perfection. "I'm suffering from grade A kitchen envy right now. You should see what I have to work with. Santorini's is about a fifth this size. And at home, I have a galley kitchen in an apartment. This is…" He sighed and stroked the massive handle. "Gorgeous."

She laughed. "Well, make yourself at home. I don't think I've ever had a chef in here who treated everything with such reverence."

"Then you've probably never had a real chef in here. Is that a sound system?" he asked, pointing to speakers in the ceiling.

"Yeah, Desmond liked to hook his phone up to them with Bluetooth."

"Sweet." He pulled open the door to a large walk-in cooler. "And this is well stocked and neatly organized."

"A lot of that is what was purchased for your mom's wedding." Grace followed him into the tight, cold space. "So, technically, this food belongs to your family."

"So I can cook…" He bent over, doing a rapid inventory of the food and a lightning-quick menu in his head. "Wow. I could make…" He straightened and looked at her. "Dinner. Tonight. For you. And me."

"That's not—"

"Please." He put both hands on her shoulders and added gentle pressure. "Rosemary-infused rack of lamb with a carrot soufflé and maybe a red cabbage slaw with hazelnut and lemon? We can eat it outside and watch the sun go down."

She gave in to a slow smile. "You *really* want to do that celebrity wedding, don't you?"

"I really want to have dinner on the terrace with you."

He felt her shudder under his touch, then try to cover her response with a sigh of resignation. "Then I'll set up a table and pick the wine."

The next hour flew by in a blur as Alex slipped into work mode, put some classic rock on the sound system, and took advantage of every aspect of the chef's kitchen.

He was vaguely aware that Grace had come back, opened a bottle of wine, poured him a glass, and taken one to the chef's table under the window to watch him work. Every once in a while, when he stopped to think, wash his hands, or wipe down the prep station, he took a sip and threw her a smile. But mostly, he was deep into the creative process, timing his cooking, tasting his work, and visualizing the outcome.

When he had two plates beautifully arranged, he carried them outside, and she brought the wine. They sat across from each other, toasting just as a nearly full moon rose over the vineyard.

"How did you do this?" she asked with no small amount of wonder in her gaze.

"Years of training."

"Not…this." She looked down at the plate. "Obviously, you are a seriously fantastic chef."

"You haven't even taken a bite yet."

"I'm eating with my eyes. But I meant…" She flicked her fingers from her to him, then at the whole ambience around them. "This."

"The moonrise was just my good luck."

She laughed. "I guess I'm not explaining myself. How did you get me here? This is so far out of my comfort zone, I feel like I'm a different woman."

It was? "Dinner at home with a friend?"

"It feels…like more."

He put down his glass and laid his hand over hers. "It is," he said softly, making her eyes widen with surprise. "It's my audition."

Picking up her fork, she slid the tines through the mustard-shallot sauce, then closing her eyes, she slipped the fork between her lips and let out the softest, sweetest, sexiest moan.

After a moment, she opened her eyes to meet his, then leaned back in her chair, probably unaware that fading light put an extra glow in her hair and eyes. "Now I know why your family calls you Alexander the Great."

"Do I get the job?"

"Yes," she whispered.

He raised his glass to the moon. "Nice work, Mother Nature."

"Mother Nature didn't make this sauce."

He laughed, and then they both ate slowly, savoring every bite. Alex was always critical of his own creations, but he was confident he'd hit this one out of the park.

"Think this is the kind of dinner your celebrity clients would like?"

"It's the kind anyone with a mouth, nose, and stomach would like. This is perfect."

"Nothing's perfect, especially in the kitchen. But..." He took a bite and nodded when the flavors melded exactly as planned. "This is close."

"To answer your question, I honestly don't know what Scooter and Blue will want on the menu. That's what's being discussed with the advance team reps. That and..." She made a face and looked at the bottle on the table. "The wine."

"So, what's your plan for that?" he asked.

"To promise them whatever they want and then figure out how to deliver. They won't be tasting anything this week. I suppose, if we make the cut, there will be a test dinner—a dry run, if you will. That's usually how it goes when you're competing with other venues for a big event."

"But still you want to blow them away on Tuesday and make the cut."

"I do." Her gaze moved past him to the vineyards that spilled out from the terrace. "It's a shame we don't have an extra twelve or eighteen months to age this year's harvest. It was a wonderful harvest, the best in the three years I've had the winery. For weeks, I've been adjusting the candida on the fermentation and keeping the sulfur dioxide synthesis to a minimum."

"Have you ever considered..." He leaned closer. "*Not* treating winemaking like a science project?"

"It *is* a science project. Every single step of the way, including where we are right now, all the way through malolactic fermentation, science is involved."

"Malo-whatic?"

She smiled. "A layman would call it barrel aging, for at least a year, maybe eighteen months."

"And you feel that long step is absolutely necessary?"

She gave a sly smile. "Oh, I don't know. Do you think the rosemary rub on this lamb was absolutely necessary?"

"Not if I was making a different recipe."

"I never change the chemistry, which, I guess, is what you call the recipe."

He finished his last bite, setting down the fork and using the linen napkin to dab his mouth. "And you press late this week, right? That means you'll have wine this week from your wonderful harvest."

"I told you I'm not a fan of first press," she said. "It's…hit or miss, and it basically happens on one night, and there's a lot of…instinct involved." She sounded like she wasn't quite sure she trusted hers.

"But that's why the end product can be magical," he countered. "In France, they go crazy for the Beaujolais Nouveau."

"Different grapes, different climate, different soil. I mean, it could be done by someone with more experience."

"You could do it. Trust your gut."

She looked at him for a long time, quiet. "I trust science and logic," she finally said. "They've never let me down."

Like people. She didn't have to say it, but he could read the unspoken words in her eyes, and it made him want to know who did that and why and how he could show her that not every person would let her down.

"Well, I live and breathe by my gut," he replied. "It rarely fails me. Plus…" He put his hand over hers and felt her fingers tense. Baby steps, he told himself. No reason to scare her. "My palate is flawless," he said, only half teasing, but definitely keeping things light. "I could help you make that wine. It could be perfect."

She smiled, leaning right back toward him. "I thought there was no such thing as perfection."

"I meant in cooking. In life, plenty of things are perfect. Your eyes, sometimes blue, sometimes green, sometimes the most haunting shade of both. Those are perfection."

Color rose, highlighting her cheekbones. "Stop it."

"Why? It's true. And those three little puppies? Perfection."

She laughed. "They are. And so's your flirting game. Everything about you, actually." She tipped her head and studied him. "What's your fatal flaw?"

"That I don't have one?" he joked.

"Everyone has a fatal flaw. Please tell me there's *something* wrong with you."

He smiled and pointed a playful finger at her. "You're flirting game's pretty good, too, you know."

She laughed, denying nothing. "Name a flaw, Alex Santorini. Fatal or otherwise."

"Okay." He thought about it for a moment, knowing this was as good an opportunity as any to share his real issues with someone he liked and respected and who had no vested familial interest. "I'm frustrated by my situation, trapped in a kitchen that's nothing like the dream I just cooked in, and I frequently wake up in the middle of the night wanting to scream that I'm thirty-six years old and haven't started my life yet. Not my professional life, anyway."

She searched his face for a moment, thinking. "Why don't you change your situation?"

"Family." He didn't hesitate one nanosecond. "My family is the one and only reason I stay where I am and can't change a thing."

"Would they stop you?"

"No, but…" He lifted the glass and turned it to watch the liquid form legs. "It would rock the foundation of our family not to have a Santorini in the kitchen. It's more than just a family-*owned* business, it's a family-*run* business. And that doesn't just mean John clicking away on his calculator and griping about how much I paid for truffle salt. The business is a restaurant, so a Santorini should be cooking." His father hadn't said that on his deathbed, but Alex knew what the man had been thinking when he'd faced the end. And he couldn't let Nico Santorini down.

"I get that," she said. "But can't you sit down and tell your family how unhappy you are? They all seem like very reasonable and loving people."

"They are, and they'd probably tell me to go fly free. But I can't. I mean, I could if someone else knew how to cook. John's a numbers guy, Cassie is running her own event-planning business, Nick's a doctor in Africa, and Theo's in the Navy. My mom's a decent home cook, but no chef. The food gene was all…" He closed his eyes, his father's face as crystal clear as the day they'd said goodbye. "It's why I grew this beard, you know?"

"For the restaurant?"

"For my dad. John and I both did. We wanted to be exactly like him. Work like him. Look like him." He rubbed the now-familiar whiskers. "And I know it sounds crazy, but I feel like I'd be letting him down to walk away from the business that my grandfather started and my father ran." He gave her a slow grin. "This is a Greek thing, trust me."

"Sounds like a bunch of Greek *excuses* for not taking a chance and following your dreams, if you ask me."

Greek excuses? He shifted in his seat and took the last drink of his wine instead of dignifying that with a response.

"Who in your family would be upset if you turned over the restaurant to another talented chef?" she asked. "Your mother? I sense her life is with Daniel now. Your siblings all have their roles."

"Yiayia, for one," he said. "It would break her heart, which is not the strongest to begin with. She had a heart attack before she moved here and never even told us. Now she looks and acts different, but I know there's a very demanding woman under that nicely pulled face, and her expectations are sky-high."

"Have you ever talked to her about it?"

He shook his head. "She's only been living here a few months. She and Gramma Finnie are so busy trying to…"

"Set me up with your twin brother," she finished for him.

He laughed, then made a fake angry face. "Don't even *think* about it."

"I'm not."

The serious, sweet way she said it made him smile. "Anyway, she may look and act nicer than she used to be, but she's still a steel-spined matriarch with her lifeblood in the restaurant. If I announced I wanted to cook French food or open a high-end gourmet restaurant, it would rock the Santorini boat too much."

"The Santorini boat or the Alex boat?" She lifted a brow to punctuate the sharp, and weirdly intuitive, question.

He brushed it off. "You asked me my flaw. I think it's that I carry a low-grade level of resentment against my family for holding me back. You might not get that because you've been able to follow your passion to own a winery with nothing and no one to stop you."

"No one at all," she said, looking down. "Not a living soul."

His whole being went cold at the way she said it. "Really?"

"And..." She lifted her gaze and met his with one that was unwavering and pained. "I would trade this winery for a family that has depth and history and trust and love in a *heartbeat*. Hell, I'd trade it for a dysfunctional lot of losers. I'd throw in my right arm and last year's harvest for a couple of moderately interesting siblings and maybe a parent or two."

He just looked at her, knowing that whatever he said would sound cavalier in the face of that kind of emptiness.

"Don't ever resent your family, Alex," she said. "Be honest with them. Do the right thing for them. But don't resent them. You've no idea what it's like not to have one."

The words hit him hard, delivered with more passion than he'd heard from her, and the timbre of her voice said she meant every word.

"I'm sorry. I had no idea. I wouldn't have made that

assumption about your family not getting in the way."

She shrugged. "Sometimes, it just seems that people think the grass is always greener, but my grass?" She gave a dry laugh. "No, it isn't. My grass was brown. More like rocks, gravel, and barren wasteland. You have four siblings, an amazing mom, and have been gifted with about a dozen more of some of the greatest people I've ever met."

He stared at her, putting two and two together and coming up with...three. Three abandoned puppies. "So, I hope I'm not overstepping my bounds, but can I make an observation about you?"

"I suppose."

"Just going on my gut—"

"Which you trust."

"Completely. That gut tells me this is your reason for not wanting to separate those dogs."

She tried to wave off the observation, but he could see it hit home. "Oh, Alex. Dr. Freud is calling and wants his armchair analysis back." She tried for a light tone, but just missed the mark.

"I'm serious. I'm pretty smart about these things."

"Yes, it would seem you are."

"So I'm right." He leaned closer. "Will you tell me?"

When her shoulders tensed and her fingers shook ever so slightly, he actually felt his heart shift a little.

"If I don't," she said, "you'll guess it all anyway or suss it out with that amazing gut instinct."

Eventually, he would. "So, what's the story? How did you grow up? When did you lose your family?"

"I grew up...carefully," she said softly. "I was told my parents were killed in a car accident when I was five, and I ended up in the foster care system."

He frowned, something not fitting. "You were *told*?"

"There's nothing, not a single shred of a paper trail, that leads to them," she said. "My mother's name was Celia, and I only know that from one intrepid investigator, though I've been through three of them over the years, and worked with a California organization that specializes in helping foster children find their birth parents."

"Did you do a DNA test? Because one of those changed our entire family tree."

"Yes, twice, but the results were really unsatisfactory."

"What did you find out?"

"When the first one claimed I'm nearly forty percent Hispanic, with ancestors in South America, it seemed like a mistake, based on my coloring. But the results were almost the same from the second test. So apparently, this blue-eyed blonde is a Latina."

"Entirely possible," he said. "In France, I worked with a brilliant chef from Argentina, and he was a blue-eyed blond."

"Argentina was on the list, but none of the potential relatives were from outside the US. The only names I was given were likely third and fourth cousins, and I contacted them. No one had ever heard of anyone named Donovan anywhere in their family tree. No one had ever had a relative in California. Another dead end."

"California? That's where you're from?"

"I guess. That's where I ended up in the foster system." She took a deep breath and let it out with a ragged sigh. "Fact is, I don't know who I am, who my family was, where or what I come from, or…anything. Blank slate."

He sank deeper in his seat, the weight of her words pushing at him, making him ashamed that he'd so casually claimed to resent a family that was…his. Real, whole, and by his side, while she…

"Brick walls," she said under her breath.

"What you put up so no one gets too close?" he guessed.

She gave a sad smile. "Yes, that, too, but I meant that someone, somewhere spent an incredible amount of time or energy or money to be sure I only run into brick walls when I dig into my past. I *cannot* track down my family."

"I can't imagine what that's like."

"I've accepted it," she said. "And I've spent way too much of my own time, energy, and money on the problem, but ended up with nothing to show for it."

"And the years in foster care? You weren't adopted?"

"Nope." She shook her head. "I was shuffled from family to family, no more than eighteen months or two years in any one place. But…" She held up a hand as if she expected pity. "I'm the first to admit, I didn't have any horrible experiences. I ended up in decent homes, with good families, just…never adopted."

The crack in her voice was like a knife in his heart. Who wouldn't want a sweet little girl named Grace?

"I was smart," she said quickly, as though staving off his pity. "And intelligence is an asset in that world. I zipped through school, no matter where they put me. Four high schools, and only because I graduated early. About six elementary schools. I ended up getting many scholarships, because it turns out the education system has an open pocketbook for foster kids. I actually *made* money going to college and got my advanced degree on grants. I outsmarted the system, and I'm fine."

But, good God, she didn't *sound* fine. Her voice was strained and thin as she told her story, her hands fisted, her gaze averted toward the end, as if eye contact would literally hurt.

"So that's why the soft spot for abandoned puppies?" he guessed, trying to lighten the conversation.

"I don't have a lot of soft spots, as you might have noticed. Attachments are…difficult. But there is something about siblings. I've always wondered…" She closed her eyes, fighting so many emotions he couldn't begin to name them all. "Alex, can we change the subject? Please?"

"Of course. I'm sorry." He took that fisted hand in his and tried to loosen it so he could wrap his fingers around hers. "What do you want to talk about?"

She swallowed, rooted for composure, and found it. "An agenda for our meeting on Tuesday?" she suggested with false brightness.

"So I really have the job?"

"Yes." The sweet laugh was back in her voice. "You have the job."

"Thank you. And as far as the agenda, I'll wing it."

"Wing it?" She looked horrified. "Not this control freak's favorite two words."

"Don't worry," he assured her on a laugh. "I'll do my homework and come prepared. Trust me, okay?"

"You *do* know this is probably the most important professional opportunity I've ever had?"

"Then you've got the ideal partner. And you did a great wedding here. You've got the venue stuff covered."

"But not the wine stuff," she said.

He squeezed her hand. "Just promise them the wine of their dreams, and we'll figure it out." Then he ran his thumb over her soft, silky knuckles, already knowing if they felt this good, the rest of her would probably drive him crazy. "You can kill yourself by burying too many feelings, did you know that? It's a scientific fact. You like those."

She angled her head and very slowly eased her hand from his, standing up to end the dinner and all the personal talk. "I'll take my chances, Alex."

Chapter Eight

Grace awoke on Tuesday morning with a tight chest, a fluttery stomach, and a low-grade throbbing in her temples. So, the usual amount of stress before a big meeting. She dressed and then set up the conference room with coffee and cold drinks, notebooks, and a collection of some of the most stunning wedding pictures taken at Overlook Glen, the whole time mentally rehearsing the tour and her pitch for the important guests.

She organized her work at the round meeting table, opened her file, and glanced at the two business cards stapled to the inside, sent with the original request for wedding information. One was formal, feminine, and printed on see-through indigo vellum with raised white lettering.

Denise Cooper, Event Manager for Blue. The pop star's famous single name was written with a flourish of a B that looked like a calligrapher had drawn it on a wedding invitation.

The other card was thin, white, and inexpensive. *Joel Rosen, In Charge of Gigs & Shit.* On the back was Scooter Hawkings's square, scratchy, industrial logo.

Grace couldn't be the first person to wonder what had brought together these two marquee names with such shockingly different styles and audiences. Rumor had it they'd met when Blue drove up to a party at a music producer's mansion in Nashville, saw Scooter, and thought he was the valet, ordering him to park her car. He played along, came into the party with her keys, and by the time the night ended, they left together.

Could they do something with that? she wondered. Great-looking models as valets? Denise Cooper wouldn't give her a clue what they wanted until they met today, and after that, she could present her ideas.

"Special delivery!"

She lifted her head from studying the file in front of her, frowning at the male voice.

Alex. And, of course, butterflies in her stomach took flight.

Pushing up, she headed toward the reception area, already hearing the barks, and her heart suddenly fluttered for a whole different reason. "You have the puppies?"

She rushed around the corner and practically slammed into Alex, carrying a large wire crate and looking like Santa himself bearing gifts.

"I swung by Waterford this morning and checked on them, and Molly said they were cleared to go. I thought they'd bring us good luck today. I hope you agree and aren't overwhelmed."

"Oh, Alex." She dropped down to look at the three of them. "I'm thrilled. Are you sure they're okay to be here?"

"Some restrictions," he said. "They shouldn't walk

on grass that has been used by other dogs, which I didn't think would be a problem. They have a special diet, which I have covered. And Garrett has started running a social media campaign using this address as their location. And if their mother shows up, they'll be with her that much sooner. She's the one thing they need the most, according to Dr. Molly."

She looked up at him, cursing the unexpected lump in her throat. "Oh, that's...thank you for getting them." She stood and lifted her arms, reaching for him in a gesture that felt oddly natural.

Of course, he folded her in his arms with nothing unnatural or clumsy about his moves. "But I can't let you think I'm an actual knight in shining armor. Truth be told, I went to Waterford before dawn to use the kitchen, since Santorini's kicks into breakfast gear pretty early. But Waterford has a double oven and a helluva better cooktop than my apartment. I ran into Molly, and she told me they were good to go today. So, I snagged 'em. Plus, I got this oversized crate so they can all be comfy and together during our meeting."

"Why were you cooking before dawn?" she asked.

"For today. Gotta show the guests what I can do. Come on. I have the Santorini's catering van outside and a ton of stuff to unload."

"But no one is expecting food today. They already told me it's a brief meeting to go over logistics, then they're driving to the next winery."

"Where they'll get lunch and forget we exist."

We. Her heart slipped around her chest for a moment. "I like the way you think, Alex Santorini. And I *love* the way you cook."

92

He put an arm around her shoulders and squeezed. "We're going to kill this, Gracie." Then he tapped the top of the crate and leaned over the pups. "Sit tight, kids."

She followed him to a white van with his restaurant's name on the side, where he opened the double doors and started hauling out coolers, platters, and canvas bags overflowing with fresh vegetables.

"What is all this?"

"This is me winging it." He winked at her. "Go big or go home, right?"

"Right." How could she argue with someone who seemed to want this business as much as she did?

After a few minutes, they had everything unloaded, and he insisted on driving the van around the side so their guests wouldn't see it and come in with the preconceived notion that they were getting Greek food.

After giving the puppies some playtime, they set up the crate in the corner of the conference room so Grace could keep an eye on them while she worked.

"What work is left to do?" Alex asked as he looked around the carefully arranged table and the wall of giant wedding photo blowups.

"I have to rehearse my speaking notes."

"Speaking notes?" He gave a dry laugh. "Now those, I don't have."

"You don't need them," she assured him. "I'll be running the meeting, and I have a very specific agenda from beginning to end."

"Aye, aye, captain." He gave a mock salute and inched back, giving her a slow up-and-down, taking in her cream-colored linen shift and dark pumps, his gaze slow and appreciative. "You do look extremely professional. And gorgeous."

She smiled. "As do you." He wore a blue chambray shirt with the sleeves rolled up, tucked into khakis. It was the most dressed up she could remember seeing him, other than in a tux at his mother's wedding.

"I trimmed. Can you tell?" He lifted his chin from side to side, showing his dark whiskers cut short and neat.

"You look…" *Hot.* "Like a very competent chef."

He smirked. "Flew by competent years ago, honey. How much time until they get here?"

"Two hours and nine minutes."

"And thirteen seconds." With one knuckle, he raised her chin and forced her gaze right on him, not that it was ever anywhere else when he was in the room. "Relax, Gracie. We got this. You rehearse your well-planned agenda and leave their stomachs to me."

Her stomach did a somersault as he inched infinitesimally closer, and she could have sworn he was about to kiss her.

"Yes, Chef," she whispered.

He backed away and headed for the kitchen.

The somersault feeling in her stomach evaporated as Grace worked on her notes, only to be replaced by a gnawing hunger thanks to mouthwatering aromas that wafted from the kitchen.

Tangy onions, sweet, buttery pastry, the earthy scent of mushrooms and red wine, lemon, basil, thyme, and nutty cheeses. It was accompanied by a music playlist that consisted of nothing but the driving country twang of Scooter Hawkings's greatest hits, alternated with the cherublike ballads sung by Blue.

The only other sound was the almost constant bark and scrapes of the dogs, who seemed content in their corner, all together.

Between songs and barks, during a brief few seconds of silence, Grace heard two voices and a car door closing through her open window.

"They're here?" Thirty...*six* minutes early? She stood and hustled to the window, but couldn't see the other side of the parking lot from that angle.

As she darted into the hall, the music from the kitchen was even louder and the aroma even stronger, and all her butterflies and tension and nerves kicked into high gear as she crossed the stone floor to open one of the two massive doors. Time to welcome the event manager and the guy in charge of *Gigs & Shit*.

But she knew instantly that's not who was heading toward her.

"Well, will you take a listen to that?" A man stopped in midstep next to a petite brunette in a flowing lavender maxi dress. He took off a black cowboy hat and cocked his head.

No, Lord, *no*. That was no man. No regular man. That was—

"They're playing your song, sweetheart."

The woman paused, listened, opened her mouth, and belted out the next line. "And that's why they call me crazy..." She beamed up at him, tossing back a lock of waist-length glorious dark hair that had to take a team of five people to color and curl. "Crazy for you." On tiptoes, she kissed him. "And I am, Scooter Hawkings, hottest human on God's green earth!"

He threw his head back with laughter. "Lord Almighty, what did I do to deserve my sweet Blue Belle?"

"Blue Belle now? An hour ago, you called me Blue *Balls*."

"'Cause we were at your parents' house." He nuzzled her neck and gave his crotch an adjustment. "You got rid of mine, thanks to that little detour back there on the back road."

Grace stood dumbfounded and slack-jawed, almost unable to process...*anything*. An old terror crept up her back, stealing her breath, pressing her chest. *Change*. God, she hated it so much.

"Hello," she managed with a croak in her voice. "This is quite a...surprise. I was expecting Denise and Joel."

Arm in arm, six-foot-two Scooter and barely five-foot-three Blue, approached Grace, both of them exuding some kind of mystical larger-than-lifeness that was probably the secret to their celebrity.

"Oh, we shit-canned those two," Scooter announced on a snort, stretching out his free hand. "James Harvey Hawkings, ma'am, but if you don't call me Scooter, I'll have to shoot you."

Grace blinked and gave a nervous laugh, but Blue jabbed him with an elbow. "Shut up, cowboy. He wouldn't shoot a mouse, and we didn't fire anyone," she said, her speaking voice just as raspy and distinctive as her singing voice. "I'm Blue, and you must be...God, I forgot what Denise said your name is."

"Grace Donovan, and welcome to Overlook Glen Vineyards." She gave Blue's delicate hand a shake. "I really wasn't expecting...you."

"I know," Blue said, sailing by to enter the winery on her own. "But Scooter and I were visiting my folks, and I thought it might be fun to do a few of the venue reviews ourselves. Wow, this place is beautiful. Scoot, get in here, honey. It's like a freaking medieval castle. Be my knight in shining armor, Sir Scooter!"

He hustled in past Grace, leaving her standing on the stone stair trying to reconcile reality with expectations, barely able to breathe through the drowning sensation that she'd lost control.

"And now they're playing some real tunes," she heard Scooter say as Alex's playlist switched to a screaming guitar and a loud cry of "Kick your boots and booties higher, we're gonna set this place on fire!"

Pivoting, Grace caught up with the couple as they made their way around the oversize reception area, toward the wide, curved stairs with a wrought-iron railing. She could do this. She *had* to.

"That makes a beautiful setting for a bridal photo," Grace said, launching into her speech, even if this wasn't where she liked to start the tour.

But they breezed right past the stairs, noses in the air, noisily sniffing.

"Holy Mother of Culinary Insanity, what is that *smell*?" Scooter asked.

"It's heaven, Scoots." Blue grabbed his arm and started tugging him toward the kitchen. "We died and went to food heaven."

"I'm happy to give you a tour and..." Grace's voice faded as they trotted off and disappeared into the hall that led to the kitchen, laughing and singing and forgetting Grace existed. "Or you can just go surprise the chef," she whispered.

She hustled to catch up, and they beat her to the kitchen with Scooter bellowing his own song as they entered. Grace was right behind them, with a perfect view of Alex as he turned from his beloved pastry oven, holding a tray.

"Greetings," he said with barely a flicker of surprise. Maybe he didn't know what Scooter Hawkings and Blue looked like. "Porcini mushroom tartlets, anyone?"

Scooter and Blue shared a jaw-dropped look like little kids who'd been offered tickets to Disneyland.

"Did he say mushrooms?" Scooter stage-whispered.

"Porcini," Blue replied excitedly.

"Tartlets!" Scooter squeezed her. "That's my new nickname for you. Tartlet."

Laughing, they powered their way into the kitchen right over to the island. Alex grinned at them, then leaned a bit to the left to see around Scooter's height and catch Grace's eye. Before she could try to explain that this wasn't the advance team, he gave her a wink that communicated more confidence and comfort than she'd ever had in her whole life.

"Chef Alex Santorini," he said, wiping his hands on his white chef's apron and then extending one as he came around the island. "Welcome to my kitchen."

"I'm Scooter. This is Tartlet."

She giggled and shook his hand. "You can call me Blue."

"They decided to come in place of the advance team," Grace said, coming up behind them. "Isn't that a wonderful surprise?"

"No surprise," Alex said. "After reading that article in *Rolling Stone* about how you show up for your own sound checks five hours before a show, Scooter? I seriously expected you today."

Scooter shrugged. "Hey, I was a roadie as a teenager with big dreams. I learned then, if you want something done right, you don't leave it to anyone else."

"And you've wanted a winery wedding since you were a kid," Alex said to Blue with a sly smile. "At least that's what the author of *Am I Blue* wrote in the authorized biography."

"You read that?" she asked. "Just for…this?"

"Of course."

He *had*? Grace hadn't even thought about reading Blue's biography. That's what Alex called *winging it*?

Alex slipped by them to sidle next to Grace, putting a light hand on her back. "We haven't talked about much else but the chance to have this wedding at Overlook Glen."

Grace drew in a breath, a little envious of his social ease, and in awe, too. "Having you here in person is incredible," she said. "Would you like to start with a tour?"

"I'd like to start with a tartlet," Scooter said, powering toward the island and eyeing the array of food. "Jeez, Louise, man. You made all this?"

With a quick squeeze to her shoulder, Alex waved everyone closer. "Just wanted to let you know what kind of appetizers we might serve for your event. So I worked up a little tasting menu." He slid one tray forward, overflowing with long pastries filled with colorful veggies and bubbling cheese. "A Provençale vegetable tart drizzled with champagne vinaigrette and a fontina and basil dressing."

"I'm actually going to cry." Blue smacked her hand over her heart. "Or dive in face first."

Alex laughed. "These are simple cheddar gougères, which are…"

Scooter picked up the puff pastry and popped it into his mouth. "Cheeseballs, French style," he said on a chew. "Oh, sweet mother naked in the backyard, that is good." He swallowed and eyed the rest of the island like a starving man.

Alex continued walking them through the platters, from onion tarts to something called a brandade de morue. "This?" he said, picking up a small round of bread and running it through the luxuriously silky spread. "Will inspire you to write more music."

Blue leaned over the dish, holding back her long chocolate-colored waves to inhale. "Get. That. In. My. Belly. Now."

They all laughed, taking a break from chattering to just stare at the food.

"Uh, I thought we could start with a walk-through," Grace tried again. "We could look at the various spots for your vows to be exchanged and sit in the conference room to discuss event logistics and enjoy all this food."

For a moment, the two guests just stared at her, expressionless, then they both belly-laughed in musical unison. Holding Blue with one arm and grabbing the tray of brandade with the other, Scooter called over his shoulder, "I'm not leaving this place right here, mama. Get this shit to the table, stat. Bring some wine. Forks?"

"Optional," Blue joked.

Grace and Alex exchanged a look of surprise, his face nothing but amusement and a willingness to go with the flow. But Grace was sure hers revealed that old monster who resided deep inside of her, the one that writhed when things went off plan and tensed when she couldn't guide them back.

After a second, Alex leaned over and whispered, "We got this, Gracie."

She stared at him for a moment, realizing that with each breath she took, she was inhaling the confidence and flexibility and pure strength he exuded. And the scent of some really tasty herbs and spices.

"We sure do," she said under her breath.

Grace might not like to pivot and fly in a new direction, but Grac*ie*? Maybe, just maybe, she could.

They ate, drank, and were so damn merry, Alex's face hurt from laughing at this odd and hilarious couple, who were so down-to-earth it was hard to believe they were megastars with millions of rabid fans.

And dear God, Scooter Hawkings could *eat*.

Alex had almost as much fun watching the big man devour every bite with gusto as he did laughing at their silly antics and constant teasing, kissing, and inside jokes. When the last of the appetizers was nearly gone, Scooter leaned back, knocked back the rest of Grace's Pinot Noir, and threw an arm over Blue's shoulders.

"Blueberry, let's go check the place out, what do you say?"

"Oh, I'll take you," Grace said, pushing up from the bench she shared with Alex. "We can—"

"Go alone." Scooter held out a *halt* hand. "If you don't mind, we like to roam on these walk-throughs."

Interesting, Alex thought. How many had they done?

"I need to just soak up the spiritual essence of the place," Blue said in her airy, birdlike voice.

Scooter snorted a laugh. "Don't even ask me what that is, but if it involves taking off her clothes and rolling on the grass, I'm all in."

"And we'll stay out," Alex joked.

"It's getting the vibe," Blue said. "I need to get married in a place that smells like…love and joy. I want my friends and family to be smothered by the feeling that what happens here is good and lasting. So, we go alone. Do you mind?"

"Not at all," Grace assured them, but Alex could feel her whole body tense next to him.

"We should take the puppies out, anyway," he said to her.

"Wait. What?" Blue choked the question.

"There are *puppies*?" Scooter practically shot out of his chair.

"I love puppies!" Blue announced. "How many?"

"Three of them," Grace said. "And they are no doubt chomping at the bit to get free."

"Release the puppies!" Scooter shouted in a dead-on *Clash of the Titans* voice.

"Oh my God," Blue whispered. "Could this get any better? Three puppies!"

Grace turned to Alex. "Want to help me round up the crew?"

"Absolutely."

Leaving their guests, Alex and Grace walked out of the kitchen, and the minute they were past the reception area and out of earshot, they stopped, turned to each other, and high-fived with both hands.

"They loved your food."

"They love this place."

They spoke at exactly the same time, then laughed. "Alex," Grace said. "This is all you. They haven't even seen the property."

"They liked the Pinot Noir," he said, coming close to mockingly whisper, "And the *spiritual essence*."

"Not as much as the reblochon tarts with fingerling potatoes, or those herb and lemon baby artichokes."

"The *artichaut poivrade* is a game changer," he agreed, putting an arm around her to walk toward the conference room and the sound of their barking charges. "And now we close the deal with the three musketeers."

She laughed again. "I never dreamed this is how I could land this event. It's all so…spontaneous and unpredictable."

She said it like the words were synonymous with *horrible* and *dangerous*.

"I happen to love spontaneous and unpredictable," Alex said. "I live for both."

Grace groaned. "Not me."

"You've got to learn to let go, Gracie. And trust me."

"I'm learning," she promised as they reached a crate that literally rocked with the excitement of three squirming, barking, dying-to-be-free puppies. The minute Alex unlatched the door, Jack and Bitsy poured out, too fast to be caught. Alex darted to snag them, but Gertie practically jumped into Grace's arms, her tail wagging at warp speed.

"Oh, my little girl," Grace crooned. "You missed us. Come and meet our famous guests."

Alex snatched Jack and called for Bitsy, grabbing her just as she reached the door. Scooping one into each arm, he turned in time to catch Gertie licking Grace's face and kneading her chest with two happy paws.

Lucky puppy.

Grace threw her head back and gave the most liberated, joyous giggle, echoing what he'd heard from that petite rock star in the kitchen. It was a beautiful sound that drew him closer to her and made him ache to do everything that dog was doing—kiss, touch, and drown in the sound of Gracie's uncontrolled laughter.

"You know, I think these three *could* seal the deal for us," she said on a sigh at the end of her long laugh.

Us. He liked that. "We're a good team," he said softly. "You, me, and the dogs." He dipped his head so they were inches apart, close enough to kiss her so easily, close enough that he could hear her soft intake of a surprised breath.

For what felt like three, four, maybe five heartbeats, they just looked at each other, and neither one moved. One more second, and he would—

"Let's see them puppers!" Scooter's booming voice broke them apart suddenly, making them turn as the big man and his bride-to-be came waltzing in with no regard for any boundaries or protocol.

"Here they are," Grace said, a little breathless. "This is Gertie. The brown one's Jack. And the frantic one is Bitsy."

Scooter put his massive hands on either side of his face. "Lordy, I'm dead. Just deceased on the ground. Are they yours?" he asked Grace.

"For the moment," she said. "They were abandoned at the winery."

"*Abandoned?*" Blue's voice cracked like she'd hit the falsetto on one of her ballads as she took Bitsy from Alex. "Someone left these darling creatures? Oh, Scooter. I want them." She kissed the puppy. "I want them all."

"Whoa, whoa," Alex said, stepping in before the man who'd give his lady the moon got any ideas. "They need to stay here," he said, getting a look of abject disappointment from the lady. "I'm sorry, but they're under the care of a local vet, and we're hoping to find their mother. But you can see them anytime you're here."

"Then I'm going to want to come back, and soon," Blue said, taking and snuggling Bitsy, who squirmed to get free. "You are my little nugget."

Holding the puppy, she looked around, her eyes widening at the wall of oversize wedding prints Grace had hung. "Oh! Look at *them*. Were all these taken here?" she asked Grace.

"Every one. Right out on the terrace and in the winery and some on the grounds of the vineyards."

She stopped in front of one, using Bitsy's little paw to point. "Love that dress, hate those flowers. Oh my gosh, that view is a perfect backdrop. I want to see that spot right there, right now."

Scooter made a face at Alex as he took Jack in his big hands. "Puppies are more fun."

Jack was practically lost against Scooter's giant chest, rolling into a ball and settling against him, as calm as Alex had ever seen him. Scooter whispered endearments into the dog's ear, like he wasn't a big lug of a mountain man cuddling a five-pound ball of fur.

"Let's go look around, Scooter." Blue handed Bitsy to Grace, who took the dog with the free arm that wasn't holding Gertie. "I want to get the feel of this place."

"Only if I can bring Jack the Ripper." At Blue's look, he added, "What? That's what he's doing to my heart, right?"

"We should hang on to the puppies," Alex said, only a little afraid these two would get a little overenthusiastic with them. "They have some restrictions on the property, but they'll be waiting for you."

The big man reluctantly gave up Jack. "I'll be back," he promised, Terminator style, before joining Blue and heading out.

As their voices faded down the hall, Grace and Alex turned to each other.

"I knew they'd bring us good luck," Alex said.

"You brought the luck," she said. "And the skill and style and...and..." She lifted the two dogs in her arms. "If my hands weren't full, I'd probably kiss you right now."

He leaned closer, over all three dogs. "Be my guest."

She gave him a peck.

"A real kiss," he urged.

"When we make the next cut for this wedding."

"That's what I need," he said to Jack. "Inspiration." But he really needed that kiss and wouldn't be happy until he got it.

Chapter Nine

The next morning, Grace was still feeling the glow of the day before. The laughter, the food, the optimism, the puppies. The *chef.*

That gorgeous, talented, passionate, confident, sexy chef who'd kept her awake with fantasies and thoughts she hadn't entertained in a long, long time.

Scooter and Blue had spent hours walking the vineyard, poking around the winery, and lounging on the terrace, playing with the puppies until all five of them were asleep in the setting sun.

Inside, Grace and Alex had cleaned the kitchen until it sparkled, then waited. And talked. And planned. And laughed. And started planning another meal for the unorthodox guests who didn't seem to want to leave. But then Scooter came in with a sleeping Blue in his arms and whispered that they had to go.

So as strange as their arrival had been, their exit was just as dramatic and…unexpected.

Alex had left soon after, hoping to get to the restaurant for Tuesday dinner service, which she couldn't believe he could cook after that long day. That night, Grace had slept with the puppies in the crate next to her bed until they succeeded in begging to be let into her bed in the middle of the night.

As soon as the sun slipped over the horizon, she took them out, spreading their purple blanket on the lawn in front of the cook's cottage to let them romp in the morning air, secured by shrubs and a small gate so they couldn't escape.

Glancing at the little house, she realized she hadn't even thought about Desmond once in more than twenty-four hours. Sighing with sadness, it made her realize that one more person had come and gone in her life, leaving not even a trace behind. Just…three dogs and one blanket.

She swallowed against an unexpected lump in her throat, guiding Gertie onto her lap for some love.

"People just seem to disappear in my life, Gert," she whispered to the dog. "It must be me."

Gertie looked up with big brown eyes, her expression so dear, Grace would have sworn she was disagreeing.

As she pulled the little creature up for a kiss, her phone buzzed. It couldn't be eight o'clock yet, she thought as she fished it out of her sweatpants pocket. She used this phone as the winery line, so calls did come in at all hours.

She gasped softly at the name *Denise Cooper* on the screen. Blue's advance person? They'd made a decision already?

Crossing her fingers, Grace took a deep breath and answered the call with her most professional voice. "Hello, this is Grace Donovan. How can I help you?"

"Hey, Grace, it's Denise. Hope you're still speaking to me after that surprise."

Grace laughed. "Of course. It was a completely pleasant surprise, I assure you."

"Really? On a scale of one to ten, how speechless were you?"

"About an eleven. And a half."

"You sure recovered well," Denise assured her. "Blue gushed last night when she called me after they finished at Foothill Ridge."

Grace almost choked. They'd left here and gone to another winery? A much bigger competitor? "Oh, that's…" Stunning. "Good to know."

"So, I hope you're sitting down."

Oh Lord. "I am."

"Blue and Scooter want to do a dry-run event at the last three wineries in the running."

There were three? "Okay, we hoped for that, although my chef did cook for them."

"Trust me, I heard," she said on a sarcastic moan. "If I had to hear the word *tart* one more time, I might have screamed. The only thing they loved more were those puppies."

Grace smiled and stroked Gertie. "They are a bit magical," she admitted.

"They must have been, because I'm happy to officially announce that Overlook Glen made the next cut."

"Really?" She gave Gertie a victory kiss. "I'm so happy to hear that."

"Don't get too happy," Denise added. "Because with that comes some significant work on your part. If you want to drop out, we understand. Foothill did, which is why we're down to three finalists."

Grace felt like her head was spinning. "Foothill

Ridge Winery? Where they went last night?"

"Yeah. But Blue didn't really love them, to be honest, and it might have been mutual. The owner was pissed they showed up so late and in person, no less. Anyhoo, when I told Foothill the parameters for the next round, they dropped out."

How bad were the parameters that Foothill would walk away from this wedding? "Then they mustn't have wanted to be selected as much as we do," Grace said.

"Good answer, but maybe you better hear me out first."

She switched the phone to her other ear, sitting up straighter. "Go ahead."

"Scooter and Blue are asking that the remaining three wineries replicate a wedding in every way. Not their wedding, mind you, since I know you didn't discuss any details about what Blue wants. But a wedding*like* event. Top to bottom, food, wine, décor, photographer, music, everything. And that one-of-a-kind wine is a must. They want you to put it together and supply at least twenty people to attend, in addition to the entourage they'll bring, which will mean about forty total for the event."

Now it didn't *feel* like her head was spinning—it really was. "Whoa, that's…"

"A metric buttload of work, I know." She sighed. "They'll cover every dime of your out-of-pocket expenses even if you don't get chosen. If you do, your venue will be booked solid for the next few years. No question about that."

And she wanted those bookings. "So, a full dry run of a wedding reception and dinner?"

"Yeah," Denise said on a laugh. "I guess you figured out by now that Scooter and Blue do things a little, uh, differently than most people."

"They are spontaneous," Grace agreed.

"And demanding. Believe me, I've worked for Blue for two years, and this is just how she rolls, and Scooter's cut from the same cloth. Don't be fooled by their goofiness and jokes. They are totally serious about their images and their brands, even for a small, private wedding. They'll be looking for that something special that makes your place stand out against Mockingbird Estates and Silverbell Vineyards. Blue's looking for something indescribable that will make the winner just jump out to her with zero doubts."

What could Overlook Glen offer that those two gorgeous wineries couldn't? They were bigger, had full-time staff, and had been hosting weddings much longer than she had.

"You want out?" Denise asked after Grace was quiet for a beat.

With Alex on her side? "Absolutely not. I think we can handle anything." She closed her fingers over Gertie's belly and watched Jack and Bitsy bat at a bush. "When are they thinking about having this event?"

"Sunday, the third."

Grace spun through a mental calendar, coming up with no Sundays falling on the third early next year. Scooter and Blue hadn't set a date, yet, but she assumed it would be sometime in the summer. "You mean…May third?" she guessed.

Denise snorted. "I mean November third."

Grace pulled her phone out and stared at her calendar app in utter disbelief. "In...*less than two weeks*?"

"Look, it's crazy, I know. But Scooter's going on tour for months, and Blue's dropping a surprise Christmas album in mid-November—if you tell that to a soul, she'll have you killed in your sleep—but she thinks if you can pull this off, then you can do anything. And, sorry, but they are celebrities and usually get what they want."

So, she had to come up with twenty people, an entire wedding menu, music, flowers, décor, and the wine made exclusively for them...all in less than two weeks? In the middle of the post-harvest press? For a moment, she just couldn't speak.

"Your chef can handle the short notice?"

For the first time in a while, she smiled. The chef was actually the least of her problems. "My chef can handle anything." *Just ask him.*

"Well, they loved him," Denise said. "And your winery, puppies, and you."

"That's good."

"And, Grace, thank you for not freaking out over this. These aren't easy calls to make, but when you work for a global superstar, this is the territory."

"Nothing makes me freak out, Denise." Except change, detours, stress, and emotional messiness. Which could be the essence of every single moment for the next two weeks if she said yes to this. But how could she say no? With Alex, she might actually be able to pull this off.

She cleared her throat and sat up straighter. "Denise, I can assure you that we'll do everything in our power to wow Blue, Scooter, and every person at the dry run."

"I like that," Denise replied with a smile in her voice. "So we'll see you on Sunday, the third of *November*, ready to be wowed."

After saying goodbye, Grace clicked off and scooped up little Gertie for a kiss. "I don't know if I want to cry or scream," she whispered. "But I know exactly who we're calling next."

Alex hadn't been a member of the "clan" that included the Kilcannon and Mahoney families for very long in the scheme of things. Only officially, by marriage, for a matter of days since his mother and Daniel Kilcannon exchanged vows on Saturday. And by association for about four months since the couple had reunited, and he and John decided to open a Santorini's in Bitter Bark.

But it was long enough to know that no matter the size or scope of an issue or a need—whether it was a "little problem" or a "family crisis"—this group gathered, planned, acted, and solved.

They also joked, teased, mocked, ate, drank, and loved their dogs throughout the whole process.

So he wasn't the least bit surprised when he shot out a group text about the event that he and Gracie had to pull off and an impromptu "meeting" got called at Santorini's late that afternoon. The restaurant was closed for dinner on Wednesdays, but you wouldn't know it looking out to the dining room where many of the tables were occupied by Mahoneys or Kilcannons of all ages.

"You'd think they never got invited to anything," John joked as he came out of his office, carrying a notebook, the day's receipts, and his trusty calculator. "Everyone is here *but* Grace."

Alex laughed as he hung the last cooking pot and started to untie his apron. "How many Kilcannons and Mahoneys does it take to pull off an event?"

"It takes Santorinis," John quipped. "Oh, and good news. Tom Bartlett's got your ass covered for a few weeks."

"Really?" Alex held up his hand to give his brother a high five, grateful that a good cook from the Chestnut Creek location could cover for him here.

"Of course he wants time and a half, plus travel, and thinks we should put him up in a hotel."

Alex snorted. "Pay the extra, cover his gas, and let him sleep on the sofa in our apartment."

"Or in your bed, since you probably won't be there."

"Why wouldn't I…" He threw his brother a look. "Thanks for the vote of confidence, man. Not sure we're there." But he was sure he wanted to be. Still, he'd take it slow with a woman as cautious as Grace.

At the sound of the door opening, Alex dipped his head to see his mother and Daniel, who held the door for Grace. Stepping inside, she froze in place and blinked at the crowd.

"She looks shell-shocked," John said. "And, oh my God, she has three puppies on leashes."

Alex snorted a laugh. "Of course she does." He took a minute to stare at the woman and enjoy that now-familiar jolt of anticipation that hit him every time they were in the same room together.

Gracie.

God, he liked her. Need gnawed at his gut, and something far more primal hit him even lower. Yeah, *slow*. If he could.

"Twenty bucks says she's going to keep those dogs," Alex mused, finally tearing his gaze from Grace to look at his brother, who was staring at him. "What?"

"Just thinking about upping my bet in the family pool."

"What family pool?"

"The one that says you and Grace are…you know. The Dogmothers' next matchmaking hit."

He closed his eyes and shook his head, remembering his conversation with Grace about family. Sometimes, the one he was lucky enough to have did drive him a little crazy.

John clamped a hand on Alex's back. "My money's on you, based purely on how much you drool every time you see her. I think you're going down, little brother."

"Little?" He jerked out of John's grasp. "By four stinking minutes."

John just laughed. "Come on, the natives are getting restless."

Alex followed John to the dining room, noticing that Grace was still standing in the doorway. The dogs had been spirited away by Molly, Pru, and little Christian.

"Welcome to the nuthouse," he said under his breath as he got next to Grace, giving her what should have been a quick hug, but holding her one or two seconds too long. Long enough to feel her whole body slightly trembling. Too much family?

"Alex, *what* is going on?"

Yeah, a lot of family. "Dearly beloved, we've come to solve a problem. It's kind of what this bunch does. Don't be intimidated."

"I'm not, but…" She glanced around, gave a quick but nervous smile, then looked back up at him. "*Everyone?*"

"You need twenty people, right? And a plan for an event we have to pull off in twelve days? I asked on the group chat if people would be willing to come to the dry run, and they all want to know what else they can do to help."

"So they came here?"

"Well…" He laughed, seeing it through her eyes. "Most of them were in town, and the restaurant is closed tonight, and they will help you, believe me. So…" Every ounce of color had left her face, and he could have sworn her eyes welled up. "What's wrong?"

She shifted so that his whole body blocked her from the family's view. "I just never expected…this."

"I know they can be overwhelming, but they just want to lend a hand."

She nodded, pulling it together. "Yeah, okay. That's good. It's just…a lot."

"They don't bite. Much." He put an arm around her and tugged her into him so she knew she didn't have to face the crowd alone, then turned her around and called for everyone's attention.

When they finally quieted down—except for the puppies, who were being passed around and kissed like they were literal babies—Alex explained the whole situation to them, from the surprise visit by

Scooter and Blue to what the couple was asking.

"Is she as pretty in real life?" Pru asked, squeezing her hands together. "I am such a fan."

"She's beautiful," Grace confirmed. "Very petite in person."

"And big in personality," Alex added.

"So what can we do to help?" John asked from a corner booth, where he sat across from Daniel and Mom, with Santorini paperwork spread out on the table.

"For one thing," Grace said, "we need as many of you as possible to attend. Full wedding attire, happy faces on, acting like you're at the best wedding reception since, well..." She pointed at Daniel. "Since yours last weekend."

"Please tell me I can wear the same suit," Trace said. "Because I only have one."

"Absolutely," Grace assured him.

"Well, I can't wear the same dress," Mom joked. "But I will tell you, Grace, your venue is wonderful. And since we're not going on our honeymoon until after the holidays, you can count on us for another."

"And us," Aidan said, an arm around Beck, his wife of a few months, then he leaned over to look at Garrett. "Assuming you don't have me flying to deliver a dog."

"I promise. But are babies welcome at this wedding? Teething babies?" Garrett asked, lifting his brows to Jessie, who bounced their nearly eight-month-old son on her lap.

"Of course," Grace said quickly. "I'm sure Scooter and Blue would love that."

"Just know that Scooter Hawkings has never met a

personal boundary he won't break," Alex warned. "I'm not sure I'd trust him not to pick up your baby and sing to it."

"He can sing to me *anytime*," Yiayia said, fanning herself and cracking everyone up.

"So, you're all in?" Alex asked, giving Grace an *I told you so* look.

"Liam's still at Waterford," Andi said. "But count on this group of Kilcannons." She patted Christian's shoulder, making him look up from Jack, who had his undivided attention.

"Can we bring these dogs?" Christian asked.

"Oh, I don't know," Grace said. "That might be—"

"Brilliant," Alex interjected, earning a wide-eyed look from her.

"Puppies? At a wedding?" she asked.

"Trace and I had as many dogs as people at ours," Molly told her. "And that was a fairy tale wedding."

"Fairy tail," Pru chimed in. "T-A-I-L."

Everyone laughed, but Alex and Grace held each other's gaze.

"They did love the puppies," she said softly.

"None of the competition will have anything like that."

"Just don't think about training them." Shane, easily one of the best dog trainers Alex had ever known, lifted Bitsy out of Pru's hands, holding her high. "Cute as Christmas, but don't expect them to be a ring bearer like Meatball was in your wedding, Molls."

Bitsy tried to lick his face and wagged her tail.

"But they are all so darn cute," Pru said, taking Bitsy back from her uncle. "I know a lot about Blue. She'd love that idea at a wedding."

"Oh, there's no actual wedding," Grace reminded her. "Just the reception. And do we really want these three hooligans running around?"

"Hooligans!" Christian howled at the word and put his little nose close to Jack's. "Who's a hooligan?"

"Then we should have an *actual* wedding." Gramma Finnie scanned the crowd like she was on the hunt for her next victim.

"Too bad I just did that three months ago," Darcy said.

"Me, too," Beck added.

Cassie, between Darcy and her cousin Ella Mahoney in their usual pack of three, sat a little straighter and cleared her throat. "What you need is an event planner, Grace," she called out. "I'm all yours, *gratis*."

"Thank you, Cassie," Grace said. "I loved your ideas for your mom's wedding. I'll take you up on that offer, but nothing's gratis. Scooter and Blue are covering all expenses."

Cassie's eyes lit. "Sweet deal."

"What else can we do?" Molly asked.

"I guess, since I have you all here, I could pick your brains for the things that stood out to you most at the wedding last weekend," Grace said, taking out a notebook. "You're all such fresh customers, it would help me to get some ideas."

This group was not shy, shouting out that they loved the way the tables had been arranged, the wall of sunflowers Grace had created for a photo backdrop, the lanterns and tree lights after dark, and the timing so the sun set during the ceremony. She took notes, then looked up at Alex.

"Not a word about Desmond's food."

"It was fine," he assured her. "But the food is the last thing you need to worry about."

After a while, the group started to break up as families headed home for dinner, but not without promises to be at the event and help to convince the celebrity guests that they were having the time of their lives.

Grace helped Alex pick up some of the glasses and cups left behind, while Gramma Finnie and Yiayia continued a game of gin rummy in one of the booths, chatting with Cassie and Pru, who had the puppies.

"Feel better?" he asked.

"A little," she said. "I just didn't expect such a huge group…thing."

"They're good people."

"No, it's more than that." She snagged a few glasses and followed him into the kitchen. "It takes my breath away to see them in action. And I get…in my own head. Even a little…"

"Jealous?" he guessed.

She nodded. "I don't want to, because it's small and wrong, but envy can eat at me."

"Don't let it." He lifted her chin with a finger, looking into her eyes. "They'll just wrap you up like you're one of us."

"That's what I'm afraid of," she whispered.

"They won't hurt you, Grace."

She searched his face, a little bit of that agony he'd seen in her eyes the other night still on display. "Until this is all over," she whispered. Then it could hurt like hell.

They were interrupted by the sound of the front

121

door opening and the cheerful greeting of the remaining women as the tall figure of a firefighter in a navy-blue shirt and khakis came in with a familiar gray Weimaraner at his side.

"Braden is here," Alex said. Of course, Cassie went straight into the man's arms for a kiss that lasted at least five seconds too long and would have gone on for more if Gertie hadn't intervened with a bark and a demand to play with Jelly Bean.

While the dogs romped, Cassie put her hand through Braden's arm and tugged him to a booth far from the others.

"So now we have people and a plan," Alex said. "What do we have to think about next?"

"The wine," she said. "And I don't think your family can all come together and solve that issue."

"Well, I have an idea about that," he said, throwing on the water to wash the glasses.

"If you say use the first press from this year's harvest—"

"Why not try it?" he insisted. "I'll stay there with you during the whole press. We can change the acidity, or whatever you do, and I'll taste it and coax the flavor out of it. Your science skills and my *flawless* gut instinct."

She laughed at that, but didn't answer.

He dipped his head a little closer. "What do you have to lose, Gracie?"

She looked up at him for a long time, holding his gaze and maybe her breath. "I don't know what it is about you," she admitted on a sigh.

"Charisma? Charm? Talent? Great ideas? A passion for perfection and my unparalleled palate?"

"Getting close," she teased, a hint of smile lifting her lips. "It's definitely in the area of your mouth."

He flickered a brow. "Oh, really?"

She touched his lip with her finger, letting her gaze drop. "It's…nice."

"Nice?" He inched closer, ready for the kiss he'd thought about taking since sometime yesterday morning. "Nice enough to kiss? We *did* make the next cut."

"Mmm. We did."

He took that as a yes, lowering his head to let their lips brush softly. He slid his arms around her, easing her into him and deepening that first fresh contact to—

"*Ahem.*"

They broke apart, turning to see Cassie and Braden, arm in arm in the kitchen doorway.

"We interrupting?" Braden asked with a tease in his voice.

"Not at all," Alex lied.

"Because we wanted to talk to you about something," Cassie said, her dark eyes sparking with happiness.

"What's up?" Alex turned off the water and stepped closer.

They looked at each other, both hesitating for a moment, then Braden nodded. "Go ahead, Cass."

"You're one hundred percent sure?" she asked.

"Honey, I'd marry you tomorrow. I love this idea."

"What idea?" Alex asked.

Cassie just grinned at him, then looked at Grace. "Look, first of all, feel free to say no. We don't want to barge in on your big opportunity." She bit her lip and looked from one to the other. "But what if there really was a wedding at this event? What would you think of that?"

Grace lifted both brows. "I think that would be...pretty awesome."

"Really?" Cassie's voice rose. "Because I know they're paying for it, so I wouldn't want to incur extra charges or make it my day, but Braden and I just talked about it and really wanted to see if you thought our getting married that day might work."

"Cassie, seriously?" Alex walked closer to his sister. "That's what you guys want?"

"Braden and I are dreading a major wedding—the money, the time, the stress. Nick won't be back for ages, and who knows if we can align that with Theo's next leave?"

"And weddings that include the entire fire department can get huge," Braden added. "Cassie said the whole family is on board to attend already, so that's everyone we *really* want."

"Not to mention we've had a *lot* of weddings in this family in the past year or so." Cassie shook her head with a soft laugh. "But, honestly, Grace, we don't want to add any burden or expense. We'd pay for anything that is wedding-related and, added bonus, I really would be your event planner at absolutely no cost at all. And I can get great prices on everything. Feel free to think about it and let us know."

Grace pressed her hands together under her chin, her blue-green eyes bright. "You know, having a wedding during the dry run will not only add realism, it would up the emotional ante and make everyone all warm and gooey. If the ceremony is simple, it could add a magical element to the whole thing."

"Are you willing to share your day with Blue?" Alex asked, wanting to be positive this was what she wanted. "Because she and Scooter pretty much suck all the air out of every room they enter."

"I know I should be more into the idea of a wedding," Cassie said with an apologetic shrug. "But I've organized a lot of them, been to more, and I am honestly overwhelmed at the idea of having one of my own. Plus, if we can save so much money..."

"We can buy a house," Braden said. "And we both think that's more important."

"But you have to both agree," Cassie insisted. "We don't want to derail this critical day."

"No one else will have an actual wedding for the dry run," Grace said. "And it sure would put love in the air, which is that indefinable 'essence' that Blue wants."

"But they're bringing twenty-some people you don't know from Adam," Alex said, determined to be the devil's advocate so his sister didn't compromise on her wedding day.

Cassie smiled at him. "My whole family will be there, and heck, maybe Blue can sing "Because I'm Crazy" for our first dance. How insane would that be?"

Alex searched his sister's face, knowing every angle, lash, and expression on that countenance since the day she was born. All he'd ever wanted to do was be sure she was happy. "If Nick's not there, who's going to walk you down the aisle?" he asked softly. "I always figured it would be Nick, since Dad died."

"You thought about that?"

"You're my little sister, Cass. Yes, I think about stuff like that."

"I could ask Daniel, if you think that's okay. He's our stepfather."

He considered that, then nodded slowly.

"You don't like the idea of Daniel walking me down the aisle?" Cassie asked.

"I just want to be sure you're not short-changing yourself when it comes to the wedding you've always wanted."

"Alex, this *is* the wedding I've always wanted. The winery is gorgeous. I'll be surrounded by people I love. And…" She looked up at Braden. "I'm marrying Einstein, the most awesome man on earth."

Braden smiled at her, pulling her in for a kiss. "Cass. You slay me."

She laughed. "Because he says things like that."

"Then I guess it's up to Grace." He turned to her, now gauging her expression, which looked pretty positive. "Unless you think it would add a layer of complication that makes you nuts."

"You know, to be honest, I might go nuts if Cassie weren't an event planner," she said, nodding slowly. "But she knows more about weddings than I do. So I say yes."

"Really?" Cassie asked.

"Really," Grace confirmed. "I think it'll be amazing."

"Thank *you*!" Cassie impulsively threw her arms around Grace and squeezed. She got that deer-in-the-headlights look in response as Grace reached up and patted Cassie's arms, clearly out of her comfort zone with that kind of emotional outburst.

"I'm so excited!" Cassie planted a sloppy kiss on Grace's cheek, and Alex had to laugh at the way she froze.

"C'mere, you." He pulled Cassie off her and gave his sister a bear hug. "You're a lucky man, Braden Mahoney," he added, extending his hand to shake his future brother-in-law's.

"I had the idea during our family meeting," Cassie said excitedly. "But I didn't want to blow in here and take over this important event and make it about me."

"It's about a wedding," Grace said. "So I love the idea of having one."

Cassie clapped her hands and pressed her lips into her knuckles as if she couldn't contain her joy. "I do want to keep it a surprise, though. Even from Mom. These things have a way of snowballing when other people get involved. Let's just keep it together and since I'm helping you plan the event, no one will question when we talk and get together a lot over the next two weeks."

"Twelve days," Alex corrected.

Cassie and Braden shared a totally goofy grin. "Twelve days!" she said on a giggle.

"Can't wait, Cass."

Laughing, they left the kitchen, and Alex turned to Grace, eyeing her carefully. "My family might be a little too much for you."

"Your family is…" She took a minute to find the right words, staring after the couple who'd just left, shaking her head. "More than anything I've ever experienced."

"In a good way, I hope."

"In a way that makes me ache a little," she admitted.

"I don't want you to ache." He went to her, sliding

his arms around her again. "Except when I kiss you. Then you can ache."

"I did," she admitted on a whisper. "But…the good kind of ache."

He placed his lips on her head, saving a real kiss for a more private time and place. "When can we press the wine?"

She laughed. "You're relentless."

"Thank you."

"I have a meeting with the wine-press team tomorrow. I'm guessing we'll start on Thursday morning. We'll be done by evening, or certainly will have enough free-run juice to test, taste, tweak, and bottle wine overnight. You up for that?"

"An all-nighter with you? Absolutely."

She leaned into him, letting her head fall on his shoulder with a sigh that sounded very much like resignation. "Don't make me feel things, Alex. It terrifies me."

He lifted her chin to bring her mouth close to his. "It doesn't have to hurt, you know."

"But it will…eventually."

He kissed her lightly. "Did that hurt?"

"No."

He kissed her again, sliding his hand under her hair. "That?"

"Not a bit."

"Then what are you afraid of?"

She put her hands on either side of his face, rubbing her fingers over his beard. "I'm afraid of…what's best for me."

Baffled, he frowned. "What's—"

"Alex!" Pru called. "Jack just took Gramma Finnie's glasses and hid them under the wet bar and Bitsy just knocked over all the menus!"

They shared a look, a laugh, one more quick kiss, and headed out.

Chapter Ten

Grace woke on press day with a low burn of excitement in her heart and three puppies in her bed. They were deeply attached to her, which was mutual, so she decided to keep them with her during the press, which took place in a huge metal-roofed barnlike building adjacent to the vineyards and the wine cellar.

Tugging them on extra-long leashes she planned to connect to the picnic table, she spied her two workers standing in the sunshine when she arrived. Ryan Perkins, a young man who'd worked in the wineries in Upstate New York before moving to North Carolina with his wife, and Jay Corbell, a fiftysomething man who spoke very little but really knew his stuff.

They'd been here for last year's press and were two of the finest wine-pressers she'd ever worked with. Right now, they were laughing with a third man.

She inched one way, then the other, unable to make out anything but a silhouette against the morning light. A familiar, strong, broad-shouldered, narrow-hipped silhouette that looked just as good in a white T-shirt and jeans as he did in a chef's apron.

Against her will, Grace's stomach did that fluttery flip thing that she'd come to expect at the sight of Alex Santorini. Although she hadn't seen him since that family meeting in Bitter Bark, they'd talked several times by phone. And he texted her frequently with ideas, pictures, and menu planning.

She'd also chatted with Cassie quite a few times, but Grace's focus had been the final days of fermentation, which had demanded her attention as they adjusted yeast levels, oxidation, and prepared for this big day.

She wasn't the least bit surprised that Alex had kept his promise to help her make wine. She was a little bothered by her physiological response to him, but hey, Mother Nature was a powerful force, and she was whipping Grace's hormones into a frenzy this week.

"Here's our boss," Ryan said, raising his paper cup in her direction.

"Good morning," she called, scanning the three men, but unable to keep her gaze from landing on Alex. "And welcome to our newest member of the press team."

"I come bearing gifts." He gestured toward a large plastic tray he'd set on a worktable, overflowing with pastries and cookies, plus a metal coffee container with a spout.

"What's all this?"

"Bougatsa, milopita, paximadia, and a loaf of vasilopita." He pronounced the words with a thick Greek accent that sounded as if he'd been raised on the streets of Athens instead of in Chestnut Creek, North Carolina.

"I have no idea what he's saying." Ryan held up a napkin-wrapped pastry. "But holy crap, this is good. So's the coffee."

"Yeah. He can stay," Jay added, taking a bite of his own pastry as he and Ryan headed over to the press. "And bring lunch," he called over his shoulder.

Alex laughed easily at that, coming closer to Grace to put a hand on her shoulder and usher her to the table. "Come and eat. Big day today. You'll need nourishment."

She eyed him, a little amused by his ability to fit into any situation and a little envious of it, too. "I'll take some coffee."

"Really?" He lifted up a layered pastry dusted with powdered sugar. "My bougatsa has actually won awards."

The sweet custard and buttery phyllo dough made her mouth water. "Okay," she said without bothering to fight the temptation. "And coffee. And…thank you for being here today. I know it's never easy to leave work."

He handed her the pastry and poured a cup of coffee. "My grill in Bitter Bark is in good hands, and I'm yours for the duration of the next week and a half."

Her heart tripped with gratitude, and she felt a smile form. "I like that," she said.

"Taste," he whispered, leaning closer and inching the pastry toward her mouth. "You'll like this even more."

She took a bite, the dough flaking and crunching, the creamy custard covering her tongue with tangy, gooey goodness. All she could do was close her eyes and moan. "Oh my…" She didn't bother to finish, enjoying the bite and finally swallowing. When she opened her eyes, he was looking right at her with an expression of smug satisfaction mixed with longing and lust. There it was, right in his eyes.

"You missed a little bit." He dabbed her lip with his finger, pulling it back to reveal a flake of pastry. Still holding her gaze, he slipped the crumb into his mouth. "Mmm. Good."

She let out a breath and reached for the coffee, wishing it were ice-cold water. "Keep that up, and it's going to be a long day, Alex."

He just chuckled. "From what these guys have been telling me, it is going to be a long day no matter what."

"And night," she said. "If we bottle the press wine."

He beamed at her. "That's my girl. And since I suspected you'll see things my way and bottle that wine tonight, I brought lunch, dinner, and a midnight snack."

"Why am I not the least bit surprised?" After finishing the pastry, wiping her hands, and taking a healthy drink of coffee, Grace took a deep breath and walked toward her team. "All right, gentlemen. Let's start the press."

Grace had been through the motions of a wine press many, many times, deeply familiar with every step. As a teaching assistant while getting her master's, she'd guided undergraduates through the process, explaining to the newbies the difference between a "crush" and a "press" and how to balance tannins, remove proteins, and add something as simple as clay so that unwanted particles adhere to it and flush out.

But today was different. From the moment Ryan and Jay opened the containers of fermented must and let her scoop out a cup of the thick, sugary, alcoholic pulp, today's press had a magical feel. The sun poured through the open doors, dappling the equipment in golden rays, giving the puppies a perfect place to rest and occasionally romp, secured by their leashes to the table and within sight.

Jay, Ryan, Alex, and Grace all donned smocks and grabbed buckets to gather the must and pour it into the bladder press. Someday, Overlook Glen might be big enough to have this step automated by a twenty-thousand-dollar stainless-steel machine like they had at wineries like Mondavi or Carlson Woods, but Grace wasn't there yet.

For now, as a small winery, this press worked perfectly, even though it would take the entire day to get through all the fermented must. The work was hard and heavy, but exhilarating. After the bin was full for the first time, the liquid started running before any pressure was even applied.

Taking a break, Alex and Grace slipped off their protective smocks and stood side by side, holding their breath as the thick spout gurgled and choked and finally spit out the first drops of pinkish juice into the container.

"This is the free run," she explained. "We keep it isolated because we'll use it later to adjust the taste of the press-run wine. It's good, though. Want to taste?"

"Of course."

She grabbed two plastic cups and handed him one, showing him how to position it under the spout at an angle to get some of the juice. They filled the cups halfway and held them up.

"I'm nervous," she admitted.

"Why?"

"This is the first taste, the one that will tell us if we had a great harvest or a good one. It'll be harsher because of the tannins and skins, but we'll know if it's thin or rich, acidic or stringent."

"Can you change all that with the press run?"

"Some, yes. But the bones of the wine are in this cup right here."

"Ready?" He lifted his glass.

"I guess so." She angled the see-through cup and looked closely.

"Can you tell by looking?" he asked.

"I can see the color is nice, the viscosity looks good, but the only thing that matters is how it tastes."

He tapped her glass with his. "Here's to your best harvest yet."

She didn't have the heart to tell him that vintners thought it was bad luck to toast the free run. Instead, she held his gaze, put the rim to her lips, and tipped the glass as he did the same thing, aware that her heart was hammering at her ribs.

The first sip was warm, rich, layered, and... delicious. She closed her eyes to be sure, holding the wine in her mouth to let it reach every taste bud, finally swallowing. As she did, something else hit her lips.

Alex's kiss was light, sweet, and unexpected.

"Wow," he whispered. "That's wonderful."

So was his mouth on hers. She let the contact linger for one second, then inched back. "It's good," she agreed. "Not too thin. This is going to be a great blending juice."

He took another drink. This time, he closed his eyes. "Fennel-scented duck breast," he whispered. "With peppercorns and thyme."

She smiled. "You're planning the menu after the first taste of free-run juice?"

"Of course. This is gonna be great wine, Gracie."

She lifted her glass and sniffed, unable to disagree or even be bothered by the nickname. For some reason, *Gracie* sounded as right on his lips as this wine. "I think it is," she agreed, turning to the machine to watch the free run pour.

The next batch was just as good, and so was the third and fourth. By the time they stopped for lunch—which Alex had indeed brought in a cooler—the four of them were a little giddy on the prospects of this year's harvest. Their hands were all purple, their clothes stained, and Grace was sure her braid was falling out down her back, but she didn't care. The morning's work had her high with happiness.

After eating the delicious sandwiches, Ryan and Jay took off for a much-needed break, and Alex and Grace grabbed the leashes to take the puppies back to the house for their lunch.

"We can go through the cellars," she said, guiding him to the underground corridor that connected the press building to the main house. "I don't like to walk them through the vineyards anyway, since grapes can be poisonous to dogs."

"Really? I didn't know that." He tugged at Jack's leash. "What a good mom you guys have."

"I'm not their mom."

"You're their foster mom," he said as they stepped into the cool, dark vestibule that led down to the barrels. "And if I know anything about anything, you'll be a foster failure."

She slowed her step, the words slicing through her. "What's a foster failure?"

"I've just heard the Kilcannons use the expression, usually in reference to their mother, Annie, who apparently failed at fostering so often they sometimes owned six dogs at a time."

"So a foster failure is someone who…keeps their dogs."

"Yeah…" His expression changed as he realized what he'd said. "I guess that means something completely different to you."

An old sadness cloaked her that not even the glorious morning could erase. No one had ever been a foster failure with her. "I just never heard the term before."

"Well, I think you're going to keep these dogs," he said, obviously trying to lighten the topic as they entered the cellars. "That is, if Scooter and Blue don't make them part of your contract."

She gave a smile, not really listening. *Foster failure*. Why hadn't any of her foster families *failed* and decided to keep her?

"Whoa, this place is so cool." Alex stopped to blink in the dim light and take in the rows and rows of barrels aging the wine. "And not just the temperature."

"I know," she agreed, taking a whiff of the oak- and vanilla-infused chilly air. "It's my favorite spot in the winery. In any winery, to be honest. The first time I stepped foot in a wine cellar, I was on a tour for an undergraduate class in botany. But that moment, my life changed."

"How so?" he asked.

"I don't know why or how, but I had a visceral reaction to the smells and the temperature." She paused to run a finger over an oak barrel. "It comforted me and still does."

"It feels like a safe place," he commented as they walked.

"But it's more than that. It's...familiar. In fact, I dream about it a lot."

"You do?"

She shrugged, the admission feeling so personal, but she still wanted to share it with him. "I have this recurring dream that I'm walking through a wine cellar just like this, and I'm holding someone's hand. It's a big, kind of fat, man's hand, and..." She gave an uncomfortable laugh. "As things are in dreams, it's weird because he has no thumb."

"No thumb? Definitely weird."

"But that doesn't matter. He's squeezing my hand, which is lost in his, and everything is so...secure." She sighed, lost as she remembered the good feeling the dream always gave her since she'd started having it as long ago as she could remember. "So, when I stepped into an actual wine cellar in college, I felt like I had been dreaming about it my whole life, and I knew that I wanted to study winemaking. And that someday, I'd want my own winery."

She paused at a row of barrels from last year's harvest that had just passed the one-year mark. It had been well over a month since she'd tasted the wine inside, but she hadn't planned to touch those for six more months. So these barrels should be ready and perfect in time for a summer wedding for Scooter and Blue, but it wouldn't be quite right for the wedding they were holding in a little over a week.

"And this right here?" She tapped the barrel. "Is our last great hope."

He gave her a questioning look. "For?"

"For the Scooter and Blue exclusive bottles, if what we bottle tonight isn't great. That's last year's harvest, aged one year almost to the day. In six months, it might be perfect. But now? I'm not sure."

"Can we taste it?"

"Yes, there's one barrel with a spigot. Later, we can get some."

They meandered through the corridor, pausing here and there for the dogs, taking time to examine the barrels, read the dates, and cool off. She was looking at a barrel when she felt Alex's gaze on her.

"What is it?" she asked.

"You're different down here," he said. "You're... softer."

She gave him a smile. "I'm hard everywhere else?"

"You're...protected." He put his hands on her shoulders and turned her toward him. "Your voice is easy, and your muscles..." He squeezed lightly. "Aren't tense. And you look..."

She let out a sigh, inching closer to him. "Yes?"

"Inviting," he finished. "You know I'm going to kiss you, don't you?"

A chill ran up and down her spine. "I hope so."

He lowered his head and kissed her lightly, holding back, barely touching, then letting his tongue graze her lip. She leaned into him, wrapping her arms around his neck, opening her mouth to taste the grapes and sunshine and saltiness of his mouth.

Here, in this sacred, comforting, eerily wonderful place, no kiss had ever felt quite so delicious.

They kissed until they were completely tied up by three leashes, trapped like captives and having their boots licked and nibbled.

"Wow," she whispered, stealing one more brush of his lips. "I thought I liked the cellars before. Now they're the site of our first real kiss."

"First of many, I hope."

Many. Why didn't that terrify her? She had no idea, but it didn't. On the contrary, she couldn't wait to get started.

Chapter Eleven

Alex might have been a touch drunk on the tastings, but he could generally hold his liquor like a pro. No, the heady sensation that had him laughing, working like a beast, and fighting every opportunity to touch Grace had nothing to do with her delicious free-run wine.

If anything was *crushed* around here, it was him. He had it so bad for this woman that it was a joke. Which might have been the reason his face hurt from laughing, and his arms hurt from scooping, and his everything else hurt from how much he wanted to get her into those dark, wine-soaked cellars again.

But Alex had learned one thing as a chef—timing was everything. And his was always impeccable.

As the sun dipped low, Alex sat on the picnic table, drinking a bottle of water, while Jack and Bitsy romped on the tabletop, and Gertie wandered around underneath. Not far away, Ryan and Jay finished cleaning the press, having transferred the free run and the press run into temporary holding tanks.

"Are you coming back tomorrow for the barreling?"

Ryan asked Alex. "Not that I'm jonesing for more of those pastries."

"I may not leave."

Jay looked up, narrowing his gaze, a little protective, Alex imagined, at the thought of a man spending the night with his boss.

"I'm trying to persuade Grace to bottle some of the press wine, and I know that work has to be done on it right away," he explained.

Ryan looked skeptical. "Lots of wineries around here do that, but it'd be a first for Overlook Glen."

"First time for everything," Alex said. And they needed that exclusive wine for the event in less than two weeks.

"Actually, not a first," Jay said. "My uncle worked for the guy that used to own this place. He said they bottled first presses all the time 'cause the grapes are that good, at least they were then. That guy grew some of the best grapes in the area."

Just then, Grace came down the path, a phone to her ear. "Thanks for checking in, Denise. You're more than welcome to park in our lot." She signed off the call and pressed the phone to her chest, looking at Alex. "They're coming in six tour buses. *Six*."

"Cool."

"This is getting so real," she whispered.

"All the more reason to make that wine tonight."

She shot him a look and then thanked Ryan and Jay for their hard work. After they left, she peered into the press, admiring how clean it was.

Alex joined her at the press, peering in to see it so shiny, the center stainless steel looked like a mirror.

"So, let's just say we were to make some press wine tonight. How would we do that?"

Leaning back, she regarded him carefully, and he braced for the argument that it couldn't or shouldn't be done.

"We *are* going to make some press wine tonight," she whispered. "Assuming you're not too tired."

"Are you kidding?" He hugged her, squeezing so tight he lifted her off the ground. "We're doing this, Gracie!"

A smile pulled at her lips as she looked up at him. "Where'd you get all that…energy and intensity, Alex Santorini?"

"My dad," he answered without missing a beat. "Nico Santorini was a beast who didn't know the meaning of 'quit' or 'slow down' or 'can't be done.'" That was, until cancer made him quit, slow down, and not do anything.

She regarded him closely for a moment. "It's not just that you won't quit. You actually believe down to the bone that we could make something extraordinary tonight."

"Without one molecule of doubt."

"One molecule of doubt, huh?" She reached up and touched his face, stroking his beard with a light touch that hit too hard. "I love it when you go all scientific on me."

He leaned closer, brushing her lips with his. "Come on, Gracie. Let's stay up all night and make magic."

She stood on her toes and kissed him. "Feed me first."

He laughed into her mouth. "Words that go straight to my heart."

An hour later, after they'd had a simple omelet dinner with the last of the bougatsa and a few shots of espresso, they gathered up the big crate and took three very tired puppies with them back to the work area.

Both of them were still purple stained up to their elbows, and even after washing, Grace had splatters of grape juice on her cheeks and all over the jeans and old top she wore. Like an idiot, Alex had worn a white T-shirt that looked tie-dyed now. But it didn't matter. With the dogs settled, the materials ready, and espresso pumping through them, they started by tasting a sample from each container.

Grace spit hers out into an empty cup, making him inch back in surprise. "I thought it was pretty good," he said.

"It's not bad. But I can't drink as much as we're going to have to taste tonight, unless you want to carry me to bed."

He gave a sly smile. "I've heard worse ideas."

She flicked his arm playfully and held out her empty plastic shot glass. "Next batch, please."

He turned the spigot for them and poured about an ounce in each glass, tasting it and following her lead to spit it out.

"Okay, okay," she said after letting it settle on her tongue. "Slightly thin. Has a little more acetobacter from the ferment. Taste the volatile acidity? We need to let a little carbon dioxide in the container. And it needs to be colder. Would you mind moving all of this into the cellars?"

He didn't question her opinion or authority, setting up a workstation at the bottom of the few stairs down to the long corridor.

They waited while she explained a little more about the carbon dioxide process, then they tasted again.

"That made a difference," he said, surprised.

"Subtle. I think we can try to add some of the free-run juice now. A very small amount. It's powerful, but it will enrich this batch. I think. We'll know in two hours."

After they blended that one, tasted the last container, and blended a different amount, there was little else to do but wait for a few hours, even though it was getting late already.

"You want to go home?" she asked.

"Are you crazy?"

"Or to the winery, my apartment? Your kitchen?"

"It's mine now?" he asked on a laugh.

"Yours to rest in, if you like. I'm going to stay here."

"Then so am I." He gestured toward a wooden bench along the wall. "You want to lie down over there?"

"I usually do," she said. "Open it up. There are some cushions in there. But it's only wide enough for one."

He lifted the top of the bench, found the cushions, and set them up for her, beckoning her closer. "You rest. I'll sit on the floor."

She didn't argue, her shoulders already sagging with exhaustion. But before she sat down, she lifted one of the cushions, put it to her nose, and sniffed.

Alex just looked at her with one raised eyebrow, making her laugh.

"I like the smell."

He took it and sniffed. "Pretty…musty."

"I think it's nice." She settled on the bench, lying on her side, her head propped on the pillow.

Alex slid to the ground in front of her, letting his head fall back on the bench, pleasantly surprised when she threaded her fingers into his hair and stroked it.

"That *will* put me to sleep," he said. "But don't stop. Please."

"Mmm." She wound some hair around her fingers and lightly scratched his scalp and feathered the hair in her hands. "You've got beautiful, thick Greek hair."

"We all do," he said. "Theo favors my mom, but the rest of us are pure Santorinis. Except Nick, who's a Kilcannon."

"I heard bits and pieces of that when I did your mother's wedding. That must have been a shock."

"You have no idea."

"How does it make you feel about Nick?"

"He's still my brother, heart and soul. A man I completely admire, respect, and often want to emulate. I don't care that our DNA is a little different. We were raised together, side by side at the dinner table, and he's always had my back."

Her fingers stilled, then fell out of his hair completely, hitting the bench with a thud. He waited a second, then turned to see if she'd fallen asleep.

Her eyes were closed, but it was because she was fighting tears.

"Gracie," he whispered, turning his whole body to face her. "I'm sorry. I keep forgetting and talking about family stuff. I forget you don't have siblings."

"I do," she whispered.

He inched back. "You do? Didn't you say there was no trace of your family anywhere?"

"This trace is in my…" She sighed. "In my memory bank."

"Really? What do you remember?"

"Their names were…Bitsy and Jack."

"Oh." He stroked back some strands of her hair that had fallen on her cheek. "I get it now."

She gave a sad smile. "I've got nothing but memories, Alex. Not very clear, either. But I just don't think I imagined those kids, and the feeling of being with them wasn't…a foster home. It was a real home."

"Tell me about it."

She settled deeper into the cushions, thinking. "They were very, very young, maybe two. And we were in big, huge, beautiful rooms. Somewhere that had to be a mansion."

"Houses seem bigger to little kids," he said.

"I know." She nodded in agreement. "But in my memory, I can see things like a pool and a giant canopy bed and rooms full of toys."

"So, you think this family was rich?"

"I have no idea. There's no trace of a Bitsy or Jack Donovan in the state of California, or at least none that could be younger siblings of mine. And I don't know where I was, what city or if it even *was* California. But…" She squeezed her eyes shut as if she were rooting for that memory. "There were hills and sunshine and…" Her eyes popped open. "Maybe vineyards. Maybe."

"And you know your mother's name was Celia. That's all you know?"

"Like I said, one of the investigators told me someone had given him that much from a sealed file."

"The files are sealed? Is that legal?"

"Yes. Trust me, I've tried. I don't want to try again, if that's what you're thinking. I don't want the disappointment. I'd rather look forward than bang into brick walls."

He stroked her cheek lightly. "Okay. Tell me more about Bitsy and Jack."

She opened her eyes and looked into his. "I can tell you that you're the first person I've ever shared that with who didn't try to tell me that I imagined them or they were probably part of the first foster home I ever stayed in, which I don't remember well."

"Of course I believe you," he said. "Tell me every single detail you remember."

She let her eyes shutter closed. "My clearest memory is a room I would describe as a nursery. Somewhere sunny, bright, and big. There's tons of toys, like a dollhouse the size of a walk-in playhouse, cars, a train, balls, just...so much stuff. I was holding a little girl on my lap, calling her my Bitsy, my itsy-bitsy sister. And there was a boy named Jack. He had dark hair like a mop on his head and dark eyes and..." She squished her face, thinking. "A woman kept rubbing his head in front of me, just stroking his hair, calling him Jackie. I remember it so clearly."

"Do you remember her?"

"I think..." She looked at him. "I remember the essence of her, not what she looked like. I remember thinking I was definitely not her favorite and some-times wanted to be."

"Could you guess her age?"

"Older, but then, everyone is to a child. My gut says she was a grandmother or nanny. She called me Gracie, but not..." She gnawed on her lip. "Not with love. But I remember squeezing that little toddler, Bitsy, because I sensed she was going to be taken from me, and I loved her so much. So much."

He searched her face, rubbing his thumb along her jawline, trying to imagine knowing that Cassie, Theo, Nick, and, God, *John*, existed but not being able to find them. "That has to hurt," he said.

"There are no words for how much."

"No other memories?"

"Flashes. A pool. Some hills. A blue book that I could read, so I couldn't have been too young. A long street that might have been a driveway or a road. That's all I remember until…my next clear memory is of a foster home at seven. That was no mansion, and there was no Jack or Bitsy."

"Did those investigators you hired go back and talk to your foster families?"

"The ones they could find and the ones who'd talk. No one had any idea where I'd come from or who my parents were. Please, Alex. Don't take me down that road again. I know you're intense and relentless, but it leads nowhere. Please."

"Okay, okay," he assured her. "Anything else you remember?"

"Just little wisps of things." She smiled and tapped the pillow. "Like this pillow, which, for some reason, takes me back to that time. I don't know how or why, but it does."

He didn't respond for a while, thinking about how complicated and empty it must be for her to have no real memories, or a family to fill in the gaps, or parents to show her pictures and tell her about her childhood. Nothing.

"No wonder you're so guarded," he mused.

She sighed and smiled. "I spent about thirteen years being shuffled from family to family, house to house, situation to situation. Every time I let my guard down and started to care or connect, I was sent away." Her voice hitched. "No one wanted me. At the risk of sounding ridiculously melodramatic, no one has ever wanted me. So it seems safer not to give in to emotions or caring or…connections."

"What about with men?"

She cocked a brow. "I've been with men. Not many, not frequently, but I've…tried."

"And failed?" he guessed.

"No one has the patience to deal with me. I expect it to end. I expect to be…sent away, or they'll leave. Like Desmond, even though that wasn't a romantic relationship. He wanted a connection, I know. But I held back, and that's probably what frustrated him. In anticipation, I sabotage the situation. I'm self-aware enough to know what I'm doing and messed up enough not to stop."

"Are you going to sabotage things with me?" he asked on a whisper.

"There are things with you?" she teased. "We're in our first week of knowing each other."

"I want there to be things with me," he said, leaning closer to her. "I want there to be lots of things."

"Like…"

"Like this." He lifted her hand and pressed his lips against her knuckles. "And this." He moved to her mouth, taking another kiss and sliding his hand into her messy braid, leaning over her to get more contact. "And anything else I can have, touch, taste, and kiss."

"Mmm." A whimper escaped her throat as her whole body rocked a little on the bench. "That could get very…messy."

"Messy is good, Gracie. It's real. It's life. It's… fun."

She let out her next breath into his mouth, firing need through him, making him pull her whole body closer, ready to lay her down right on the cellar floor. He coasted a hand down the length of her body, lingering on each curve and dip, itching to get under her clothes.

"The wine," she whispered. "We need to taste the wine."

"Can't it wait?"

"It'll be ruined." She kissed him again, harder this time. "And so will I."

He laughed softly. "Let's check the wine, then."

He broke the next kiss slowly, reluctant to let go. She took a second to clear her head, too, finally sitting up and straightening her top, her eyes dark with the same arousal he felt. "You're awfully tempting, Alex."

"I'm a firm believer in giving in to temptation."

She laughed. "I have no doubt of that."

He stood and reached for her, pulling her up and into his arms. "Come on, Gracie. Let's taste the wine."

Keeping his arm around her, he walked her back to the first blend and poured them each a tiny taste. He held it up, but she shook her head.

"Bad luck to toast a taste," she said. "Ask any vintner."

He tipped his head in agreement, then sipped when she did. Instantly, he noticed the difference. She must have, too, because her eyes widened. And she swallowed this one.

"It's better," he said.

"Richer," she agreed. "Almost as if it's been aged."

"It doesn't have to be aged."

"I know, I know." She held the tiny cup to her nose and sniffed, her eyes closed in deep thought. "It just is missing...something. The micro-oxidation that you can only get from a barrel."

"Micro-oxidation?" He smiled. "I think it's missing a whisper of mellowness and a touch of permanence."

"So we agree it's missing something."

He nodded, frowning, tasting again, and feeling more than thinking about the missing ingredient and how to get it. "Last year's harvest," he said softly.

"It's not quite ready."

"But if you blended it with this, it might add that age that's missing."

She shrugged, at least considering the idea. "I suppose we could try. Wineries do mix years sometimes. I wouldn't want to sell it as an Overlook Glen label, but—"

"But if it hits the mark, we can make it for Scooter and Blue."

She nodded, her eyes bright with the willingness to try. "Let's get some and blend it."

They did, moving like a team in harmony, tasting, testing, and getting it close to right.

"One hour," she said. "The molecules of the two different wines need an hour to merge and come together."

"Merge and come together." He felt his mouth lift

in a smile. "Exactly what we should be doing while we wait."

"Stop it." She laughed. "We're not having sex in the wine cellar."

"Give me one good reason why."

She breezed by him to the crate where Gertie was clawing for release. "I'll give you three. Our little friends need some playtime."

"*I* need some playtime."

She chuckled and opened the crate door, and almost immediately the three puppies shot out.

"Whoa!" Alex pivoted and snagged Jack, then ran after Bitsy, while Gracie, as always, cuddled little Gertie.

The namesakes of her childhood memory.

When he had both of them, he brought them back and settled on the floor so they could face each other and keep the puppies somewhat contained and able to crawl, play, lick, and love.

"Everything I want to be doing with you," he joked, lifting Bitsy to motorboat her sweet little belly.

"I'm excited, Alex," she said, looking over Gertie's head.

"Exactly. So put them back into the—"

"About the wine." She lowered the dog. "I really feel like this might be the answer. We might have a wine I've never made before that's amazing. I wouldn't have thought of that without you."

He winked at her. "Let's wait until we taste it."

"I have a good feeling about this."

"Look at you, making wine with feelings instead of oxygen."

As giddy as their three little pets, they played with the puppies for a while, laughing more than they talked, slipping into an easy rhythm, exchanging the dogs back and forth.

"I can't wait much longer," Grace said, checking her phone to see the time. "It's been fifty minutes."

"Okay, you stay there," he said, easing Jack toward her. "I'll get our taste."

He poured two tasting cups full and brought them back, grateful that the puppies were settled quietly in Grace's lap. "Here you go. No toasting."

She took the cup and held it up for a sniff. "Oh God, Alex."

"What?" He sat down on the ground close to her, careful not to spill his wine.

"It's good," she said. "I think it's great."

He had to agree based on the aroma. "You ready?"

"I'm ready."

They both closed their eyes and drank. And swallowed. And stayed perfectly silent for a few heartbeats, each waiting for the other to respond.

Finally, he opened his eyes to meet her smile.

"You like it, Gracie?"

"It's the best wine I've ever made."

Satisfaction washed over him. "I think it's damn good. It's perfect. It's exactly what we're going to serve and bottle for our dry run, which will be anything but *dry*."

She pressed a hand to her mouth as if her joy couldn't be contained.

"And you know what this wine deserves?" he asked. "Its own label. Let's make them for the bottles."

"I have Overlook Glen labels. I don't think they expect named wine for the dry run they threw at us with zero notice."

"Exactly. Remember, we're going to wow them. What were you going to call it? Blue Hawk?"

She shrugged. "That was just one idea."

"We need something amazing." He picked up Jack and nuzzled his chunky neck. "Jack Wine."

"Gertie's Choice," she joked.

He laughed. "Bitsy...Bitsy Noir."

"You're on to something, but we're just not there yet."

"Three dogs..." Grace said.

"Three Dog Night!" He snapped his fingers. "That's it. That's the wine. The wine we made in this cellar with our three puppies. Three Dog Night."

"Like the band?"

"It's actually a real thing. My buddy from Australia used to say if it was freezing at night, it'd take three dogs in bed with you to stay warm. Then it's a three-dog night."

Suddenly, all of the puppies barked and made a rush for Alex, climbing onto his legs and chest, pawing their way up. "What do you think, puppers? Want a wine named after you?"

Jack barked wildly. Bitsy turned so hard, she slid off his thigh and nestled between his legs. And Gertie snuggled into his neck and slathered him with kisses.

And Grace? She just watched with a look that told him she'd trade places with those dogs in a heartbeat. And God knew he wanted her to.

Chapter Twelve

Oh Lord, her back hurt.

Grace blinked her eyes open, expecting the normal morning light that poured into her room, but there was only darkness. The cool, comforting darkness of…the wine cellar.

She sat up, realizing she was asleep on the bench, covered with the purple blanket that belonged to the puppies. Blinking, waiting for her eyes to adjust, she slid her gaze to the crate in the corner, expecting to see the dogs, but the door was open, and they were gone.

"Oh God." She straightened and stood, wincing at the knot in her back, memories of the night before coming back. They'd finished blending, carefully mixing last year's Pinot into this year's first press and free run to create more than enough wine for fifty bottles.

Alex—the world's most relentless person—insisted on carrying each five-gallon container out to the bottling station near the press. At about four thirty, she'd nearly collapsed, and he told her to rest for a few minutes on the bench.

That was the last thing she remembered.

Well, that and the...fun. The laughter. The easiness. A few too many congratulatory kisses and the sexy undercurrent that hummed between them. In fact, if she hadn't been worried about the chemical balance and oxidation of the wine, they'd probably be waking up next to each other upstairs in her room, balancing a whole different set of chemicals.

She froze midstep at the thought.

That's where this was going. She knew it. He knew it. Hell, those puppies knew it. It would be hot and crazy and passionate and...messy. She'd develop feelings and an attachment, and then he'd leave, or she'd run, or life would separate them, because that's how it always happened to Grace Donovan.

It's been a wonderful year, Grace.

We love having you, Grace.

Oh, honey, you're like our own daughter. But...this is best for you.

There was always a but. No family, no love, no *explanation*.

The back door swung open, blinding her with a flash of morning light and a familiar silhouette.

"Good morning, gorgeous."

She laughed, pushing back some hair, feeling anything but. "Did you ever sleep?" she asked.

"Not a wink. But the wine is almost bottled and..." He angled his head. "I mastered the screw-top machine."

"Pretty sweet, isn't it?"

"I admit I get the appeal."

"Where are the puppies?" she asked, looking past him.

"I've got them leashed up out there, all their business done and morning meals completed."

"On zero sleep? Who are you, Superman?"

He shrugged. "When I'm going hard on a project, I don't need sleep. This wine, Gracie." He did a chef kiss with his fingers. "We nailed it."

"You did," she corrected. "I would never have thought to use wine aged a year to blend with this."

"Three Dog Night is going to be a huge hit. Would you think I'm out of my mind if I asked for a blank label? I've got the idea for a design in mind and wanted to sketch it out. I have a friend who did some marketing work for Santorini's, and he texted that he could probably produce something for us in time for the big event, but he needs the measurements and your logo."

Her jaw loosened. "Did you work any other miracles while I slept like a baby?"

"Managed not to join you, and *that* is a miracle." He tapped her nose. "Labels?"

"They're in the office." She shot her thumb toward the winery, hearing Ryan's truck rolling up outside. "I need to go to my apartment for a few minutes, so let's get Ryan and Jay started on the barrels, and I'll show you the labels."

A few minutes later, she and Alex returned to the main house, both of them moving with a surprising spring in their step despite the long night of bottling.

"Your enthusiasm is infectious," she told him as she unlocked the door to her office.

"I'm stoked for this. I have so many ideas for the menu. And you have to figure something out with Cassie to have those puppies in the wedding."

"The wedding Scooter and Blue don't even know is happening."

He gave her a squeeze as they walked in. "We're going to kill this, Gracie."

She just laughed, infected by his spirit.

"This is a great office," he said, looking around the room full of scarred, antique woods and ancient file folders, sun pouring through a window that looked out at the vineyards.

"I haven't renovated it," she said, seeing the room through his eyes. "I like the feel of it, imagining owners over the years running Overlook Glen from here, on this oak furniture. And look at this. It's really cool."

She stepped to a large wooden cabinet with three long, flat drawers and pulled one open. "Every label of every wine ever made here. One of these days, I'm going to go through all of them, pick the best, and make a collage for the reception area. But these are from the last twenty years or so." She waved her hand over the array of wine labels, each in small stacks, all with the Overlook Glen logo and different types of wine and names.

Alex picked up a pack and fluttered through them. "Very nice."

"Next drawer is even older, and the blanks are in the bottom drawer." She swallowed, aware of how close he was and suddenly wanting very much to brush her teeth before he turned and kissed her. "I'm going to run up to my apartment and clean up for the day," she said. "Make yourself at home."

"I will, thanks."

She slipped out, closing the door and darting up the

curved stairs to her apartment. There, she flipped on the shower, brushed her teeth, jumped under deliciously hot water, letting it sluice over her aching bones. Most, not all, of the grape stains lightened on her hands and forearms after she washed and shampooed, moving quickly and thinking about coffee and how much work it would be barreling all day.

Fun with Alex, though, whom she suspected wouldn't leave her side.

Yep, it was getting messy. And dangerous. And...wonderful.

Wrapping the towel around her and squeezing the water out of her hair, she opened the bathroom door and froze.

Alex stood in her room, right in the middle of it, holding something in his hand, his expression kind of...ravaged.

"What?" She barely breathed the word.

"I found something."

"The perfect label?" But even as she guessed it, she knew that whatever he held, which was the size of a label, had visibly upset him.

He shook his head. "I think you need to..." His gaze dropped over her. "Dress?"

Frowning, she took a step closer. "The towel won't fall off."

He inched back, covering what was in one hand with the other. She looked down at his hands, staring at his purple wine stains, trying to see what it was. "Grace." His voice was gruff and low. "This is going to upset you."

"What is it?" A hot tendril of worry wended its way through her chest, at war with a punch of frustration that he wouldn't show her what he was holding. "Alex, you're scaring me."

She waited for him to laugh, to be his easy, comfortable, and comforting self, to make a joke and punctuate it with a kiss that she was more than ready for now.

But he stayed dead silent.

Turning, she went back into the bathroom, grabbed a robe from the back of the door, and slipped into it, letting the towel fall as she yanked the tie tight. If he wanted her dressed for whatever label he thought would upset her, fine.

"What is it?" she asked when she stepped out, catching him looking at what he held. Then he lifted his gaze, his perpetually tanned skin the closest thing to pale she'd ever seen.

He came closer, reaching for her hand, tugging her to sit down on the bed.

"I pulled the bottom drawer too hard, trying to get to the back, and it fell out."

"That's okay. I'm sure we can fix—"

"And I found this." Very slowly, he finally handed her a picture with rounded corners and slightly washed-out colors.

She took it, angled it away from the sun that shone on its glossy surface and looked at the image of a woman holding a baby, a tiny Mary-Jane-wearing towhead who couldn't have been two years old, the vineyards in full bloom behind them.

"Someone who lived here once?" she guessed.

"Turn it over." The order was barely a rough whisper.

Suddenly, as something hot and scary shot through her stomach, her hand started shaking, paralyzed and light purple and unable to do what he said. Instead, she looked up at him. "Why?"

"Because you need to see what it says." He put a hand on her leg, pressing lightly. "Brace yourself, honey."

Swallowing hard, she turned it over and read the scripted handwriting in faded ink.

Celia and Gracie Overlook Glen Harvest Oct. 1988

She stared at the words, so utterly and wholly wrong and impossible and... "What?" She choked. "How is this possible?"

She'd never been here before. She had no ties to this winery. She'd found it by luck...hadn't she? She could still remember the call from her real estate agent, who'd gotten hold of this gem of a listing she could snag for a song.

Chills exploded all over her body.

This couldn't be a coincidence. Not even a chance. Then...who? Her mother? Her grandfather? Who wanted her to have this property, but hadn't wanted to *raise* her?

"I don't understand," she whispered as her head grew light, and the world seemed to black out around her. "I don't..." She squeezed her eyes shut. "I can't handle this right now, Alex. We have wine to deal with."

Grace thought *he* was strong and relentless? Alex watched in awe as Grace moved through what had to be the most difficult day in a life that had clearly had its fair share of difficulties. Nothing—not even discovering lies and truths so deeply intertwined that it was impossible to tell one from the other—would stop the process of barrel-aging the rest of the wine that had been pressed the day before.

Through it all, her back was straight, her jaw locked. Her pretty mouth stayed tight, and her aquamarine eyes had lost all the luster he'd enjoyed the night before. Even her approach to bottling was different than yesterday's.

Maybe it was his imagination, but she seemed more scientific today, too. She clung to her notes and used calculus—literal calculus, on a piece of paper with a calculator—that turned winemaking into math, with formulas for carbon dioxide and airlocks and measurements of oxygen molecules.

He got it, though. Science made sense to Grace Donovan, especially when a thirty-one-year-old photograph and the writing on the back made none.

She'd been born here? Her mother had lived here? Or she'd visited, at least. There was obviously some connection with the winery she'd acquired by what she'd thought was luck and timing. So, who was pulling the strings and why?

If Alex wanted to know, he couldn't imagine the need for answers that burned in Grace. She might cover it with math and stoicism, but he knew that under that cool surface, she was churning. And all he wanted to do was help her figure it out.

Because he'd felt the revelation rack her body, and he'd heard the sobs he'd finally helped calm to a whimper. He'd waited outside her room while she washed her face and dressed, and he'd marveled when she stepped out with that mask firmly in place, refusing to discuss what that picture had revealed.

Other than a woman who looked very much like her and was named Celia and had to be her mother.

But while they transferred the wine into waiting oak barrels and rolled them into open slots in the cellar, all those questions plagued him, too. And no matter how sleep-deprived he was, he cobbled together a plan to find out the truth. She deserved that and nothing less.

As he and Ryan returned from the cellar, having stored the last of the barrels, the sun was dipping, but the day wasn't done. He found Grace at the picnic table, playing with the dogs, whispering to Gertie.

When he slid next to her and smiled, she just looked at him.

"Gracie," he whispered, getting a kick of pain when she flinched a little at the name. "Let's start with the real estate agent who listed the house. Do you know who that was?"

She bit her lip, nodding. "It must be on the contract, right? My agent handled everything. It was fast and easy and…" She closed her eyes. "Purposeful."

"Can you reach your agent?"

"I should be able to. Her name's Donna Morgan, and she's with a huge national firm, but her office is in DC. She actually specializes in winery properties, mostly in Virginia, but also all over the East."

"Let's call her, and if she doesn't know the previous owner's name, then get the listing agent. You have every right to know who owned this property before you."

Just then, Jay came closer, wiping his brow and opening a bottle of water. "Bib Hunnicutt," he said, angling his head in a silent apology that acknowledged he'd overheard their conversation. "Is something wrong, Grace?"

On the bench, Grace's fingers curled around Alex's hand, squeezing him. "Bib," she whispered, paling a little.

"That's what everyone called him," Jay said. "Old Bib, which must have been a nickname for something that's long forgotten."

"You knew him?" she asked, her voice stretched thin.

"Nah, but my uncle knew the Hunnicutts pretty well. Him and his wife, Bonnie. People talked around here when they died within a year of each other. Cancer, both of them. They say she knew she had it, but didn't tell him or do anything about it. She just nursed him to the end, then hers was so far gone, she died about eight or nine months later."

"When was this?" Alex asked.

He shrugged. "They died a little over three years ago, I guess. They pretty much kept to themselves, though. Didn't socialize much with neighbors or folks in town."

"I...had no idea who owned this property," Grace said after processing all that. "My Realtor just told me the owners had both passed, and an attorney was handling the sale."

"Then we'll find that attorney," Alex said softly, getting a slightly surprised look from Jay.

"Was something wrong with the barrels? The press? What's your issue with the Hunnicutts?" Jay asked.

"Curiosity," Alex answered easily for her. "I'm fascinated by the history of this winery and the families who've owned it in the past."

"You could talk to my uncle," he said. "He worked here back in the seventies and early eighties."

"But not 1988?" Alex asked.

Jay frowned. "I'd have to check," he said. "Seems to me he moved to another place in the mid-eighties, but sometimes his stories all ramble together. He's eighty-two now, and I don't always, you know, pay attention."

Alex gave him an understanding smile. "Does he live around here, Jay?"

"Oh yeah. He lives just outside of Bitter Bark in that Starling apartment complex for seniors."

"Do you think he'd talk to us today?" Alex got a quick look from Grace. "Why wait?" he asked.

Jay looked from one to the other, nodding slowly. "I can call him and tell him you want to stop by. Just remember, his memory is a little shaky at times. Although, he usually remembers the weather fifty years ago, but he can't tell you what he had for breakfast."

"We'll be gentle," Grace said, turning to him. "I do need to know the history of the family that owned this winery."

"Sure thing. And good news, we're done with the barrels," he said. "Ryan and I will handle the cleanup, if you like." He waited a beat. "I'll call my uncle."

He stepped away, pulling out a cell phone. Alex slipped his arm around Grace and eased her closer. "I'll drive you there. On the way, we'll call the agent who sold you the property. We'll ask all over town until we figure this out. We'll find out who your mother was."

Just then, Gertie climbed up on Grace's lap for some love. "And I thought we just wanted to find *their* mother."

"Her, too," he teased lightly.

She was quiet for a moment, then leaned away to look at him. "Bib. I remember that name. I remember saying it. Bib."

"Maybe you do have family, Grace." And if so, there was nothing he wanted more than to help her find out about them, even if they were gone.

But that just made her look sadder. "If I do, or did, they didn't want me. Why not?"

"We have to find out the whole story before we start making assumptions."

"But I don't want to—"

He put a hand over her lips. "This isn't foster families in California. This is the reason why you bought this winery, which has a connection to your birth and your mother. You have every right and reason to find out what it is."

She just stared at him.

"And who knows?" he added. "It might lead you to Bitsy and Jack."

Her eyes filled as she put her arms around him and laid her head on his shoulder. "I know I shouldn't feel this way about you. I know it's going to hurt like a bitch at some point in time, but this is the kindest thing anyone's ever done, and I...you...we..."

"Shhh." He pulled her into him and kissed her forehead. "One emotional land mine at a time, sweetheart."

She melted a little in his arms, then looked up at him. "I'm scared about what I'm going to find out."

"Hey, what's that saying? The truth will set you free."

"Or shatter you into a million pieces, never to recover."

"There's the attitude." He tapped her nose.

She managed a shaky smile as Jay came back over, holding a piece of paper. "He's very excited to have company," he said kind of sheepishly. "Guess I should visit him more often. His name's Lou Corbell."

Alex took the paper. "We'll give him your best, Jay. And thanks."

A few minutes later, they were headed to Bitter Bark with the dogs in the back and hope in their hearts.

Chapter Thirteen

"First stop, Waterford Farm."

Grace turned to look at Alex, blinking away the fog that had descended over her throughout the day and refused to budge. She wasn't sure she could take an onslaught of Kilcannons, Mahoneys, and Santorinis right now. "Why?"

"I texted my mom, and she reminded me that Daniel Kilcannon has lived here his whole life, and—"

"You told her?"

"Not in detail. I texted her earlier today and told her we found something at the winery that has made it urgent you learn more about the previous owners." He slid her a look. "We tell each other everything in my family."

"Well, obviously, in mine? We don't." She heard the bitterness in her voice, but didn't care.

"Hey." He closed his fingers around her hand. "We're in this together."

"Thank you." She turned and looked out the window at the passing fall colors, thinking about... everything. "I wonder how long I lived here. If I lived here. If the Overlook Glen people were family or friends." A punch of pain hit her chest. "There is really nothing worse than not knowing your roots or history."

"Yes, there is."

She looked at him, not sure what that would be.

"Grace, you just found a connection to the very home where you live. Someone, somewhere had to have orchestrated your purchase of that winery, and they did it, I'm guessing, because they loved you."

"Or felt guilty as hell."

"Or missed you. Maybe they watched you all your life, but for some reason you don't know, couldn't reach out to you."

"Creepy."

"The point is, you ended up exactly where you belong, and that should fuel your fire to make Overlook Glen a world-class winery and event venue, just to make all that worthwhile."

His voice deepened with passion, and his vision, when articulated, made sense. Kind of.

"I don't doubt you want all the answers," he continued. "And I'll help you find them. But you were a baby at Overlook Glen, and now you're the owner, and that should give you some kind of, I don't know, circular joy."

She gave his hand a squeeze. "I love your attitude about life, Alex. I'd love for it to rub off on me."

He smiled back. "Let me rub."

She laughed, possibly for the first time since he'd stood in front of her with a photograph that changed her life. "What else was in that drawer?" she asked.

"Blank labels. The picture was caught in the side,

slipped down and almost invisible. I don't even know how I saw it."

"I've been in that file plenty of times," she said. "But I never really looked much in that bottom drawer."

"Did you clean out the whole office? Search for anything else?"

"It was empty when I moved in, except for the label drawers and some files that I don't think I kept." She grunted. "Damn. There could have been answers in those files."

He patted her hand. "We'll get answers, Gracie. We won't stop until we get answers."

A wave of appreciation and affection rolled over her, making her eyes well for the fortieth time that day. "Why?"

"Because you need them," he answered without a moment's hesitation.

"No, I mean, why are you helping me? Because you want to sleep with me?" The question was out before she could check herself, and the look she got nearly gutted her.

"Do you really think that's what I'm made of?"

"No." She shook her head. "I don't, and I'm sorry I even said that. I just…I'm not used to people caring."

"Because you don't let them."

She ran a hand through her hair and let the truth hit her. "I told you, it's hard for me. I made connections at every family as a child. I tried. I hoped. I let people in, and then wham, I got sent away." She mentally swore at the crack in her voice, sick of her own sob story. "All I'm saying is trust doesn't come easy, and emotional connections are scary to me."

He took her hand again, holding it with that relentless grip of his. "They're scary for everyone."

"Have you ever been hurt? Abandoned? Left behind?"

He didn't answer for a moment. "My dad died holding my hand," he finally said. "He was my hero. Bigger than life. The one person I wanted to impress. He was…everything to me."

There was every bit as much pain in his voice as hers.

"And because of that," he added, "I feel paralyzed in my job. Unwilling to hurt him, even though he's gone, by pursuing my own dreams because I think it will be an insult to his."

She stroked his knuckles with her thumb, wanting to offer sympathy, but not entirely sure how to do that. "I'm sure he was very proud of you and would have supported whatever you wanted to do."

His only response was a tight smile and a nod as they pulled into Waterford Farm. "He's gone, so I'll never know."

The canine rescue and training work was in full swing, with at least a dozen dogs of various sizes romping around in what looked like chaos in the main pen. But there were enough trainers in there for Grace to guess it was at least controlled chaos, with tall, handsome Shane Kilcannon in the middle, calling out orders to the trainees and their dogs.

Darcy darted by with a quick wave, two standard poodles on leashes with fresh coiffed hair, and a small group stood outside the veterinary office with a few more dogs. Even from the distance, Grace could make out the youngest of the Kilcannon brothers, Aidan, deep in conversation with his brother Garrett and his father, Daniel.

As if sensing they were in a place for even more fun, Gertie, Jack, and Bitsy woke up and started barking and clawing at their crate, ready to play.

"When we head out to Jay's dad's place, let's leave the dogs here," Alex suggested as they parked. "We might not be able to bring them into the apartment complex."

"Good idea." She turned and smiled. "They won't mind."

It was a challenge even leashing the squirmy, excited pups, who wanted to shoot out of their confinement and wreak havoc on the training pen. But Grace and Alex managed to carry the puppies so they didn't come into contact with the grass, where they could contract a disease. They walked to where Daniel and his group stood on the porch in front of the vet office, all surrounding a big black dog, who sat obediently while they talked.

After saying hello, Aidan put his hand on the dog's head. "You're just in time to say goodbye to Rio the Rottie. I'm flying him to Savannah in about an hour to take him to a new home."

"Hello, Rio the Rottie." Grace bent over to put a hand on his massive head, getting the sweetest look in return. That didn't last long, though, as the three puppies instantly squirmed and barked, demanding the dog's attention.

"They can play with him," Daniel said, taking Jack from Alex's arm. "They all love it." He set the puppy down on the wooden slats of the porch, so Alex did the same, and suddenly puppies were all over Rio, licking, clawing, and demanding his attention. But Gertie was clinging to Grace for dear life, so she held on to the puppy and watched the others.

Jack jumped up, and instantly Rio dropped to the ground, rolled over, and stretched out as if he were their personal playground.

And the only thing anyone could do was laugh, which felt so good to Grace.

"They're obviously getting well socialized," Daniel said, reaching to pet Gertie. "And how's this pretty girl doing?"

"She's a little shy," Grace said, sounding a lot like a mom making excuses. "But sweet as can be."

"Please tell me you're here because you changed your mind about letting them be adopted individually," Garrett said. "I have a family that desperately wants one, would take two, but refused three."

Grace looked up at him. "I can't separate them."

Without hesitation, Alex put a strong and supportive arm around her shoulders. "I'm not even sure we can part with them at all."

At the quick and surprised look they all gave him, he must have realized he'd said *we* and held up a hand. "They're a major part of the big event," he added. "We've even named the exclusive wine after them."

"So what brings you two out here?" Daniel asked.

"Actually, we hoped to talk to you," Alex said. "Do you have some time?"

"Can I bring this angel?" he asked, reaching for Gertie, who went to him without hesitation.

"I don't think they'll miss her for a few minutes." Grace pointed at the tiny puppies literally walking over Rio's belly, making the big dog let out a musical whine. "Is it okay to leave them here?"

"Sure," Aidan said, looking across the field. "Here comes Darcy, so expect them to be on the Waterford Farm Instagram in the next hour. Puppies are social media gold."

"I'm just going down to watch Liam's bite training," Daniel said, cocking his head toward a part of the property Grace had never been. "Come along."

They went with him, making small talk as Grace took in the gorgeous colors of the trees and the crisp autumn air. At the bottom of a hill was another large and long pen, where three men, all in head-to-toe protective gear, worked with several big, menacing-looking German shepherds.

"So how are the plans for the big day going?" Daniel asked.

"Pretty well," Alex said, "but in the process of getting ready, we realized it would be great for our clients to know a little of the history of Overlook Glen, to add color and depth to the event."

Grace blinked at him, grateful for the smooth, if surprising, explanation.

"Great idea," Daniel agreed, lifting his head as Gertie bathed him in doggy kisses. "This one is special," he said.

"They all are," she agreed.

"So," Alex continued. "We were wondering if you knew the previous owners of Overlook Glen, since you've lived here your whole life. I believe the guy's name was Hunnicutt."

"George and Bonnie? Wasn't that their name? He had a nickname, though."

"Bib," Grace supplied.

"Yeah." Daniel snapped his fingers as the name clicked. "That was it. Bib Hunnicutt. Annie knew them better than I did," he said, adding, "Annie was my first wife," for Grace's benefit. "They took one of her foster dogs, if I recall correctly, but then..." He frowned, shaking his head. "My memory is fuzzy on this, but I seem to remember they couldn't keep the dog for some reason. Mind you, we are going back a good thirty years."

"Thirty years?" Grace asked. That meant she would have been two, about a year before that picture had been taken.

He slowed his step and studied Gertie for a moment, obviously thinking. "Something like that. Maybe thirty-one. I seem to recall Liam was about ten, and Annie was fostering a snow-white American Eskimo named Candy that they wanted, but something happened, and they returned her to us." He gave a soft laugh. "Not sure that's the history or color you're looking for, Grace, but beyond that, I didn't know the family."

"Do you know if they had kids?" she asked.

"I don't, I'm sorry." As they reached the fence, he lifted a hand and waved Liam over, who said something to one of the other trainers, then he took off his helmet, walking closer, greeting all of them with a simple nod.

"Hey, Liam," Daniel said. "Got a challenge for you."

Dark brows drew together as he looked from one to

the other, then down to Gertie. "Sure, I'll train her. I could have her sniffing out bombs and drugs in no time."

Daniel inched the dog away as if he expected his bite-suited son to take her. "Not yet, you won't. The challenge is to see if your memory is better than mine. I'm thinking of Candy, an American Eskimo your mother fostered."

His eyes flickered with a genuine response. "I loved that dog," he said. "Sweet and smart as a whip. Wasn't happy when Mom adopted her out."

"To the people who owned Overlook Glen, right?" Daniel asked.

"Yeah," he said, looking at Grace. "In fact, I was thinking about it at the wedding. The place has really changed since then. You've done a great job."

"Grace is looking for historical data on the property," Daniel said. "Wondering if you can remember anything about the owners."

He tipped his head, thinking. "Sorry, I was pretty young. All I remember is they sent Candy back after a week. I remember because I had to go out there with Mom to get her, and I was so happy, but damn if someone else didn't adopt her right away."

"So you were there?" Grace stepped closer to the fence, closing her fingers over the wire. "You met them? Did they have kids?"

He shook his head. "I don't know, sorry. To be honest, I only have one bizarre memory of that place."

"What is it?" She probably sounded a little desperate, but didn't care. She was.

"It's strange." He gave a dry smile. "Not sure it's something you want to, you know, share with your clients. I just remember because I was a kid, and I must have gaped at the guy, and in the van on the way back, my mom lectured me about not staring at…imperfections."

"Imperfections?" A cold chill ran up her back, and an image flashed in her head. That hand, holding hers in the cellar, that hand that was missing a…

"He didn't have a thumb."

"Oh." The sound squeaked out, and Alex drew in a breath, too. "On his left hand," she whispered. "That was Bib Hunnicutt?"

She felt Alex's hand on her back add a knowing pressure, somehow connecting them in this new, thin, shocking line in her life's story.

"Yeah." Liam nodded. "I think Mom said he had an accident during a harvest one year."

The chills wouldn't stop, rising and falling up her back. That man who held her hand and protected her and made her feel so loved and safe was Bib Hunnicutt.

But *who was he*?

"And he owned the winery," she said.

"Yes, and oh!" Liam's face brightened. "His wife, Bonnie? She sent me home with a lemon bar, and to this day, I've never eaten anything that good." He grinned at Alex. "No offense, Chef."

"I remember the lemon bars," she whispered, practically knocked over by the power of the memory.

"I didn't realize you had a connection to the previous owners," Daniel said, sounding surprised. "You spent time there as a child?"

"I did," she said. "I'm just trying to piece the memories together." She smiled at Liam. "You really helped, thank you."

He nodded, then turned when the dogs barked behind him. "I gotta go. Good luck figuring this out."

"Yes, of course, thank you," Grace said, turning to Alex, certain her color was high as the news had left her head reeling and her heart pounding. "I remember the lemon bars," she repeated, the revelation so powerful, she could feel tears threatening. A real memory from before any foster homes!

"I'll have to make them for you," he said.

For a moment, her whole world shifted in so many ways. There was a person, a connection, in the past. And the connection she was making—the one right in front of her—just said the kindest thing she'd ever heard.

All she wanted to do was throw her arms around him and never let go.

All of that—every dip on the emotional roller coaster—was terrifying and thrilling and real.

"Let's get back to those puppies," Daniel said. "And if you like, Grace, I can call a few acquaintances in town who knew the Hunnicutts and ask for more information."

"Yes, please do." She slipped her hand into Alex's and squeezed, fighting tears of wonder and joy.

Grace on a mission was as attractive—maybe more so—than Grace dealing with her issues. Alex could practically feel her humming with determination as she coaxed him quickly out of Waterford once they got the puppies set up in the kennels for play, food, and rest.

Her eyes were the color of broken sea glass, sharp with focus and hope, as she left three messages for the real estate agent who'd sold her the property three years ago.

"I remember his hand. I can feel it holding mine," she said, not for the first time, as they pulled up to the Starling Senior Living Center just north of town. "I knew this man, Bib Hunnicutt, and I trusted him."

"Is it possible he was your grandfather?"

She closed her eyes. "Then why did I go into the foster system if they only died three years ago?" She glanced at him as they climbed out of his Jeep. "Why didn't Bib and Bonnie Hunnicutt want me?"

"You don't know that they didn't want you," Alex said. "Maybe they didn't know where you were."

"But he knew where I was when he made sure I got his property." She slipped her hand into Alex's. "Maybe Mr. Corbell can help."

Tugging her closer, Alex planted a kiss on her head. "You need answers."

"Like I need my next breath," she replied, leaning into him. "And if I don't like what they are, then…I'm no worse off than when I didn't have any."

Jay must have told his uncle they were coming, because he showed up moments after the woman at the reception desk called his apartment, entering the lobby in a crisp white shirt, dark pants, and a jaunty red bow tie. His silver hair was thin to the point of baldness, but he'd combed the six or seven strands over his head and looked mighty happy to have company.

"So you're the pretty lady who bought Overlook Glen," he said, moving slowly toward them, slightly hunched by age. "My nephew tells me you're doing a good job with the old place."

"Hello, Mr. Corbell." She shook his hand and introduced him to Alex, then they all sat in a small grouping of chairs near a window.

"We're looking into the history of Overlook Glen," she said without preamble. "Jay tells me you worked there years ago."

"Harvests, mostly. Just when the hands had to come in. Mostly, they came from out of state or another country, then moved on, so you didn't get the same men twice, but since I was a local, I went every year. I liked the Hunnicutts."

She leaned forward. "Did you know them well?"

"Oh, well enough. Not like we had dinner or anything, but Bib, he paid on time, and Bonnie was so sweet. Loved to bake for the help."

"Did they have children?" Alex asked.

Lou snorted. "Not sure Miss Celia was ever a *child*."

"*Who?*" They asked the question at exactly the same time.

"Their girl, Celia. If ever there was a wild child, she was it. Trouble from the day she was born, as I recall."

Grace just stared at him, speechless, her fingers digging into the armrests of the chair.

"What else can you tell us about her?" Alex prodded. "When she married? Where she lived?"

He drew his thick gray brows together. "I stopped doing their harvests and lost touch, but I can tell you that child never met a rule she wouldn't break." He started laughing, which turned into a cough.

"Can I get you water?" Grace asked, glancing at a table with small bottles of water.

He managed to nod, and as she got up, the old man watched her carefully, frowning. When she came back, he took the bottle, but he'd caught his breath. He pointed the bottle at Grace. "She looked like you," he said. "You could be her daughter."

"I think I am," she whispered.

That made the old man slap one hand against his water bottle. "Well, howdy. And you bought the winery? How's that for a neat little circle in life? So they left it to you, then. Very nice." He studied her some more. "Course, I didn't know your mama had a baby, but I can't say I'm surprised. She did like the boys." He gave a yellowed grin. "How is she?"

"She...passed away. Many years ago in an auto accident. I think."

"Oh." His whole face dropped. "Hadn't heard that."

But wouldn't it be news if a local girl died in a car accident?

"She was always such a spirited thing. Coming down to the vineyards, wanting to help with the harvest. Course, her father wouldn't let her on account of his accident." He held up his thumb. "Never stopped him from hard work, though."

"I don't suppose you have any pictures of him, Mr. Corbell? Or of her as a child?"

Lips tight, he shook his head. "My wife was a cleaner-outer," he said. "Never kept anything, didn't put any sentimental value on much. When she passed, we had the emptiest attic in North Carolina. So, sorry. I don't have anything from back in those days. Just my memories."

"They've been really helpful, Lou," Alex said. "Thank you."

He grinned. "Bring me a bottle of wine one of these days, young lady. I might be able to dig up more memories for you."

"I will," she said, standing up as he did. "I promise I will." In a move that might have been the most uncharacteristic thing Alex had ever seen her do, Grace reached out and circled the old man in a genuine and warm embrace. "And thank you."

He patted her back and gave a smile over her shoulder at Alex. "She's soft, you lucky dog."

Alex just smiled. She was soft today, that was for sure.

After they said goodbye, he put his arm around Grace and walked her out. "So, what do you think, Gracie?"

She looked up at him, with a light he'd never seen in her eyes before. "I think...I woke up an orphan who's spent all but the first few years of my life in foster homes with nothing that resembled a family. And now, because of you, I know I had grandparents who loved me enough to make my dream of owning a winery come true. I may never know why or how, but...I know who." She stopped, turned, and wrapped him in a hug much like the one she'd given old Mr. Corbell. "How can I ever thank you for that?"

"You're not going to quit looking for answers, are you?"

She inched back, her eyes misty. "Absolutely not."

"Good, because I want to help you."

"Why?"

He lifted her chin and kissed her lightly. "Because I like happy, sweet, soft, emotional Gracie."

She melted into his arms with a sigh that matched her description perfectly.

Chapter Fourteen

G race stared at the text from Donna Morgan, the real estate agent who'd found Overlook Glen for her.

No owners listed on contract. Calvin Etheridge had power of attorney over everything. Retired two years ago. His office is closed, phone number disconnected. You can try the North Carolina Bar Association—that's my best idea. Sorry. Best of luck!

A mix of emotions swirled inside her. Retired and disconnected.

It was like the search for her family that had consumed her for a few years during graduate school. Always, *always* a brick wall forced her to stop. But this was one of the most tangible leads she'd ever had. This man had known her grandparents.

She'd find him. She *had* to.

The bar association wouldn't be open until Monday, so she'd have to wait to make any calls. Anyway, Cassie Santorini was on her way over to discuss and plan her surprise wedding, and the big event eight days away was still Grace's most burning priority.

But she had time for one thing. She tapped out a text to Alex, telling him the man's name and sharing her excitement, finishing up just as the formal bell to the front of the winery rang.

When she opened it, she found Cassie in the doorway next to the Weimaraner whom Grace had seen at the restaurant earlier in the week.

"Jelly Bean's the best man, and since Braden's on duty at the fire station right now, this dog is my partner in crime. Okay if he comes in?"

Grace laughed and petted the sleek gray head, forcing herself to focus on the business at hand, not Calvin Etheridge, retired and disconnected. "He's one of the most handsome groomsmen I've ever seen, and he's more than welcome today and on your wedding day."

"My wedding day." Cassie let out a musical laugh, pushing some thick black hair over her shoulder. "I'm so in love with this idea, Grace. You can't imagine how excited we are."

"So am I. And very glad you could come today, because we have very little time left." Grace tapped her heart as her chest tightened. "But we can do it."

"I really don't want you to worry about my end of things," Cassie said, pausing in the reception area to take in the scope of the two-story room. "I love everything about this place," she said, her voice a hushed whisper. "The minute I walked in here with my mom, I wanted to have my own wedding here, but..." She rubbed her fingers together in the universal gesture for money.

"Not to worry about that," Grace assured her. "I got a do-not-exceed budget for the 'dry run' from

Blue's people and..." She looked skyward with a laugh. "They don't want to spare any expense. Even without exceeding, you'll be thrilled."

Cassie gave a little squeal. "I'm so happy. Does that mean I can pick some kind of gorgeous flowers?"

"Flowers, décor, cake, music, whatever you want. We've got the food and wine covered, obviously. Do you need a tour?"

"Jelly Bean does," Cassie said on a laugh as the dog ambled toward the curved staircase and took one step up. "JB. Stay."

Instantly, he turned around, returned to her, sat, and stared up.

"Wow, how do you get them to do that?" Grace asked. "I have three puppies in a crate in the back who mock me when I say 'stay.'"

"First of all, your dog has to have a genius IQ." She put her hand on Jelly Bean's head and bent over to kiss him. "Which this man does. Forgive me if I brag, but there is nothing, and I do mean *nothing*, you can't train this dog to do, as long as he doesn't have to tell two scents apart. That is his only flaw."

"And you definitely want him in the wedding?"

Cassie sighed and rubbed his head. "We kind of do. We have another dog, too, but Jazz is really a working arson dog and wouldn't be right here. But JB? He's the one who brought us together. Well, JB and our grandmothers."

"Let's go in the conference room and look at some ideas I pulled for you, and you can tell me that story." She tossed a look over her shoulder at Cassie. "I definitely got the impression your grandmother is a bit of a matchmaker."

"She is," Cassie confirmed. "Along with Gramma Finnie. They call themselves the Dogmothers and are trying to pick up where my stepfather left off. He was the Dogfather. Have you heard of all his successes?"

"Bits and pieces," Grace said as they entered the conference room, making the puppies clatter in their crate. "Here they are."

"Babies!" She went right to them, with Jelly Bean at her side. The little dogs went nuts at the sight of him, and he instantly lay down in front of the crate. "Can I take them out?"

"Yes, but be prepared that we won't get a thing done but running after them."

"Jelly Bean will watch them." Cassie unlatched the gate, and out spilled the furballs, led by Bitsy, who literally rolled into Jelly Bean's paws. Jack went straight to the big dog's behind for a sniff, and Gertie inched closer cautiously, glancing up at Grace as if she sought permission.

"Could they *be* any cuter?" Cassie folded to the floor and reached for Gertie, lifting her for a kiss. "Are you completely in love?" she asked.

"I'm pretty enchanted," Grace admitted, abandoning the table full of wedding ideas to watch the dogs play. "They are worming right into my heart."

Cassie looked up. "Kinda like Alex?"

"Whoa. Didn't waste any time, did you?"

She gently put Gertie on the floor next to Jelly Bean and reached for Jack. "Hey, he's my big bro, and I ran into him at Santorini's this morning. Speaking of enchanted." She grinned. "Never thought I'd hear him wax romantic about making wine, but there you have it."

"He enjoyed the winemaking." Grace couldn't hide her smile.

"He enjoyed the wine*maker*."

A thrill Grace didn't even recognize zipped up her spine as she remembered how sweetly they'd parted yesterday after spending hours talking about nothing except the discovery of her mother. When he left, Grace had collapsed after the sleepless night before, a new kind of peace settling over her all night.

Had he mentioned that to his sister? That he'd helped her get one step closer to solving the black hole of her family roots? "Did he say anything else?"

"Just that I should butter you up." Cassie took one of the leashes that hung on the crate and dangled it in front of Bitsy, making her jump and play more like a kitten than a puppy.

"Butter me up?"

"So when he calls and asks you to dinner tonight, you'll say yes."

Grace laughed. "I don't think you'll have to do much buttering."

Jelly Bean put his paw over the leash, bringing it down and making Bitsy bark in his face. He barked right back, and she startled, then rolled onto her back, making Cassie and Grace laugh.

"Told you he could keep them in line." Cassie pushed up, abandoning the dogs. "Like I said, he can do anything. I'm counting on him playing the role of the entire wedding party. Otherwise, we have to ruin the surprise, and I really don't want to."

Grace thought about that, watching the puppies play. "Alex and I really wanted to include the puppies in the event somehow, because Blue and Scooter went bananas over them. But they're so small, I don't know how."

"One as ring bearer, one as a maid of honor, one as a flower girl? With JB as the best man!"

"It's a dream," Grace agreed. "But I'm afraid we'll lose all control of these three. They are absolutely *not* trained."

"Jelly Bean can teach them," she said, utterly confident. "I'm telling you, he's brilliant."

Grace inched back, not believing Cassie could be serious. "They're not even six weeks old. They'll run all over the place and get lost in the vineyard."

"On leashes?"

"Who's going to…" Grace read the other woman's expression, shaking her head in disbelief. "Jelly Bean?"

Cassie held her hand out. "Five bucks he can do it. Braden and I might have to work with him and the pups for a few days, but he can do it. He'll bring them down those steps with me right behind them at least." Her dark eyes flashed with joy. "Oh God, *that* is the wedding I want!"

Just then, Grace's phone chirped with a call, stealing her attention. "Let's…think about it." She turned to get the phone, getting that little thrill again at the name on the screen. "It's Alex," she said to Cassie.

"Tell him I slathered you in butter and please say yes."

Smiling, Grace answered, a little surprised at how her heart kicked up at the sound of his voice.

"Tonight, Gracie. Ricardo's in Bitter Bark, seven o'clock sharp."

She laughed and looked at Cassie, who was back on the floor with the dogs. "I guess I have to say yes to that demand," she quipped.

Cassie reached over her shoulder to give a thumbs-up without even turning around.

"That's only if you want to run into Cal Etheridge for an impromptu conversation."

"*What?*" At the sound of Grace's shocked voice, Cassie turned to look at her, and Gertie started barking. "How did you...what?"

She heard his easy, confident laugh. "Gramma Finnie came into Santorini's after I got your text, and I asked her if she knew Cal Etheridge. Turns out Ruth, his wife, was in Gramma's needlepoint club. She assured me that Cal and Ruth go to Ricardo's for lasagna every Saturday night and sit in the same booth at seven o'clock. I got a reservation, and since I know the owner, he gave me the booth across from theirs."

She choked softly into the phone, stunned. "Alex...I..."

"Just say yes to him!" Cassie popped up, holding Gertie. "That way, Braden and I can puppysit and start training the wedding party tonight."

"Did you hear that?" Grace asked Alex.

"I did," he said on a laugh. "She had me at 'just say yes.' You can explain the rest to me tonight. I'll pick you up at six thirty."

Grace opened her mouth to try to form a sentence, but why bother? Cassie was staring at her, Alex was waiting for her, and Gramma Finnie might have just helped solve the biggest mystery in Grace's life.

"Yes," she whispered into the phone. "There's really no way to fight this family. It's a force of nature."

"Then just hang on for the ride, Gracie, and don't fight a thing."

"I feel like Ethan Hunt," Alex said as he opened the heavy mahogany doors to the Italian restaurant that qualified as an institution in Bitter Bark.

Grace looked up at him, a question in eyes that looked particularly sparkly tonight, thanks to evening makeup and a bubbling excitement for what they might learn. "No clue who that is."

"You've never seen the *Mission: Impossible* movies with Tom Cruise?" He leaned close to her ear as they stepped into the darkened restaurant. "Your mission, Ms. Donovan, should you choose to accept it, is to act like this meeting is a total coincidence, tell him your real estate agent mentioned the lawyer's name only once, but you have a photographic memory, then use all your charms to get him to break attorney-client privilege."

She blinked at him. "And if I don't choose to accept this mission?"

"Then I..." He leaned down and kissed her forehead. "Will cover for you." He turned to the hostess, who broke into a wide smile. "Mr. Santorini, how nice to see you again." She looked down at her chart, frowning. "I thought you like that table by the window for two, but someone put you in the back with the booths. I'll just—"

"No, no, the back is fine," he said, holding up a hand. "I actually requested that."

"Okay." She pulled some menus, then glanced at

Grace. "It's noisy back there and not as intimate."

Of course, he'd never sit in the noisy booths with a date, and he'd brought a few here. "This is great, thanks," he said, taking Grace's hand and whispering, "We like noisy and the right company."

Grace's return smile was a little nervous as she looked past the hostess, scanning the booths for their target. All Gramma Finnie had told Alex was that Cal Etheridge was as bald as the proverbial cue ball, and then she'd whispered that Ruth was a little terrified of him.

A portly, hairless man shoveled lasagna in the booth next to where they were seated, accompanied by a petite, older woman who picked at a salad. Bingo.

Alex and Grace slid into the seats across from each other, both of them glancing at the next table, but getting not so much as a look in return. Grace's eyes asked the obvious question. How to meet them?

"I got it covered," he promised, taking his napkin from under the silverware. "Ricardo will be out before we order. He always comes to say hello."

"I've been here before, and he never says hello to me."

"Fellow chef," he said softly, unable to be heard by anyone else. "He knows I won't order until he stops by to tell me what's fresh and good. I do it for him when he comes to Santorini's, and it isn't nearly as fancy as this place. We'll chat for a minute, and I'll…figure something out to get the introduction."

A slow smile pulled at her glossy lips. "I honestly couldn't have picked a better partner for this," she said, reaching for his hand. "Thank you, Alex."

The compliment warmed him, and he turned his

palm to capture her narrow fingers in his. "My pleasure."

"Is it? I mean, you could be working on the menu for the event."

"I have the menu planned."

"Or hanging with your family."

"Tomorrow's Sunday, and I'll see them all at Waterford Farm."

"Or on a date."

He squeezed her hand. "And just what do you call this?"

"*Mission: Impossible*?" she teased.

"A perfect description for this date."

"Because we're so different?" She eased her hand out of his and slowly opened the menu.

"Because getting your attention wasn't easy. And I still have to wonder if I ever would have if you hadn't needed help with the puppies and a chef for the event."

"I told you, you had my attention from the moment I saw you." She nibbled on her lower lip, holding his gaze.

"Yeah, yeah. I scare you with my, what was it? Passion. Oh, and there are some guideposts that trip you up. I remember the conversation." He inched his menu to the side and leaned over the table to whisper, "And yes, Gracie. This is a date."

"There he is!" A man's voice boomed from behind him, making Alex turn to see the big smile and snowy-white hair of Ricardo Mancini, wiping his hand on a chef apron before patting Alex on the back. "My fellow Mediterranean brother in the kitchen. It's always an honor to cook for you, Chef."

"And an honor to eat here." Alex stood to shake his hand and add a quick hug, then turned to introduce Grace, an idea forming and making him say the next sentence loud and clear. "This is Grace Donovan, owner of Overlook Glen Vineyards."

The minute he said the words, the woman in the next booth whipped to the right to look at them, as he'd suspected she might, and let out a soft gasp. Instantly, Alex turned to her. "I take it you've been there and know what an awesome place it is," he said smoothly, while Ricardo greeted Grace.

The woman's eyes widened as she looked at her husband, who seemed to have trouble swallowing his bite.

"No, no," the lady said. "We…"

Ricardo turned his hundred-watt smile on the other diners. "Ruth, Cal, I didn't see you there. How are you?" He stretched his hand out to the woman and did his back-pat thing to the man. "You've got to be some of my most loyal guests. Do you know Alex Santorini, owner of the new Greek place in town? He's also French-trained and puts my pedestrian Italian to shame."

They had no choice but to exchange introductions and handshakes, and include Grace, who slipped out of the booth to say hello, sending a quick look of victory and gratitude to Alex. He responded with a nod to remind her of her mission.

He saw her swallow some nerves and the smile falter on her face as she shook the bald man's hand. "Calvin Etheridge?" she said. "The attorney?"

"Former," he said brusquely, avoiding eye contact. "Retired now."

"But I think we've done business together."

"Small world," Ricardo chimed in, backing away to let them chat, pointing at Alex. "Fra diavolo is on point tonight, if I must say so myself."

"Done, Chef. Thanks." He turned to put a hand on Grace's back, subtly keeping her right in place at the Etheridges' table.

"Yes, I'm sure you handled the sale of my winery," she insisted, even though the man was obviously trying to brush her off. "I never forget a name. Calvin Etheridge. Surely you recall the Overlook Glen sale."

Cal and Ruth shared a look that Alex easily interpreted: He didn't want his wife to say a word.

The lawyer dabbed at his mouth with a red napkin, then set it down and fixed his dark gaze on Grace. "Miss, I don't discuss business over dinner, especially now that I'm retired."

"But I only wanted to thank you."

He nodded. "You're welcome. Enjoy your dinner."

Grace's back straightened, and her chin lifted imperceptibly. "And I wanted to ask if you would be kind enough to share some of the history of the place. I haven't met anyone who knew the owners. The Hunnicutts, was it?"

His eyes narrowed as he glared at her. "Anything I could tell you, if I wanted to, which I don't, is private and confidential under attorney-client privilege. Please don't ask any more."

"But can you tell me anything about…them? Their family? Their children?" Her voice rose with a subtle note of desperation, pulling Ruth's attention.

"They've both passed," the woman whispered, staring hard at Grace.

"Did you know them?"

"I…did."

"Ruth." Her husband's voice was rich with warning.

"Well, it's a sin to lie, Cal. I knew them."

Cal whipped his napkin off his lap and tossed it on his plate. "We're finished here," he said, pushing out of the booth so abruptly that Alex and Grace had to step out of his way. "Let's go, Ruth. Let these nice people have their dinner."

Color drained from Ruth's face as she removed her napkin and reached for her purse. Cal marched toward the front of the restaurant, unconcerned as a few heads turned to follow him.

As Ruth stepped out, Grace blocked her.

"Anything," Grace whispered. "Please tell me anything at all."

Ruth looked past Alex as if she expected her husband to lunge back and grab her, then put a hand on Grace's arm. "If I could, I would. But I promised Bonnie. She was my friend."

"Oh, please. Anything, any answers."

"Obviously, you've found the answers. I can't add anything, except you are the living, breathing image of your mother."

"Why didn't they contact me? The Hunnicutts? Why didn't they—"

"Ruth!" The booming voice echoed through the restaurant, getting the attention of every diner.

"I'm so sorry, Gracie. I promised. Right in church during our Bible study, in the eyes of God. I can't break that promise." She hustled away, holding up a hand to quiet her husband, leaving Grace standing in open-jawed shock.

"She called me Gracie," she whispered, her eyes filling. "She knows…everything."

He pulled her into his arms and slid them into the booth, both on the same side. "I heard. We'll find out more. Take a breath, honey. Have a glass of wine. We'll get to her somehow. Our mission is not yet accomplished."

Chapter Fifteen

She shouldn't be here. Grace shouldn't be pulling into Waterford Farm on a Sunday afternoon when she had a to-do list a mile long and a weight on her heart so heavy it had hurt to wake up that morning.

But Alex had asked her to come, and he wanted her here. And even though he used the lure of a conversation with Gramma Finnie about Cal Etheridge, she would have come without that opportunity. Because he'd been wonderful last night.

Over a dinner she barely remembered eating, he'd calmed her with kind words and unwavering attention. Afterward, they'd taken a walk through Bushrod Square, and he'd shared a story on the very spot where his mother and her brand-new husband had actually broken up in college, unaware that she was a few days' pregnant with Nick.

The family lore touched her, and when she'd wondered about her own mother and grandparents walking through the square, he'd let her imagine that and helped her through the threat of tears.

When he took her home and they reunited with the

puppies, he'd marveled with his sister and her fiancé at how they'd managed to teach Jelly Bean to hold the leash of one puppy, confident they'd have him holding all three by next Sunday.

And when Cassie and Braden left, Alex had kissed Grace good night, stroked her hair, and held her for a long time, but then he left, too, sensing that this wasn't the time to suggest he spend the night.

He recognized internal turmoil when he saw it, and his respect touched her.

But she did take the puppies up to her apartment, where she snuggled with all three of them as she finally fell asleep.

With all that fresh in her mind when she woke, it was an easy decision to text Alex that she'd come to Waterford for the family Sunday dinner. How could she not? How could she resist him...or the family that somehow enveloped her in warmth?

It was bittersweet, sure. But she'd started to get over the gnawing envy, which had already shifted to admiration. And her feelings for Alex? She'd gone well past admiration and was fast slipping into...

She let out a noisy sigh at the sight of him on the Waterford lawns.

Her feelings were fast slipping into something dangerous and risky and thrilling and *real*. She could end up hurt. She could end up annihilated. She could end up...loved.

Alex stood with a group of family members and dogs just outside of the kitchen porch of the big house, turning as she pulled into the drive, his smile visible almost immediately. He broke away and hustled down the drive, giving her a moment to admire the way his casual white button-down shirt fit his broad shoulders and how the hair that fell over his collar fluttered in the breeze. Every step he took was confident, masculine, and sexy.

She had no idea how much longer she could resist the man, or if she wanted to.

"Hey." He opened her car door and leaned over, kissing her right on the mouth as if it was the most natural thing in the world. "You made it."

"We all did." She pointed her thumb into the back, where the puppies scrambled in excitement to see Alex.

"Hey, kids." He opened the back door and grabbed the leashes that hung over the crate. "Molly just told me they're good to go on the grass now, so we can walk them."

He had them leashed up in no time, while Grace opened the other side and pulled out a bag. "I brought another surprise," she said, holding up one of the bottles. "Unlabeled, but it's Three Dog Night. I thought we could share the first few bottles with your family."

"My buddy dropped off the labels at Santorini's this morning." He grinned at her. "We can put them on these bottles."

She came around the car, laughing at how tangled the three puppies already were in the leashes, but between the two of them, they got the knots undone and took the crew toward the house. Of course, there was a multifamily welcoming committee, led by Pru and Christian, who pounced all over the dogs.

As Grace greeted everyone, Alex went to his car to get the wine labels, and almost immediately Cassie sidled up next to her.

"Talk to you for a sec?" she whispered.

"Of course. Everything okay?"

"Oh yeah, I just want to ask you a favor." With all the attention on the puppies, they slipped a few feet away toward the empty wraparound porch. "Would you go dress shopping with me?"

"Oh, of course, but are you sure you don't want to take someone you're close to? One of your cousins? Though I know that would ruin the surprise for them." She'd noticed that Cassie was tight with Ella and Darcy and wondered if she'd bring those two in on the wedding plans.

But Cassie shook her head. "There is no such thing as a secret in this family," she said. "I love them all to death, but everyone's so damn close, there's no way to keep anything quiet. I'm determined that they are all stunned and shocked on Sunday. So, some day this week? There's a great dress store in Chestnut Creek where I grew up."

"Can you get a wedding gown in a week?"

"Nothing formal or traditional. Off the rack is fine for me, and it doesn't even have to be a big old wedding gown. If it's subtle enough, I'll wear it to the event. If not, I'll slip away and change there. Oh, I did talk to the pastor at church today. Him, I can trust." She laughed. "I think."

"And you don't want anyone else in the wedding?"

"Just my Jelly Bean and the three stooges. But honestly, I'll need a second opinion on the dress."

Grace nodded. "I'd love to go. I'm honored."

Cassie gave her an impulsive hug and kiss, which Grace was almost getting used to with this family, breaking away as Alex arrived.

"Come on, let's take these inside, and we can all gather for the first labeling."

"Family labeling?" Grace joked.

"Family everything." He took the bag with the bottles of wine and led her inside. There, even more of them were all grouped around the kitchen table, where Katie Santorini—now Kilcannon—flipped through a large book, holding baby Annabelle with the ease of a woman who had had five babies and the joy of someone ready to be a grandmother.

"Perfect timing," she said, greeting her son and Grace. "The wedding photographer dropped these off yesterday. Overlook Glen looks amazing, and he did a great job."

"Good to hear, since I hired him for the event next week," Grace said, leaning over to see a gorgeous shot of Katie coming down the curved stairs. "Oh wow. You look amazing."

She smiled up at Daniel, who'd come to stand behind her, sipping a cup of steaming-hot coffee. "I look happy, that's for sure," Katie said.

"And amazing," Daniel added, putting a loving hand on her shoulder.

"And we've got something to make everyone happy," Alex announced, pulling out a wine bottle. "The very first bottles of Three Dog Night, which will be the custom blend for Scooter and Blue. Check out the labels." He produced the labels, spreading them on the table with much fanfare and *oohs* from the crowd.

"They're perfect," Grace said, admiring the sleek purple and teal design that included the shapes of three dogs. "And if we don't get picked to do their wedding, we can still sell this wine using this label."

"If you don't get picked?" Yiayia flattened her hands on the kitchen table and narrowed her eyes at Grace. "How can you have any doubts? Alex is cooking, and this entire family is behind you."

"And you have the most beautiful venue," Katie added, flipping the photo book to a page that included the winery's breathtaking view. "I looked at the other two wineries, and they might be a little bigger and more established, but they're slick and inauthentic. I can see Blue getting married at Overlook Glen."

A chorus of agreement rose, strong enough to make Grace laugh. "Okay, okay. I'm buying into this family's confidence."

As they chattered, Alex cleaned and dried one of the bottles and made some space on the counter to affix the label, with the group around them growing as he made a huge deal about the first label.

"You're nothing if not enthusiastic, lad," Gramma Finnie noted, tugging Grace's hand to ease her onto the bench next to her. "Did you find the lawyer?" she asked softly.

"We did, but he couldn't shed much light on things for me," Grace told her. "I'd love more time with Ruth."

Gramma played with the top button of a black-and-white cardigan. "My needlepoint group has disbanded, or I'd invite you, lass."

"Her husband was loath to share anything with me about Overlook Glen's former owners," Grace said, choosing her words carefully, as Cassie's warning about family secrets was still fresh in her head. "Of course, he's saddled with attorney-client privilege. But Ruth?"

Gramma gave an unladylike snort. "She's a good Christian woman, but if that man says, 'Bark,' Ruth asks, 'How loud?'" Gramma rolled her eyes. "Your best bet is to get her alone."

"Any ideas?" Grace asked.

"Let me think on it, lass. And, oh my, would you look at that!"

Alex lifted the bottle to a round of applause and cheers, including one from Grace. Three Dog Night was a spectacular-looking bottle of wine.

"And now we drink it," he said. "Feel free to open the other one, but I'm going to take Grace on a walk, along with the three puppies who inspired this wine, and open bottle number one. Yes?" he asked her.

As if she could say no.

As they were headed out the door a few minutes later, Yiayia snagged Alex's arm and squeezed. "Hang on a minute, boyo."

Grace turned and looked from him to his grandmother, then said, "I'll get the dogs outside," as if she'd read the request for privacy in Yiayia's eyes. Alex certainly saw it.

"What's up?" he asked.

"I have some treats for you." She dragged him to the coffee counter and handed him a small basket. "I made some kataifi." She sang the word the way his father and grandfather used to. "It's the one thing I can make better than you."

He smiled. "No argument, Yiayia. Yours are absolute nests of deliciousness, and mine are…"

"Well, I wouldn't use pistachio." She sniffed. "I think that's where you went wrong last time."

He had to laugh, taking the basket. "There's the Yiayia you've been hiding all these months."

She angled her head and looked sad. "I'm trying," she said, the honesty in her eyes touching him. "Have you talked to Garrett yet?"

"No, I haven't even seen him. Why?"

"He's had a call about the puppies. Someone who claims they lost them and wants them back."

His eyes widened. "Really?"

She tsked and shook her head. "There are unscrupulous people out there, and Garrett says they have to produce the mother, and the puppies need to respond to her. He's not just going to hand them over to anyone who might sell them off."

The very thought of that gave him a sick punch in his gut. "I'll talk to him."

"And Grace? Will you tell her?" Yiayia asked, looking out the window. "Because she's getting mighty attached to those pups."

He followed her gaze, getting a glimpse of Grace sitting on the purple blanket as Gertie climbed on her lap and Pru handed her baby Fiona to hold. As she threw her head back with a heartfelt laugh, the puppy nuzzled the baby. Christian sat on her other side, playing with Jack, and Pru was running around trying to grab Bitsy's leash.

He couldn't hear what Grace said, but whatever it was, it made Christian giggle and lift Jack high in the air. As if on instinct, Grace reached up to make sure the puppy was safe in the little boy's hands.

Attached. Oh yes, she was. And if the puppies'

mother showed up? "That might break her heart," he whispered out loud. The poor woman had had a life of broken attachments. "But it would be best for the puppies."

"Maybe the owner will let her keep them, after all," Yiayia said.

Or maybe the owner wouldn't. "We'd have to do the right thing," he said, slipping the bottle of wine into the basket and closing the lid.

Yiayia reached up, patting his beard. "You're so much like your father, you know."

He turned to her, surprised by the comment. "I know."

"Except he would never close that lid without checking out my kataifi."

He laughed and tapped the basket. "I'll check it out in my mouth, Yiayia. But right now, I'm trying to think of how to prepare Grace if she has to say goodbye to those puppies."

Yiayia nodded. "I was wrong about John," she admitted softly. "It kills me to be wrong, but I was. She's good for your soul."

He winked at her. "And the rest of me." With a quick kiss on her forehead, he went out to find Grace and tell her the news.

But as he walked toward the little scene on the grass, he slowed his step. Maybe the owner would fall through. Maybe Garrett would decide it was a scam. Maybe he could delay her heartbreak somehow.

Because right now, right this moment, Grace was so soft and changed and different from the woman he'd tried to flirt with at his mother's wedding. Her walls were down, her deep childhood pain—even though he suspected he'd done nothing but dredge it up again—seemed gone for the moment. It wasn't just the puppies, but they were such a big part of it.

In a few moments, they'd gathered up the dogs and the blanket, handed the baby back to Pru, and started down the walking path with all three tugging on their leashes.

As they headed down the hill toward the lake, Grace looked around in wonder as more views of Waterford Farm spilled out for acres and acres. "Pru was just telling me how Daniel started Waterford as a canine facility so he could honor his late wife and get all his kids back to Bitter Bark."

"But it was their home first and Gramma Finnie's before that. Has she told you the story of how she came here?"

"Not yet," Grace said.

"She will, and she likes you, so you'll get the long version."

"I'll look forward to it." She gave a wistful sigh. "What a way to grow up, though, at a place like this."

"No kidding. Even I get a little envious of how the Kilcannons lived, and I grew up in a big family. It's *Little House on the Prairie* with dogs."

She slipped her arm through his and tugged him closer. "I'm not feeling that kind of envy," she assured him. "In fact, for the first time in years and years, I feel hope. Gramma Finnie said she'd think about how I could somehow talk to Ruth Etheridge."

"That'd be great."

"That'd be…life-changing. You have no idea, Alex. I just want to know something. Anything. A connection to her."

"You do realize that you're most likely living in the house where she grew up," he reminded her. "If that's not a connection, I don't know what is."

"It is," she said, but didn't sound too convinced. "I just want to know something more about her. Something tangible. And my father, whoever he was."

They reached the lake and found a large spot of grass, spreading the blanket for them and the dogs. Grace watched and cheered him on, taking pictures as he ceremoniously unscrewed the wine, joking about how he really could be wrong about some things, then lifted the basket lid to show Yiayia's pastries.

"Yes, she kicks my butt in the kataifi department," he told her.

After he poured the deep burgundy-colored wine into two plastic cups, he handed her one.

"Are we allowed to toast the first sip of Three Dog Night?" he asked.

"Absolutely."

He lifted his glass and held her eyes. "To connections," he whispered. "The ones you're missing and the ones you're finding."

She let out a sigh of appreciation. "You did that for me, Alex. You singlehandedly helped me make these connections, so yes, I'll drink to that. And to you."

They tasted the wine at the same moment, both of them letting out a soft whimper of delight when the flavors hit their tongue.

"It's amazing," he said. "The best Pinot Noir I've ever tasted."

She inched back and held the cup up, looking through the clear plastic with awe. "You did that, too!

The best Pinot Noir that has ever had the Overlook Glen label, at least since I've owned the place."

Just then, Bitsy launched toward Grace, nearly knocking the wine out of her hand, making them laugh.

Grace was way too happy right then for Alex to announce the puppies might have to be returned to their mother. He'd talk to Garrett when they went back to the house and suss out how serious this lead was. In the meantime, he just wanted to bask in the glow of a woman enjoying a rare moment of pure peace.

"More pictures." She got her phone out and leaned into him to snap a selfie. "And one with the dogs. You. And the wine."

She unleashed the puppies and let them crawl all over him, making him laugh and lean back on the blanket.

"Oh, that's perfect," she exclaimed, standing over him and snapping pictures. "With the wine bottle at a jaunty angle, the label nice and visible. I can use this in Overlook Glen marketing."

Gertie snuggled between his outstretched legs, and Jack climbed up on his chest, and Bitsy stopped moving for one minute, turning toward the camera, making Grace squeal as she got the shot.

"Oh, Alex." She dropped to her knees on the blanket and scooped up Gertie for a kiss. "I love these dogs so much. I want to keep them."

Oh boy. Just when the owner showed up. "I could have called that the minute I found you with them," he said.

She let Gertie lick her face, laughing at his response. "Well, you'd have been right. These are my three little orphans," she whispered into Gertie's ear. "I'll take care of you. In fact, I'm going to make first-press wine every year, and it will always be called Three Dog Night. It will be your legacy, my loves."

Alex sat up and took a deep drink of that wine, hoping like hell this wasn't another attachment that would break her heart and already trying to figure out a way to protect her from that.

Chapter Sixteen

"Training day!" Grace announced to the puppies as she carried Bitsy and Gertie downstairs on Tuesday morning, joining Jack at the bottom to leash them. "Jelly Bean is in the house."

They couldn't have understood that, but the excited tone in her voice had all three of them barking, and Bitsy jumped at the bottom step and pawed at the marble, trying valiantly to get up onto it.

"No, sister. You can't do steps yet. But maybe your genius-level friend can teach you." Grace opened the winery door to find Braden and Cassie embracing in the parking lot, with Jelly Bean waiting patiently next to them.

Behind her, the puppies barked and shot out the door, their leashes dragging.

"Whoa! Watch out!" she called to the couple, breaking them apart.

Grace went after Gertie, who was an easy catch. Braden snagged Jack, and Jelly Bean somehow managed to get Bitsy's leash in his mouth and bring her to a stop. She turned and barked at him, then collapsed on the ground, rolled over, and offered her belly while her little legs paddled in the air.

"Well, one of them is submissive," Braden joked.

"Not the one I would have thought," Grace said. "But he certainly seems to have her under his spell."

"One down, two to go," Cassie said, patting Braden's arm. "Got your work cut out today."

"I can handle it," he said. "I got treats and time. And you…" He tapped her nose. "Need to find a dress that will make you happy."

"You make me happy, Einstein," she replied, getting up on her tiptoes for a quick kiss from her tall, handsome firefighter. "But a dress will be nice. You ready, Grace? I have an appointment, but I can change it if you want to wait for Alex."

"He just texted and said he was hung up with a vegetable distributor who's supplying a lot of the food for Sunday," she said. "He won't be here for a while, so you might miss your appointment if we wait."

"You guys go," Braden said. "I'll take the dogs out back and start working." He gave a whistle to Jelly Bean, who got up from his resting place next to Bitsy and tugged on her leash, then guided her into the house.

Grace handed over the other two, grabbed her bag, and headed out with Cassie, still amazed.

"Jelly Bean has actually calmed Bitsy. It's stunning."

"I'm telling you, he's Lassie. Have you heard about the time I fell down the steps and he saved me?"

As they drove to the town of Chestnut Creek, Cassie shared story after story about her family and the Kilcannons, each one a little more sweet and romantic than the next. The whole time, Grace waited for the punch of envy or the twist of deep-seated resentment that families like these even existed while she'd grown up with a revolving door of strangers.

But she didn't have any. Mostly, she laughed and sighed and asked questions. By the time they reached Chestnut Creek, Grace felt that same sense of hope welling up that she'd felt after that brief conversation with Ruth Etheridge.

Maybe the idea of family wasn't a dead end. Maybe she could learn about her history, parents, and grandparents. And maybe, if she spent enough time around the Santorinis and Kilcannons and Mahoneys... maybe...

Don't go there, she warned herself. For one thing, it would be falling in love with Alex for the wrong reasons. But even if this very young, budding romance evolved, what if it ended, leaving her alone again? With one more *lost* family?

Was she crazy? Why would she even take a chance like that?

"Grace." Cassie put her hand on Grace's arm, her tone clear that she'd been trying to get Grace's attention.

"Oh God, I'm sorry. I was zoned out...planning this event. What?"

"We just passed the wedding store. Park anywhere." Cassie gave a squeeze. "I feel ya, sister."

But she doubted Cassie did. Still, she put away her thoughts and headed into the hushed coolness of a formal wedding and dress shop, greeted by an attractive redheaded woman who held out two glasses of champagne.

"Ms. Santorini and…" She lifted a strawberry-colored brow. "Best friend or sister? Based on the difference in your looks, I'm saying best friend."

They looked at each other and gave a quick laugh. Grace opened her mouth to set the record straight, but Cassie threw an arm around her and gave a typical squeeze. "For today, she's my sister." Then she winked at Grace. "Someday. Who knows?"

A scary, tempting, delicious zing shot through her. Without giving it much thought, Grace put her own arm around Cassie and squeezed, not really able to remember the last time she opened her heart even a crack for a deep friendship. The few friendships she'd had growing up had always ended, so she'd avoided any as an adult.

But this woman? This dark-eyed, quick-witted, big-hearted Greek goddess who exuded everything Grace ever wanted to be? Yes, she could be a friend…or a sister.

"For today," Grace agreed, hugging with one hand and lifting the champagne with the other. "We are sisters."

"I am Penelope, and I will be your sister, too. Now, do we want froufrou fem, sexy sleek, or don't-give-a-damn hippie cool?"

Cassie laughed and looked at Grace. "I have no idea. What do you think?"

Grace bit her lip and looked up and down at Cassie's beautiful feminine figure, glossy black hair, and ebony eyes. "You need a gorgeous dress that suits a bride, but isn't a cliché. Something with a splash of the unexpected, a touch of traditional, and a neckline that will make Braden Mahoney cry."

Penelope hooted and grabbed Grace's hand. "Oh, honey, you have the job. And I know just where to start. This way, ladies. Cassie, there's your dressing room. Grace, there's your viewing perch. I'll start the dress party."

The next two hours passed in a blur of satin and lace and a feeling of comfort, connection, security, and joy. There was laughter from down in the gut, a tear from deep in the heart, and the dizzying new sensation of being connected at the soul. It was two solid hours of whatever God had had in mind when he invented the idea of a sister. And nothing had ever felt quite like it in Grace's entire life.

Alex spent some time in the winery kitchen and then gave up cooking to sit on the terrace and watch Braden miraculously teach Jelly Bean to walk puppies on a leash, which involved a lot of running after Bitsy and plenty of peanut butter.

But mostly, Alex checked his watch and waited for Garrett to arrive with the puppies' owner.

"How's he going to know if this so-called owner is legit?" he asked Braden, giving voice to the question burning in his head.

Braden eyed him from his position on one knee in front of Jelly Bean, holding the end of Jack's leash in one hand and a spoonful of peanut butter in the other. "Not too many people are going to show up who don't have a legitimate claim, but I suppose it could happen. My guess is we'll know by how the puppies respond to the mother and how she takes to them."

"Will she be nursing still?"

"I guess it depends on how long these pups have been separated from her. If they were out on their own for a few weeks and they were her only pups, I imagine she wouldn't. I know at the fire station, when someone's claiming a lost dog or cat, we can always tell how they respond to what we've named it. They get really put off if you call little Fluffypants something like Henry."

"I'll have to watch for that," Alex said.

"And, if I know Garrett," Braden continued, "he'll be eyeing the owners more than the dog. He's a good judge of character, so trust him."

Gertie meandered over to Alex and looked up, begging for love.

"C'mere, little girl." He scooped her up. "Are you tired from training?" She licked his neck and nestled deeper against him. "Missing your mom?"

Braden looked up. "And if it is the pups' real mom, what's your plan?"

"I'm going to ask if the puppies can stay through the big event. Maybe invite the owners to attend and meet the celebrities. Then I'll gently break the news to Grace." *Very gently.*

In his pocket, his phone buzzed, showing a text from Garrett.

I'm on my way in, and I think the owner is right behind me. Meet us in front with the pups.

"Here we go, baby," he whispered to Gertie, giving her a little squeeze. "Hope they have hearts." Then he gestured to Braden, who was already up and leashing Jack. "Let's go."

Still carrying Gertie, with Jack and Bitsy on leashes that Jelly Bean held in his mouth, they all went to the front of the winery to meet the new arrivals. Alex was only a little surprised how hard his heart kicked his ribs, because he so wanted this to be a mistake.

The wrong mother. The wrong owners—or at least people who'd understand that these puppies had a family and a home. Maybe they'd leave the mother with them.

Because if Grace came home, and the puppies were gone, she was going to be knocked for a loop. He probably should have warned her that this could be happening, but she seemed so happy to be going out with Cassie to shop for wedding dresses. He didn't want to mar that experience for her.

Garrett was already out of his screaming-yellow Jeep and walking toward the winery when Alex and Braden stepped outside. He turned and pointed to a red pickup rumbling into the lot.

"I've talked to this guy by phone," he said as Alex came closer. "His name's Marty Casper, and he's a breeder from outside of Winston-Salem. He says one of his Labs gave birth about a month ago to six puppies, and these are three of them."

"And what? He lost them, and they walked damn near a hundred miles to this winery?" Alex snorted in disbelief.

"I guess we'll hear what he has to say." Garrett stuck his hands in the pockets of his denim jacket and watched the truck, his dark eyes narrowing in distrust. "Could be an unethical dog breeder? Puppy mill? I don't know. I'm not handing those puppies over unless I'm one hundred percent confident this guy's the owner and he's brought their mother."

"And you think you'll know that?" Alex asked.

Garrett shot him a look. "Want to help?"

"Of course."

"I'm going to try to check to see if the dog he brings is chipped, without telling the owner. You distract him with the puppies, and I just need to run the reader over the dog he says is the mother."

"Chip or no chip, will you let him take the puppies?"

"If this feels like a real family reunion—and believe me, we'll be able to tell—then we might have to, so brace yourself for that. If he brings pictures of the puppies, some kind of paper trail, like a vet record, yeah. If not, then we'll keep the dogs and tell him to provide proof. Either way, if the dog's chipped, we'll have some information."

Nodding, Alex rubbed Gertie's little head while she pressed her nose into his neck as if she sensed something was up.

The battered pickup stopped about fifty feet away, close enough for them to hear a deep dog bark from the back cab. A bone-thin man in a ball cap and sunglasses climbed out, lifting the front of a filthy T-shirt with a faded Tabasco bottle on it to wipe sweat from his face. After a minute, he opened the back door, and almost immediately a large black Labrador jumped out and trotted past him.

Jack and Bitsy responded instantly, tugging at their leashes and barking, but Gertie didn't stop her tongue bath of Alex's neck.

"You know this lady?" Alex whispered to the dog, gently turning her head. "Is this your momma, little girl?"

She didn't move. She stared at the other dog, silent, still, and even a little scared. Jack and Bitsy barked as the dog approached them at a fairly rapid clip.

"Sugar!" the man called. "Stop!"

Sugar ignored the order and continued right to the pups, even as Braden bent over and lifted them. The bigger dog looked up, snarled, and barked loudly. She was black from head to toe, a color that didn't appear on one inch of the puppies' bodies.

Jelly Bean replied with a bark, too, but his sounded more like a warning.

So what the hell did all this mean?

Alex walked closer to join Garrett, who went to greet the man.

"I'm Marty," the man said. "You Garrett Kilcannon?"

Garrett nodded and gestured to Alex. "This gentleman and the woman who owns this winery have been taking care of the puppies," he explained.

A few feet away, the barking continued, with Sugar trying to get to the puppies. Braden, and Jelly Bean, held them off.

"She won't hurt them," Marty called. "Just wants to get reacquainted."

"When did she whelp?" Garrett asked.

"Whenever they were born," the guy said with the raspy laugh of a heavy smoker. "'Bout six weeks, I reckon."

"I'm going to go look at her," Garrett said, heading toward Sugar. Marty started to follow, but Alex stepped in front of him, purposely blocking his way.

"This is Gertie," he said, showing the dog to Marty.

The other man didn't react to the name at all. And Gertie turned from him and shoved her snout against

Alex's neck. Marty took a step to follow Garrett, but Alex blocked him again. "She doesn't seem to remember you," he said.

"She's a pup," the other man said, his voice rich with condescension.

"But no recognition," he said, refusing to let the man see past him just in case Garrett was trying to get a read on the dog's chip. "Isn't that strange?"

"What's strange is that my puppies are out here."

"How did you lose them, anyway?"

The man's rugged jaw locked as if he were trying not to lose his cool. "They were *stolen*," he said, looking hard at Alex. "You want to tell me how *you* came to have them?"

"They were abandoned on this property."

Marty shuttered his eyes as if he didn't believe that and took a wide sidestep closer to where Braden and Garrett stood with the two puppies and Sugar. Garrett glanced at Alex with a surreptitious flick of his brows, as if to say he'd successfully read a chip.

The older dog had stopped barking, and Braden gently eased Jack and Bitsy to the ground, holding their leashes tight and short. Jelly Bean stayed right next to them, his eyes on the new arrival.

Sugar leaned over, sniffed Jack, then walked around to get a whiff of Jelly Bean's butt.

"Poor things," Marty mumbled. "Been away from Mom awhile."

"You have pictures?" Alex asked. "Of their birth? With Sugar?"

He got another deathly glare from Marty. "What the hell do I look like? An Instagrammer?"

Garrett stepped closer to Marty and Alex, but kept

his eye on the interaction among the dogs. "Most people take pictures of newborns," he said.

"Babies. Not puppies." Marty looked from one to the other. "You telling me you don't believe I own those pups?"

"I'm not sure," Garrett said, drawing the words out and giving Alex a real twinge of hope that he wouldn't have to give up the puppies. "They aren't exactly bonded."

Marty mumbled a curse and marched to the dog. "Sugar," he said gruffly. "That's your kid." He reached down to turn the dog's head toward Jack, and she took a wary step backward.

"How about this guy?" he asked, trying again to make Sugar look at Bitsy.

"That's a girl," Alex said.

Marty just shrugged. "Come on, Sugar."

Sugar walked away from him and the puppies, sniffing the ground and following a scent on the asphalt parking lot.

"Sugar!" Marty hollered. "Get back here!"

"Hey." Garrett put a hand up. "Not necessary. I don't think these dogs are related. If they are, this reunion is a little strange."

Marty turned his head and spit on the ground. "They've been separated for three weeks. She mighta forgot her offspring."

"Then she's one darn unusual dog," Garrett said, bending over to pick up Bitsy and carry her closer to Sugar, but the bigger dog backed away and barked, heading to Braden to sniff the hand that had been holding a spoonful of peanut butter for the past hour.

"She goes nuts for treats," Marty told them. "She

isn't going to care one whit about those dogs if she thinks there's food somewhere."

Did he really expect them to believe that? Alex and Garrett shared a look, confirming that both men had the same thought.

"We called this one Lulu." Marty bent over to pet Jack. "She looks just like her father."

"She's a *he*," Alex said.

"They were too young to know that when they were taken from me," Marty said defensively.

"And a breeder would know that," Garrett added, his arms folded as he stared at the man.

Alex almost breathed an audible sigh of relief.

"That's BS, pal," the man said. "You obviously don't know shit about dogs."

Garrett stepped closer. "Look, if you can't provide pictures of these puppies when they were born, or even shots of any others in the litter, and some legal proof of ownership, like a receipt from a vet, I'm not going to—"

"How much?" Marty asked, looking from one man to the next. "What's the price, boys?"

Alex felt his fingers tighten in Gertie's soft fur. "We don't have a price, Marty," he ground out.

"Look, they're obviously mutts and not a purebred like Sugar, but they have sentimental value to…my daughter."

Not a chance. "These dogs aren't going anywhere but to their mother." Alex put his hand on Sugar's head, leaning over to let the bigger dog have a sniff of the puppy he still held tight. Sugar turned away and went back to Braden's pocket. "Which this dog *isn't*."

Marty stared him down one more time, then looked at Braden and Garrett. Finally, he shoved his sunglasses on his face and snapped his fingers at Sugar. "I'll see if my daughter took any pictures," he said. "Let's go, Sugar."

When the dog didn't move, he stomped his foot. "Sugar!"

Garrett cringed at that and put a strong hand on Sugar's head. "Come on, girl," he said gently, with the dog-whispering calm that all the Kilcannons seemed to possess.

She turned and followed Marty to the truck, her tail and head down as if she were still sniffing. Or just sad.

"Least-interested mother I've ever seen," Garrett said under his breath as Marty reached his truck.

"Plus, that guy is an asshole."

"That, too. But I read the chip. I'll check the name and address of the owner. I can tell you this much, Sugar is not their mother."

Braden reached down to rub Jelly Bean's head. "Good protection work, JB. You love these little puppies, don't you?"

Alex didn't know about Jelly Bean, but *he* loved the puppies, and he couldn't wait for Grace to come back so he could celebrate this dodged bullet.

Chapter Seventeen

After stepping in to play the role of "sister" and then hearing how close she'd come to losing the puppies, Grace wasn't sure her day could get any better. Garrett called Alex late that afternoon and informed him that the chip reader did link a black Lab to an owner named Martin Casper, although the name listed for the dog was Maggie, not Sugar. They decided if he came back with proof, they'd reconsider.

So Gertie, Jack, and Bitsy didn't have their mother, but each day—each hour—it felt more like they were where they belonged.

Then Alex suggested he cook up a few dishes he was considering for the wedding so she could taste each and every one, which turned into hours of cooking, laughing, talking, sipping wine, and eating some of the most outrageously good food Grace had ever had.

By ten o'clock that night, they relaxed on the terrace with an empty bottle of wine, full stomachs, sleepy puppies, and a feeling of contentment as heady as the wine.

They settled next to each other in two rattan patio chairs, looking out over the valley in the moonlight, the puppies between them, sleeping contentedly on their blanket.

"You can only pick one," Alex said, holding up a finger. "No questions, comments, or changes. Pick one."

Grace slid him a questioning look. "Trick question or a psychological game?"

"Wedding planning, Gracie. Just trying to pare down the offerings for the big day. You've sampled it all by now, so we have to eliminate one dish in each course."

"Okay." She tucked her feet up and turned to face him, taking in his strong profile. "Hit me."

"Pizza wedges with smoked caviar or baked goat cheese salad?"

"Hmm. I think—"

"Don't think, just feel." He grinned. "So I guess it is a little bit of a psychological game."

"Pizza."

He nodded. "Agree. What about potato egg pie with bacon and crème fraîche or porcini mushroom tartlet?"

"The tartlet that Scooter inhaled? I think you know the answer to that one."

"Yeah, but the egg pie is sin on a plate."

"Everything you make is sin on a plate," she teased, eyeing him a little longer than necessary just for the sheer pleasure of it. "You, actually, are sin…in a chair."

He sent back an evil, playful, flirtatious grin. "The tartlet wins. How about winter squash soup versus the sweet potato soup with turmeric?"

"Hmm. I think they're too similar. Give me more of a choice. What about that chicken soup with lemon you made?"

"Chicken with tomato and caramelized lemon?" He nodded. "Yeah, excellent call."

"Next?" She took a sip of wine, enjoying the game. The moment. The *man*.

"Braised lamb shank with peppers or ham steak in Madeira sauce?"

"The lamb, I think."

"Then dessert. Nectarine pavlovas or banana and chocolate cream pie parfaits?"

"Uh, wedding cake? Cassie already ordered it from her favorite bakery in Chestnut Creek."

"But there has to be a fruit option, too."

She laughed. "No stone unturned, huh? I'll go with the pavlovas because they sound so pretty, but did you make them? I don't remember."

"Not yet, but I will tomorrow. Actually, I can make them tomorrow morning for breakfast."

She lifted a brow, aware of a low hum of heat in her blood. "Tomorrow…morning?"

He smiled and reached for her hand across the space that separated them. "Too soon?"

"Too…scary."

He looked at her for a long time, that intensity in his eyes deepening with each passing heartbeat. "You're still scared of me, Gracie?"

"No," she whispered with complete honesty. "I'm not scared of you. I'm scared of…not you."

He frowned. "Not following."

"When it's over. When you're gone. When I'm alone in that bed again."

"Such optimism." He gave her fingers a slight squeeze.

"Optimism has never worked well for me."

"We're so close," he whispered. "How can I get those last few bricks down from that wall you've built around yourself?"

"I don't know," she confessed. "They're pretty sturdy and permanent."

"But are they Alex-proof?"

She laughed softly. "So far."

He was out of his chair in an instant, right onto his knees next to her, stunning her with the speed and grace of the move. "You can't avoid something because you're scared of it being over, Grace."

"Can't I?" She raised a brow. "I can and I have, ever since…" She dug through her memory and came up with… "The Sweetley house."

"The whatly house?"

She closed her eyes and set her glass down. "Long story."

"I have all night."

She peeked at him from under her lids.

"At least, I hope I do. With nectarine pavlovas at sunrise."

"Sunrise?"

"We have to be at the farmers' market outside Holly Hills by seven a.m. They get the best food and produce on Wednesdays, but you have to be there early. The puppies will love it. So, it only makes sense for me to stay tonight. I'll sleep right here under the stars…with you and Gertie and Jack and Crazy Ass. Yeah?"

She opened her eyes completely during his little speech, studying his face, memorizing every detail of his eyes and nose and mouth, already knowing how that beard felt against her cheeks and wondering about what it would feel like against her thighs.

"Oh, Hurricane Alex. I'm not sure even my brick walls can withstand you."

"That sounds…promising." He leaned in and kissed her. "But I don't want to force those walls down, Gracie. I want you to…" He stood, easily bringing her with him. "Step out of that hiding place and into…" He folded her in a hug. "My arms."

"Mmm." She tilted her head back, melting into him. "That sounds nice."

"It could be." He kissed her, angling his head and running his hands up and down her back. "It would be." She lifted her chin so he could press kisses along her jawline and throat, letting out a sigh of pleasure as he grazed and nibbled her collarbone.

So good. This would be so good.

"So…long hot kisses on my lap in that chair or…" He worked his way back to her mouth, sliding his hands into her hair. "Tell me about the Sweetley house?"

She drew back, a frown pulling. "Another game of choice?" she guessed.

"Yep. Essentially, make out or talk? Your call."

As if there was any contest. She wanted to fall back into that chair with him, wrap her arms and legs around him, and let the clothes fall where they may.

"I'll talk," she said on a resigned sigh. "But let's do it in the chair."

He laughed and turned her around so he could sit first and bring her onto his lap, but just as he was going down, he jumped up again.

"Where's Bitsy?"

She blinked into the dim light at the blanket where there were two sleeping dogs. "Bitsy?" She spun around. "She was just there." Wasn't she? How could she have walked away and they didn't see?

"Bitsy?" she called again, grabbing her phone to shine the flashlight around the whole terrace.

"Where are you, doggo?" Alex's words were drowned out by Jack's barking, alerted to something exciting. Gertie just launched toward Grace's leg, pawing to be picked up.

"C'mere, baby." Gracie reached down and gathered the puppy in her arms, pressing her little body to her chest, getting as much comfort as she gave. "Could she have walked off the terrace?"

"I don't know how we'd miss that." Alex started toward the perimeter, shining the beam of his phone flashlight over every inch. "We gotta put a bell on that girl. Bitsy! Stay with those two," he called to Grace as he headed toward the steps that led to the path and the vineyard. "I'll look around here."

"Maybe she went back to the cook's cottage?" Grace suggested, hating the thought of the little puppy running through the dark. "Hush, Jack." She dropped onto the chair, clinging to Gertie, worry crawling up her chest.

She could hear Alex calling for Bitsy, his voice taut with concern.

"Where did she go?" Grace whispered to the dogs, scanning with her flashlight again. Which landed on a slightly open French door leading into the reception area. "I thought I closed that."

Hoping she'd find Bitsy inside, she urged Jack

forward and carried Gertie, setting her down as they stepped inside. "Bitsy?" she called. "Come on, let's look around."

She couldn't have gone up the stairs, so Grace headed down toward the kitchen, searching in all the puppies' favorite places, near the treats and their water bowls, but there was no Bitsy.

So she went to the other side of the building, past the closed door to her office, into the conference room, checking under every table and chair.

"Grace?"

"Did you find her?" She ushered the dogs into the hall, heading back to meet Alex in the reception area, her heart dropping when she saw his empty hands. "Oh God."

"Where could she have gone?"

Jack hustled to the curved stairs, one of his favorite play places, all wound up now for fun and games. Alex was on him in a second.

"Oh no you don't, big guy." He lifted Jack from the second step, then paused, looking up. "She can climb, you know."

"No, she can't."

He turned and gave her a look. "Jelly Bean, the great and powerful wizard, taught her today."

"Oh my God." Each holding a dog, they tore up the twenty-five marble steps side by side to the second floor. Every door was closed up there, and the long hall that looked down into the reception area was empty.

"Third floor?"

"My apartment." They went up the conventional flight of stairs to the third-floor landing, where the door to the living area of Grace's apartment was open, as always. They stood in the entry vestibule for a moment, silent except for their breathing, when they heard the tiny mew.

With a quick look, they darted toward the dimly lit bedroom, and there was Bitsy, asleep in the crate, the door wide open.

"Bitsy!" Grace practically fell on her with a whimper of relief.

"She put herself to bed," Alex said on a laugh, dropping onto the bed and letting Jack down. "I can't believe she came all the way up here."

The other two dogs were all over Bitsy, licking and sniffing and wagging their tails as if they'd been separated for a month instead of a few minutes. Grace honestly didn't know whether to laugh or cry.

"You stay with them," Alex said. "I'll go get their blanket. They can't sleep without it."

She looked up at him, almost drowning in one of those waves of affection that washed over her. "Alex…"

"It's okay." He held up a hand. "I'll be back. You promised me the Sweetley story."

He touched the top of her head as he left, the gesture so gentle and tender, her heart felt like it might explode.

"Now there's a good man," she whispered to Gertie, who'd found her way onto Grace's lap. "A very good man."

He returned with the blanket and the promise that everything downstairs was locked tight.

"So, you're staying?" she asked as she spread the purple blanket over the pillows in the bottom of the crate.

"I can sleep in another room, if you prefer."

She straightened and turned to find him stretched out on top of her comforter, shoes off, his head cradled in strong arms. "I prefer you right there," she said, latching the puppies in their crate. "And I will tell you the story, but I warn you…"

"One of us is going to cry?"

She laughed softly, climbing next to him on the bed. "The puppies will, at about two o'clock. And I let them sleep in the bed with me."

"Then it'll officially be a three-dog night."

She wrapped her arms around him, slid her leg over his, and laid her head on his chest.

"Where should I start?"

"Wherever you want."

She thought for a moment, about the homes before the Sweetleys', but they all ran together. Until that one. "The Sweetley family was the first home that made me…hope. They made me believe I could have a family."

"Tell me about them." He stroked her hair, coaxing the story out of her with each gentle touch.

"They had an adopted son and a dog named Bailey. I was eleven when I got there, and my bedroom had butterfly wallpaper and butterflies on the bedspread. Oh, and a big butterfly-shaped rug on the floor." She sighed at the memory of digging her toes into that rug and wanting to just…stay. "I thought I was in heaven."

"And they were nice people?"

"As sweet as their name. I lived there for eleven and a half months."

"What happened?"

233

"I don't know," she said honestly. "They talked about adoption, and my social worker was certain I was going to stay, but then one day, a new social worker came. A man with short hair and a black tie and a pinched face. He said I had to leave."

"Why?"

She shook her head. "That's what happened, Alex. Every single time. It was like a switch was thrown, and the possibility of adoption just fell apart, every time."

"Tell me about the other ones. In fact, tell me everything you want from beginning to end."

She took a deep breath, closed her eyes, and started from the earliest home she could remember, spilling out her story and her heart.

Eventually, she talked herself to sleep on Alex's chest, somewhere long after the Sweetleys.

She woke once, in the middle of the night, to find him opening the crate to put the puppies on the bed. They all slept together, Grace and Alex still dressed and two little furballs tucked between them and another on her chest.

She couldn't remember ever being quite so content in her whole life. Maybe once, with the butterfly carpet.

Chapter Eighteen

Alex opened his eyes just before dawn, torn between the pull of the kitchen and the thought of making a nectarine pavlova…and the woman sleeping next to him and the thought of making *love.*

He was ready in every way possible. His body screamed for her, his heart ached for her, and his passionate Greek soul just wanted to create glorious food and spoon-feed it to her to take away all that pain.

Grace sighed in her sleep, nestling closer, moving just enough to wake Gertie, who was tucked into Grace's side. The little puppy pawed at the comforter, pressing down for a stretch. That woke Jack, then the maniac started prancing up and down Alex's stomach.

So much for morning sex.

"Oh, hello." Grace blinked her eyes open and laughed when Gertie licked her cheek. "Who is this?"

"Not me, I'm sorry to say." Alex lifted Gertie's little body so he could have access to that same cheek. "But I'm just as furry."

Smiling, she put her hand on his beard, scratching her fingers. "Have you ever thought about shaving it?"

"John and I grew them when my dad died," he told her. "Nico Santorini had a beard, and his father, my Papu, Nikodemus Santorini, had a beard."

"And your other brothers?"

"They don't work in the restaurant. But John and I decided it was a way to honor and remember him, and now?" He shrugged. "It's been two years, and this beard is a part of me." He frowned, holding her blue-green gaze. "You want me to shave it?"

"My opinion shouldn't matter."

"It does." He moved a puppy aside and came closer to her. "I like you so much, Grace," he whispered.

She held his gaze, her eyes moving over his face as the words sank in. "Even after you heard my sob story?"

"Your sob story just makes me understand—and like you more. It makes me want to…" He tugged at her shirt. "Tear down all the walls."

"Yeah." She let him lift the shirt and reveal some skin, holding his gaze as he placed a hand on the dip in her waist. "I like you, too, Alex," she admitted. "I like you…a lot."

Turned on by the tremble in her voice, he eased her closer, lining up their fully clothed bodies and forcing Gertie out of her hiding place between them.

He leaned in and kissed her lightly, gliding his hand a little higher. "So, we like each other." He broke the kiss and closed all the space between them. "Now what?"

She gave a soft, throaty laugh. "We make like?"

He smiled at that, rocking just enough to let her know how badly he wanted her. "Is that sex, but with your clothes on?"

"That's…" She moaned as he pressed some kisses into her throat and tugged the T-shirt higher. "Nice."

So nice.

He kissed her again, letting their tongues tangle and taste, finally reaching the soft fabric of her bra, hungry to get it off and touch every inch. She rolled onto her back, inviting him on top of her, kissing and rocking as he slid his hand under the band and cupped her sweet, small breast.

"Alex." She arched again, moving against him as need gripped her, too. "Wait."

He stilled instantly, moving his hand away and bracing himself over her. "I'll wait," he said. "As long as you like."

"I don't *want* to wait," she said roughly, the emotional battle she was fighting visible all over her pretty face. "I want you, but…"

"Listen to me," he said. "People don't automatically push you away just because you start to care about them."

She closed her eyes. "Is that what you got out of my story?"

"Yeah," he said without hesitation. "And that you blame yourself for that. And expect it from everyone."

"How could I not?" she asked. "When the same thing happens to you six, eight, ten, twelve times, you start to see a pattern in life. People don't…want *you*."

"Gracie." He smoothed a lock of her fair hair, curling it behind her ear. "I want to change your mind and convince you that's wrong."

"Quite a risk, Alex. What if we try and…fail? Then you'll just be another one."

He wanted to say he didn't fail, but there was no

guarantee this would work out. They hadn't known each other for long. "So you just…give up? Never take a chance? Is that how you want to live your life? Alone?"

"I don't *want* to."

He looked at her for a long time. "Then don't."

On a sigh, she eased him up, and he braced for the rejection, but then she grabbed the bottom of her T-shirt, yanked it up, and flipped it to the floor. Instantly, Jack pounced on it like he'd been given a new toy.

But Alex was the one who just got the prize.

"Oh." The word slipped out as he looked down at a thin cotton bra that revealed the outlines of her breasts. "Then you made your decision."

"Yup." She laughed and pulled at his shirt, so he got rid of it, too, then fell back down to cover her in kisses and get that bra off.

Blood thrummed in his head, and her breath grew tight and a little frantic, and somewhere, in the distance, he heard Jack bark.

"Puppies," she muttered, pushing him up a little to look around the bed and floor. "I see two."

"*Damn* it." He rolled over just in time to catch Bitsy flying out the door. "I'll get her. Don't you even think about moving." As he climbed off the bed, his phone dinged from the night table with a call. At dawn? "Please don't be a Santorini's emergency." Because that was the only thing that would make him walk away right now. Maybe. If it was burning down. He grabbed the phone and read the caller ID with a frown. "Huh? It's Gramma Finnie."

"Does she usually call you this early?"

"No. I hope Yiayia's okay."

"I'll get Bitsy. You talk to Gramma."

Swearing softly, he tapped the screen and put the phone to his ear as Grace took off after the wayward dog. "Hey, Gramma. What's up?"

"Ruth Etheridge is up," she said without preamble. "And posting on Facebook."

He straightened as Grace came back in with Bitsy in her arms, his gaze devouring the leggings and bra, her entire sexy body revealed in the formfitting clothes.

"And…" What had the old woman said? He couldn't even think he ached for her so much. "Facebook? What?"

"Alex, are you awake? I know you're an early riser."

He looked down at the tent in his pants. "I've…risen," he said dryly, making Grace bite back a laugh. "Now what did you say about Ruth Etheridge?"

Grace sucked in a breath. "What?"

"Oh, good, you're with Grace," Gramma said. "Put the lass on the phone, or put me on speaker."

He pulled the phone away and mouthed, "Sorry," as he tapped the screen. "Okay, Gramma, you're on speaker. Grace and I were just…"

"Menu planning," Grace said quickly.

He smiled and reached for the strap of her bra, snapping it playfully. "So what did Ruth Etheridge post on Facebook?" he asked.

"Her whereabouts, that's what. And, Grace, didn't you say you wanted to spend more time with her away from her husband, to find out about the history of your winery?"

"I did." Her eyes lit up and so did her smile. "Thank you for remembering, Gramma Finnie."

"'Tis nothing, lass. I have the memory of a steel trap," she said without a drop of irony. "Ruth posted that she's lookin' forward to morning choir practice because they have a new song set or somethin', but I happen to know she attends First Baptist of Bitter Bark, and one of my dear friends is a regular there. And she just told me that lunchtime choir practice starts at noon. Do with that what you will, lass."

What would she do with that? Alex eyed Grace and watched her nod slowly. "Thank you, Gramma Finnie," she said. "I really appreciate your sleuthing work."

"Not to worry. I was just firing up my computer to write my blog this week."

Grace blinked. "You blog?"

"Like a beast," Alex joked.

"I'm writin' up the story of my son's second wedding," she said. "My sweet old readers are lovin' the romance of it all."

"I bet they are," Grace said. "And I promise I'll get you some kind of exclusive interview when we get Scooter and Blue's wedding. I owe you one, Gramma."

"That would be wonderful, but you don't owe me a thing, lass. 'Tis my pleasure to put a smile on your pretty face."

After they said goodbye, Grace reached for Alex's hand. "Will you go with me?"

"Yes. We'll all go together." He rubbed Bitsy's head. "To the farmers' market, then to Bitter Bark."

She let out a sigh and pressed her hand against

his chest. "Let's give this a little more time," she whispered.

He nodded, knowing that he'd lost her to the possibility of what she'd learn about her mother today.

"Maybe one more wall can come tumbling down when I talk to Ruth."

He leaned over and kissed her. "There's no rush, Gracie. I'm not going anywhere." He put a hand on her cheek. "I promise."

She almost forgot how nervous she was to talk to Ruth while they shopped and laughed their way through the farmers' market with three puppies who attracted a lot of attention. But by the time they got to Bitter Bark at eleven thirty, the knot in Grace's stomach started to burn.

"I want to talk to her alone," she said as they walked through the square toward the stately white church next to the town hall. "Do you mind?"

"No, I get that," Alex said. "I'll stay right here with the puppies, on this bench. Are you going to go into the church?"

"I was hoping I'd catch her outside, but I don't know if she walks or will park in the back."

"You go to the back of the church and watch the parking lot," he said. "I can see the steps from here, and if I see her, I'll text you immediately."

She smiled up at him. "It's a plan. Thank you, Alex."

He gave her a quick kiss. "Go…ambush."

She backed away, then darted across the street,

walking through the alley between the two big buildings. Just as she reached the parking area behind the church, she saw Ruth and another woman climbing out of a compact car.

She swallowed hard, her palms damp. She hadn't expected anyone else to be with her, but she couldn't back down now. This was the only living person she'd ever met who knew her mother. She had to talk to her.

"Mrs. Etheridge?" she called as she approached. "I don't know if you remember me. I'm—"

"Gracie," she said softly, slowing her step to stare and take her own shuddering breath. "Of course I remember you." She turned to the woman she was with. "Sheila, I'll meet you in there. I want to talk to this young lady."

A warm rush of relief rolled over Grace as the other woman smiled and headed toward the back door of the church.

"Thank you," Grace said. "I hope I'm not completely overstepping my bounds."

"You are," the other woman replied without a trace of humor. "But I haven't stopped thinking about you since the other night."

"Mrs. Etheridge—"

"Ruth. Call me Ruth."

Grace nodded. "Ruth, I've never in my life met someone who knew my mother. I have so many questions about her."

Ruth's brows crinkled with a perplexed look. "You don't…" She shook her head as if this news didn't compute. "You don't know your mother?"

"She died in a car accident, I believe."

Her eyes flashed. "Celia's dead?"

"I assumed you knew. She died when I was very little."

"All those years, and Bonnie…" The color drained from her face. "Oh, I'm glad she didn't know that pain. Though that girl certainly put her through enough."

"That girl…my mother?" Grace guessed.

Ruth searched Grace's face, thinking. "Did your father raise you, then? Did she ever find him?"

Grace shook her head as frustration rolled through her. "I don't know who my father was," she said. "I was put into the foster system at five and told my parents were killed in a car accident. That's all I know. I didn't even know I was related to the former owners of the winery until I found this." She flipped open her bag and pulled out the picture. "Celia and Grace in 1988."

When Ruth took it, Grace noticed her hands were shaking. "Oh, yes, there she is. The wild child."

"That's what someone else called her."

"I thought you hadn't talked to anyone who knew her." Suspicion darkened her voice.

"I talked to a man who once worked at the winery. He met her as a little girl, but I don't know how to find anyone else who knew the Hunnicutts."

"They were recluses, that's why. After Celia left with the…with you."

"So she had a baby and ran away?" Grace tried to put the pieces together, but nothing quite fit.

An older couple approached the church, and the woman said hello, eyeing Grace as they passed. Another car pulled into the lot, making Ruth look from side to side as if one of these witnesses could tell her husband what she was doing.

"Come inside," she said quickly, gesturing for Grace to follow. She opened the heavy door that led to a linoleum-floored hallway. With another flick of her hands, Ruth ushered her down that hall, then into a room furnished with undersized desks and chairs, the walls decorated with rainbows and Noah's Ark animals.

"Cal signed a piece of paper that binds him legally," she said. "He cannot, under any circumstances, reveal what Bonnie did and why."

"What did Bonnie do?"

She huffed out a breath. "Made sure you got that winery, that's what."

"But, Ruth, how did she know who and where I was, and why didn't she reach out to me?"

Ruth stared at her, her pale blue eyes moving over Grace's face while she struggled with her secrets. "I don't know everything," she said. "But Cal told me enough, and I was friends with Bonnie for years before..." She bit her lip. "Before Celia left and shattered the hearts of those two people."

"When did she do that? Why?"

"When you were two. Why? Because she got wind of where your father was."

"Who is he?" Grace asked, her voice taut from the lump in her throat.

"Now that, I don't know," Ruth said. "Bonnie and Bib didn't know, either. A harvest worker, is all. A man who showed up for one harvest and..." She tipped her head to the side as if she couldn't even say it. "Made young Celia think she was in love, though I just think she was in one of her rebel phases, then he disappeared before he even found out she was with child."

Her father was a harvester? Who came and went from winery to winery? "So she ran away to find him? And took me?"

She nodded. "Left in the middle of the night from that little cottage where she was living with you."

Grace had lived in the cook's cottage as a baby?

"Might as well have ripped her mother's heart out of her chest and stomped on it."

Grace put her hand to her mouth, holding back all responses until she had time to process this information.

"Celia ran off to God knows where, and no one, not Bonnie or Bib or anyone, ever heard from her again. Course now you tell me she died." She let out a mournful sigh. "You can only imagine what that did to those poor God-fearin' people. Bad enough that Celia got herself pregnant by a virtual stranger. Then she left and never told them where she went or called them again."

"She must have died without calling them, and they never found out."

She gave a look that said even death didn't absolve Celia of her sins. "Bib and Bonnie became shadows, I tell you. They never left the winery, just grew grapes, made and sold wine, and stayed to themselves. Emotionally, they were ruined."

Grace stared at her, finally getting some pieces of the puzzle together, but still missing so much. "Then how did they find me to arrange for me to be able to buy the winery? And why didn't they contact me before they died?"

"I don't know."

The words cut through her. "But I *have* to know. And I have to know why."

Ruth shook her head. "If Bonnie told my husband, he didn't tell me. All I know is that Bonnie came to him not long after Bib passed and just a month or so before she did, and she insisted on one thing—that you get the winery."

"How could she be sure I would buy it? Or could?"

Ruth shrugged. "Once you saw it, did you ever consider not buying it?"

Not at that price. But how would Bonnie know that she'd buy it? And why wouldn't Bonnie come directly to her? "I wanted it from the first," she admitted.

"Bonnie must have hoped that's what would happen," Ruth said.

"And you're sure she never knew her daughter had died?"

"I don't know what she knew. We lost touch years ago. But, dear, I've just not only told you everything I know, I've risked my marriage and my husband's reputation to do it."

Aching for more answers, Grace reached out and took the woman's hand. "Why did you do that?"

She didn't answer for a long time, looking hard at Grace. "I didn't care much for your mother," she said. "She wreaked havoc wherever she went, ruining lives, breaking hearts, and living her life as selfishly as a person could."

Grace's heart broke a little. She'd longed for any detail about her mother, but now that she had it, she didn't want it. At least, she didn't *like* it.

"But your grandmother? And Bib? The finest people God has ever put on this earth. They didn't deserve what that girl put them through, but I think..." She gave Grace's hand a squeeze. "I think all that bad business must have skipped a generation, because you don't seem a bit like Celia. You remind me more of Bonnie. And I know why she wanted to be sure you got the winery. Because she loved you. Good enough reason, if you ask me."

Did she? If she loved Grace, why didn't Bonnie reach out to her while she was still alive? Why make posthumous arrangements through a lawyer?

"And I think," Ruth continued, "if Bonnie could whisper in my ear today, she'd tell me to help you. So I did. With everything I know, but there's no more."

Grace nodded, acknowledging that. "Thank you, Ruth. I won't break your confidence, I promise. I won't get your husband in trouble, and I won't bother you again."

Ruth nodded and backed away, reaching for the door, but then she turned to look at Grace.

"How did you get the name Donovan?" she asked.

"I don't know," Grace said. "It's just what they told me my name was."

Ruth made a face as though she understood what kind of empty existence that must have been. "Well, your birth name is Graciela Bonita Hunnicutt. I remember the day you were christened, right here in this church. It was a private service, but I worked in the front office and sneaked into the sanctuary to watch. Bonnie told me you were named after both your grandmothers. Bonnie's name was Bonita, so your other grandmother was Graciela. From somewhere in South America, I suppose."

This new and unexpected revelation nearly knocked her over, drowning her like a rogue wave that came out of nowhere.

"Goodbye now." With a nod, Ruth slipped out, leaving Grace alone in the room. After a minute, she pulled out a chair sized for a first grader and sat in it, dropping her head in her hands, trying to process it all.

Graciela Bonita Hunnicutt. Her grandmothers. For the first time in her life, Grace felt connected to a family. By blood. A woman named Bonnie. A South American grandma named Graciela. They were her people, her ancestors, her roots. Finally, Grace wasn't completely...*untethered.*

Buoyed by the news—overjoyed by it, actually—she practically ran back to the square to tell Alex that one more brick had just fallen and smashed into a million pieces. Maybe the last brick in the wall she'd built around herself.

Grace Donovan might be guarded, cold, and scared of Alex's passion. Grace Donovan might not trust anyone to stay with her. Grace Donovan might not be capable of love.

But Graciela Bonita Hunnicutt?

That was a whole new person.

Chapter Nineteen

Once, in his early days of cooking, Alex had popped a raw Komodo Dragon pepper into his mouth, and his entire head nearly exploded from the heat. Grace's expression as she ran to him across the square reminded him of that moment, as though whatever was going on in her head was too much for one person to bear.

But she wasn't in pain, as he had been. From Bitter Bark all the way back to the winery, she hummed with a new kind of passion and power, her eyes glinting as she told him every bit of her conversation with Ruth. Six times.

Her fingers grasped him over and over, squeezing his arm, his hand, his leg with every shared revelation.

She crackled with this little, but profound, new understanding of who she was, and it was clearly important that he share the true meaning of the moment with her.

"I don't think I've ever seen you this…electrified," he said on a laugh as they climbed out of his Jeep and headed toward the winery.

She turned, practically dancing, flipping her long

blond hair over her shoulder. "I should have trusted those DNA tests more because Ruth thinks my grandmother was from South America. I very well may be a Latina, Alex," she announced, flipping her hair back. "What do you think of that?"

He reached for her, pulling her into a hug. "It's hot. You're hot. On fire."

"Mmm." Up on her toes, she planted a deep kiss on his mouth, softening against him and threading her fingers into his hair. "I am. I am…" She dug her nails in a little and dragged them over his neck, sending a cascade of need right through him. "I am a new woman."

"I liked the old one."

"Yeah? You're gonna go nuts over the new one," she teased, biting his lip. "Let's go upstairs."

"Now? In the middle of the day?"

She drew back. "You do not strike me as the kind of man who cares what time it is." With a sly look, she bowed her back slightly. "There's no one here. The puppies are tired. And I am…" She kissed him again, with no question of her intent.

"Graciela," he whispered into her mouth.

"Yeah." She practically melted, pulling him toward the door at the same time that she corralled the leashed puppies. They weren't so cooperative, so while she got her key in the lock, Alex picked up Gertie and Bitsy and tugged Jack's leash once the door was open.

They stood in the reception area to kiss again, with Gertie smooshed and Bitsy squirming between them.

"They need a nap," Alex announced, setting the dogs on the floor.

"So do I." Grace linked her free arm through his, easing him toward the steps. "Or at least an afternoon in bed."

She didn't have to ask twice. They made it up the stairs in record time, considering they had three puppies and had to stop to make out at least twice. The second time, Grace ripped off his T-shirt, which hit the stairs to her apartment. In the doorway, Alex got hers off. And her bra.

The puppies scampered right into their crate, which Alex shifted to the living room, and then he closed the door to find Grace already on the bed, shimmying out of her jeans.

"They don't need to see this," he joked, stepping to the bed to help her.

"It could scar them for life." She lifted her butt so he could pull off her jeans and see all of her. "Oh, Gracie," he whispered when she fell back on the bed, wearing nothing but a burgundy lace thong and a smoky, expectant expression. Every muscle in his body tightened, hardened, and ached for her. "Graciela," he corrected.

She propped herself on her elbows, her bare breasts sloping like perfect teardrops, beckoning him. "Alexander the Great."

He laughed. "That's what they call me."

"You are, you know," she said softly, her voice so sweet he left his jeans on and knelt on the bed to get closer to her.

"Haven't proven that yet."

"Oh, but you have. Over and over again." She pressed her hands on his chest, looking up into his eyes. "You're one sexy wall-removing..." She scraped her hands down his chest. "Puppy-saving…" Lingered over his abs, tracing the muscles. "Family-finding…" Reached his zipper and dragged it down. "Gourmet-cooking…" And pushed his jeans over his hips. "Great, great, oh, *very* great…man."

He wanted to laugh, but her first touch made him hiss in a breath and push her back down on the bed, kissing everywhere he could get his mouth as she helped him finish undressing. Her hands were magic. Her mouth was fire. Her skin was like silk and her body as womanly and warm and inviting as he'd imagined.

"I have a condom," he muttered into a kiss, working his way down her bare stomach, lost in the sensation of her skin against his mouth.

"We can use it…in a minute." She pushed him further, opening herself to his hands and mouth, rolling under his touches and kisses, whimpering as he easily brought her to a climax that just made him need to be inside her even more.

"Gracie. Gracie." He whispered the nickname into her damp skin as he pressed kisses on her hips and navel and suckled her breasts.

She could barely moan in reply, clutching his shoulders in desperation. "Please, Alex. Please."

With every breath labored and dragged out, she caressed his body as he sheathed himself, her touch making heat pool low in his back and deep in his belly. Need built and blinded him, making him close his eyes to focus everything on how incredible she felt.

When he settled on top of her and she wrapped her legs around his hips, he opened his eyes, his pounding heart jumping when he saw the tears spilling from the sides of her eyes.

"Gracie." He touched a tear, stilling the steady rocking of both their bodies. "Why are you crying?"

"I…can't explain it," she said gruffly. "I don't want to." She gripped his hips and guided him to where she wanted him. "Just make love to me, Alex. Fill me up with all your passion and intensity and let me be…"

"Graciela." He breathed her name as he entered her, the sweet satisfaction of the first stroke of their joined bodies like hot cream melting all over his body.

Her next breath caught in her throat as her eyes closed and her fingers tightened on his shoulders and her legs gripped him like a vise.

They moved in harmony, in a perfect rhythm that kept building to a boil that he couldn't contain. She lost control first, biting her lip as she peaked, pulling him along, helpless from the pleasure of it all and blind with sweat.

As he fell over the edge, he murmured her name, her new name, over and over, squeezing her body, utterly lost for what felt like an eternity, until he let go and dropped next to her, spent and satisfied.

Time passed. Pulses slowed. Bodies cooled. And when he opened his eyes to look into hers, Alex really did see someone completely different. Beautiful, at peace, and satisfied…but different.

"Hey." He slid off her and touched her cheek, still damp from sweat and maybe those tears. "I got to be the first man to make love to Graciela Bonita Hunnicutt."

She stared at him, but her eyes dimmed a little for the first time since she'd come running across the square.

"You okay?" he asked, pulling her against him.

"I am. Better than okay. Just…" Her voice faded.

"Just what?"

"It's like starting all over again, you know? Like when I would go to a new home, and I was so hopeful, and then…"

"What's starting all over again? This new name? This new information about your family?"

She gave him a wry smile. "This new man," she said softly. "This wonderful man who is going to make me want everything and then…"

"Gracie. I'm all in. Long haul."

She breathed a sigh. "Too good to be true." She stroked his beard, holding his gaze. "That's the story of my sad life." She smiled. "What's yours?"

He thought about it for a moment, lost in her eyes. "I came in second."

"Is that…" She glanced down at their bodies, still pressed together. "A bad dirty joke?"

That made him chuckle. "No, it's the story of my life. Second best. Second to John, always, in birth, in life, in school, and in my father's eyes. Second in my class in France, too."

"I thought you never lost at anything."

"It's not about winning or losing. It's…just what happens to me." He smiled. "But it won't happen with Scooter and Blue, I promise. You think things are too good to be true, and I think I'm second-best, but together?" He squeezed her against him completely. "We are unstoppable."

On a long, sweet exhale, she curled into him. "You are great, Alexander. In every imaginable way."

Grace opened her eyes at the sound of Alex's soft snore. No, that was Jack, but Alex *was* sound asleep next to her. Before they'd both crashed, he'd opened the door to the living area to make sure the puppies knew they were close by, so it was easy to hear the noisy one.

She stayed still for a moment, looking around her room for the first time since she'd learned her real name. And all she wanted was…more. Now that she knew a little bit, she wanted to know more.

With a quick look at Alex, she slipped out of bed silently, grabbed a pair of sleep pants and a tank top, then tiptoed out of the room. Glancing at the crate, she saw Bitsy and Jack rolled into a ball, almost making one dog. But Gertie was standing, looking sad and needy.

"Okay, baby," Grace whispered, quietly unlatching the crate to grab the little puppy. Bitsy stirred and opened her eyes, but she must have decided sleeping on Jack's belly beat a visit with Gracie and closed them again.

Taking Gertie, Grace slipped down the stairs, feeling a pang of guilt when she realized the most important event in her life was in four days and she was spending hours in bed.

"Well, I needed that," she rationalized to Gertie. "All the deliveries are tomorrow, then the setup, then the final touches." With the exception of a few phone calls, and maybe one more meeting with Cassie, they were just about ready to roll. Friday and Saturday would be crazy, though.

So it wasn't work that took her into her downstairs office. Setting Gertie on the floor with a quick check to make sure there was nothing the puppy could chew or choke on, Grace walked to the window that offered a breathtaking view of the vineyard.

Why would Celia run away from here? Leave her parents and home, take a small child? And never come back or contact them? Were there answers anywhere?

She glanced around the office, cursing the day she'd cleaned out the old file cabinets, not that interested in the former owners.

Sitting at the desk, she opened her laptop and opened Google, forming her search words.

Celia Hunnicutt…Bitter Bark, North Carolina.

The first and only thing that came up was a news story from the *Bitter Bark Banner* that a local teenager had been arrested for drunken driving.

The wild child.

She googled George and Bonnie Hunnicutt, and in addition to small bits of news about Overlook Glen in the local paper and small wine periodicals, the only real information was in their obituaries. She pored over every word of those.

Neither mentioned a daughter or granddaughter, no relatives at all, in fact. Bonnie died eight months after Bib, also of cancer.

During that eight-month period, Grace had been searching for a winery to buy. Was that how Bonnie located her? Some connection in the winery world? Then how long had she known that Grace Donovan was Graciela Hunnicutt? Who told her?

"You left me."

Startled at the voice, Grace turned from her laptop to see Alex standing in the doorway, wearing nothing but unbuttoned jeans. "You were asleep and I…"

"Want information more than you want…"

"I want both," she assured him, looking at his bare chest and abs and that trail of dark hair that led down to his zipper.

He pointed to the laptop screen. "Obituary? Smart place to start." He came around the desk, slowing his step to reach down and pet Gertie. "What did you find out?"

"Not much. Not enough. It'll never be enough. I need to know how Bonnie found me, how she knew I was looking for a winery, and why, oh God, *why* didn't she contact me in person?" She heard the ache in her voice, felt it deep in her chest. She'd just buried that pain in the euphoria of finally knowing her real name and the bliss of sex with Alex. But it was back, and it was real.

Instantly, his strong hands were on her shoulders, turning the chair at the same time he sank down to crouch in front of her.

"Honey, at some point in your life, you're going to have to let go."

She stared at him, knowing he was right but that he was asking the impossible.

"We'll keep researching and looking, but once you know all you can know, you're going to have to accept what you don't know and not let it define you."

"How can I do that?" she asked on a ragged whisper.

"I'm not sure, but I can tell you this, you don't have to do it alone. I'm right here."

She pressed her hand on his face, stroking the soft whiskers of his beard. "Why are you doing this for me?"

"Why would you even ask that?" He gave a soft laugh. "I like you. I like us. I like holding you and sleeping with you and cooking for you and watching you…bloom. Do I need more reason than that?"

She shook her head, then gestured toward the computer. "My mother was arrested for drunk driving at sixteen."

He rolled his eyes. "You told me that Ruth said you were more like your grandmother than your mother. She was a wild teenager, thankfully."

"Thankfully?"

"The result of her wildness is you," he said, leaning in for a kiss. "And I couldn't be happier about that. And someday, you'll stop questioning and searching and doubting and realize that you are right where you're supposed to be, and you're who you're supposed to be. And then, Graciela, you'll be free."

"I want that," she said, gripping his arms to underscore the statement. "I want that so much."

He kissed her again and pulled her out of the chair. "Come back to bed," he said, wrapping her in an embrace. "We're just getting started together."

She practically melted at the thought and followed him back to bed.

Chapter Twenty

B y one o'clock on Sunday, Alex was so deep in the zone that he didn't even hear Grace come up behind him in the kitchen and wrap her arms around his waist. But that pulled him away from the tartlet shells in the Blodgett oven, and he turned in her arms, meeting the gaze of the woman he'd spent every waking and sleeping minute with for four days. He fell right out of the zone and into her mesmerizing blue-green eyes.

"We are one hundred percent ready outside," she announced. "Tables are set and scaped, the flower wall is ready for photos, and the name cards are hanging on the find-your-seat tree. Want to check it out?"

"Yes." He gestured for one of the three cooks he'd hired for the event to watch the shells, wiped his hands on his apron, and headed out with her. He stood in the open French doors that led to the terrace, letting out a soft, "Oh wow," at the sight. "Gracie, you knocked it out of the park."

"I had a lot of help from Cassie, I have to say. But I'm really proud of the tablescapes. I think they'll do your food justice."

"I know they will."

They walked through the tables hand in hand, stopping to fix a wineglass or straighten some silverware.

"Oh my gawwwwd!" They both turned at the sound of a female squeal, laughing when they saw Cassie's face as she stood in the doorway to the terrace. "Grace! Alex!"

Her arms were loaded with dress bags and a small suitcase, her hair up in a knot on her head, nothing but joy on her pretty face. Alex honestly couldn't remember seeing his little sister quite this happy.

"This is a-freaking-mazing!"

They hustled over to her, Alex taking her armloads of stuff while Grace slid in for a big hug. "You had so many wonderful ideas," Grace said. "I think this is the prettiest wedding set I've ever seen."

Cassie pulled back and scanned the whole area again, her eyes welling up. "Oh man, I wish Dad was here."

The words caught him by surprise, choking him. "Yeah, me, too, Cass."

She reached up and hugged him, nearly knocking the dress bag out of his hand. "He's here in spirit, Alex," she whispered. "And I don't think he'll mind that Mom's new husband is walking me down the aisle for a surprise wedding, do you?"

Alex almost answered truthfully. Nico Santorini would have blown like a torched flambé if he'd known another man—who was now married to his Katie—was giving away his only daughter.

"Have you asked Daniel yet?"

She shook her head. "I didn't want to ruin the surprise."

"Are you a hundred percent sure that's what you want to do?"

She didn't answer for a moment, but blinked hard enough for a tear to threaten.

"I'm going to take that as a no," Alex said, setting the dress bag on the closest chair and reaching out to hold his sister. "Are you just super emotional, or are you upset about something?"

"I wish he was here," she said, fighting a sob. "I can't believe I'm getting married and he's not here."

Alex squeezed her again, holding his sister tight until he swallowed the lump in his own throat. "Let me do it, Cassie."

She eased back and looked into his eyes. "Walk me down the aisle?"

"Please, let me do it for Dad."

She threw her arms around him. "I would love that, Alex. And since you already know, I won't have to make up some lame excuse to get Daniel away from Mom and…" She kissed his cheek. "You're the most like him of anyone in the world anyway."

The compliment warmed him, and after one more hug, he let go, turning to Grace, who'd watched the whole exchange and looked as teary as Cassie.

"Not you, too?" he joked, dabbing at her cheek.

"I'm fine," she said, looking from one to the other. "Jealous as hell, but fine."

He opened his arms wide and pulled them both in for a bear hug. "Listen, my girls. You need to dry your eyes. This is a huge day for us."

They both laughed, looking up at him.

"You," he said to Cassie, "are going to be the most breathtaking bride whoever walked down the aisle on her brother's arm. Your joy will be palpable, and our honored guests will be able to see exactly what their own wedding will be like. Also, you're tying the knot with an awesome man, and I will expect to be Uncle Alex soon."

Cassie giggled, obviously relieved and happy with her decision.

"And you…" He turned to Grace. "Are going to orchestrate the most incredible, jaw-dropping, flawless event in the long and wonderful history of Overlook Glen that will no doubt result in you landing a celebrity wedding that turns this place into the number one venue in the state of North Carolina."

She beamed at him. "I believe I will. And you?"

"I am going to…" He looked from his sister's deep, dark eyes into Grace's haunting turquoise gaze. "Prepare a feast worthy of you two amazing, beautiful ladies."

With another hug and a cheer, they set off to do all that and more.

From the moment the first of the Kilcannons, Mahoneys, and the rest of the Santorinis arrived, Grace felt like she was wrapped in a cocoon of love and protection, sharing secrets and inside jokes with extended family, and no matter where she turned or what she needed, someone was there for her.

This must be what having a family is like.

Well, duh, it was, but the constant sense that there was a net to catch her if she fell was utterly foreign to Grace Donovan.

But not, she thought as she approached Gramma Finnie and Yiayia in the reception area, for Graciela Bonita Hunnicutt.

"Hello, ladies," she said, reaching out to them. "It's our *other* power couple of the day."

Yiayia gave a loud laugh and elbowed her best friend. "Did you hear that, Finola? We are a power couple." Then she frowned. "I wanted to bring Gala and Pyggie, but Alex said there were only four dogs allowed today. Why does Jelly Bean get special treatment?"

Because of the surprise wedding. "He's babysitting the puppies," she answered smoothly, sliding a hand around one arm of each lady. "Let me take you to the cocktail bar."

"Oooh, a cocktail bar," Yiayia teased. "Fancy."

"It is. Alex thought of it, of course."

Yiayia broke into a slow smile. "Of course he did. Isn't my grandson wonderful?"

"And she means Alex, lass, not John." Gramma Finnie squeezed Grace's hand with her narrow little arm. "Not that John isn't wonderful, because he is. But he's not for you, and you should forgive us for not seein' that from the start."

Grace just laughed, looking from one to the other. "Nothing to forgive. You two are awesome."

Yiayia slowed her step, narrowed her eyes, and slid her arm free as she openly studied Grace. "You've changed," she announced.

A soft flush rose to her cheeks. "Have I?"

"Everything about you is softer." Yiayia put a hand on Grace's cheek. "Is it love? Or just really good sex?"

"Agnes!" Gramma Finnie choked, and that flush on Grace's cheeks burned deep and hot.

"It's…"

Alex came up behind her, sliding his hands around her waist and leaning in to whisper in her ear. "Scooter and Blue have arrived," he said. "The tour buses just pulled into the side lot." He added a kiss on her cheek. "It's show time, Gracie."

A million chills cascaded over her as she tilted her head, turned a little, and let their lips brush.

"Does that answer your question, Agnes?" Gramma Finnie asked.

"Yes, it's both."

Alex inched to the side. "Both what?"

"Both exciting and nerve-racking," Grace answered with a quick clap. "Our guests of honor are here," she called to the group that started to congregate around them.

More than twenty family members closed in a circle around Grace, some clapping, some cheering, some looking serious. Beyond them was her team of servers hired for the event, their faces familiar, too, as they'd worked many weddings at Overlook Glen. And out from the kitchen came Alex's staff of cooks, enlisted by him to help on the event.

"This is it," Daniel Kilcannon announced, quieting the group with his natural, paternal authority. "Are there any last-minute instructions, Grace?"

Next to her, Alex draped his arm over Grace's shoulders. "Go, team, go?" he joked.

She smiled and took a moment to let her gaze slide over all the faces, some growing more and more familiar and comforting. Cassie stood next to Braden, her dark eyes on fire with her secret nearly bubbling out. The tall, handsome Kilcannon men were shoulder to shoulder, some holding babies or the hand of a woman who'd had the good fortune to marry into this clan.

Braden's firefighter brothers and his younger sister stood near him, still in the dark about the real wedding they were about to witness, but every one of those firefighters had shown their support by arranging to have the day off just because Grace and Alex needed them here. That alone stunned Grace.

John, Alex's twin, whispered something to his mother, Katie, who laughed lightly.

"I don't have any instructions," Grace replied, swallowing an unexpected tightness in her throat. "Except to say thank you so much for doing this. Thank you for taking the time, getting dressed up, and showing the most…" Damn it, her voice cracked. "Amazing support."

"That's what families do," Liam called out.

"Also, free booze," Shane joked.

"It's like a party for no reason," little Christian said. "Just please don't make me dance again like I did at Grandpa Daniel's wedding."

Everyone laughed, and Liam ruffled his son's hair. "You might have to dance once, bud."

"And the food better be good, Alex." John pointed at him. "'Cause your customers have missed you."

Grace felt Alex stiffen, then he laughed. "It'll be good," he said, sounding uncharacteristically humble.

A few more quips and jokes from the sidelines, then the greeter working the door came hustling in, holding up her hand, giving the signal that the VIPs were walking across the parking lot and about to enter.

"Let's do this," Alex called. "Spread out and have fun!"

As if on cue, the small musical quartet started playing, and the "guests" meandered around the terrace and began to laugh, talk, and seem entirely natural. Alex gave Grace one more kiss, then took his crew back to the kitchen.

Then, Grace squared her shoulders and walked to the reception area just as Scooter Hawkings and Blue entered, both of them singing at the top of their lungs.

All Grace could do was laugh, holding out her arms when Blue came to her for a hug. How could she not be joyous today? This could never have happened, even if Desmond had stayed. They'd have been paralyzed by the celebrities' challenging requests.

Like Foothill, Grace might have dropped out of the running rather than try to scare up twenty-some strangers willing to "act" like they were at a wedding. And then to hold an actual ceremony that wouldn't leave a dry eye in the house?

"Can I just say that your invitations were precious to the point of tears," Blue said as she gave Grace a second hug. "There were puppies!"

"Where are my little beasts?" Scooter asked, giving another bear hug to Grace, as if they were lifelong friends.

"They're part of a surprise," Grace said, her gaze shifting to nearly two dozen people coming in from the lot. As she took in the faces and ages, she frowned. "All people who work for you?" Because there were at least three kids, a couple who had to be

266

in their seventies, and a woman who looked like a carbon copy of Blue in thirty years.

"Family, mostly," Blue said. "They all want a say in the wedding venue."

"Opinions are like assholes," Scooter mumbled. "Everyone's got one. But hell, since we're paying, we figured we'd see how they act at a shindig and make sure we'll keep them. Right, Ma?" he called to the Blue look-alike.

The woman just angled her head and smiled. "I'm the mother of the bride, and I get to have a say. And I say…" She stopped as she entered, taking in the two-story reception area, the curved steps with a flower-wrapped railing, and the view to the vineyard beyond. "Momma likes this one."

There was a flurry of introductions—Grace finally got to meet the famous Denise, who stayed very much in the background—and a blending of two more families.

Blue took Grace's hand and pulled her closer for a formal introduction. "This is my father, Reverend Herman Wisniewski, so now you know why I don't use my nearly unpronounceable last name, and my mother, Valerie, who is the epitome of a pastor's wife, so she is obviously scandalized by my choice of husbands."

"Not scandalized at all, Lydia," the woman said. "Scooter treats you like the princess you are."

Grace's eyes widened, and Scooter hooted.

"I'm marrying a woman named Lydia Miriam Wisniewski. Isn't that the wildest thing you ever heard?"

"Blue was her first word," Valerie explained. "And it stuck as her nickname. The fact is the good Lord knows who you are, no matter what you call yourself." She added a look to her future son-in-law. "He even knows you, Scooter."

"Doubtful," Scooter quipped.

"Knows and loves," Blue's father assured him.

With more laughter and chatter, questions and answers, the party made its way to the terrace, where Blue slowed her step and took Grace's hand.

"It's beautiful!" she exclaimed, looking at the chunky farm tables with their glorious flowers, candles, and linens. "And who are all these people having so much fun?"

It didn't take long for the new arrivals to be swooped up and folded into the party and a festive, bright atmosphere to rise from the crowd while servers cruised the crowd with Alex's amazing appetizers and the cocktail bar started to flow.

The moment that happened, Grace's crew went to work, knowing exactly what had to be done. With the entire group of guests captive on the terrace, the French doors were closed and drapes drawn, the chairs were brought out from storage by a setup team, and the huge two-story reception area was transformed for the surprise wedding.

"Let's go," Grace said to Cassie, grabbing her by the arm to sneak her out and up to the apartment to dress, since the bridal dressing suite was open for anyone who wanted to tour it. Alex was able to take a break and snag Braden, so the two of them went to the conference room where tuxedos, and four dogs, were waiting.

Upstairs, Cassie's hands were shaking as Grace slipped her into a white gown and tied a deep blue satin ribbon into a bow around her waist.

"She's going to think we picked this color for her name," Cassie said. "But all the Greeks in the audience will understand."

"And there are plenty of Greeks out there," Grace agreed as she reached for a tulle veil that floated like air around her dark hair.

"Just one missing," Cassie said on a rough whisper.

At the hitch in Cassie's throat, Grace turned to see if the other woman was crying. Not yet, but darn close.

"Oh, Cassie, I know you miss your father," she said, reaching out to hug her. "Would you like me to go downstairs and get your mother? She should be here. She deserves this moment with you."

"You think?" Cassie dabbed under her eyes. "It's supposed to be a surprise."

"You've kept the surprise long enough. You can't do this—put on this veil and step into those shoes—and not have your mother here." Now it was Grace's voice that caught. "I know I'd give…anything. Anything in the world for…that." Even if she was *the wild child.*

Cassie tipped her head and sighed. "Grace. You are so kind, so thoughtful. You're like a sister. Yes. Please get my mother."

The words nearly took her breath away. "Don't move. I'll be right back."

Grace rushed to the terrace, where no one yet had a clue regarding what was about to happen. Scooter was telling a story to a few of the Kilcannons, making them roar with laughter, and Blue was sipping a cocktail, chatting with Pru, who was gaping like she was staring at a real, live enchanted princess.

Grace spotted the tall, white-haired figure of Daniel Kilcannon and his new wife right by his side.

"Katie," Grace whispered as she came up to her. "I need you."

"Of course!" She excused herself and stepped aside, a question in her brown eyes. "Is everything all right?"

"Very much so. Come with me."

Without any more explanation, she slipped Katie through the kitchen and down the hall, and of course, she saw the chairs set up, all facing the bottom of the stairs.

"What is—"

"Shh." Grace grabbed her hand and tugged her up the stairs. "You'll see."

If she figured it out, she didn't let on, staying quiet as Grace led her into her apartment. As she entered, Grace stepped back to let her go to Cassie.

"Oh my God! Cassandra Santorini, what are you doing?"

"Mommy." Cassie waved her hands at her face as if that could stave off the tears, then the two women rushed to each other and hugged while Cassie explained.

"Honey, this is the most wonderful surprise."

"Are you sure?" Cassie asked. "It seemed so quick and smart and cost-effective, but now I'm all nervous and excited and hoping you understand that we didn't get to plan my wedding together."

"I got married two weeks ago, and we planned plenty. This is perfect. You're perfect. I love you so much, Cassie. You're the greatest gift God could have given me."

Grace bit her lip so hard she was surprised it didn't bleed. What did it feel like to be loved like that?

"Mom, I miss Daddy."

"I know, I know." She let out a sigh. "Who's going to walk you down the aisle?"

"The stairs, actually. I asked Alex. And Grace... where is Grace?"

"I'm here," she said, stepping into the room. "I just wanted to give you two a little privacy."

"Why?" Cassie said on a laugh. "You're family now."

She threw the words with the sweet flippancy that made Cassie who she was, without having any way of knowing what they did to Grace. They soothed like a balm and warmed like the sun and gave her a feeling of hope that transcended any envy she might have fought off in the last few minutes.

Just then, a soft bark at the door made Cassie gasp again. "That's Jelly Bean! And the puppies."

Sure enough, Alex was right outside with the rest of the wedding party. Alex in a tuxedo, which just wasn't fair. "Cass told her?" he asked when he heard his mother's voice.

"A girl needs her mother on this day," Grace said, hating the thickness in her throat.

Alex touched her chin with a light fingertip, silent, but the sympathy and warmth in his eyes were all she needed.

"I'll make the announcement," Grace said. "You stay here while Katie finishes up the bride. Oh, where's Braden?"

"He's on the landing downstairs."

She started to take off, but Alex snagged her arm

and pulled her closer for a kiss, taking a moment to deepen the connection and make the kiss count.

She eased back, barely able to breathe from the excitement of the moment and the meaning in that kiss. "I could never have dreamed of doing this without you, Alex," she confessed.

"Don't dream of doing anything without me."

She sighed and let her eyes shut. "You make me dizzy with hope."

He laughed softly and kissed her again. "More dizziness, straight ahead, I promise."

She stepped away, aware that Katie and Cassie were a few feet away, witnesses to the whole exchange. With a quick laugh, she headed out, stopping at the landing where Braden stood in his tuxedo, with a blue tie the same color as Cassie's satin bow.

But the real showstoppers were the three puppies, two with ribbons, one with a bow tie, all on three bright blue leashes. Next to them, Jelly Bean stood as serious as if he really were the best man.

"I'm dying," Gracie said on a laugh. "And about fifty people downstairs are about to as well. Nervous?"

Braden grinned, his handsome face a little pale, but his deep-blue eyes shone with…with something she'd just seen in Alex's expression. Damn the hope that nearly swallowed her.

"I'm not nervous," he said. "I'm about to marry the sweetest, funniest, most beautiful, good-hearted woman God ever made. I can't believe how lucky I am."

"All you need now is an audience." With an impulsive kiss on the cheek, she practically flew down the stairs, did one last check of the room, and greeted the pastor, who was waiting just outside. Then she took a deep, deep breath and threw open the French doors.

As rehearsed with the quartet, the music stopped, and of course, the crowd quieted.

"Ladies and gentlemen," she called out. "What is a wedding without, well, a wedding? I invite you all to witness the marriage of Cassandra Santorini to Braden Mahoney."

The gasps and cheers and applause were deafening. It took a good ten or fifteen minutes for the crowd to process it all, for the families to gather into natural groups, and for the whole fifty of them to file into the room and take seats. People peppered Grace with questions, the new guests got caught up in the excitement, and Scooter and Blue kindly let the whole Kilcannon and Mahoney clan take the front rows, since it was their family marrying.

There, Daniel Kilcannon sat with an empty seat next to him after Grace told him Katie would be right down.

After a moment, Braden came down the steps to stand at the bottom under the canopy of flowers, taking the time to first greet his brothers and sister and his mother, Colleen, who sat on Daniel's other side, holding Gramma Finnie's hand. On the other side of Gramma, Yiayia was openly crying with happiness.

Finally, when the room grew quiet, the quartet played a sweet slow song, and Grace stepped off to the side and slipped into a chair at the end of a row where Scooter and Blue sat.

Katie came down the stairs first, holding some of Cassie's flowers, tears in her eyes as she made the same walk she'd made a few weeks ago as a bride.

When she reached the bottom, she hugged Braden long enough that most of the eyes on them were damp with tears, then she sat next to Daniel in the front row, whispering excitedly in his ear.

And then, with one loud bark announcing their arrival, Jelly Bean came to the top of the stairs, gripping three leashes tightly in his mouth. The crowd nearly lost it with more applause and laughter, which set Bitsy into a little bit of a tizzy, but Jelly Bean masterfully led the three puppies down the stairs with only a little bit of nonsense and mayhem at the end.

"That's it," Blue said, leaning over to Scooter, but talking just loud enough for Grace to hear. "My decision is made."

Before Grace had a minute to hold on to that news, the quartet started the traditional "Wedding March," eliciting a new round of oohs and awws as Cassie appeared at the top of the stairs, holding her bouquet of blue and white flowers with one hand, clinging to the strong arm of her older brother with the other.

As they came down the stairs, Alex searched the crowd, smiling at his family. But then his gaze landed on Grace, where it stayed, unwavering and certain, just like he was. An unfamiliar and precious sensation rolled over Grace as she held the eyes of Alex Santorini.

Warmth, security, optimism, connection…forever. She felt it all and wanted more.

Grace was only vaguely aware that a tear trickled down her cheek as Alex shook Braden's hand and gave him a brotherly hug and then took his sister in his arms and whispered something in her ear that made her smile.

The young couple stood facing each other in front of the pastor, the room still and silent and expectant.

"Dearly beloved…"

Grace looked at the faces of a family she longed to be a part of and the one man she suspected she already loved. They *were* dearly beloved. As dangerous as that was, she couldn't change it now.

Chapter Twenty-One

Before Alex opened his eyes on Monday morning, he reached for Grace, already aching to start this day the way they ended the last one…by making love.

When his hand thudded on an empty mattress, he cursed softly and opened his eyes, blinking into the morning light. Bright, late light. He rolled over and checked out the puppy crate, which was empty. No surprise, since it had been, as always, a three-puppy, two-person night sometime after two a.m.

Checking his phone for the time, he was mildly startled that it was nearly ten, hours after he ordinarily woke, but he was more interested in the message from Garrett Kilcannon.

Found a forum post about a couple from Asheville whose dog and three puppies were stolen a few weeks ago. Following up but haven't reached them. There's a reward, so watch for frauds. They could show at any time. Will keep you posted.

He closed his eyes for a moment, then pushed up. He'd have to tell her, but not until they celebrated their outstanding success.

The whole shindig had gone on until nearly midnight, when the last of the tour buses had rolled out, taking away a very happy Scooter and Blue and their giant entourage. Then the Irish and Greeks kicked into high gear to celebrate Braden and Cassie's wedding, with more dancing, laughing, kissing, and congratulating the bride and groom.

The food, every stinking morsel of it, was as close to perfection as possible, and Scooter and Blue's parting shot—which came after many *actual* shots— was a request that Alex chuck it all and move to Nashville to be their private chef. And the Three Dog Night wine was everyone's favorite, with glasses raised for an hour of toasts that slid pretty quickly into roasts.

Everything—every single thing, from the surprise wedding to Cassie and Braden's first dance to Blue's signature ballad to the way Alex and Grace had fallen into bed together last night—had been perfect.

Alex couldn't remember ever feeling so complete, so whole, so utterly where he belonged. Here. With her. Cooking for the most demanding clientele and working together as a team.

So where was she, and why couldn't he hold her and tell her that right now?

The dogs, of course. They probably had to go out, and Grace had kindly let him sleep.

And now he kindly wanted to hold that woman and tell her all about his ideas for their future. He rolled out of bed and pulled on a pair of sweats and a T-shirt from a pile of his clothes that had started slowly growing on a chair in her bedroom.

He didn't mind that, either. Sleeping here every

night, waking up with her. Yes, their romance was new, and they were a little infatuated, but now what? The "event" was over. She'd hire another chef. He'd go back to Santorini's. They could see each other when they had time, which would be tough, or...

As he walked down the stairs, moments from yesterday filtered through his mind, none as clear as when he'd escorted his sister to her groom, his gaze on Gracie. His lost girl, his orphan, his lover, his friend. His...everything.

He wanted her to be everything. Not exactly sure how that happened, but it had.

The realization propelled him to the terrace, which needed some serious attention and cleanup, but showed no signs of woman or dogs. He tried the office, the kitchen, even the front of the winery, but no Gracie.

He walked down to the path, and as he got to the bottom, he heard a dog bark by the cook's cottage. He followed the sound and found the puppies playing in the yard and the front door wide open.

He bent down to love on Jack and Gertie, smiling at Bitsy, who romped around the perimeter of the little grassy area.

"Your momma inside?" he asked Gertie as he lifted her and kissed her head, then set her back down. They stayed on the grass, close to the door, already having learned this small freedom.

In the cottage, he found Grace sitting on a stool at the kitchen counter, sipping a cup of coffee, her look far away.

"There you are," he said, stepping inside. "Everything okay?"

"Yeah." She smiled at him, pulling herself to the present from wherever she had been. "Just tired. You?"

"Wiped."

"I figured. It's why I let you sleep in."

"I missed you." He came around the counter to stand behind her. "You like to come down here, don't you?"

"Guilty. The dogs like the yard, and I'm…digging for a memory."

He looked around the small and sparsely furnished rooms, which were clean and bright, but utterly devoid of personality. More like a short-term rental than a home. But this was where she'd spent her first two years of life.

"You were awfully young when you lived in this little house. I doubt you'll remember anything."

"I guess you can't remember what happened when you were two," she agreed, glancing at the cushy sofa in the living room. "But I can't help imagining what it was like to toddle around this place with my mother, the wild child. Did I sleep in that bedroom with her? Sit in a high chair right here? Take my first steps on this very floor?"

He wrapped both arms around her, rocking her back into his chest. "You remember walking through the wine cellar with your grandfather, right?"

He felt her sigh in his arms.

"We'll find out more, Grace," he told her. "I promise I will help you learn everything you can about your family, and your father's family, too."

She dropped her head back and smiled up at him. "I know you will, but I came to a shocking realization this morning."

"What is it?"

"I can let go. I can stop dreaming about people I probably made up or who were undoubtedly foster siblings that a five-year-old girl imagined were her real brother and sister. I can let Bitsy and Jack be dogs, not ghosts from my past. And I can stop wondering why I lost everyone I cared about."

"Wow." He stroked her hair and pressed a kiss on the top of her head. "How'd you come upon this epiphany?"

"Yesterday," she said softly, turning on the stool to face him. "I saw these families—yours and your new stepfamily and even Scooter's and Blue's—and I realized that all I've ever done was ache to be part of something like that, and I've spent a lot of years longing for something I'll never have. I want to stop."

He searched her face. "You could have it. With me."

Her whole expression softened. "I've known you for two weeks, Alex."

"Two of the best weeks of my life."

That made her smile, spreading her legs a little to let him get closer. "Yeah, no argument there."

"Best connection, best sex, best food, best... friend."

"Oh." She locked her hands around his neck. "You're going to make me cry."

"Go ahead, cry all you want. And tell me I'm crazy since we hardly know each other. But I am crazy, Gracie. I'm crazy about you and what we did yesterday. I'm wild about the possibility of doing it again and again and again. I want to work as a team, live as partners, and..."

She stared at him for a long moment, her chest rising and falling with slow breaths. "What are you saying?"

"That we have something special, and I want more of it. A lot more. For a long time. For as long as we can go and then beyond." He lowered his face to kiss her, taking advantage of her height on the stool to press their bodies together and hit the perfect spot.

"Alex," she murmured into the kiss, lifting her knees to wrap her legs around his hips. "You know what's amazing?"

He slid his hands from her shoulders down to her chest, caressing her breasts and instantly growing harder against her. "This. You. Us." He gave up on trying to form a full sentence and kissed her again, sliding his hand under her T-shirt to touch warm, sweet, silky skin.

"What's amazing," she said, leaning back to speak but arching on a sigh so he could have full access to her body, "is that I'm not scared."

His hand stilled as he looked at her, sensing down to his bones how much that statement meant.

"I know I could get hurt," she said. "I know I could face down one more time when I'm not someone's forever, but it's worth the risk." She swallowed hard. "*You* are worth the risk."

He let out a breath, shuttering his eyes closed. "I won't hurt you, Gracie. I won't—"

"Shhh." She put a finger over his mouth. "You don't have to make any promises now." She pressed her hands against his cheeks and pulled him in for a kiss. "Just make love to me, Alex. Give me my first real memory in this house. Make it you and me and—"

He cut her off with a kiss and easily lifted her from the stool. She laughed in surprise as he slipped his hands under her backside and turned. "Bedroom? Living room? Right here on the counter?"

"Somewhere...close. Fast. *Now*."

He chose the sofa, which was a soft place to fall and a little short for his six-foot frame, but it didn't matter. Neither of them opened their eyes except to look at each other as they undressed as quickly as possible. There was no foreplay, no finesse, none of the sweetness they'd enjoyed every other time.

This was raw pleasure and real...love.

Whether she'd agree or not, Alex knew it. He knew it. And as he gripped her body and they joined as one, he had to fight not to say the words out loud.

They'd get there. He'd tell her. Now he just wanted to christen this cottage with a new kind of hope for her and help Grace let go of all the pain and doubt and disappointment that darkened her life.

He whispered her name as she straddled him, taking him inside her as he pressed his mouth to hers with each fiery kiss. She reached a climax almost instantly, gasping for air, then greedily hunting the next, bringing him along with sexy words and long kisses.

Afterward, they clung to each other, spent and satisfied and shaking.

"I used to think you were too intense for me," she admitted on a ragged whisper.

"I used to think you were too cautious for me," he replied.

She laughed softly. "I knew all that intensity would make you a stunning partner, though." She threaded her fingers into his hair. "I just worried I couldn't handle a lover like you."

"Partner. Lover." He curled his lip at the words. "Do better, Gracie."

"Better? What are you looking for, Alex? An official title?"

"Yeah." He wove a strand of her hair around his finger, knowing he had a tendency to be impulsive and impassioned by the feelings of the moment. But this was real, and he didn't want to wait one minute more to confirm that. "I want to be yours. Your boyfriend. Your man. Your...however far we can take this thing, Gracie."

For what felt like way too many heartbeats, she looked at him. Her teal-toned eyes deepened and softened and then lit from the inside.

"I would love that, Alex." She kissed him lightly, with a sigh that brushed his lips. "I want you to be first in my life. The one—"

Outside, Jack barked, his low pitch always recognizable.

"And outside, there are two, three, and four in my life," she joked, but then Alex remembered Garrett's text.

"Listen, Gracie—"

Jack barked again, this time with enough power to make them sit up and untangle.

"Maybe Bitsy is straying." She gave him a soft nudge, and he instantly reached for his sweats.

"I better get her before she ends up lost in the vineyard."

"You're a good man, Alex Santorini. I can tell just by the way you love those puppies."

And by the way he loved her.

He stared at her, then lightly touched her lips. He wanted to tell her he loved her. Right here, right now. "Gracie, I…" Was it too soon? Would it scare her?

"What?"

Jack barked again, prodding Alex to stand and find his T-shirt. "When I get back."

"Give me a hint," she teased, playfully reaching out to flutter her fingertips on his abs.

He took a breath. Maybe he should start with something a little less stunning than *I love you*. He didn't want to rush that. But she had to know. "Gracie, I want—"

"Look at what we have here!"

A woman's voice floated in through the front door, making Gracie gasp and pat the sofa for her clothes. "Oh my God, someone's here. Who could be here?"

Shit. Alex knew exactly who it was. The *owners*. Or at least someone who claimed to be.

"Hello? Is anyone here? We're trying to find Grace."

As her eyes popped, Alex pulled on his T-shirt, looking at her completely naked body. "I'll talk to them." He smoothed her hair and added a kiss, because if these were the puppies' real owners, it wasn't going to be easy for her. "And no matter what happens, Gracie, you can count on me."

She frowned, not following.

"Hello?" A man's voice this time, loud and impatient, and too close for Alex to take the time to explain with Grace naked on the sofa.

So he pivoted and headed to the door, spying a couple who'd come down the terrace steps and were walking toward the cottage. Bitsy had run to them, and Gertie was making her way closer. Jack, a natural protector, had stayed on the grass, barking out the alert.

Alex picked him up as he walked closer. "Good boy," he muttered, his gaze locked on the couple. The woman, a slender blonde in an expensive-looking linen jumpsuit, picked up Gertie, turning as Bitsy went romping by.

The man managed to snag the little puppy just as Alex reached them, physically blocking the path to give Grace time to dress.

"Thank you," Alex called as he got closer. "Bitsy's a wild one."

"Bitsy?" the woman asked with way too much interest. "You call her *Bitsy*? Oh, let me hold that one." The couple exchanged dogs and the woman cooed at the one squirming in her arms. "Bitsy?" she repeated with no small amount of shock.

Of course. The real owners would react to the "new" names for their puppies, exactly as Braden had said.

Something told him there was nothing untoward about this couple. They looked completely legit, and if they answered all the questions and provided the information Garrett had asked the other guy who'd tried to take them, he and Grace would have to let the puppies go.

"I'm Alex Santorini," he said, looking from one to the other. At their questioning look, he added, "I'm the chef here."

"We need to see Grace Donovan."

"Regarding?" As if he didn't know.

The woman, who looked to be younger than thirty, with stunning bone structure and flawless skin, nibbled her lower lip and stroked the puppy she held in her arms, seemingly unconcerned that Bitsy might dirty her white outfit.

"Regarding why you call her Bitsy," the woman said, her expression serious enough that Alex knew without a doubt that these were the puppy owners, come to smash Gracie's heart.

"Hello, can I help you?" Grace came down the path, looking pretty damn together for a woman who'd just lost her heart, body, and soul on the living room sofa. Her T-shirt was smooth, her jeans buttoned and zipped, her hair back in place.

"I'm Grace Donovan," she said as she approached, extending her hand to the woman. "I'm the owner of Overlook Glen. Are you here for a tour? To talk about our venue?"

The woman didn't speak for a moment, but stared at Grace as they shook hands, her gaze penetrating to the point of being rude. After an awkward beat, the man next to her, who looked about as young as his female companion, reached his hand out, his dark brown eyes narrowing in a serious expression.

"Jack Carlson of Carlson Woods Winery."

It was Grace's turn to suck in a soft breath and stare. "Jack...Carlson...Woods?" Her voice rose with shock, and Alex got that. Carlson Woods had to be one of, if not *the*, largest Napa Valley wineries. A household name, synonymous with wine, both inexpensive and high-end.

"Oh." Grace squeaked the word. "Carlson...Mr. Carlson. It's...an honor to meet you."

"This is my sister, Libby."

"Libby Carlson." Grace let out a nervous laugh. "My goodness. I'm a little starstruck. What brings you all the way to North Carolina?"

Siblings. Well that explained why, despite different hair and eye coloring, they bore a striking, undeniable resemblance to each other.

"Well…" Libby let out a sigh and clutched the puppy she held a little tighter. "Bitsy." She petted the dog's head. "You named her Bitsy."

"Yes," Grace said. "That's Bitsy and Gertie and…" She put her hand on the puppy in Alex's arms, her fingers trembling. She must have guessed why they were here. "This is Jack."

"Jack?" Libby gasped.

"Are you here to claim them as yours?" Alex asked, sensing he knew the answer but surprised these wealthy winery owners from California would manage to lose three puppies. So he clung to a shred of hope as he added, "If so, we'll need to see pictures of the mother and of the pups when they were born. You'll need proof, ma'am, no matter who you are."

The two people shared another look, and the man nodded imperceptibly at his sister, silently communicating, just like he and John did.

"I have pictures of…the mother," Libby said. "And the newborns." She took a step closer and put a hand on Grace's arm, close enough for Alex to see this woman was shaking, too. "I have pictures of you at four and five, when Jack and I were just babies."

"Excuse me?" Grace barely breathed the words as goose bumps rose visibly on her arms.

"I go by Libby now," the woman said, her voice

thick with emotion. "But the last time I saw you, I was Bitsy." She stroked Grace's arm. "I'm your sister, Gracie. We're your brother and sister, and I guess…" She lifted the puppy in her arms. "You've missed us, too."

"My brother and…" Grace swayed, but the other woman tightened her grip to hold her steady.

"We've come to ask you to come home to California, to help run the largest winery in the country, and *finally* live with your family, where you belong."

Every drop of blood drained from Grace's face as her eyes fluttered, looking like she might truly faint.

As Alex looked at her, something she'd said during their very first dinner together came floating back from his memory.

I'd trade it for a dysfunctional lot of losers. I'd throw in my right arm and last year's harvest for a couple of moderately interesting siblings and maybe a parent or two.

Right then and there, he knew he'd just lost her forever.

Chapter Twenty-Two

The blood rushing in Grace's head made it impossible to hear anything. The woman's words sounded like she was talking underwater. Nothing made sense. Nothing.

Except…

"Bitsy?" It was all Grace could manage.

The other woman laughed, revealing a stunning smile, dimples, and dancing green eyes that looked like Alex's freshly cut mint. And…her mother. And even, in some weird way, the image Grace saw every day in the mirror.

A *sister*. Chills exploded again while her throat felt like it was closing.

"You can call me Bitsy, if you like." She tightened an already viselike grip on Grace's arm. "After all, you named your dog after me."

"And me." The other man stepped forward, grinning with those same dimples, his hair and eyes as dark as Alex's, but somehow looking just like his sister. "Little Jack," he said softly.

Grace just stared at him, wondering if this tall man was making a joke by calling himself *little*.

He gave an uncomfortable laugh. "I've been told that when I was a baby, you used to read a book to me called *A Big Day for Little Jack*."

"It was blue," she whispered, shock still pressing so hard on her chest it actually hurt. "With a bunny on the cover. I remember the book."

How is this possible?

Both Jack and Libby laughed, a little nervous and excited, but Grace couldn't even smile. She couldn't even think. Looking for help, she glanced at Alex, who seemed to have taken a few steps back, his gaze moving from one to the other as he, too, tried to take in this news.

"Why don't I let you three talk?" he suggested. "I'll take the dogs, and you can go sit down and… catch up."

"On twenty-five years?" Bitsy asked on another laugh. "That's a lot of catching up to do."

"I need answers." The words tumbled out of Grace's mouth, rough and serious, making all the laughing stop.

"Of course, I—"

"Now." She held up her hand to make her point. "Were you in foster care? Why were we separated? How long have you known? And why did a grandmother I don't remember essentially arrange to give me this winery? And how did you find me when I couldn't find you?"

"Grace." Alex put his hand on her shoulder, the touch warm and welcome. "I'm sure they'll tell you everything you want to know and then some."

"We have the answers," Jack said. "You might not like them, but we're here with pictures, documentation, letters, and explanations. You deserve all of it and more, Gracie. Some terrible and unfair things have happened to you."

She blinked, surprised that her eyes were dry and that the rushing blood had finally leveled off in her head. Thinking clearly for the first time in a few minutes, she turned to Alex, the echo of their conversation still fresh in her mind.

"Don't leave me," she whispered. "I want you with me."

His gaze softened, and he melted into a smile. "Of course."

She slipped her arm around him and faced the others, almost expecting a fight. "Alex is my…" Partner? Lover? *Do better, Gracie.* "My boyfriend."

"Then, by all means," Jack said, putting a brotherly hand on Alex's shoulder. "You should hear this, too."

"Let's find a table on the terrace," Alex said, leading them that way.

Somehow, Grace took steps, followed, and found the next breath. Somehow.

"It's a darling winery," Bitsy mused as they walked, the comment reminding Grace that not only were these two strangers the very children of her foggiest memories, they were the *heirs to the Carlson Woods Winery fortune.*

The very thought slowed her step. How did that happen? How was that even fair?

"I know, I know," Bitsy whispered, taking her hand and giving it a squeeze. "I'll tell you everything. Just brace yourself."

As they found a clean table on the terrace and made small talk about the wedding that was hosted there the night before, Alex got the puppies inside and came back with cold drinks for everyone. Grace gave him a silent look of gratitude, taking his hand when he sat next to her.

Once settled, Jack leaned forward and flattened his hands on the table. "You, Grace Hunnicutt Carlson, have been the victim of a very bad man."

She blinked at him. "Grace...Carlson?"

"That's your name," Bitsy said. "After your mother married our father, you became a Carlson, even if the adoption never happened officially. You're a Carlson to us."

"*What?*"

"Wait a second," Alex said, squeezing Grace's hand. "Start slow and clear and from the beginning."

Jack inhaled and exchanged a look with Bitsy, who nodded. "I'll try not to interrupt," she promised. "But I'm excited, and I want you to be, too, Gracie."

Grace felt the first smile since...since she'd been entangled and naked with Alex a few minutes ago. As much as she ached to go back to that sweet moment and life-changing conversation, she knew this one would change her life, too. But Bitsy's enthusiasm was infectious and seemed genuine.

"So, I'm guessing you know nothing," Jack said to Grace. "Blank slate?"

So, so blank. "All I know is that the Hunnicutts lived here and had a daughter, Celia, who had a baby, Grace, who I guess...is me. Celia disappeared with her baby, presumably on a search for my father, a harvest worker. At some point, I was put in foster care, told my parents were dead, and all access to any files was locked down."

Jack let out a deep, disgusted sigh. "You can thank my grandfather for that."

"From the beginning," Alex insisted, his frustration evident.

Jack nodded. "Celia Hunnicutt is your mother—and ours—and she ran away from here with you and went to California to find a man whose name no one has ever known. He was your father, and yes, he was a harvest worker. Her search took her to Carlson Woods in Napa, where she met our father, John Carlson, the sole heir to the winery business. They had a whirlwind romance, eloped, and less than a year later, Celia gave birth to twins." He made a gesture that included him and Libby. "Elizabeth Deanna and John Carlson the Fourth."

"Bitsy and Jack," Grace whispered.

The fancy house. The many toys. Was that the Carlson Woods mansion in Napa Valley? She'd seen pictures in *Architectural Digest* and driven past the winery many times on trips to the wine country. She'd never visited, though.

"JJ and Deanna, our paternal grandparents, were not happy with this turn of events," Jack continued. "JJ especially didn't approve of the marriage, despised our mother, and did his level best to hide you from the world. Grandmama Dee might not have agreed, but she never went against JJ's wishes."

"He…hid me?" Something cold and ugly crawled up Grace's chest and lodged in her throat.

"JJ felt you were…tainted." Jack cringed as he made the admission.

"Oh, cut the crap, Jack," Bitsy interjected. "JJ Carlson was a raging, appalling, horrific racist who believed Grace wasn't worthy of the name Carlson because her father was an Argentinian harvest worker. He hated you, Gracie. Could barely stand our mother, but since she procreated Jack…" She flipped her hand and held it out dramatically to her brother. "She produced the male Carlson heir that he wanted. So, he tolerated her because our father, John Carlson the Third, worshipped the ground Celia walked on. And he loved you, Gracie," she added. "My grandmother told me our father loved you very much."

Her head was whirling with all the names, information, and stunning revelations.

"Your grandmother is Dee Carlson? The socialite?" Grace dug into her mental files about the world-famous family and winery. Easily pushing eighty, the woman was revered and respected in the oenology industry, known for her philanthropy and largesse.

"She didn't agree with any of her husband's decisions," Bitsy said. "But the one thing my grandmother lacks is a backbone and the will to fight anything her husband and his powerful family wanted. He was the boss, the last say in everything. And then our parents were killed in a car accident when we were two years old and you were five." Her expression softened with sympathy. "Our grandparents became our guardians, and any protection you had disappeared."

"JJ—your grandfather—is the very bad man you talked about?" Grace asked Jack.

"He *was*." Jack looked at her directly. "Grandpapa JJ died about a month ago, and Grandmama Dee finally came clean about exactly what he'd done."

"And that's when we learned we have a sister," Bitsy said. "Which is the most thrilling thing that's ever happened to me."

Grace wanted to hold on to that comment, but the earlier one stuck in her head. "What exactly did he do?"

"When Mom and Dad died, JJ disowned you, put you in the foster care system as an orphan he claimed was 'left' at the winery, the illegitimate offspring of an unknown harvest worker. He changed your last name, and he paid off so many people to seal files and shut mouths and not ask questions that he financed a small industry. But money talks, and he had millions and millions and *millions* of dollars."

She felt all the blood chill in her veins. "Why did he do that? What the hell was wrong with him?"

Jack's eyes shuttered. "He made every decision based on what he thought would further the success of Carlson Woods Winery. He believed that you might have someday inherited the winery over me. He thought your background could ruin our name. He…"

"He sucked donkey balls," Bitsy interjected. "And I hope he's frying in hell this very minute."

Grace nodded in agreement. "Yeah, I hope he is."

"He made sure you never got adopted," Bitsy added. "He paid people to freeze the process and stop it. Every time a family wanted to adopt you, he made sure the 'system' wouldn't allow it."

Grace tried to gasp, but the air caught in her throat. "What?" The word came out as a sob, tearing at her.

"I'm sorry," Bitsy said, reaching to put her arms around Grace. "I'm ashamed to carry his name. I'm sorry."

For a moment, Grace couldn't talk. All she could do was let this news wash over her while she clung to Alex's hand. A man she'd never met—but, freakishly, admired professionally—had prevented her from being happy. He'd stolen every chance for her to have a family.

"Why?" she croaked. "Why stop an adoption?"

"He thought a family might want to really dig for your past and maybe find out too much, or even pay someone more than he had." Jack shook his head. "He lived in fear that someone would find out the truth and come after those millions. He lived in fear that *you* would."

"Corrupt son of a bitch," Alex muttered, his voice thick with contempt.

"He was," Jack agreed coolly.

"But not Grandmama Dee," Bitsy added. "She had no spine, she couldn't stand up to him, but she did follow you your whole life. She knew everywhere you lived and when you moved. She knew everything, without telling her husband or us."

Grace leaned back with this new assault of information. "She...followed me?"

"She tracked you, using PIs and such. She kept an eye on the Hunnicutts, too. When Bib died, she secretly contacted Bonnie to tell her where you were so she could find you and be your family."

"Why did she wait so long to contact Bonnie?"

"Fear of being caught by her husband. But her sources told her that Bib wasn't the only one seeing an oncologist regularly. She suspected Bonnie was sick, and guilt ate away at her, so she reached out."

"But Bonnie didn't reach out to me," Grace said, trying not to let this new offense hurt too much.

"I have the letters between them," Bitsy said. "You'll understand when you read them. Bonnie knew she only had a few months to live. After putting Bib through chemo and all the treatments, she opted to follow him without a fight. But she didn't want you to go through the pain of finding her, then losing her right away."

"And this winery?"

"Grandmama Dee told her you had been looking at wineries—she knew because of the PIs. So that's why Bonnie contacted an attorney and arranged for you to buy this one for a song."

With every new piece of the puzzle that fell into place, Grace grew more and more stunned by the picture that emerged. "My whole life, I've been... manipulated," she whispered. "And watched. And changed. And *broken*."

"Grace, please." Bitsy grabbed her arm. "We *just* found out, or you would have never been put through this! We have a sister! Can you imagine how we felt?"

"Yes," she whispered, searching the other woman's face and seeing...family. "I can imagine." She bit her lip, looking at Jack. "I didn't dream you," she marveled. "All these years. Bitsy and Jack. I thought...I made you up. Like imaginary friends."

"Nope, we're real," Bitsy said with a huge smile, but Jack's expression was far more serious.

"Grace," he said. "I know this has to be...shocking. Appalling, even. We're appalled at our grandfather. All we want to do is make it up to you."

Alex snorted softly. "Not sure you can give the woman back the twenty-five years she spent wondering who she was and why no one wanted her."

"I realize that," Jack said, looking at him. "But we mean to try."

Bitsy leaned forward. "Come to California, Gracie," she said. "Live near us, with us. I run the day-to-day operations of Carlson Woods, and Jack is now the CEO. You have a degree in oenology, and that qualifies you as our head vintner. Grandmama Dee told me how smart you are and how young you were when you graduated."

Grace's stomach took an unexpected turn that this virtual stranger knew so much about her.

"You want me in California to help run one of the largest wineries in the world?"

Bitsy nodded, beaming at her. "We are fully prepared to divide the company into three pieces, since Jack and I are in line to split everything fifty-fifty. You are one-third of the Carlson heirs."

She looked from one to the other, one more shock wave going through her. "Divide it? You'd do that?"

"For our sister?" she exclaimed. "We couldn't spend that much money in our lives if we tried, and we don't want to. It's yours."

"But you'll have families of your own," Grace said. "If you don't already."

"We don't," Jack told her. "But you *had* a family, Gracie, and it was taken from you. You have every right to sue us and smear us and make JJ Carlson look like the demon he was. But we're not doing this to protect the brand," he added quickly. "We've talked about it for three weeks. Libby—er, Bitsy—and I want you, Gracie. We want the big sister who was taken from us."

Bitsy sidled up closer, practically draping herself on Grace. "I love you already," she said. "You look like all the pictures I have of our mom. Your mom. You look just like her, and I…" She blinked teary eyes. "I never want to spend another day without you as part of my life. We can be close for the rest of our lives, working together, living in Napa, traveling, building the business, and, eventually, having families that love each other. Wouldn't you like that, Gracie? Wouldn't you?"

She opened her mouth to say, *Are you kidding?* but glanced at Alex, and suddenly that answer wouldn't sound quite right.

"California…" She whispered the word and saw him nod imperceptibly.

"It's far, Gracie."

"Then you come, too," Bitsy insisted. "Are you guys serious? Been together long? Grandmama Dee didn't know about a boyfriend, so I guess she didn't know everything."

"She didn't know anything," Grace said quietly, pushing up because she just couldn't sit there and have her world turned upside down and inside out for one more minute. "She didn't know how many nights I cried because I didn't even know who I was. She didn't know what it felt like when yet another mother or father looked at me and told me that going away was 'for the best.' She didn't know how I woke up in the middle of the night and remembered two little babies that I knew were connected to me but couldn't find."

"And now we're here," Bitsy whispered, looking up as tears started to roll down her cheeks. "Trying to make up for the sins of our grandfather. Please, Grace. Jack and I want to make it up to you in some way."

Grace just stared at her, her entire being ripped in half. "I need to think," she whispered. "I need some air. Some time. Excuse me."

Without waiting for any of them to say a word, she took off, darting down the stairs and breaking into a run toward the vineyard. The air rushed over her ears, quieting the volcano of emotions that threatened to send her to the ground, weeping for everything she'd lost and, suddenly, inexplicably, found.

"Grace! Gracie!" At the sound of Alex's voice, she slowed her step, but didn't stop, because facing him would cause just as much turmoil. He'd confessed his feelings, bared his soul, and brought her to the brink of a feeling she hadn't even thought possible.

But...her siblings were here. They wanted her. They ached for her, too.

"Grace, please."

The pain in his voice broke her stride, and her heart. Catching her breath, Grace stopped and turned, watching Alex close the space between them with long strides.

"Not alone," he said, barely huffing from the run. "You aren't going to spend one minute of this storm alone."

"Oh, Alex." Her chest cracked with gratitude as he took her in his arms, pulling her so close she could feel their hearts beat in wild and perfect rhythm. "I can't even process what they just told me. In my craziest imaginings, it was nothing, *nothing* like this."

He held her tight, stroking her back, soothing her with a calming hush.

"It's the most unfair thing I've ever heard," he said. "I'm so furious. I can't even imagine how mad you are."

Mad? Maybe. Sad and deeply disappointed, too. She leaned back to look him in the eyes. "I can't change the past, Alex."

"But you can change the future." He couldn't hide the hurt, or fear, in his voice. Changing the future meant leaving here, starting a life three thousand miles away, and throwing herself into a brand-new family.

"What should I do?" she asked on a broken breath.

"Not make a decision standing out here, that's for sure." He grazed his thumb over her cheek. "You keep talking to them. You find out your history, your family, your roots. Don't turn them away, don't make any rash decisions, and don't worry about me."

"How could I not? What you said in the cottage when you—"

"Shhh." He put a finger over her lips. "I'm not in this equation."

"Of course you are." She tightened her grip on his arms. "I feel the same way you do. You said you want to be mine. You want to plan things together...to..." She shook her head. "I can't remember your exact words."

"That's because you've had another, far more memorable, conversation since then."

"Not more memorable," she said. "Alex, I really care about you."

He nodded, shushing her again. "You need to concentrate on them now, Gracie. Your brother and sister. They're genuine. They're real. And they are the family you've wanted for years. And...wow." He gave a dry laugh. "They're offering you a life that has to be something you've dreamed of. One of the biggest wineries in the world? The best job in the world for you, and a fortune to boot."

"I don't care about all that, just the family."

"But all that *is* the family. *Your* family."

She glanced around at the grapevines, then looked up at the stone building that was her home. Now...and long ago. "This is my family, too. My maternal grandmother wanted me to have this. My stepgrandfather wanted me to be miserable."

"You have to take all of that into consideration," he said. "And talk to them. Get to know them. You have *siblings*, Gracie. And they genuinely want a relationship with you."

"I do, too," she said, giving in to a burst of joy at the thought of it. "I have siblings. Bitsy and Jack."

He gave her another hug. "Just make me one promise, okay?"

What did he want? A guarantee that she'd stay or—

"Let those brick walls remain on the ground and out of your way, Gracie." He brushed some hair back from her face, running his knuckles over her jaw. "This is your first real chance to let someone new in."

"You were my first chance for that."

With a tight smile, he planted a kiss on her forehead. "Just promise me. No walls for your siblings."

"I promise."

"Good girl." With one more quick kiss, he stepped back. "I'm going to give you some time and space. You need it. Then we'll talk."

Without letting her argue, he hugged her and left.

Grace took a few more minutes in the vineyard, closing her eyes and visualizing a big pile of bricks smashed on the ground. Then she metaphorically climbed over them and walked back up to the terrace to spend the first day of the rest of her life with her brother and sister.

Chapter Twenty-Three

The group text came into Alex's phone just as he reached the outskirts of Bitter Bark. At the stoplight, he read the message, which was a callout to anyone near Yiayia and Grandma Finnie's house. They'd had a power outage, lost their Wi-Fi, and had no idea how to get their internet connection back up.

At that moment, he needed a distraction more than anything.

I'm two minutes away, he texted back, turning onto Dogwood Lane, where they'd lived in a two-story Victorian for the past several months. The house was charming enough, but had turned into a minor money pit that needed a lot of work.

Fortunately, a Mahoney firefighter or Kilcannon dog whisperer was never too busy to fix a broken appliance, rebuild a set of stairs, or lend a hand on some other repair. And the Santorinis were no different, pitching in with the same frequency.

Family.

He took his—and the extended clan it had organically become—for granted. But what must this discovery be like for Grace? Especially after searching for years and then learning that she really did have a family, and no ordinary one at that, after thinking she was alone and orphaned? He couldn't begin to climb into Grace's head and empathize, but he could give her the breathing room she needed to deal with the mind-boggling changes.

Enough room to decide if she would take the job and life and family they were offering.

That punched him in the gut, making him slam the driver's side door as he climbed out. Just as he got close to what he wanted, his opportunity got yanked from him.

The same thing happened in France, when he was on the precipice of a dream career...only to learn Dad had cancer, and his family needed him. Family first, always. There wasn't any question about that.

And surely Grace would come to that conclusion and leave to go live her life as an heiress and world-class vintner at an internationally acclaimed company owned by the blood family she'd longed her entire life to find.

Alex didn't stand a chance.

"There's my Alexander." Yiayia stepped out of the front door, a smile he still didn't quite understand putting very few creases in her face. "Come to save the day for Gramma Finnie."

Taking the two front steps in one bound, he gave her a cursory hug and kiss on the head. "I'm helping both of you, as I understand it."

"Pffft." She flicked some white-tipped nails at him. "I don't need internet to make kalitsounia. And now that you're here, I don't need anything but a hand in the kitchen."

"Why are you making cheese pies?"

"To take to the restaurant for a lunch special. That part-time cook John brought in from Chestnut Creek *isn't Greek*." She whispered the last two words as if Charlie Hopkins had committed a felony.

"He's a good cook and knows the Santorini's menu inside out." He frowned at her. "Which doesn't include kalitsounia."

"It's a *special*, and we seem to be getting in each other's way."

He slowed his step. "You keep getting...how often are you there, Yiayia?"

"Every day since you've been gone."

"Really don't trust Charlie, do you?"

She just shrugged and ushered him into the little office off the front room. "Finnie took the dogs for a walk, but she's tearing her short white hair out because she's trying to post her blog."

Smiling, he sat down at the desk and eyed the router. "Gramma and her blog." Shaking his head, he added, "She's a hoot."

"She's a woman on a mission to get five thousand followers."

He jerked back and angled his head. "That many people care about Gramma Finnie's Irish sayings?"

"That's not what she writes about anymore." She pointed at the computer. "Ever since we moved here, she's really spread her wings. The blog isn't about being a granny at Waterford Farm. It's called 'The Dogmothers,' and it's hilarious. I'm so proud of that little lady."

He tapped a few keys and checked the status of the lights on the router, easily figuring out how to bring the Wi-Fi back. "What does she blog about?"

"Our lives, my recipes, the dogs, the family. This week, she's writing about the surprise wedding that wouldn't have happened if not for us."

"For you?" He choked softly. "Grace and I made it happen. And Cassie and Braden."

"And who do you think made Cassie and Braden happen?" She leaned a hip on the desk and gave him a sly look. "Once you and Grace make it official, we'll be two for two."

His heart dropped. "Don't check off another win just yet, Yiayia." The router lights flickered, then burned steadily while he checked the monitor. "But you do have internet."

"Finola will be delighted," she said. "Now come into the kitchen and cook with me."

He started to dig for excuses, but she put a hand on his shoulder and pressed. "Who knows how much time you have left to roll a kalitsounia with your old Yiayia?"

That made him laugh. "There's the master manipulator who's run this family with an iron fist."

"No, no." She held up that fist, then loosened her fingers. "Not anymore. I'm trying so hard. I haven't forced my will on anyone in…days. I haven't been nasty in weeks. I haven't said an unkind thing about anyone, and can I remind you that I not only approved of Cassie's marriage to a non-Greek, I *orchestrated* it?"

Small exaggeration, but he let it go. "You are a changed woman," he agreed. "Why is that?"

"In the kitchen." She jabbed him in the arm playfully. "And I might tell you."

He pushed up, not bothering to find that excuse. Few things centered him like a good pastry, and he actually enjoyed cooking with his grandmother. She wasn't as good as his father or grandfather had been, but she could hold her own and then some.

After he got some coffee, Gramma Finnie came in with the doxies and showered him with love and gratitude for the internet fix.

"My ladies are gettin' anxious," she said after they made some small talk, blowing him a kiss on her way out. "My blog is usually up by this time on a Monday."

When she was gone, Yiayia let out a noisy sigh, loud enough that he knew he should ask what was the matter. "You have an issue with her blogging?"

"My issue is just another thing I'm trying to change," she said, handing him a rolling pin and inching him toward the counter. "I'm jealous. It's a sin, I think. Isn't it?"

"Haven't checked lately, but since when have you been worried about what's a sin?"

"Since…I have." At her own workstation, she broke some eggs over a glass bowl, suddenly more interested in the ricotta-and-feta filling than him.

"Come on, Yiayia. I know you don't like to acknowledge it, but you are a different woman than the one I grew up fearing."

Her wooden spoon slowed. "Oh, you all know I had a little work done." She tapped what used to be a deep crease between her eyes. "That's why I don't frown anymore."

"You don't frown anymore because you aren't mad at everyone," he said. "What changed?"

She sighed and stirred some more. "I knocked on heaven's door, and it was locked."

"You mean..." He looked up from the dough, thinking back to when she'd gone to the hospital last spring after fainting in the basement. Cassie had gone, too, having broken her foot falling down the old basement steps while going to help her.

"Before that," she said, following his thoughts.

"That's right. You had a heart attack in Florida that you conveniently forgot to tell your family about."

She shrugged. "It was enough to change me into the nice lady you see in front of you." She pointed the spoon at his board. "And if you don't roll those to perfection, I won't be nice anymore."

He laughed and concentrated on his pastries.

"Now tell me everything, grandson," she said.

"Everything?"

"Why Finola and I won't be two for two as matchmakers, and don't even try to make me think that's not why you have that sad look around your eyes. I know your face, Alexander. I know when your passionate soul is hurting."

He glanced up, only a little surprised at her keen insight. *That* certainly hadn't changed. "It's a long story."

"Pastries take time. Talk."

He shook his head. "No, it's really a long story, and frankly, not mine to tell. Suffice it to say that Grace might have a better offer."

She snorted softly, as if there was no one better. An hour ago, he would have agreed. But then Bitsy and Jack Carlson showed up.

"What exactly were you offering her?" Yiayia asked.

He gently kneaded the dough, liking the feel of it under his fingers, the sense of exactly how thin it should be to flake around the filling she made. While he did, his mind went back to earlier this morning...in the cottage.

All he'd really had time to offer her was a restaurant in the winery. But that was just the beginning, the tip of the iceberg. He wanted everything and had been about to tell her that when...

"Not enough," he admitted in answer to Yiayia's question. "And what I did offer wasn't really... feasible."

"What was it?"

He gave her a steady look, wondering how she'd react. No time like the present to find out. "I was thinking about starting a restaurant in the winery."

"Another Santorini's?" Her brows lifted with interest that he knew he was about to dash.

"No," he said simply. "A place where I could make and serve the French food and experimental recipes that I love."

Something flickered in her eyes. Disapproval? Disappointment? No, she didn't look anything but... interested. "How would you cook at both places?"

"I don't know," he said honestly. "But I know I'd figure it out. Chefs can own two places, and I don't have to be at Santorini's constantly."

Then she frowned, her mind, still sharp in her eighties, whirring. "That's what you offered this beautiful lady who has made you so happy? A *restaurant*?"

He grinned at her. "Worked for my grandfather when he wanted you."

"Is that all you want from her? That kitchen in her winery?"

"No, Yiayia. I want…whatever she's willing to give," he admitted as he looked around for the right knife to cut the dough.

Without a word, Yiayia opened a drawer and handed him a pizza wheel, a versatile tool if there ever was one. "Does she know that?"

"I think she knows that's where I want to go, but…" He made one perfect square and started on the next. "She might want to go…somewhere else."

"I see." She poked her baby finger into the filling and tasted it. "My sweet Nikodemus would tell me this needs more salt, but he'd be wrong."

He smiled at the irony of her calling her late husband *sweet*, but no doubt she'd romanticized his memory, and he wasn't about to change that. "I can still hear his booming voice in the kitchen," he said, conjuring up an image of his loud, somewhat scary Greek grandfather. "'Three ingredients, Alexander. Three. Olive oil, lemon, and rigani. You can feed the world with three ingredients.'"

She laughed and pushed the bowl of filling toward him. "He loved you very much, you know. And always knew you'd be the one to follow in Nico's footsteps, not any of the others. Not in the kitchen."

"What if I didn't?" he asked softly. "What if I didn't follow in my father and grandfather's footsteps?"

She wiped some fallen ricotta from the counter, silent.

"That would break your heart, wouldn't it?"

"*My* heart? Is that the heart you're worried about,

Alexander?"

"And Dad's," he admitted. "I feel like I made a promise to him that I'd stay with Santorini's, like a good Greek son. Family is first, Yiayia. Family business, too. And I…"

Still holding her wooden spoon, she came around the counter and pointed it at his face, suddenly looking very much like the Yiayia he'd feared as a child.

"*You* don't want to leave Santorini's, Alexander. You can blame some imaginary deathbed promise, you can throw some guilt at me, or heck, you can pretend you need to be there for John. But the truth is, you choose to stay because you're terrified of leaving the comfort of that restaurant. Of the family. Of the world you've built behind that grill."

He stared at her, every imaginable argument rising up. How could she say that? All he'd ever wanted was *more* than Santorini's, but…but…

He stayed there, paralyzed.

"And you try to be him." She reached up and touched his beard. "But you are not Nico, no matter how hard you try, and you are not John or Nick or anyone else. You are Alexander the Great, and that's exactly who your father wanted you to be. Has it ever occurred to you that he'd be more honored by you leaving and doing your French thing than by staying and feeling resentful?"

"But what if I fail?" he whispered.

She gave a slow smile. "What if you don't?"

If only he could do it with Grace, instead of alone. If only…

"Anyway, I wish you *would* open that restaurant," she said, coming closer to whisper, "Then I could work at Santorini's, and Gramma Finnie wouldn't be the only old lady with something important and meaningful to do."

"That's what you want?" he asked with an astonished laugh.

"Yes, it is. I believe I'm on this earth for a few reasons, and cooking Greek food is one of them. So please stop talking and start rolling so I can finish this kalitsounia."

He did, smiling, thinking, and wondering if he'd spent these years making excuses because he was too afraid to try.

It still felt like a dream when Grace woke the next morning. She had stayed up until the very late hours, talking with Jack and Bitsy, though they'd ultimately declined her invitation to spend the night at the winery. They'd sensed her need to be alone, to unpack all she'd learned, and to make a decision about her future.

Could that future be a job as the head of oenology at Carlson Woods Winery—essentially one of the top vintner positions in the world—and a home in Napa Valley, living and working side by side with a brother and sister who wanted her desperately? Yes, it very well could be. She could keep Overlook Glen, of course, even rebranding it as a Carlson Woods property if she wanted.

A month ago, there would have been no decision to make. She'd have flown "home" on their private jet as soon as she squared things away here. She'd have embraced the new life and gone on to forgive, if not forget, what JJ Carlson did to her.

That was before Alex.

Instead, she sat at her desk, with puppies at her feet, reading the exchange of letters between her grandmother and her stepgrandmother as they'd decided her fate without consulting her. The women became real and so did the heartache.

Aching to talk to Alex and share it all, she reached for her cell phone just as someone rang the formal bell at the front of the winery, giving her a familiar thrill.

"He came to us, of course," she whispered to the dogs, grabbing Gertie for a kiss. "Come on, kids. Let's go see the man we…"

Did she love Alex Santorini? Maybe. If she didn't already, she knew she would soon.

Holding Gertie, with Jack and Bitsy at her feet, she headed into the main reception hall and opened the front door, already smiling.

But that smile disappeared at the sight of a middle-aged man with hair pulled up into a sloppy man bun and an equally silver-haired woman next to him.

Before she could greet them, the woman reached out and nearly grabbed Gertie out of her hands.

"Reesie!"

Instinctively, Grace jerked back. At her feet, Jack and Bitsy started barking like crazy.

"Dottie! Tucker!" The man dropped to his knees to reach for the dogs. "Look how big you got."

Grace stared at them, knowing exactly who these strangers had to be, but already welling up with resentment and bracing for a fight.

"I simply can't thank you enough," the woman said,

beaming at Gertie. "You've taken such good care of them."

"They're..." *Yours*. She couldn't say it. They weren't anyone's but *hers*.

"We rushed home as soon as we found out where they were."

"How...who..."

The man stood, bringing Jack with him, tucking the dog into his chest. "But you don't have Sugar, their mother? They were all stolen at the same time."

"They were stolen?"

"Please?" The woman held her hands out for Gertie again. "She was my favorite from the moment she was born."

Reluctantly, Grace handed over the dog.

"There's my little Reese's Peanut Butter Cup!" she cooed. "I missed you, baby girl."

Trying to turn her resentment into resignation, Grace pushed the wooden door wider and gestured for them to come in. She knew what had to be done, but not without a little due diligence first.

An aching wave of need for Alex hit so hard, it nearly knocked her over.

"I'm Grace Donovan," she said. "And you are?"

"Mark and Jennifer Sanderson," the man said. "We've been in Phoenix, then Dallas, then Nashville at competitions, and Jennifer lost her phone."

"And someone forgot to bring his."

"The point is, we had no idea Sugar and the puppies were stolen, even before we—*I*—lost my phone, because our caretaker was too afraid to tell us, certain he could find them just by looking."

"But of course he didn't," the woman said. "I knew

he was incompetent when you hired him, Mark."

"But affordable," Mark said. "It wasn't until we ran into a breeder in Charlotte who'd seen the puppies on the lost-dog sites and wondered if they could be ours."

"Whoa, *whoa*." Grace held up her hand, as lost with this avalanche of new information as she had been yesterday. "Are you breeders? Competitors?"

"Both," Jennifer said. "We breed specialty mixes for working-dog competitions and show our best all over the country. It's just the two of us, so when we leave town, we put a caretaker in charge. We hired a new one, a total mess, and Sugar and the puppies were stolen right from under his nose. They're valuable, you know, so when he finally came clean, we put a reward out. A week or so later, our friend saw the puppies online and put two and two together."

Her husband stepped forward. "How did you get them, ma'am?"

"They were abandoned on the property," Grace said. "A few weeks ago. We had a local rescuer post the information, hoping to find their mother."

"Well, we still don't have their mother," the man said, still petting Jack with genuine affection.

"Might never have her," Jennifer added bitterly.

"But we'll still pay you the reward," he said.

"Oh, no." Grace shook her head. "I don't want a reward. But I will need proof of ownership." She felt a little silly even asking it, but Garrett had urged her to be thorough if anyone showed up.

"We have papers, pictures, and all the proof you need," Mark said, lowering Jack to the ground next to Bitsy. "Look at that dot, Jenn," he said, patting the spot on her back as she turned in a circle that could be described only as happiness before he picked her up. "That's why we called her Dottie."

"I call her Bitsy, and she's…" Wild. Wonderful. *Mine*. "Really sweet."

He smiled, then put her down, but Bitsy barked and licked his leg, clearly familiar with the man. Gertie was lathering love on the woman's neck, the way she did when she utterly trusted someone.

"Here are their papers." Mark pulled an envelope from his jacket pocket, sliding out some folded documents. "Proof that they were born on September nineteenth at our home in Asheville." He opened the papers, each one with a picture of a puppy printed on it. "These are signed by a local vet, and we've already filed these with the United States Dog Agility Association, so they'll back us up with copies. I've been involved with the organization for thirty-five years. We've filed a report with the Asheville Police regarding the theft, too, and can get them on the phone to verify who we are."

As he talked, Grace flipped through the papers, the proof of their ownership more obvious by the minute. Then Jennifer pulled out her phone and tapped on a picture of her husband holding all three of the puppies in a small crate…with a purple checked blanket at the bottom.

"*Oh*." That left no doubt at all, and her heart fell. "These are your puppies."

"Of course they are!" Jennifer crooned, lifting Bitsy. "My little orphans."

The word hit hard. "You have no idea where their mother might be?" Grace asked.

She shook her head, sadness in her blue eyes. "She might show up on the competition circuit, but she'd have a new name and trainer, and we'd have a hell of a legal battle to prove she's ours."

"Was she chipped?"

"Of course," Mark said.

"Here's a picture." Jennifer flipped to another shot, showing a dark brown Lab with white markings. "Shug-Shug has won her last five agility competitions and will make someone money." She gave a sigh. "That was Sugar's competition name, Shug-Shug. If I wanted her to do anything at all, I just said, 'Shug-Shug, go!' and she would. Such a good girl."

Mark shook his head. "I just hope the bastards who took her don't breed her again, because she's all done. We just hadn't had a chance to get her fixed after this litter."

Grace studied the image of the dog who had Jack's fur color, Bitsy's cute markings, and Gertie's eyes.

"If I see or hear anything," she said, "I'll let you know."

"Do they have anything we should take with us?" Jennifer asked, leaving no doubt what their intentions were—to take the dogs. "We're anxious to get them home to Asheville."

"Just…that blanket. I'll go get it." She went into the office and got the whole crate, her heart literally aching as she lifted it and carried it back.

"I just don't know how to thank you," Jennifer said, pressing a kiss into Gertie's head. "They seem so healthy and happy."

"They are. I've had them to a vet. They've had shots. I guess I should get you all that information."

She looked from one to the other. "Can you come back and get them tomorrow, and I'll have the shot records and…"

Jennifer angled her head. "I'm not leaving here without my puppies," she said. "I'm sure you've grown attached to them, but they are ours, and this is for the best."

Grace's eyes shuttered. "Of course. I understand."

She walked with them to their van, got their card and phone number, and took pictures of all of the paperwork they'd brought with them. Finally, she took the time to say goodbye to each of the puppies.

Jack, the leader. Bitsy, the wild one. And Gertie, the neediest of all.

As they drove off, her vision blurred with tears until all Grace could do was sit on the stone steps of the winery and call the only person who could comfort her right at that moment. She didn't need space or time. She needed Alex.

Chapter Twenty-Four

After Grace called, Alex walked straight out of Santorini's during the lunch rush. John didn't argue, and Yiayia was already on her way in. And as he drove well over the speed limit to Overlook Glen, he cursed himself for not remembering to tell her about the reward offer Garrett had discovered for three puppies that looked like theirs. But, still, there was no guarantee these were their rightful owners. So who were these clowns who *took the puppies*?

Grace had been upset, and it had been a little hard to follow her explanation, but he knew one thing: She needed him.

He practically two-wheeled it on the turn to the winery, squealing into the front lot to see Grace sitting on the step to the entrance, her head in her hands. Instantly, he felt his heart shatter, knowing just how much she loved those puppies. They both did, but Grace had been on such a roller coaster of emotions, he wasn't going to make it worse by accusing her of giving up the puppies to the wrong people.

She pushed up as he got out of the Jeep, both of

them rushing a little to meet halfway and fold into each other's arms.

"I can't believe they're gone," she whispered on a ragged breath.

"I know, I know." After a hug, he pulled back to search her ravaged face and red-rimmed eyes. "I forgot to tell you that Garrett spotted a reward for three puppies online. He's been trying to reach the owners, but hasn't yet."

"Because the woman lost her phone."

"How convenient. And impossible."

She bristled as if she'd expected the pushback. "They knew the dogs, the dogs knew them, they had all the paperwork."

"I know they *said* all that, but—"

She took out her phone and tapped the screen. "I took pictures of all the paperwork, which looked legitimate to me. And here's the guy with each of the puppies moments after they were born."

He squinted at the image, recognizing newborn versions of Jack, Bitsy, and Gertie. "Yeah, that looks like them."

"And here's what they filed with an organization that oversees competition dogs, which I did just look up, and it is real. And this?" She slid to the next shot. "A copy of the police report they filed after they found out the dogs had been stolen. They're valuable."

"If they're valuable, why leave them?"

"Apparently, their mother is the most valuable, quite the winner of working-dog competitions. I guess the puppies are still an unknown, since they are mixed breed." She angled the screen and showed him a shot of a brown Lab with markings that looked like Gertie's and Bitsy's. "Here's their mother, Sugar."

He drew back, frowning. "The mother's name is Sugar?"

"Yes, but they call her Shug-Shug." She eyed the picture with a sigh. "And they have no idea where she is or who took her."

"But I might."

That made her jerk her head up to look at him. "You do?"

"The guy who tried to take the puppies a while back? His dog, the one he claimed was the mother, but Garrett didn't think she was? He called that dog Sugar."

"But it wasn't her?" She pointed to the phone.

"Not even close. Garrett's chip reader said the dog was named Maggie. But maybe he called her Sugar because he knew the real mother's name because he stole her."

"We have to find out. Did that chip reader have an address?"

He already had his phone out, tapping Garrett's contact. "If you had to go from Asheville to Winston-Salem on back roads, looking for a place to dump puppies, you'd pretty much go through this area."

She made a face as if the very idea of *dumping* the puppies hurt. Then her eyes flashed. "Then the owners, who didn't find out the dogs were gone for a while, put up a reward, and that's probably why he came back for them." She squeezed his arm with urgency, her voice cracking. "We have to find their mother, Alex. Those babies need to be together with their mother, no matter who owns them. We owe that to our puppies."

He put an arm around her shoulders and pulled her into his chest while he got Garrett on the phone and gave him a fast explanation, then got Marty Casper's address.

"If you go after that dog, be careful," Garrett added. "That guy was a jerk. Could be a jerk with a gun."

"We'll be careful," he promised Garrett.

"You could contact the Winston-Salem Police and send them out there."

He could, but that would tip the guy off that they knew he'd taken the dog. "I might," he said. "Right now, I just want to do some recon."

In a matter of minutes, they were on the road, silent but holding hands. With a sigh and a soft laugh, Grace leaned into him.

"What was that movie? *Mission: Impossible*?"

He chuckled. "Your mission, Gracie, should you choose to accept it, is to locate, abduct, and return a dog to her rightful owners and precious puppies."

"Oh, is that all?"

"No, it's not." He squeezed her hand for a long time, both of them knowing they had another big mission to undertake. "You also have to make a life-changing decision about whether to give up your winery business and move to California for the best job in your industry and the family you've always dreamed of."

"Oh yeah, that." She slipped her hand from his and rubbed her arms as if she were cold, turning to stare out the windows. "I almost forgot."

He snorted. "Right." He took her hand back. "What are they like, really?"

"Pretty darn wonderful." She sounded like the

admission pained her. "Genuine. Warm. Deeply concerned and surprisingly racked with guilt, considering they didn't know I existed until fairly recently. They're ashamed of their grandfather, a little disgusted by their grandmother, and seem to really want to not only make it all up to me, but hand me the moon as compensation for my years of anguish. You don't even want to know how much money a third of Carlson Woods is."

No, he didn't. "Then you're going." It wasn't a question. It couldn't be.

For a long moment, she didn't answer. "It's not that simple," she finally said. "And we didn't finish our conversation."

The conversation where he'd come *this close* to telling her he loved her? Not now. Not ever. He couldn't complicate her already far too complicated life with that admission. He couldn't make anything more difficult for her.

"You were going to tell me something," she urged. "Something you wanted. Something that mattered."

"Yeah, well…"

"Alex." She stroked his knuckles. "I want all the information I can have before I make a decision."

"There's no decision, Grace." He forced all the emotion out of his voice, sounding like he was discussing a menu item, not the rest of her life. He couldn't steal her happily ever after just because he wanted her in his. "It's a fairy tale ending for a really rough life. You get the name, the business, the fortune, and the love of a real family." He smiled at her, forcing himself to make it authentic because she really deserved this. No one deserved it more. "It's perfect."

She just stared at him. "What about you?"

He'd just come in second, like always. "Me? Well..." He shifted in his seat and passed a slow-moving truck on the highway. "I do kind of have an idea." A kernel of one, but he could get behind it. "But it involves you."

She let out a little shuddering breath, her fingers still on his. "Really? What is it?"

"I had this interesting conversation with my grandmother yesterday after I left the winery." He glanced at her, seeing a light in her eyes he knew he'd put there. That glimmer of happiness and hope hadn't been evident the night he'd hunted her down and pretended to want a different wine. It hadn't been there when he'd found her with three lost puppies. It hadn't been there when Scooter and Blue had shown up to turn their world upside down.

But it was there now. Bright blue-green, warm with affection, glistening with...love. But she could find love again. But her real family? One of the largest wineries in the world? No, this was too good to take away just because they...had a crush on each other. It was too soon to be more than that. Right?

"What did you and your grandmother the match-maker talk about?" she asked on a tease.

It would be so easy. *Yes, she matchmade us right into each other's arms. Don't go, Gracie. Let's make a life together and forget your real family and fortune and...*

He swallowed. "My grandmother, the secret line cook."

"Excuse me?"

"Turns out, Yiayia has been rooting for me to leave my job so she can take it over."

She turned in her seat a little. "Leave your job?"

"But she accused me of being so comfortable at Santorini's that I'm actually afraid to leave and pursue my culinary dreams." He added a smile. "I think you called it a 'bunch of Greek excuses.'"

She nodded. "So…what are you going to do?"

He was going to stop being afraid. "When you go to California, I'm wondering if I might buy your winery here and turn it into a farm-to-table restaurant like the one where I trained in France."

A shadow of disappointment crossed her face. "That's what you want to do? If I…leave?"

He threw her a grin he suspected didn't reach his eyes. "I love that kitchen, Gracie."

She closed her eyes and smiled. "I know you do. Well, we'll see. I haven't made my decision yet." She leaned forward and turned on the music, effectively ending the conversation. Connected to his playlist, the system jumped right to Blue's famous song that Cassie and Braden had danced to. But today, the lyrics were personal, and cut right into Alex's heart.

And that's why they call me crazy…crazy for you.

He didn't want her. He didn't love her. He didn't see the possibilities here or in California for a life together.

Grace squeezed her eyes against the sting of tears as they reached the exit for Winston-Salem, trying hard to think about the job at hand and not the heartache in her chest.

Had he really been about to ask to buy the winery yesterday morning? She'd never know now, because Bitsy and Jack showed up, and everything changed. Her chance at happiness was snatched away by the very thing she'd always thought would make her happy—a reunion with her siblings. But they wouldn't accept just a reunion. That wouldn't be enough for them. They wanted a sister, a sibling, a life near and with one another.

And, on some level, so did she. But she also wanted Alex, which was insane since she'd known the man about two weeks.

"Okay, the GPS says we take the next left and head into the hills." He squinted into the light and handed her the phone. "Can you look on satellite and give me the lay of the land?"

She did, zooming in as much as she could. "It's a farm kind of place, lots of woods, a little house and smaller structures around it. Can't tell what they are."

"Kennels?"

"Maybe."

"Could be a puppy mill," he said, sounding disgusted.

"Is that illegal?"

"If you can prove they're harming the dogs, then yes. If they are presenting themselves as 'breeders' for profit, then no, not illegal. But unscrupulous. Frequently awful. Not Waterford Farm, that's for damn sure."

"Do they steal dogs?"

"If they have value, yeah, someone horrible might do that. It can be an ugly business that skirts the law." He reached for her. "And it might be upsetting to you."

"I just want to find this dog," she said. "How can we do that without tipping him off?"

Alex considered that, turning onto the next road as the GPS instructed, but this one wasn't paved, and the brush around them grew thicker.

"This guy knows me, so the second he sees me, he'll be tipped off."

"Then I'll go looking for the dog alone."

"Like hell you will."

"Alex, he has no reason to hurt me. You drop me off and stay on the outskirts of the property. I'll keep you on the phone and tell him my husband is driving around, and I'm looking to buy a Labrador, female, still old enough to breed. What's the worst that could happen? He'll send me away? Maybe he'll have Sugar, and I'll recognize her markings. I'll make an offer and buy her for a buttload of money..." She gave a wry smile. "Since I have that now."

He almost laughed. "Offer a million, Ms. Carlson."

"I'll offer more than he can say no to, if it's her. Then she's ours, and we'll take her back to her puppies."

He studied her for a long moment. "I don't think so."

"He's not going to hurt me, Alex." She narrowed her eyes. "But we have no idea what he could do to Jack, Bitsy, and Gertie's mama."

He searched her face, thinking. Then, suddenly, he pulled over and stopped the Jeep on the side of the dirt road. "I'm coming with you."

"He'll recognize you, and then we're in trouble."

He reached over the console, grabbing a small leather bag from the floor of the back seat. "I started carrying this when I stayed at your place. Didn't think I'd need to shave in the car, but I can do it."

"You're going to *shave*?"

"And there's a hat back there. He won't recognize me."

She inched back, taking it in. "You're going to shave the beard you grew to honor your father?"

"To save the mother of the puppies we love." He zipped open the case and grabbed some small scissors. "Probably won't hurt as much if I trim it all off first." He tilted the rearview mirror and tried to situate himself to see in it.

For a moment, she just stared at him, trying to imagine him without a beard. But instead of seeing him, she just fell a little harder and deeper in love with this man.

"Let me help," she whispered, taking the scissors from his hand. "I can do this for you."

He turned to her, holding her gaze. The only sound was the snip of the blades and their soft breaths as his whiskers floated to the floor and seat. Neither of them said a word, but Grace had never felt more connected to anyone.

Her mind spun with how much she wanted to tell him her true feelings, but he'd already made his own known. This wasn't forever to him. This wasn't more than a fun romance with sex and laughter and a chance to cook in a kitchen he loved. This wasn't—

"Gracie," he whispered. "I love you."

The scissors froze, and she moved her gaze from his chin to his eyes.

"I know you're leaving and starting your life where you should be and with the family that wants and loves you," he said. "And that's what should happen. But I want you to know that I've fallen in love with you. You are a lovable woman, and don't let anyone or any history tell you differently."

"Alex…"

The sound of an engine behind them stole their attention as a rusted-out red truck came rumbling up the hill. It slowed as it passed, but not much, kicking up dirt and stones and heading up the road. In the back of the truck bed was an empty dog crate, very much like the one they kept the puppies in.

"That's Marty Casper," Alex said.

"Oh God," she said.

"Let me finish fast." He grabbed a razor and dry-shaved himself so quickly, he nicked his skin three times. With each stroke of the razor, a new man emerged. His jaw was as defined as she'd imagined, his cheeks hollow, his face as handsome bare as it was bearded.

And he loved her. "Now what should I do?" she whispered.

"We," he corrected. "I'll tell you what we're going to do." Dabbing at the spots of blood with the sleeve of his T-shirt, he threw the bag into the back, grabbed a ball cap that said Eat Greek on it, and whipped out some sunglasses from behind the visor. "Let's get this mission accomplished."

She wanted to laugh, to cry, and to repeat those three sweet words right back.

But Gracie just smiled, touched his bare cheek, and nodded in agreement.

Chapter Twenty-five

His face stung like a son of a bitch, but Alex didn't care as they parked outside a filthy brown ranch house that looked like it had been built in the 1940s and had never been painted since then. There was no "lawn" to speak of, just dirt and brush and an old refrigerator under what might have been a laundry line at one point.

The front porch railing was broken in several spots, and the windows were so dirty, they looked fogged.

But none of that mattered to Alex. All he cared about was the constant, endless, steady barrage of barking that came from way in the back, behind so many bushes he couldn't see what was there. But he could hear what had to be dozens of dogs.

"Should we knock or try to find our way back?" Grace asked, inching closer to him.

"We should—"

The front door swung open, and a woman in jeans and a filthy T-shirt stepped out. "Yeah?" she called.

He whispered under his breath, "Just follow my lead, and don't question if I sound a little dumb. The dumber I am about dogs, the more they'll trust us."

He touched his hat and took a few steps closer. "Afternoon, ma'am. I was told I could buy a Labrador dog here."

"Who sent you?"

Shoot. He took a breath and a chance. "Friend of Marty's. Preferred I didn't use his name, but he told me about Maggie. Is she available?"

The woman practically spit. "Maggie? You don't got enough money to take my Maggie."

Just as he'd hoped. "Well, we do have money, for the right dog. One that can still breed. A Lab, right, honey?" he asked Gracie.

"I like brown ones," she said.

"But we'll take anything," he added, not wanting to give away that they even knew there was a brown one there. At least, he hoped there was.

"We got some Labs," she said, turning to the house. "Martin! There's a couple here for a dog."

She disappeared into the darkness of the house, and Grace and Alex stood stone-still for a beat, not sure what to expect next. Then the scrawny man Alex instantly recognized as the one who'd been at the winery stepped out, wearing the same damn Tabasco shirt he was last time. Something told Alex he hadn't changed it since then.

"Lab only?" he asked without preamble.

"Or Lab mix," Alex said. "Just breedable."

The man took a few steps down and scrutinized him long enough to make Alex's heart kick up a notch. He couldn't recognize him, could he? Without the beard? And with sunglasses and a hat?

"Jakey said someone might come by," the man finally said.

Alex silently blessed Jakey, whoever he was. He nodded, wanting to keep conversation to a minimum. "Lab?"

"I'll get her." He started walking around the side of the house, but Grace inched forward.

"Can we see all that you have?"

Alex almost grunted. Not only did he not want her to see what might be back there, he wanted to get the dog and get out, fast.

Marty turned and stared at her. "No phones," he said, then gestured for them to follow.

As they rounded the house, the barking got louder, and they finally reached an open area between woods where two long rows of open, filthy, roofless pens were filled with about a dozen or so dogs of every breed. At least two were visibly pregnant. Some slept, some howled, some paced, and a few fought with their roommates, but every one of them had a desperate, miserable look on its face.

Nope. It sure as hell wasn't Waterford Farm.

"She can breed," he said, stopping at a pen that held two dogs, neither one of them brown, and if they had Lab in them, it was about one-tenth.

Next to him, he felt Grace shudder, silent as she looked around.

"Don't tell me," the guy said. "You want puppies."

She shook her head. "Just a…"

Alex squeezed her hand. "A Lab we can breed," he said.

"You a breeder?" the man asked, squinting at him. "'Cause you look familiar."

He shrugged. "We're thinking about getting into the business."

Marty snorted and jutted his chin at Grace. "Ain't for the faint of heart."

Wordlessly, Grace squared her shoulders and looked him in the eye. "My heart's not faint," she said. "I just want to adopt a dog. Can you show us all the Labs you have?" She glanced around at the pens. "I don't see...what I want."

"I got one more," he said. "But I'll tell you right now, she ain't cheap. She shows and makes a fortune. I'm not giving her to you for less than five grand."

Alex had done enough research these past few weeks to know that was sky-high, but not out of the realm of reality for a dog who could win financial prizes at competitions.

"I can write you a check," Grace said.

"Cash only, dollface."

"Then we'll get cash," she ground out. "We'd like to see the dog."

He hesitated a minute, his attention on Alex, sizing him up for the money, maybe. Or remembering where they last met. "Show us the dog," Alex said coolly.

"Come on." He took them to a small barnlike building on the other side of the house, pushing open the door to let some light in.

A brown dog was lying on the ground, chained to a stationary tub, her distinct white markings barely visible through the dirt on her fur.

"Oh." The sound came out of Grace's mouth like a soft whimper.

"She's a little, uh, too energetic," Marty said quickly. "Can't be trusted loose."

Alex tamped down the anger that rose in him,

knowing that showing any emotions would tip their hand and trying to figure out how he could get five thousand in cash and come back.

"Hey there," Grace said, breaking away to walk up to the dog. "What's your name?"

"It's Coco," the man said, and Alex prayed Grace wouldn't react to the name not being Sugar.

But he had nothing to worry about. She folded down next to the dog and stroked her. "Hello, Coco. You are a pretty girl."

"Coco" lifted her head with mild interest.

"You can breed her right quick," Marty said. "She hasn't whelped for a while."

Liar. Alex swallowed the word and went up to the dog, who was the exact color as Jack.

"How many times has she been bred?" he asked.

"Just once. I had her since she was a pup."

More lies. Alex watched Grace, waiting for any kind of reaction to what she had to know were lies, but she just continued to stroke the dog's head, cooing into her ear. Finally, she looked up at Marty.

"If you'll take a check, I'll give you seven thousand right now. I want this dog."

The man frowned a little, the greed making the creases in his face even deeper. "I don't..."

She flipped open a small handbag on her shoulder, pulling out a checkbook. "Name your price, sir. I can afford it."

And the truth was, she could.

He huffed out a breath, silent long enough for Alex to hear his own heartbeat kick. Was this dude smart enough to know that if she could afford it, she wouldn't get her breedable Lab here at this disgusting mill? Marty had to know the dog was stolen, maybe had stolen it himself. So…how greedy was he?

"Eight-five," he said.

Oh, he was very greedy.

"Done." She opened the checkbook and slipped out a pen. "Who should I make it out to?"

"I'll fill that part out," he said, his voice tight with the very idea that he was about to have eighty-five hundred dollars.

"Unchain her," Alex said, itching to get out of there with the dog.

The other man walked over and flipped the latch on the chain, and the dog instantly rose with the relief of having the weight off her. Alex squeezed his fists, willing himself not to lose it while Grace scratched out the check and signed it with a flourish, standing up with a quick glance of victory to Alex.

The minute she did, Alex's heart dropped with a stunning realization. If Marty looked at that check, with her name, address, or Overlook Glen Winery on it anywhere, their cover would be blown.

He slipped his hand into the dog's collar. "Let's go," he said, as much to Grace as the dog, hustling toward the door.

"Bye," Grace said brightly. "Thank you."

The man didn't answer as Alex rushed the dog to the door, using his free hand to grab Grace and shepherd them both along as quickly as possible without drawing undue attention from Marty.

Just as they stepped outside, Alex glanced over his shoulder in time to catch Marty staring at the check in his hand, and even from this distance, he could see those frown lines deepen. He looked up, looked back down, and Alex didn't wait for it all to click into place.

"Move it!" he ordered Grace, tugging at Sugar's collar to get her to run. But the dog just stopped and looked up at him, clearly terrified of her next ordeal.

"Hey, wait a second!"

"I'm taking you home, baby. Run, Gracie!"

The dog refused to budge, and Alex sure as hell didn't want to yank her.

"Shug-Shug!" Grace said on a loud whisper. "Go!"

She did, instantly, trotting a few steps.

"Hold on right there, you two!"

The dog froze at the man's angry voice, cowering in fear. Alex bent down and wrapped his arms around Sugar's belly, getting a loud bark in his ear, but he managed to hoist her in his arms. Grace ran a few feet ahead of him, pushing branches out of the way as they rushed over the path to the front of the house.

"Keys are in the ignition," Alex called. "You drive!"

"Hey! I know who you are!" Marty called. "Get back here! You can't have Sugar! Suzanne! Stop them!"

Without missing a beat, Grace yanked open the Jeep's back door for Alex to get in, then whipped open the driver's door to dive behind the wheel.

"Don't you dare take that dog!" the woman called as she ran out of the front door, directly at Alex. He nearly stumbled from the weight of the dog, but righted his foot fast enough to reach the car before she did.

"That's my dog!"

But he shoved Sugar into the back seat and threw himself on top of her, managing to pull the door closed.

"Go, Gracie! *Fast*!"

The woman pounded on his window, screaming, and Marty came running out from behind the house, hollering at them. When Grace hit the accelerator and revved the engine, it was enough for the woman to fling herself away from the Jeep.

Grace took off, spitting dirt and whipping the wheels around toward the road, but when Alex turned, he saw Marty climbing into the red truck.

"He's gonna follow us," he called. "Can you handle it?"

"Are you kidding? To save this dog?" She floored the gas pedal. "Hang on, you two!"

As she tore down the rutted road, Alex watched out the back, but they had a good hundred or more yards on him. "Turn here!" he ordered as they reached the first dirt intersection that he remembered, a road barely wide enough for two cars.

She swung the wheel to the left, making the Jeep fishtail wildly, slowing them down in the process. Sugar sat up and started barking loudly, barely drowning out Grace's swearing as she fought to right the wheels.

She managed to get them straight and shot down the road, but Marty made the turn with ease, gaining on them.

"Oh my God, Alex!"

At her shriek, he turned to look out the front in time to see something bright yellow roaring up the road directly at them. And a black truck right behind it.

"We're going to hit them!" She slammed on the brakes, making Sugar slide right off the seat onto the floor.

"What the…" He slapped his hands on the back of the seat. "That's Garrett! And Liam. Stop."

As soon as she did, Garrett's bright yellow Wrangler slid up next to them. Grace got the window down, and Alex leaned forward, spying Shane in the passenger seat.

"Block the guy in the truck. Hold him off. We're calling the cops! Go, Gracie!"

Gracie hit the gas without a second's hesitation, sailed past Liam, who instantly pulled up next to Garrett, the two of them wedged side by side on the road. As Grace took the next turn, all Alex heard through the open window was the long blast of a horn, then old Marty screaming his lungs out.

By the time they reached the main road, he'd called the Winston-Salem Police, and they waited, silent and breathless, until the squad cars flew by, sirens blaring and lights flashing.

And then Grace climbed into the back seat, threw her arms around him and Sugar, and dropped her head back to laugh with the giddy, heady sense of victory.

"Mission accomplished, Alexander the Great."

Alex just held her tight while Sugar lapped his weirdly smooth cheek.

By now, Grace realized that no matter the crisis or situation, this family gathered, usually at Waterford Farm. They laughed, rehashed, ate, drank, hugged, patted one another's back, and included as many dogs as people in the whole process.

But this evening was a whole new level of family

bonding, rehashing, and high-fiving, following the arrests of Martin and Suzanne Casper for the thefts of Sugar and four other animals, plus charges of animal abuse and cruelty.

Connor and Declan Mahoney, Aidan Kilcannon, and Trace Bancroft had followed Liam, Shane, and Garrett to the Caspers' puppy mill, and they'd rescued every single dog there. Waterford opened its kennels and vet offices, while Daniel, Molly, and several vet techs checked each and every new arrival.

Waterford Farm had just acquired fourteen new dogs, several of them pregnant and more of them sick. And one of them belonged to Mark and Jennifer Sanderson, who finally had a working phone and were on their way to pick up their beloved Shug-Shug.

The rest of the family, spouses and children, arrived in waves, demanding details and crushing their loved ones with hugs. John came, too, having closed Santorini's, and brought the two grandmothers and plenty of food. The atmosphere was charged, festive, victorious...and once again, Grace burned with that age-old jealousy.

Which was *crazy*. Not only was she used to this clan and made to feel a part of it, she had her own family waiting for her in California.

Still, she burned. If not with jealousy, then with a hungry, achy need she didn't understand.

"Have some tea, lass." Gramma Finnie put a knotted hand on Grace's shoulder, then sat next to her at the giant farmhouse table in the kitchen so they could look into each other's eyes. "Or would a nice shot of Jameson's be fixin' you up just fine? You sure deserve it after what you did today."

"No Jameson's, thank you."

Yiayia slid in on her other side, offering a plate of pastries. "Then how about some kalitsounia? My darling Alexander helped me make them." She leaned in to press her shoulder against Grace's. "He's the best, isn't he? Especially with his handsome face back on display."

"Yes, he's wonderful."

"Such a husband he'll make," she added.

"Agnes, will you please try some subtlety?" Gramma Finnie chided, pressing her bony arm against Grace. "We don't have to push you now, lass, do we?"

She sighed and smiled from one to the other, wondering if now would be the time to tell them that she'd found her family and...

"He proved himself today, though, didn't he?" Yiayia asked. "You know he'd do anything for you."

"We all would," Gramma added, clearly the more controlled one in the odd relationship. "This family just adores you, lass."

"And I adore you all," she said quickly. "I've never seen anything quite so...cohesive." She gestured toward the little groups gathered around the kitchen, with a few of the Kilcannon men reliving their day's adventure, while Katie and Daniel each held a baby and listened, laughed, and had an opinion or two.

"'Tis a fine clan," Gramma Finnie said. "You'll find none better."

"And you need a clan," Yiayia added. "There's nothing like being surrounded by Greek love on Easter."

"Or the Irish on Christmas."

"Or all of us on every single Sunday." Yiayia

squeezed Grace's hand. "As my friend said, I'm not known for my subtlety, but I am quite revered for my honesty. Some say I'm honest to a fault."

"There's nothing wrong with honesty," Grace reassured her.

"Then listen to me. Yes, Alex is an extraordinary man, and I haven't seen him as happy as he's been these last few weeks since…since he left for France, I guess." She frowned, glancing around the room as if she wanted to find him, but he'd left a few minutes ago to check on Sugar.

"And I don't know you as well as I'd like to," Yiayia continued, "but you do seem to fit well with him. And with us. And, dear girl, you need a family."

"I…" *Have a family.* "I know."

Gramma took her other hand and rubbed her knuckles. "The Irish say, 'Without love, there is no family, and without family, there is no love.'"

Yiayia put an elbow on the table, leaning forward to look past Grace to Gramma. "That sounds suspiciously like Socrates, Finola."

Grace laughed softly. "I'm sure the sentiment is the same in any culture."

And so very true.

"Our point is this," Yiayia said. "You are alone in this world, and you don't have to be. This is your family, right here, ready to love you. That's all."

Grace swallowed, knowing she should tell them what had happened this week. That she wasn't alone anymore, that she had a family, and that they loved her, too.

"Family is everything," Gramma said. "I don't know who said that, but they were right."

Yes, they were. Real family, right? Blood family? Family that she'd searched for and finally found? Family that—

The kitchen door popped open, and Alex stood there, his newly shaved face still a little rough and red. "The Sandersons are here," he announced. "And they brought the puppies."

"Oh." Grace pushed up and slid out from behind the table when Gramma stepped aside, but the older woman grabbed her arm.

"I'm prayin' they pay back your good deed by givin' you those sweet pups."

"You and me both, Gramma. But what I really want is to see them back with their mother." She smiled at Yiayia, then Gramma. "Because you're right, family is everything, whether you have two legs or four."

The grandmothers shared a victorious glance, and Grace didn't have the heart to tell them their speeches and quotes had hit her heart...and maybe, as much as she was tempted to slide into this family, the right thing to do was stay with her biological family. Just like the right thing to do was reunite the puppies with their family.

"Come on." Alex reached for her hand. "Molly's bringing Sugar. She's a little undernourished and has a slight infection on her paw, but she's going to be fine."

They headed out into an early evening chill, and the entire family spilled out behind them. As they all walked down the driveway in a pack of twenty or more, Molly, Pru, and Darcy joined them from the vet's office, with Sugar walking slow but steady between them, her hair glossy from a good brushing and a big pink bandanna around her neck.

Just then, the Sandersons' van rolled into Waterford, slowing and then stopping near the crowd, and Grace recognized the couple who climbed out, both of them beaming at the dog.

"Shug-Shug!" Jennifer ran to her, and Sugar barked noisily, her tail swishing as she rushed to her mistress, a small limp barely slowing one happy dog.

"And here are your babies!" Mark opened up the side door to the van, and the puppies bounded out, Jack in the lead. He started toward his mother, but stopped and barked at Alex, waddling right over to him instead.

"Jacko!" Alex reached down and picked him up, but the minute he did, Jack barked again, with a little confusion in his eyes as he looked at Alex.

"That's right, no beard," Alex said on a laugh. "Small sacrifice to save your mom. Now go see her."

Grace rubbed Jack's head. "Go on, honey. It's a big day for little Jack." As she said the words, her eyes welled up, and the sudden ache for her own "little Jack" hit her hard. Yeah, he was her little brother, and she'd missed his whole life. Now she could share the rest of it.

Bitsy was running in circles, making her way to her mother, and Gertie walked a little slower, wary of the crowd and noise.

"Oh, baby." Grace went up to her and lifted the sweet little puppy, inhaling her familiar smell. "I'll take you to her." She walked a few steps closer to Sugar, who was already lapping her tongue over Jack to the cheering and hollering from the family as everyone congregated around the reunited mother and son, snapping pictures and soaking up the beautiful moment.

Sugar stopped her ministrations of Jack and looked up, barking once, then reaching a paw out to Gertie.

"You two remember each other?" Grace asked as she dropped to her knees in the grass. "Gertie, this is your mama." She cursed her tears, wishing them away, but really not being able to do anything about her emotions. "She's missed you, Sugar."

Sugar barked and crawled a little closer, instinctively less aggressive with Gertie than she had been with Jack. Gertie gave a quick lick to Grace's hand, then squirmed out of her hold to get to her mother. She rolled over, spread her paws, and let her mother kiss every inch of her.

Finally, Grace looked into Jennifer Sanderson's eyes, not at all surprised to see the older woman openly weeping.

"Thank you," Jennifer said. "Thank you for all you did for these puppies and Sugar."

Grace just nodded, not trusting her voice.

"I know you want them kept together," Jennifer whispered. "Always, as a threesome."

"Please. It's the only thing I ask."

"I promise I will never let them be separated. Never."

"Thank you." She reached for Bitsy, who finally made her way over and circled her siblings to get closer to Mom. "And if you'd call them by the names I've given them," Grace added. "It would mean so much to me."

"We are," she said. "This guy only answers to Jack, and Gertie is Gertie for life. And this one." She squealed as she picked up Bitsy and rubbed her nose against her fur. "Is my itsy Bitsy."

Just as Grace's heart couldn't take another minute, Alex came up behind her and put his hands on her shoulders. "You okay?" he asked.

She looked up at him, trying to smile through the tears. "I'm happy for them."

"They belong together," he said.

"Families do," she whispered. He gave her shoulders a squeeze and nodded, as if he already understood her decision. But she'd have to tell him. She'd have to tell them all, and that wouldn't be easy.

She stood and let the others have a chance to love the dogs and talk to the owners, inching away from the crowd with Alex. They stood off to the side under a tree, taking a minute to listen to the laughter and barking.

"You're leaving, aren't you?" he asked softly.

Her heart dropped. "Well, I did get a pretty solid lecture about the importance of family from your grandmothers."

"Big help they are," he said on a dry laugh. "I think they meant *my* family."

"They did, but..." She looked up at him, then touched his strong, hollowed cheek with her palm. "If I don't go, I'll always wonder what it might have been like."

"If you do, I'll always wonder what it might have been like."

She held his gaze. "Did you mean what you said in the car when you shaved?"

"Yes," he said. "And is there any chance you feel the same?"

Yes. Every chance. But she held the words in her heart. Because they'd be three thousand miles and worlds apart, both attached to families that meant everything, and two weeks just wasn't enough time to make huge decisions or declare love.

"I'll never forget you, Alex," she said softly, hating the disappointment that darkened his eyes. "And yes, you can have the winery. It's yours. Make it the restaurant of your dreams, and I'll…I'll…"

"You'll have the life and family you've always wanted," he finished.

"Then this…" She swallowed and then said the words she hated most in the whole world. "This is what's best for us."

He just closed his eyes, exactly like she had every time a family had sent her away. And one more time, Grace Donovan had to leave a place she wanted to call home.

Because it was best for her.

Chapter Twenty-six

"**G**ot another request for that falafel burger, Alex." Cassie tapped her order pad on the stainless-steel pass-through. "Why did you take it off the menu again?"

"Because it's cheesy."

"There's no cheese in it."

He threw a look at his sister, not entirely sure if she was kidding or not. She was.

"It's not what I want to cook," he said, working like hell to keep the tightness out of his throat.

Cassie leaned forward. "So what are you waiting for? Christmas? It's a month away, you know."

"I'll be here for Christmas," he said. "Didn't you hear that we got picked for the big charity dinner on Christmas Eve?"

"One dinner, with half the town helping out." She narrowed her dark eyes and pointed her pen at him before he could respond. "It's been a month since she left. You've got backup and full family support. Yiayia loves coming in here like a little kid getting her birthday wish. And that banquet kitchen is just sitting there, taunting you to come and cook." The sharpness went out of her tone and expression. "Don't be a stubborn Greek man like your father." She grinned. "Especially since you ditched the beard and don't even look like him anymore."

He let out a sigh. "I'm just not ready yet." What good was his dream restaurant without his dream woman? Four weeks, and he was no closer to getting over her than the day they'd had their last bittersweet goodbye and she'd handed him the keys to the winery.

Libby and Jack had been there that day, cheering her on, acting like it was just fine for her to leave him for them, encouraging him to come and visit. As if that was what he wanted.

Then they took her off to a private jet, and Graciela Bonita Hunnicutt Carlson started her new life.

And Alex Santorini stayed stuck in his old one, searching for a way to climb out of the misery hole he'd fallen into.

"Just go and start the work," Cassie said. "You know this entire family will help you if you need anything at all. Remodeling?"

"It's ready to go," he said. "I could hold a dinner there tonight. All I need is a sign, food, and..." He grinned. "My favorite waitress."

She tipped her head, ignoring the compliment. "You don't want to do it without her, do you?"

"That would be pretty stupid, wouldn't it? She's a millionairess living with her family, doing her dream job, and she sounded pretty happy last time I talked to her." But then, so had he. All an act.

Cassie turned as the bell dinged. "Please, God, tell me this is the last table. And by the way, your favorite waitress has a meeting in Chicago next week with her biggest client, so John better find more help, and fast."

"We got you covered, Cass," he assured her. "Go, do your thing, and we'll do ours."

"Alex." She reached across the counter. "This isn't your thing, and we've all known that for a while now. You have the answer, the location, the desire, the talent, everything."

Not everything. "Go get that table, Cass."

She pivoted and headed out, a little squeal in her voice telling him that whoever had come in was a friend. Scraping the flattop, he thought about the winery…just sitting there, waiting for him.

It was the ideal location for a jaw-dropper of a restaurant. The kitchen was ready to go. He could do a few pop-ups, test a menu, build a staff, and start his dream. Was he so afraid that he couldn't leave this damn grill?

"Why'd you eighty-six the falafel burger, Alexander?"

He turned at the sound of his grandmother's voice, peering at her through the pass. "My father turned over in his grave and nixed it."

"Pffft. I just mastered that thing. Come on out here. We've got something to show you."

"Something?" He put the spatula down and rounded the pass.

"Some*one*."

Why did his heart literally skip a beat like he was a teenager in love? Why did he take the five steps to the dining room with hope in his heart? Could she be here? Could Gracie be—

"Surprise, lad! We've got an early Christmas present for you!"

Gramma Finnie sat in her favorite booth, holding three leashes and wearing a grin so big it made her bifocals crooked.

"Jack! Bitsy! Gertie!" He practically pounced on the puppies, who were noticeably bigger with more-adult snouts and larger paws. They all barked in unison, wagging tails, and pulling at the leashes. "What are they doing here?" He instantly looked around for the Sandersons, but the restaurant was nearly empty, and the few remaining guests were beaming at the little dogs.

"I just told you, lad, they're an early Christmas present from Agnes and me."

"What?" He folded onto the bench next to Gramma, reaching down with hands aching to grab all three of them. Gertie was in his hands first, of course. Little Miss Needy.

"That Jennifer Sanderson started following my blog," Gramma Finnie told him. "Of course I wrote about the reunion and all that." She made a smug face. "Most hits I ever had, thank you very much."

He brought Gertie to his lips for a kiss. "But how did you get the dogs? They were all ready to start training them for competitions."

Yiayia tsked as she took the seat across from him. "They said it was going to be too expensive, but you know what I think? I don't think these puppies have been happy since they left you and…you."

You and Grace, she had started to say.

"Anyway," Gramma continued. "She made a promise to Grace to keep them together, and she was worried that even if she found someone who adopted all three, they might decide to separate them after

351

some time. And Jennifer did not want to break her promise to Grace. So she got in touch with me, and we said we'd take them right away. Agnes drove all the way to Asheville in her Buick, with me, of course, and now we have them."

"Wow." He picked up Jack and just had to laugh. "Way to go, Dogmothers."

"You want them, don't you?"

Without Grace? What kind of fun would that be? "I want..." *Her*.

"They'll keep you company at the winery while you're running your restaurant," Yiayia said, the old manipulative gleam in her eye. "They need you, Alex. The world needs that restaurant. And you need to spread your big beautiful Greek wings and fly out of here so that I can run that grill." She leaned closer. "It's one of the reasons I'm on this earth," she whispered, repeating that same phrase she'd used before, so it must be important to her.

For the longest time, he just stared at his grandmother while Jack licked his clean-shaven face. Bitsy pawed at his shoes. And Gertie rolled over and waited for someone to rub her belly.

No more *Greek excuses*. This was what Gracie would want him to do.

"Thank you," he said softly, putting an arm around Gramma Finnie and holding Yiayia's gaze. "I will do that."

"You're welcome," Yiayia said. "Now go take them to the winery."

"Now?"

"What better time? I'm here to finish up for you, and they'll be most comfortable there, and...and..."

"And you need to see it again," Gramma Finnie said. "You'll feel different once you do."

"It's hard to go there without Grace," he admitted. "I miss her so much."

Yiayia threw a look at Gramma Finnie. "Can I, for a change, be the one with a saying?"

"Be my guest, Agnes."

She patted Alex's hand. "The Greeks say Μου λείπεις."

"I miss you?" he guessed, easily understanding her pronunciation.

"It means 'you are missing from me.'" She gave him a look. "Is that more like what you're feeling?"

"A perfect description." He looked from one to the other. "You're sweet not to have given up on me. But, ladies, you better work your Dogmother magic on John next. You'll have better luck."

Yiayia shook her head. "It's time for a Mahoney," she said. "We've agreed to alternate matchmaking on our grandchildren."

"But you didn't matchmake me with anyone but..." He looked down at the dogs. "The three best dogs in the world."

Gramma Finnie gave him a light jab. "Take them home, lad. Where they belong. To the winery."

The words touched his heart, making him close his eyes and give up the fight. "You're right," he said. "I'll take them there."

"Now," Yiayia insisted.

"I have to—"

"Never ever say no to your Yiayia. It's Greek law."

He laughed. "Got it." With a kiss for both of them, he gathered up his three dogs and headed out to start his life with them. Alone, but maybe someday Grace would come back. And they'd be waiting.

He clung to that thought all the way to Overlook Glen, until he pulled into the parking lot and realized exactly why he'd been sent there.

Grace stood at the center of the terrace, turning slowly, trying not to be flattened by memories. She'd been gone for a month, but not one day in California could match the feeling of looking out at the Blue Ridge Mountains and wandering through the grapevines of Overlook Glen.

When Denise had called to tell her the news, she'd had zero hesitation about coming back for one last event. But she couldn't do it alone.

Would Alex help?

She pulled out her phone for the fiftieth time since she'd arrived, imagining how the conversation would unfold. Was it wrong to call him and announce that she was there? Would he be thrilled? Furious? Frustrated?

How would he feel when he found out she'd be here for only a few weeks?

How would *she*? Because leaving him once had been hard enough. Leaving him twice might be impossible. Especially now that she realized California might be home to her family and dream job, but those weren't the only things that *made* a place home.

Overlook Glen was truly her childhood home, and it still felt like where she belonged.

Alex certainly hadn't taken her up on the offer to

turn the winery into his restaurant. Not a single thing had changed since the day she'd left with Libby and Jack. The winery had barely been stepped in and was starting to look as barren as the November trees and as lifeless as the winter skies above her.

That saddened her, especially because in their few phone calls, he'd seemed to be happy about the idea. But then, she'd been telling him how happy she was at Carlson Woods, when in truth...

She closed her eyes and turned toward the vineyards, drawing her strength from the hills and valleys. Then she tapped her phone, found his name, and waited to hear his voice.

"Hey, California girl," he answered with more joy than it was fair for him to have. "How's the land of milk and honey and really good wine?"

She laughed, mostly because the sound of his voice was like an adrenaline injection to the brain. Yeah, yeah, Mother Nature had wired her to be attracted to him. And she knew the feeling was purely science and chemistry...but, good God, it was real.

"I don't know," she said. "I'm actually not there right now."

"Is that so?"

"Listen, Alex, are you sitting down?"

"Not at the moment," he said, sounding as if he was definitely walking somewhere. She closed her eyes and imagined him on the streets of Bitter Bark, maybe in the square or leaving Santorini's after a long lunch rush.

Why wasn't he here?

Because she hadn't asked yet. "Well, I have news. Big news."

"Yeah?"

"Remember how Scooter and Blue joked about a little hanky-panky on the way to Overlook Glen?"

"I believe he mentioned blue balls in the most Scooter-like way."

"Yeah, well, he wasn't shooting blanks," she said on a laugh. "Blue is expecting a baby, and she got pregnant that day."

"Get out! That's awesome." After a beat, he asked, "Is that why you called?"

"Well, not just that, but they want to move up their wedding. In fact, they want to get married in two weeks."

He laughed. "That sounds familiar."

"At Overlook Glen."

He didn't answer for a few seconds, except for a muffled sound she didn't catch. "Did you hear me, Alex?"

"Go," he whispered. "Right there, right now."

What was he talking about? "Alex? Are you—"

She heard a sound in the distance behind her. And another. A bark? Whipping around, she caught sight of the French doors opening wide, but no one was there. Except three little—not so little!—puppies running wildly toward her.

"Oh my God! Alex! Alex, you won't believe who's..." And then she saw him, strolling through the doors, a phone to his ear. "Who's...here."

"I am," he said softly into the phone. "And you, Gracie, are the most beautiful thing I've seen in a month."

On a laugh, she lowered her phone, dropping it onto the nearest table as she started toward him.

Walking, then faster, then they both ran, meeting halfway in a full-body press and a kiss that felt like it could go on forever.

"You're home," he said against her lips.

"I'm…home." Of course she was. How could anywhere else ever be home? But… "How did you know I was here? And what are the puppies doing here?" She eased away, still holding him, watching Bitsy romp and Jack inspect and Gertie just stare up at her with abject joy on her little face.

"They're home, too," he said. "My grandmothers adopted them and just gave them to me as early Christmas presents."

"No!" She pressed her hands to her mouth, a little overwhelmed.

"And I think they might have given me you as a Christmas present, too. Did they know you were here?"

"No, but…" She smiled. "Blue put an Instagram post up about it, and I know Pru follows her, so… yeah. They could have known I'd be back today."

"And you called me…" He wrapped her in his arms. "To say you're never going back?"

She bit her lip and looked up at him. "Alex, I've missed you."

"Gracie, you've been missing from me."

She frowned. "That's…"

"Greek. And a very great lady who wants nothing more than for us to be together reminded me of it today."

She melted into him. "I have been missing from you," she agreed. "And you've been missing from me."

"I love you," he whispered as he stroked her hair. "I love everything about you and all the stuff I don't even know yet."

"I love you, too. I have, for a long time."

His fingers stilled as he searched her face. "So, what are we going to do?"

And just like that, clarity and answers and certainty fell over her. The fight was over. Love won.

"We are going to hold an amazing wedding in two weeks," she said, as everything fell into place with no more doubts, all questions answered. "Then we are going to watch these babies grow into beautiful dogs who will be the mascots of this winery and restaurant."

He lifted his brow at the last word. "Both?"

"Why not? Alex, I love you so much. I don't want to live three thousand miles from you or Overlook Glen. I love getting to know my new family, and I want to be part of their lives, of course. But I don't want to live there. I want this tiny winery, where I was born. I want this North Carolina life that feels right. And, oh my goodness, I want you. Just you. Forever and ever." She pressed her hands to his face. "Yes?"

He threw his head back and laughed. "Yes!" He took her hands and brought them to his lips, kissing her knuckles. "So, Graciela, your mission, should you choose to accept it, is to live right here with me and our dogs, making wine and food and...our very own family unlike any other. Do you accept this mission?"

"With my whole heart and soul. With all the passion you have found in me. With everything I have and will ever be."

He wrapped his arms around her and lifted her off the ground, twirling her in a circle in the middle of the terrace.

Jack barked and tried to herd them inside. Bitsy ran around in circles. Gertie found a piece of sunshine and pressed her belly to the ground, staring at both of them with a look of complete contentment on her face.

Christmas is coming to Bitter Bark!
Don't miss the Dogmothers Holiday novella…
Dachshund Through the Snow!

Want to know the minute it's available?
Sign up for the newsletter.

www.roxannestclaire.com/newsletter-2/

Or get daily updates, sneak peeks, and insider information at the Dogfather Reader Facebook Group!

www.facebook.com/groups/roxannestclairereaders/

The Dogmothers is a spinoff series of
The Dogfather

Available Now

SIT...STAY...BEG (Book 1)

NEW LEASH ON LIFE (Book 2)

LEADER OF THE PACK (Book 3)

SANTA PAWS IS COMING TO TOWN (Book 4)
(A Holiday Novella)

BAD TO THE BONE (Book 5)

RUFF AROUND THE EDGES (Book 6)

DOUBLE DOG DARE (Book 7)

BARK! THE HERALD ANGELS SING (Book 8)
(A Holiday Novella)

OLD DOG NEW TRICKS (Book 9)

Join the private Dogfather Reader Facebook Group!

www.facebook.com/groups/roxannestclairereaders/

When you join, you'll find inside info on all the books and characters, sneak peeks, and a place to share the love of tails and tales!

The Dogmothers Series

Available Now

HOT UNDER THE COLLAR (Book 1)

THREE DOG NIGHT (Book 2)

DACHSHUND THROUGH THE SNOW (Book 3)

And many more to come!

For a complete list, buy links, and reading order of all my books, visit www.roxannestclaire.com. Be sure to sign up for my newsletter to find out when the next book is released!

A Dogfather/Dogmothers Family Reference Guide

THE KILCANNON FAMILY

Daniel Kilcannon aka *The Dogfather*
Son of Finola (Gramma Finnie) and Seamus
Kilcannon. Married to Annie Harper for 36 years until
her death. Veterinarian, father, and grandfather.
Widowed at opening of series. Married to Katie
Santorini (*Old Dog New Tricks*) with dogs Rusty and
Goldie.

The Kilcannons (from oldest to youngest):

• **Liam** Kilcannon and Andi Rivers (*Leader of the
Pack*) with Christian and Fiona and dog, Jag

• **Shane** Kilcannon and Chloe Somerset (*New Leash
on* Life) with daughter Annabelle and dogs, Daisy and
Ruby

• **Garrett** Kilcannon and Jessie Curtis
(*Sit...Stay...Beg*) with son Patrick and dog, Lola

• **Molly** Kilcannon and Trace Bancroft (*Bad to the
Bone*) with daughter Pru and son Danny and dog,
Meatball

• **Aidan** Kilcannon and Beck Spencer (*Ruff Around
the Edges*) with dog, Ruff

• **Darcy** Kilcannon and Josh Ranier (*Double Dog
Dare*) with dogs, Kookie and Stella

THE MAHONEY FAMILY

Colleen Mahoney

Daughter of Finola (Gramma Finnie) and Seamus Kilcannon and younger sister of Daniel. Married to Joe Mahoney for a little over 10 years until his death. Owner of Bone Appetit (canine treat bakery) and mother.

The Mahoneys (from oldest to youngest):

• **Declan** Mahoney and…

• **Connor** Mahoney and…

• **Braden** Mahoney and **Cassie** Santorini (*Hot Under the Collar*) with dogs, Jelly Bean and Jasmine

• **Ella** Mahoney and…

THE SANTORINI FAMILY

Katie Rogers Santorini

Dated **Daniel** Kilcannon in college and introduced him to Annie. Married to Nico Santorini for forty years until his death two years after Annie's. Interior Designer and mother. Recently married to **Daniel** Kilcannon (*Old Dogs New Tricks*).

The Santorinis

• **Nick** Santorini and…

• **John** Santorini (identical twin to Alex) and…

• **Alex** Santorini (identical twin to John) and Grace Donovan with dogs, Bitsy, Gertie and Jack

• **Theo** Santorini and…

• **Cassie** Santorini and **Braden** Mahoney (*Hot Under the Collar*) with dogs, Jelly Bean and Jasmine

Katie's mother-in-law from her first marriage, **Agnes "Yiayia" Santorini,** now lives in Bitter Bark with **Gramma Finnie** and their dachshunds, Pygmalion (Pyggie) and Galatea (Gala). These two women are known as "The Dogmothers."

About The Author

Published since 2003, Roxanne St. Claire is a *New York Times* and *USA Today* bestselling author of more than fifty romance and suspense novels. She has written several popular series, including The Dogfather, The Dogmothers, Barefoot Bay, the Guardian Angelinos, and the Bullet Catchers.

In addition to being a ten-time nominee and one-time winner of the prestigious RITA™ Award for the best in romance writing, Roxanne's novels have won the National Readers' Choice Award for best romantic suspense four times. Her books have been published in dozens of languages and optioned for film.

A mother of two but recent empty-nester, Roxanne lives in Florida with her husband and her two dogs, Ginger and Rosie.

www.roxannestclaire.com
www.twitter.com/roxannestclaire
www.facebook.com/roxannestclaire
www.roxannestclaire.com/newsletter/